Edward Gibbon

Autobiographies

Printed verbatim from hitherto unpublished MSS.

Edward Gibbon

Autobiographies
Printed verbatim from hitherto unpublished MSS.

ISBN/EAN: 9783337011291

Printed in Europe, USA, Canada, Australia, Japan

Cover: Foto ©Raphael Reischuk / pixelio.de

More available books at **www.hansebooks.com**

THE AUTOBIOGRAPHIES

OF

EDWARD GIBBON.

*PRINTED VERBATIM FROM HITHERTO
UNPUBLISHED MSS., WITH AN
INTRODUCTION BY THE EARL OF SHEFFIELD.*

EDITED BY

JOHN MURRAY.

WITH PORTRAIT.

LONDON:
JOHN MURRAY, ALBEMARLE STREET.
1896.

INTRODUCTION BY THE EARL OF SHEFFIELD.

THE centenary of the death of Edward Gibbon (died January, 1794, aged fifty-six) was recorded by a public commemoration held in London in November, 1894, at the instance of the Royal Historical Society. The distinguished committee of English and foreign students, who were associated on that occasion, invited me to become their President, as representing the family with which Gibbon had been so intimately connected, and which still retained the portraits, manuscripts, letters, and relics of the historian. The exhibition of these in the British Museum, and the commemoration held on November 15, reawakened interest in the work and remains of one of the greatest names in English literature; and a general desire was expressed that the manuscripts should be again collated, and that what was yet unpublished might be given to the world.

As is well known, it was my grandfather, the first Earl, who made the historian almost his adopted brother, gave him a home both in town and in country, was his devisee and literary executor, and edited and published the famous Autobiography, the letters, and remains.

All of these passed under Edward Gibbon's will to Lord Sheffield; and, together with books, relics, portraits, and various mementos, they have been for a century preserved by my father and myself with religious care and veneration in Sheffield Park. The original autograph manuscripts of the *Memoirs*, the *Diaries, Letters, Note-books*, etc., have now become the property of the British Museum, subject to the copyright of all the unpublished parts which was previously assigned to Mr. Murray. And it is with no little pleasure and pride that I have acceded to the request of the publishers that I would introduce these unpublished remains to the world, and thus complete the task of editing the historian, to which my grandfather devoted so great a portion of his time, not only as a testamentary duty, but as a labour of love.

The connection of the historian with my grandfather, his early friend, John Holroyd, and the members of the Holroyd family, forms one of the pleasantest and also most interesting passages in literary history. It was in no way interrupted by Lord Sheffield's public and official duties; it was continued without a cloud to obscure their intimacy, until it was sundered by death; and the Earl, who survived his friend so long, continued to edit and to publish the manuscripts left in his hands for some twenty years after the death of the historian.

By a clause in the will of Edward Gibbon, dated July 14, 1788, his papers were entrusted to Lord Sheffield and Mr. John Batt, his executors, in the following terms:—

"I will that all my Manuscript papers found at the time of my decease be delivered to my executors, and that if any shall appear sufficiently finished for the public eye, they do treat for the purchase of the same with a Bookseller, giving the preference to Mr. Andrew Strahan and Mr. Thomas Cadell, whose liberal spirit I have experienced in similar transactions.   And whatsoever monies may accrue from such sale and publication I give to my much-valued friend William Hayley, Esq., of Eastham, in the County of Sussex.   But in case he shall dye before me, I give the aforesaid monies to the Royal Society of London and the Royal Academy of Inscriptions of Paris, share and share alike, in trust to be by them employed in such a manner as they shall deem most beneficial to the cause of Learning."

In pursuance of the directions contained in the will and of many verbal communications, Lord Sheffield, in 1799, published the *Miscellaneous Works of Edward Gibbon, with Memoirs of his Life and Writings*, in 2 vols., 4to.   A third volume was added in 1815, and a new edition of the whole, with additions, appeared during the same year in 5 vols., 8vo.   In 1837 another edition, in one large 8vo volume, was published.

By a clause in his own will, Lord Sheffield directed that no further publication of the historian's manuscripts should be made.

" And I request of my said trustees and my heirs that none of the said manuscripts, papers, or books of the said Edward Gibbon be published unless my approbation of the publication be directed by some memorandum indorsed and written or signed by me.   And I also request the person entitled for the time being to the possession thereof not to suffer the same to be out of his possession or to be improperly exposed."

This direction has been strictly followed by my father, the second Earl, and by myself; and it is believed that no person has ever had access to any of the manuscripts for any literary purpose, excepting the late Dean Milman, who, when editing his well-known edition of the *Decline and Fall*, in 1842, was permitted to inspect the original manuscripts of the Autobiography, on condition of not publishing any new matter.

The commemoration of 1894, however, again raised the question whether such an embargo on giving to the world writings of national importance was ever meant to be, or even ought to be, regarded as perpetual. Whilst persons named in these papers or their children were living, whilst the bitter controversies of the last century were still unforgotten, whilst the fame of Edward Gibbon had hardly yet become one of our national glories, it was a matter of good feeling and sound judgment in Lord Sheffield to exercise an editor's discretion in publishing his friend's confession and private thoughts. Now that more than a hundred years have passed since his death, no such considerations have weight or meaning. And the opinion of those whom I have consulted, both professionally and as private friends, amply corroborates my own conclusion, that it is a duty which I owe to my own ancestor and to the public to give to the world all the remains of the historian which for more than a century have been preserved in the strong room of Sheffield Park.

The unlocking of the cases in which these manuscripts were secured was quite a revelation of literary workmanship, and has led to a most interesting problem in literary history. The manuscripts of the historian are all holographs—the text of the famous Memoirs being written with extraordinary beauty of calligraphy, and studied with the utmost care. But, singularly enough, none of the texts are prepared for immediate, or even direct, publication. The historian wrote, at various intervals between 1788 and 1793, no less than *six* different sketches. They are not quite continuous; they partly recount the same incidents in different form; they are written in different tones: and yet no one of them is complete; none of them seem plainly designed to supersede the rest. There is even a small seventh sketch, from which one of the noblest and most famous passages that Gibbon ever wrote has been excised, and inserted in the published Autobiography.

Lord Sheffield executed his editorial task with extreme judgment, singular ingenuity, but remarkable freedom. He was assisted in preparing the manuscripts for publication by his wife and by Lady Maria Holroyd, his eldest daughter, who became by marriage the first Lady Stanley of Alderley. This very able and remarkable woman, of whose abilities the historian expressed in letters his great admiration, evidently marked the manuscripts in pencil handwriting (now recognized as hers) for the printer's copyist. These pencil deletions, transpositions, and even additions, correspond with the Autobiography as published by Lord Sheffield. Quite a third of the whole manuscript is omitted, and many of the most piquant passages that Gibbon ever wrote were suppressed by the caution or the delicacy of his editor and his family.

The result is a problem of singular literary interest.

A piece, most elaborately composed by one of the greatest writers who ever used our language, an autobiography often pronounced to be the best we possess, is now proved to be in no sense the simple work of that illustrious pen, but to have been dexterously pieced together out of seven fragmentary sketches and adapted into a single and coherent narrative. The manner and the extent of this extraordinary piece of editing has been so fully explained in the address of November 15, published by the Centenary Committee, that it is not necessary for me to enlarge upon it further.

No sooner had the discovery of the process by which Gibbon's *Autobiography* had been concocted been made public, than a general desire was expressed to have the originals published in the form in which the historian left them. It was no case of incomplete or illegible manuscripts, nor of rough drafts designed only as notes for subsequent composition. The whole of the seven manuscripts are written with perfect precision; the style is in Gibbon's most elaborate manner; and each piece is perfectly ready for the printer—so far as it goes. It was impossible to do again the task of consolidation so admirably performed by Lord Sheffield. Nothing remained but to print the whole of the pieces *verbatim*, as the historian wrote them, not necessarily in the order of time of their apparent composition, but so as to form a consecutive narrative of the author's life.

The reader may now rest assured that, *for the first time*, he has before him the Autobiographic Sketches of Edward Gibbon in the exact form in which he left them at his death. The portions enclosed in dark brackets are the passages which were omitted by Lord Sheffield, and in the notes are inserted the passages or sentences, few and simple in themselves, which Lord Sheffield added to the original manuscript. For various reasons it was found impracticable to print the six sketches in parallel columns; but the admirers of the historian and all students of English literature will find abundant opportunity for collating the original texts with each other, and with the text as published by the editor, and now for a century current as one of the masterpieces of English literature.

The *Letters* of the historian, the bulk of which were addressed to Lord Sheffield and his family, were published in part by my grandfather in one or other of the editions of *The Miscellaneous Works of Edward Gibbon*. But in this collection many letters were omitted, and most of them were printed with some omissions and variations. These omissions have now been restored; and the *Letters*, like the other papers of our author, are now for the first time given to the world in the form in which they were composed.

I cannot pretend to any rivalry with my grandfather in the matter of the skill with which he performed the task of editing and selecting for publication the remains of his friend. But I can assure the reader that *every piece contained in this volume as the work of Edward Gibbon is now printed exactly as he wrote it without suppression or emendation.* And in transferring these literary treasures to the nation, and in giving them to the world, I feel that I am fulfilling the trust which the historian reposed in my grandfather, and am acting in the spirit of the lifelong friendship that bound him to my family.

I cannot conclude these prefatory remarks without acknowledging to the fullest extent the obligation I am under to Mr. Frederic Harrison for the assistance he has given me in the preparation and composition of this Preface.

PREFACE.

LORD SHEFFIELD has, in his introduction, told the history of the documents contained in this volume so fully, that I will only call attention to one or two minor points respecting the manner in which they are now presented to the public.

It was my first intention to append to the autobiographies a very few explanatory notes, but when the preparation of the proofs had made some progress, I came upon a series of memoranda—I can hardly give them the name of formal notes—in the historian's own handwriting, which were numbered consecutively, but otherwise bore no clue as to the part of the memoirs to which they referred.

I soon found that they belonged to Memoir F, which had been placed first of the series. In dealing with them three courses were open: (1) To omit them altogether; (2) to affix them to the passages to which they referred, and leave them to tell their own tale; (3) to elaborate them, by finding out the meaning of the very brief and enigmatical sentences of which for the most part they consist.

After much deliberation, and taking counsel of

several competent advisers, I decided to adopt the third course, in the hope that, by so doing, I should help to place the reader in a position to understand the working of Gibbon's mind, and the method of his composition, without constant reference to other books.

The explanation of these memoranda, such as it is, has been a work of considerable labour; on these grounds I would ask the indulgence of the reader and the critic if the notes do not possess that finish which perhaps it would be impossible, in the circumstances, to impart to them.

The numbered notes to Memoir E are Gibbon's own; a few of Dean Milman's notes, and almost all of those supplied by the first Lord Sheffield, have been retained throughout.

In reproducing the autobiographies it has been my endeavour to give a literal transcription of the manuscripts, including Gibbon's own spellings, and misspellings of various words.

I wish to record my thanks to Mr. Francis B. Bickley, of the British Museum, for the skill and care with which he has collated the proofs with the original manuscripts; and to the President of Magdalen College, to the officials at the Heralds' College, to Mr. H. R. Tedder, F.S.A., and to Mrs. Salmon, for the assistance which they have afforded me in clearing up many obscure points and allusions.

JOHN MURRAY.

CONTENTS.

THE AUTOBIOGRAPHIES OF
EDWARD GIBBON.

CHAPTER I.*

Throughout these autobiographies the portions hitherto unpublished
are inserted in [   ].

MY family is originally derived from the County of Kent,[1]
whose inhabitants have maintained from the earliest
antiquity [2] a provincial character of civility, courage, and
freedom. The southern district of the country, which
borders on Sussex and the sea, was formerly overspread
with the great forest Anderida,[3] and even now retains
the denomination of the *Weald,* or Woodland. In this
district, and in the hundred and parish of Rolvenden,
the Gibbons were possessed of lands in the year one
thousand three hundred and twenty-six; and the elder

---

[1] Cambden in Kent, masterly work—style and spirit
pictoresque—Latin Edition—original text—my Edition, 1607.

[2] From Cæsar, Will. of Malm. John Sarisb.—provincial
marks lost—progress of Society—isle of Sky superior to Old
Kent.

[3] Anderida — Cambden finds that Newenden-sea has
retired.†

* Memoir F, the latest and most perfect. Written in 1792-3, brought
down to 1753.

† See Appendix, 1, p. 96.

branch of the family, without much encrease or diminution of property, still adheres to its native soil. Fourteen years after the first appearance of his name, John Gibbon is recorded as the *Marmorarius*, or Architect, of King Edward the Third; the strong and stately castle of Queenborough,[4] which guarded the entrance of the Medway, was a monument of his skill; and the grant of an hereditary toll on the passage from Sandwich to Stonar, in the Isle of Thanet, is the reward of no vulgar artist. In the visitations of the Heralds, the Gibbons are frequently mentioned: they held the rank of Esquire in an age when that title was less promiscuously assumed: one of them, under the reign of Queen Elizabeth, was Captain of the militia of Kent; and a free school in the neighbouring town of Benenden proclaims the charity and opulence of its founder.*   But time, or their own obscurity, has cast a

---

[4] Queenborough. Castellum et munitissimum quod Rex Ed. III. posuit, ut ipse scribit situ amœno ad terrorem hostium et solatium Populi.†

* Canon Joy, Vicar of Benenden, has kindly furnished me with particulars of the benefactions of the Gibbon family:—

"1602. Edmund Gybbon of Benenden, Esqre, gave a Free School, house, and lands near the Beacon Hill, estimated at 80 acres, towards the maintenance of the master of the School.

"In the wall of the S. Chantry Chapel (evidently not *in situ*) is a small brass with the following inscription: 'Under this stone doeth lye buried ye body of Edmond Gibbon, late of this P̄ish of Benninden, who dyed ye last of January in Anno Dni. 1607, who was ye principall founder of Free Scole of Benninden, and gave the living that thereto belongeth.'

"1677. Edmund Gybbon of Hole, Esqre, gave a house and lands in Benenden, called Sarnden, computed at 70 acres, for the maintenance of an Usher for the School.

"1699. The Feoffees by Sale of Timber off the said Farm, purchased a house and lands, estimated at 16 acres, near the Beacon Hill, for an additional maintenance for the Usher.

"1713. John Gybbon of Hole, Esqre, gave an Exchequer annuity of £14 per annum out of the excise of beer, etc., which will expire in 1791, for a further augmentation to the Schoolmaster, provided he be neither Vicar, Curate, or Reader, and if he be, then for the use of poor Girls."

The school founded by Edmund Gibbon in 1602 is still (1896) the boys' school.

† Cf. Memoir A, p. 358.

veil of oblivion over the virtues and vices of my Kentish ancestors : their character or station confined them to the labours and pleasures of a rural life; nor is it in my power to follow the advice of the poet in an enquiry after a name—

> " Go ! search it there, where to be born, and dye
> Of rich and poor makes all the history "— [5]

So recent is the institution of our parish registers.[5a] In the beginning of the seventeenth century a younger branch of the Gibbons of Rolvenden migrated from the Country to the city, and from this branch I do not blush to descend. The law requires some abilities; the Church imposes some restraints, and before our army and navy, our Civil establishments and Indian Empire, had opened so many paths of fortune, the mercantile profession was more frequently chosen by youths of a liberal race and education who aspired to create their own independence. Our most respectable families have not disdained the counting-house or even the shop; their names are enrolled in the livery and companies of London; and in England, as well as in the Italian commonwealths, heralds have been compelled to declare that Gentility is not degraded by the exercise of trade.

The armorial ensigns which in the times of Chivalry adorned the crest and shield of the soldier are now

---

[5] Pope, M. E. iii. 287.

[5a] Registers first Lord Cromwell, 1538. Anderson. Vol. i. p. 367—few so old—series broken.*

*An Historical and Chronological Deduction of the Origin of Commerce from the earliest accounts to the present time, by Adam Anderson. London, 1764. " By order of Thomas Cromwell, Earl of Essex, Vicar-General of Henry VIII., upon the dissolution of Monasteries, every incumbent minister in all the parishes in England was compelled to keep a register of all Weddings, Christenings, and Burials."—Vol. i. p. 367.

become an empty decoration, which every man who has money to build a carriage may paint, according to his fancy, on the pannels. My family arms are the same which were borne by the Gibbons of Kent in an age when the College of Heralds religiously guarded the distinctions of blood and name: *a Lyon, rampant, gardant, between three scallop-shells, Argent on a field Azure.*[6] 1 should not, however, have been tempted to blazon my coat of arms, the most useless of all coats, were it not connected with a whimsical anecdote. About the reign of James the First, the three harmless scallop-shells were changed by Edmund Gibbon, Esq., into three *Ogresses*, or female cannibals, with the design of stigmatizing three ladies, his kinswomen, who had provoked him by an unjust law-suit.* But this singular mode of revenge, for which he obtained the sanction of Sir William Segar, King-at-arms, soon expired with its author; and on his own monument in the Temple Church, the Monsters vanish, and the three scallop-shells resume their proper and hereditary place.

[Our alliances by marriage it is not disgraceful to mention. Blue-mantle Poursuivant, who will soon be introduced to the reader's acquaintance, enumerates the Phillips de la Weld in Tenterden, the Whetnals of East-

---

[6] Arms. In Latin by G. †

* Those who are acquainted with heraldry are aware that the word *ogress* is a synonym for a *pellet* or *roundle.* These roundles are supposed to represent little coloured cakes or wafers used in the Crusades, and according to their colour they are in English heraldry termed: Bezants (gold), Plates (silver), Pomeis (green), Torteaux (red), Golpes (purple), Guzes (sanguine), and Pellets (black). In substituting pellets for scallops, Edmund Gibbon was guilty of a delicate heraldic pun which his descendant would appear to have taken in a literal, not a technical sense (cf. p. 360).

† The father of Lord Chancellor Hardwicke married an heiress of this family of Gibbon. The Chancellor's escutcheon in the Temple Hall quarters the arms of Gibbon, as does also that, in Lincoln's Inn Hall, of Charles Yorke, Chancellor in 1770.—SHEFFIELD.

Peckham, the Edgars of Suffolk, the Cromers, the Bercleys of Beauston, the Hextalls, the Ellenbriggs, the Calverleys, the Whetnalls of Cheshire—modestly checking his pen lest he should seem to indulge the pride of pedigree : "nam genus et proavos," etc. As such pride would be ridiculous, it would be scarcely less ridiculous to disclaim it; and I shall simply observe that the Gibbons have been immediately or remotely connected with several worthy families of the old gentry of England. The Memoirs of the Count de Grammont,[7] a favourite book of every man and woman of taste, immortalize the Whetnalls or Whitnells of Peckham : " la blanche Whitnell et le triste Peckham." But the insipid charms of the lady, and the dreary solitude of the mansion, were sometimes enlivened by Hamilton and love ; and had not *our* alliance preceded *her* marriage, I should be less confident of my descent from the Whetnalls of Peckham. · The Cromers in the fifteenth century were twice Sheriffs of Kent and twice Lord Mayors of London. But] the chief honour of my ancestry is James Fiens, Baron Say and Seale, and Lord High Treasurer of England in the reign of Henry the Sixth, from whom, by the Phelips, the Whetnalls, and the Cromers, I am lineally descended in the eleventh degree. His dismission and imprisonment in the Tower were insufficient to appease the popular clamour ; and the Treasurer, with his son-in-law Cromer,* was beheaded (1450), after a mock tryal, by the Kentish insurgents. The black list of his offences,

---

[7] Grammont, C.—Court at Tunbridge—merry times.†

* CADE. "Go take him away, I say, and strike off his head presently : and then break into his son-in-law's house, Sir James Cromer, and strike off his head, and bring them both upon two poles thither." —2 *Henry VI.*, iv. 7.

† See Appendix, 2, p. 96.

as it is exhibited in Shakespeare, displays the ignorance and envy of a plebeian tyrant. Besides the vague reproaches of selling Maine and Normandy to the Dauphin, the Treasurer is specially accused of luxury for riding on a foot-cloth, and of treason for speaking French, the language of our enemies. "Thou has most traiterously corrupted the youth of the Realm" (says Jack Cade to the unfortunate Lord), "in erecting a grammar school: and, whereas, before, our fore-fathers had no other books than the score and the tally, thou hast caused printing to be used; and, contrary to the King, his Crown, and dignity, thou hast built a paper-mill. It will be proved to thy face, that thou hast men about thee, who usually talk of a noun and a verb, and such abominable words as no Christian ear can endure to hear."* Our dramatic Poet is generally more attentive to character than to history; and I much fear that the art of printing was not introduced into England till several years after Lord Say's death:[8] but of some of these meritorious crimes I should hope to find my ancestor guilty; and a man of letters may be proud of his descent from a Patron and martyr of learning.

In the beginning of the last century, Robert Gibbon, Esq., of Rolvenden in Kent, who died in 1618, had a

---

[8] Caxton, 1471—Westminster. Those who believe in Harlem and Corselis cling to Sh. and allow Lord Say an experiment. Origin of printing, I believe, by Nichols, 1776, pp. 19, 20, 2nd ed. 8vo. after 25.*

* 2 *Henry VI.*, iv. 7. On this passage Blackstone writes: "Mr. Mœrman in his *Origines Typographicæ* hath availed himself of this passage in Shakespeare to support his hypothesis that printing was introduced into England (before the time of Caxton) by Frederic Corsellis, a workman from Haerlem in the time of Henry VI." The whole question is fully discussed in Timperley's *Encyclopædia of Literary and Typographical Anecdote*, 1842, pp. 144, *et seq.*

son of the same name of Robert, who settled in London in trade and became a member of the Cloth-workers' Company. His wife was a daughter of the Edgars, who flourished above four hundred years in the County of Suffolk, and produced an eminent and wealthy Serjeant-at-law, Sir Gregory Edgar, in the reign of Henry the Seventh. Of the sons of Robert Gibbon who died in 1643, Matthew did not aspire above the station of a linnen-draper in Leadenhall Street, in the Parish of St. Andrew's, but John has given the Public some curious Memorials of his existence, his character, and his family. He was born the third of November, in the year 1629; his education was liberal, at a grammar-school, and afterwards in Jesus College at Cambridge, and he celebrates the retired content which he enjoyed at Allesborough in Worcestershire, in the house of Thomas Lord Coventry, where John Gibbon was employed as domestic tutor, [the same office which Mr. Hobbes exercised in the Devonshire family.[8a]] But the spirit of my kinsman soon emerged into more active life; he visited foreign countries as a soldier and a traveller; acquired the knowledge of the French and Spanish languages; passed some time in the Isle of Jersey; crossed the Atlantic, and resided upwards of a twelfmonth (1659) in the rising Colony of Virginia. In this remote province his taste, or rather passion, for Heraldry found a singular gratification at a War-dance of the native Indians. As they moved in measured steps, brandishing their Tamahawks, his curious eye contemplated their little shields of bark,

---

[8a] The comparison is his own—quotes the words of Mr. Hobbes.[*]

[*] Cf. Memoir A, p. 367.

and their naked bodies, which were painted with the colours and symbols of his favourite science. "At which I exceedingly wondered; and concluded that Heraldry was ingrafted *naturally* into the sense of humane race. If so, it deserves a greater esteem than now-a-days is put upon it." His return to England, after the restoration, was soon followed by his marriage, his settlement in an house in St. Catherine's cloyster near the Tower, which devolved to my grandfather, and his introduction into the Heralds College (in 1671), by the style and title of Bluemantle Poursuivant at arms. In this office he enjoyed near fifty years the rare felicity of uniting in the same pursuit his duty and inclination; his name is remembered in the college, and many of his letters are still preserved.[9] Several of the most respectable characters of the age, Sir William Dugdale, Mr. Ashmole, Dr. John Betts, and Dr. Nehemiah Grew were his friends; and in the society of such men, John Gibbon may be recorded without disgrace as the member of an Astrological Club. The study of hereditary honours is favourable to the Royal prerogative; and my kinsman, like most of his family, was a high Tory in Church and State. In the latter end of the reign of Charles the Second, his pen was exercised in the cause of the Duke of York;[10] the Republican faction he most

---

[9] Mr. Brooks Lancaster Herald.*
[10] Moral verses.†

* There never has been a Mr. Brooks, Lancaster Herald, but from a passage in Memoir A (p. 356) it is evident that Mr. John Charles Brooke, who was Rouge Croix in 1773 and Somerset Herald in 1778, is meant. It is very probable that Gibbon heard from him of the large amount of work done by his kinsman at the College of Arms, and of the high estimation in which that work was held—an estimation which survives to the present time.

† This refers to the verses scattered through the other works of

cordially detested; and as each animal is conscious of its proper arms, the Herald's revenge was emblazoned on a most Diabolical scutcheon.[11] But the triumph of the Whig Government checked the preferment of Blue-Mantle; and he was even suspended from his office till his tongue could learn to pronounce the oath of abjuration. His life was prolonged to the age of ninety, and in the expectation of the inevitable though uncertain hour, he wishes to preserve the blessings of health, competence, and virtue. In the year 1682 he published at London his *Introductio ad Latinam Blasoniam,* an original attempt which Cambden had desiderated to define, in the Roman idiom, the terms and attributes of a Gothic institution. His manner is quaint and affected; his order is confused; but he displays some wit, more reading, and still more enthusiasm, and if an enthusiast be often absurd, he is never languid. An English text is perpetually interspersed with Latin sentences in prose and verse; but in his own poetry he claims an exemption from the laws of prosody. Amidst a profusion of genealogical knowledge, my kinsman could not be forgetful of his own name; and to him I am indebted for almost the

---

[11] Diabolical blazon—defence of false heraldry.*

John Gibbon, viz.: *Edouardus Confessor Redivivus, The Piety and Vertues of Holy Edward the Confessor, Revived in the sacred Majesty of King James II., published* 1688; *Unio Dissidentium, Heir Apparent and Presumptive made one,* 1680; *Day Fatality, or some observations of Days lucky and unlucky. Penn'd and Published whilst His present Majesty the most Serene King James II. was Duke of York,* 1678.

* " Tutus sit Augustissimus Rex Carolus, Sancti Fœlicis Festos, prospero natus; Celsissimus Illustrissimus Dux Jacobus, quem Stellam Borealem ante multos annos prædixêre Vates; et universa Stirps Regia, à Turba Fanatica Antimonarchicâ: Quibus Symbolum et Insigne est, Bellua multorum Capitum, *coloris Diabolici* (viz. nigri) in Campo sanguineo (Armes pour enquerir, ut dicimus Gallicé)."— Gibbon, *Introductio Ad Latinam Blasonian,* p. 165 (cf. p. 371).

whole of my information concerning the Gibbon family. From this small work, a duodecimo of one hundred and sixty-five pages, the author expected immortal fame; and at the conclusion of his labour, he sings in a strain of self-exultation—

> " Usque huc corrigitur Romana Blasonia per me
>   Verborumque dehinc barbara forma cadat
> Hic liber in meritum si forsitan incidet usum
>   Testis rite meæ sedulitatis erit.
> Quicquid agat Zoilus, ventura fatebitur ætas
>   Artis quôd fueram non Clypearis inops."

Such are the hopes of authors! In the failure of those hopes, John Gibbon has not been the first of his profession, and very possibly may not be the last of his name.[12]

His brother, Matthew Gibbon, the linnendraper of Leadenhall Street, had one daughter and two sons; my grandfather Edward, who was born in the year 1666, and Thomas, afterwards Dean of Carlisle. According to the mercantile creed that the best book is a profitable ledger, the writings of John the herald would be much less precious than those of his nephew Edward: but an author professes, at least, to write for the public benefit; and the slow balance of trade can only be pleasing to those persons to whom it is advantageous. The successful industry of my grandfather raised him above the level of his immediate ancestors; he appears to have launched into various and extensive dealings: even his opinions were subordinate to his interest, and I find him in Flanders cloathing King William's troops; while he

---

[12] Oblivion—From Wolfenbuttel to Lausanne.*

* This memorandum is explained by a passage in Memoir A, p. 356; cf. C, p. 214.   John Gibbon died in 1718, æt. 89, and is buried in St. Mary Aldermary, Bow Lane.

would have contracted with more pleasure, though not, perhaps, at a cheaper rate, for the service of King James. During his residence abroad, his concerns at home were managed by his mother Hester, an active and notable woman. Her second husband was a widower of the name of Acton; they united the children of their first nuptials: after his marriage with the daughter of Richard Acton, Goldsmith, in Leadenhall Street, he gave his own sister to Sir Whitmore Acton, of Aldenham; and I am thus connected by a triple alliance with that ancient and loyal family of Shropshire Baronets. It consisted, about that time, of seven brothers, all of Gigantic stature; one of whom, a pygmy of six feet two inches, confessed himself the last and least of the seven: adding in the true spirit of party, that such men were not born since the Revolution. Under the Tory administration of the four last years of Queen Anne (1710–1714), Mr. Edward Gibbon was appointed one of the Commissioners of the Customs; he sat at that board with Prior; but the merchant was better qualified for his station than the poet, since Lord Bolingbroke has been heard to declare, that he had never conversed with a man who more clearly understood the commerce and finances of England. In the year 1716 he was elected one of the Directors of the South-sea company; and his books exhibited the proof that, before his acceptance of this fatal office, he had acquired an independent fortune of sixty thousand pounds.

But his fortune was overwhelmed in the shipwreck of the year twenty, and the labours of thirty years were blasted in a single day. Of the use or abuse of the South-sea scheme, of the guilt or innocence of my grandfather and his brother-Directors, I am neither a competent nor a disinterested Judge. Yet the equity of modern times must condemn the violent and arbitrary proceedings which would have disgraced the cause of Justice, and would render injustice still more odious.[13] No sooner had the nation awakened from its golden dream, than a popular and even a parliamentary clamour demanded their victims; but it was acknowledged on all sides that the South-sea Directors, however guilty, could not be touched by any known laws of the land. The speech of Lord Molesworth, the author of the state of Denmark, may shew the temper, or rather the intemperance, of the House of Commons.[14] "Extraordinary crimes," exclaimed

---

[13] Tindal and Anderson *—a private narrative—negociations—false hopes to the last.

[14] Molesworth in B. B., his Denmark, erroneous, partial, and arising from personal pique.†

* Adam Anderson was chief clerk of the Stock and Annuities to the South Sea Company. He wrote an important work, *An Historical and Chronological Deduction of the Origin of Commerce from the Earliest Accounts to the Present Time*. Died 1765.

The History of England, by M. Rapin de Thoyras. Continued by N. Tindal, M.A. Vol. iv. pt. ii. 1747. Pp. 630–649 contain a full account of the proceedings of the Houses of Parliament in the winding-up of the affairs of the South Sea Company. On January 21, 1720, Mr. Gibbon, along with several of his co-directors, was, by order of the Committee of the Lords, taken into custody, and his papers were seized. Among other charges, it appeared that a fictitious stock, amounting to £574,000, had been disposed of by the directors to facilitate the passing of the South Sea Act in Parliament. Of this, £50,000 went to the Earl of Sunderland, and £10,000 each to the Duchess of Kendal and the Countess of Platen, Mr. Gibbon being one of the distributors.

† Robert, first Viscount Molesworth (1656–1725), Envoy Extraordinary to Court of Denmark, 1692, where his conduct gave considerable offence to the authorities. He sat in the Irish, and subsequently in the English Parliament, and in all his actions showed a strong controversial spirit. His *Account of the State of Denmark as it was in the Year* 1692 was published in 1694. On the meeting of Parliament at the close of 1720, the House as well as the country was in a ferment in consequence of the collapse of the South Sea Scheme. Shippen moved an amendment to the address in a violent speech, and in seconding the motion Molesworth used the words quoted. Cf. Memoir A, p. 376.

that ardent Whig, "call aloud for extraordinary remedies. The Roman lawgivers had not foreseen the possible existence of a parricide. But as soon as the first monster appeared, he was sewed in a sack, and cast headlong into the river; and I shall be content to inflict the same treatment on the authors of our present ruin." His motion was not literally adopted; but a bill of pains and penalties was introduced—a retroactive statute to punish the offences which did not exist at the time they were committed. Such a pernicious violation of liberty and law can only be excused by the most imperious necessity; nor could it be defended on this occasion by the plea of impending danger or useful example. The Legislature restrained the persons of the Directors, imposed an exorbitant security for their appearance, and marked their characters with a prævious note of ignominy; they were compelled to deliver upon oath the strict value of their estates, and were disabled from making any transfer or alienation of any part of their property. Against a bill of pains and penalties it is the common right of every subject to be heard by his counsel at the bar: they prayed to be heard, their prayer was refused, and their oppressors, who required no evidence, would listen to no defence. It had been at first proposed that one eighth of their respective estates should be allowed for the future support of the Directors; but it was speciously urged, that in the various shades of opulence and guilt, such an equal proportion would be too light for many, and for some might possibly be too heavy. The character and conduct of each man were separately weighed; but instead of the calm solemnity of a judicial enquiry, the fortune and honour of three and thirty

Englishmen were made the topic of hasty conversation, the sport of a lawless majority; and the basest member of the committee, by a malicious word or a silent vote, might indulge his general spleen, or personal animosity. Injury was aggravated by insult, and insult was em-bittered by pleasantry. Allowances of twenty pounds or one shilling were facetiously moved. A vague report that a Director had formerly been concerned in *another* project, by which some unknown persons had lost their money, was admitted as a proof of his actual guilt. One man was ruined because he had dropt a foolish speech, that his horses should feed upon gold; another, because he was grown so proud, that, one day at the Treasury, he had refused a civil answer to persons much above him. All were condemned, absent and unheard, in arbitrary fines and forfeitures which swept away the greatest part of their substance. Such bold oppression can scarcely be shielded by the omnipotence of Parlia-ment; and yet it may be seriously questioned whether the Judges of the South-sea Directors were the true and legal representatives of their country. The first Parlia-ment of George the First had been chosen (1715) for three years: the term had elapsed; their trust was expired; and the four additional years (1718–1722) during which they continued to sit, were derived, not from the people, but from themselves; from the strong measure of the septennial bill, which can only be paralleled by *il serrar di Consiglio* of the Venetian history.[15] Yet candour will

---

[15] In 1298, 470 annually chosen at Michaelmas: voted perpetual and hereditary for all the actual, and of the last years, if they had 12 votes in the Quarantia—Families broken, new ones added—Stability of Venice—Amelot de la Houssaye sur le Gouv. de Venise, Tom. i. pp. 3, 4, 6—

own that to the same Parliament every Englishman is deeply indebted : the Septennial Act, so vicious in its origin, has been sanctioned by time, experience, and the national consent; its first operation secured the house of Hanover on the throne, and its permanent influence maintains the peace and stability of Government. As often as a repeal has been moved in the house of Commons, I have given in its defence a clear and conscientious vote.

My grandfather could not expect to be treated with more lenity than his companions. His Tory principles and connections rendered him obnoxious to the ruling powers: his name is reported in a suspicious secret; and his well-known abilities could not plead the excuse of ignorance or error. In the first proceedings against the South-sea Directors, Mr. Gibbon is one of the few who were taken into custody; and in the final sentence the measure of his fine proclaims him eminently guilty. The total estimate which he delivered on oath to the house of commons amounted to one hundred and six thousand five hundred and forty-three pounds five shillings and sixpence, exclusive of antecedent settlements. Two different allowances of fifteen and of ten thousand pounds were moved for Mr. Gibbon; but, on the question being put, it was carried without a division for the smaller sum; [and as a Philosopher I *should* mention, without a sigh, the irreparable loss of above ninety-six thousand pounds, of which, in a single moment, and by an arbitrary vote, I have been ultimately deprived. The provision

---

Supineness of Dand. and Muratori—a Genoese galley more important? *

* See Appendix, 3, p. 97.

reserved for his wife could not be very considerable;
but the valuable gift which he afterwards received from
his friend and companion, Mr. Francis Acton, was understood in the family to be the restitution of an honourable
trust. Against irresistible rapine the use of fraud is
almost legitimate; in the dexterous anticipation of a
conveyance some fragments of property might escape;
debts of honour will not be annulled by any positive
law, and the frequent imposition of oaths had enlarged
and fortified the Jacobite conscience.] On these ruins,
with the skill and credit of which Parliament had not
been able to despoil him, my grandfather, at a mature
age, erected the edifice of a new fortune: the labours
of sixteen years were amply rewarded, and I have reason
to believe that the second Temple was not much inferior
to the first. [A large stock of money was vested
in the funds, and in trade, and his warehouses at
Cadiz were replenished with naval stores for which
he had contracted to supply the Court of Madrid.]
But he had realized a very considerable property in
Sussex, Hampshire, Buckinghamshire, and the New
River Company, and had acquired a spacious house, with
gardens and lands at Putney,[16] in Surrey, where he resided

---

[16] Putney—Cits—Mallet.*

* "Just there, where our good-
natured Thames is,
Some four short miles above St.
James's,
And deigns with silver-stream-
ing wave
Th' abodes of Earth-born Pride
to lave;
Aloft in air two gods were soaring,
While Putney cits beneath lay
snoring,
Plunged deep in dreams of ten
per cent.

On sums to their dear Country
lent;
Two gods of no inferior fame,
Whom ancient wits with rever-
ence name,
Though wiser moderns much dis-
parage—
I mean the gods of Love and
Marriage."

—Mallet, *Cupid and Hymen; or,
The Wedding Day.*

in decent hospitality. [His portraits represent a stern and sensible countenance; his children trembled in his presence; tradition informs me that the independent visitors who might have smiled at his anger were awed by his frown; and as he was the richest, or wisest, or oldest of his neighbours, he soon became the oracle and the tyrant of a petty Kingdom. His own wrongs had not reconciled him to the house of Hanover; his wishes might be expressed in some harmless toasts; but he was disqualified from all public trust; and in the daily devotions of the family the name of the King for whom they prayed was prudently omitted. My grandfather] died at Putney in December, 1736, at the age of seventy, leaving Edward, his only son, and two daughters, Hester and Catherine.

My father, Edward Gibbon, was born in October, 1707: at the age of thirteen he could scarcely feel that he was disinherited by act of parliament; and as he advanced towards manhood new prospects of fortune opened on his view. A parent is most attentive to supply in his children the deficiencies of which he is conscious in himself: my grandfather's knowledge was derived from a strong understanding and the experience of the ways of men; but my father enjoyed the benefits of a liberal education as a scholar and a Gentleman. At Westminster school, and afterwards at Emanuel College in Cambridge, he passed through a regular course of Academical discipline; and the care of his learning and morals was entrusted to his private Tutor the celebrated Mr. William Law. But the mind of a Saint is above or below the present World, and while the pupil proceeded on his travels the tutor remained at Putney, the much-honoured friend and spiritual director of the whole family. My father resided some time at Paris to acquire the fashionable exercises; and, as his temper was warm and social, he indulged in those pleasures for which the strictness of his former education had given him a keener relish. He afterwards visited several provinces of France, but his excursions were neither long nor remote, and the slender knowledge which he had gained of the French language was gradually obliterated. His passage through Besançon is marked by a singular consequence in the chain of human events. In a dangerous illness Mr. Gibbon was attended at his own request by one of his kinsmen of the name of Acton,[17] the younger brother of a younger brother, who had applied himself to the study of Physic. During the slow recovery of his patient, the Physician himself was attacked by the malady of love: he married his mistress, renounced his country and religion, settled at Besançon, and became the father of three sons, the eldest of whom, General Acton, is conspicuous in Europe as the principal minister of the King of the two Sicilies. By an uncle, whom another stroke of fortune had transplanted to Leghorn, he was educated in the naval service of the Emperor; and his valour and conduct in the command of the Tuscan frigates protected the retreat of the Spaniards from Algiers. On my father's return to England, he was chosen, at the general election of 1734, to serve in Parliament for the borough of Petersfield, a burgage tenure of which my grandfather possessed a weighty share till he alienated, I know not why, such important property. Prejudice and society connected

---

[17] Acton I want some memoirs.*

* Cf. Memoir A, p. 372 *sqq.*

his son with the Tories, or, as they were pleased to style themselves, the Country Gentlemen; with them he gave many a vote, with them he drank many a bottle. Without acquiring the fame of an orator or statesman, he eagerly joyned in the great opposition which, after a seven years' chace, hunted down Sir Robert Walpole, and, in the pursuit of an unpopular Minister, he gratified a private revenge against the oppressor of his family in the South-sea persecution.

The union to which I owe my birth was a marriage of inclination and esteem. Mr. James Porten, a Merchant of London, resided with his family at Putney, in a house adjoining to the bridge and Church-yard, where I have passed many happy hours of my childhood. Of his son Stanier, and of a daughter Catherine, who preserved her maiden name, I shall hereafter speak: another daughter married Mr. Darrel, of Richmond, and her two sons are opulent and worthy; the youngest and handsomest of the three sisters was Judith, my mother. [In the society of Putney the two families lived in friendly and frequent intercourse; the familiar habits of the young people improved into a tender attachment, and their mutual affection, according to the difference of the sexes, was ardently professed and modestly acknowledged. These sentiments were justified by a more perfect knowledge of each other: my father's constancy was neither chilled by absence nor dissolved by pleasure; and after his return from his travels and his election into Parliament, he seriously resolved to unite himself for ever with the object of his choice.

" Notitiam primosque gradus vicinia fecit:
Tempore crevit amor, tædæ quoque jure coissent

> Sed vetuere patres. Quod non potuere vetare,
> Ex æquo captis ardebant mentibus ambo." [18]

Such is the beginning of a love tale at Babylon or at
Putney. On the present occasion, however, the opposition of the two fathers was not equally strenuous or
sincere. The slender fortunes and dubious credit of Mr.
Porten would have been pleased with such an alliance,
but he was provoked by a sense of honour to imitate
the reluctance of his wealthy and ambitious neighbour.
The usual consequences ensued : harsh threats and tender
protestations, frowns and sighs; the seclusion of the
Lady, the despair of the Lover, clandestine correspondence
and stolen interviews. At the distance of forty years,
my aunt, Catherine Porten, could relate with pleasure
the innocent artifices which she practised to second or
screen her beloved sister; and I have found among my
father's papers many letters of both parties that breathe
a spirit of constancy and love. All their acquaintance,
the whole neighbourhood of Putney, was favourable to
their wishes; my paternal grandfather yielded a tardy
and ungracious consent, and as soon as the marriage
ceremony had been performed, the young couple was
received into his house on the hard terms of implicit
obedience and a precarious maintenance. Yet such were
the charms and talents of my mother, with such soft

---

[18] Ovid, Metamorph., iv. 59—happened in the lifetime of
Cadmus—told by one of the Minieides at her work—no connection with Greek fables—source unknown—No Roman
invented—quoted by Hyginus (C. 242. p. 351, Edit. Var. in
4° Lugd. Bat. 1742) after Ovid.*

* " Pyramus in Babylonia ob amorem Thisbes ipse se occidit" (Hyginus, *Fabulæ*, etc.); but there is no reference to Ovid.

dexterity did she follow and lead the morose humour of the old Tyrant, that in a few months she became his favourite. Could he have embraced the first child of which she was pregnant at the time of his decease, it is probable that a Will executed in anger would have been cancelled by affection; and that he would have moderated the shares of his two daughters, whom, in resentment to his son, he had enriched beyond the measure of female inheritance.

Of my two wealthy aunts on the father's side, Hester persevered in a life of celibacy, while Catherine became the wife of Mr. Edward Elliston, a Captain in the service of the East India Company, whom my grandfather styles his nephew in his Will. Both Mr. and Mrs. Elliston were dead before the date of my birth, or at least of my memory, and their only daughter and heiress will be mentioned in her proper place. These two Ladies are described by Mr. Law under the names of Flavia and Miranda, the Pagan and Christian sister. The sins of Flavia, which excluded her from the hope of salvation,* may not appear to our carnal apprehension of so black a dye. Her temper was gay and lively; she followed the fashion in her dress, and indulged her taste for company and public amusements; but her expence was regulated by œconomy :† she practised the decencies of Religion, nor

---

* "I shall not take upon me to say that it is impossible for Flavia to be saved: but thus much must be said, that she has no grounds from Scripture to think she is in the way of salvation." The whole description of her character, which is too long for quotation here, occupies the greater part of chap. vii. of Law's *Serious Call.*

† Her income was £200. "If she lives ten years longer . . . she will have spent sixty hundred pounds upon herself, bating only some shillings, crowns, or half-crowns that have gone from her in accidental charities." — Law's *Serious Call.*

is she accused of neglecting the essential duties of a wife
or a mother. The sanctity of her sister, the original or
the copy of Miranda, was indeed of an higher cast. By
austere pennance Mrs. Hester Gibbon laboured to attone
for the faults of her youth, for the profane vanities into
which she had been led or driven by authority and
example. But no sooner was she mistress of her own
actions and plentiful fortune, than the pious virgin abandoned for ever the house of a brother, from whom she was
alienated by the interest of this World and of the next.
With her spiritual guide, and a widow lady of the name
of Hutchinson, she retired to a small habitation at Cliffe,
in Northamptonshire, where she lived almost half a
century, surviving many years the loss of her two friends.
It is not my design to enumerate or extenuate the
Christian virtues of Miranda as they are described by
Mr. Law. Her charity, even in its excess, commands our
respect. "Her fortune" (says the historian) "is divided
between herself and several *other* poor people, and she
has only her part of relief from it." The sick and lame,
young children and aged persons were the first objects of
her benevolence; but she seldom refused to give alms to
a common beggar: "and instead" (I resume Mr. Law's
words) "of driving him away as a cheat, because she
does not know him, she relieves because he *is* a stranger,
and unknown to her. Excepting her victuals, she never
spent ten pounds a year upon herself. If you was to see
her, you would wonder what poor body it was, that was so
surprizingly neat and clean. She eats and drinks only
for the sake of living; and with so regular an abstinence
that every meal is an exercise of self denial, and she
humbles her body every time that she is forced to feed

it."[19] Her only study was the Bible, with some legends and books of piety which she read with implicit faith: she prayed five times each day; and as singing, according to the serious Call, is an indispensable part of devotion, she rehearsed the psalms and hymns of thanksgiving which she now, perhaps, may chant in a full chorus of Saints and Angels. Such is the portrait and such was the life of that holy Virgin who by Gods was Miranda called, and by men Mrs. Hester Gibbon. Of the pains and pleasures of a spiritual life *I* am ill-qualified to speak; yet I am inclined to believe that her lot, even on earth, has not been unhappy. Her pennance was voluntary, and, in her own eyes, meritorious; her time was filled by regular occupations; and instead of the insignificance of an old maid, she was surrounded by dependents, poor and abject as they were, who implored her bounty and imbibed her lessons. In the course of these Memoirs I shall not forget to introduce my personal acquaintance with the Saint.

At an advanced age, about the year 1761, Mr. Law died in the house, I may not say in the arms, of his beloved Miranda.] In our family he has left the reputation of a worthy and pious man, who believed all that he professed and practised all that he enjoyned. The character of a Nonjuror, which he maintained to the last,

---

[19] Second edition of Serious Call in 1732—Butterfly in Caterpillar, pp. 92–189.*

* These quotations are isolated passages taken from different parts of the same chapter.

"If a poor old traveller tells her that he has neither *strength*, nor food, nor money left, she never bids him go to the place from whence he came, or tells him that she cannot relieve him, because he may be a *cheat* or she does not know him, but she relieves him for that reason, because he is a stranger and unknown to her."—*Serious Call*, chap. viii.

For the Butterfly in Caterpillar, see Memoir A, p. 383.

is a sufficient evidence of his principles in Church and
state, and the sacrifice of interest to conscience will be
always respectable. His Theological writings, which our
domestic connection has tempted me to peruse, preserve
an imperfect sort of life, and I can pronounce with more
confidence and knowledge on the merits of the author.
His last compositions are darkly tinctured with the
incomprehensible visions of Jacob Behmen, and his discourse on the absolute unlawfullness of stage-entertainments [20] is sometimes quoted for a ridiculous intemperance
of sentiment and language. " The actors and spectators
must all be damned : the play-house is the porch of Hell,
the place of the Devil's abode, where he holds his filthy
court of evil spirits : a play is the Devil's triumph ; a
sacrifice performed to his glory, as much as in the
Heathen temples of Bacchus or Venus, etc." But these
sallies of Religious phrenzy must not extinguish the praise
which is due to Mr. William Law as a wit and a scholar.
His argument on topics of less absurdity is specious and
acute, his manner is lively, his style forcible and clear ;
and had not his vigourous mind been clouded by enthusiasm, he might be ranked with the most agreable and
ingenious writers of the times. While the Bangorian

---

[20] A small pamphlet in 1726 *—scandalized by Apollo and
Daphne †—all sober persons condemned Masqs—Nonj. and
Presb. Collier and Prynne—Rousseau, a Phil. less absurd ‡—
Excellent casuist c'est à vous à me le dire.

* *The Absolute Unlawfulness of
the Stage Entertainment fully demonstrated.*

† This was a pantomime, or
entertainment, of which the vocal
parts appear to have been composed
by Lewis Theobald, and are quoted
by Law in his pamphlet. *Apollo
and Daphne* was performed at
the Theatre Royal, Lincoln's Inn
Fields, in 1726, and at the Covent
Garden Theatre in 1734.

‡ Probably refers to Rousseau's
letter to d'Alembert on his article
Genève in the Encyclopédie, and
especially on his project for the
erection of a theatre for comedy in
that town. Published 1758.

controversy [21] was a fashionable theme, he entered the lists
on the subject of Christ's Kingdom and the authority of
the Priesthood: [22] against the plain account of the sacrament of the Lord's supper he resumed the combat with
Bishop Hoadley,[23] the object of Whig Idolatry and Tory
abhorrence; and at every weapon of attack and defence,
the Nonjuror, on the ground which is common to both,
approves himself at least equal to the Prelate.[24] On the

---

[21] Bang. Con. 1715–20—Hoadly answered Snape, Hare,
Potter, Sherlock (Biog. B., tom. vii.), disdained Law. Disdained?—three letters, 1rst eighth edition.*

[22] By the pen of an angel, says Adams (I. A. L., i. c. 17)
—I think out of character.

[23] A Demonstration of the gross and fundamental errors
of a late book,† 2d Edit. 1738 — a darker Enthusiast;
"the Religion of reason the very state of hellish minds"
(p. 196).

[24] Christian Div. to Whig. pol.—yet Religion and liberty
—Berkeley much above Hoadley (Warton on Pope, ii. 264)—
a Saint to a Priest, a Genius to a Disputant.‡

* The principal interest of the
Bangorian controversy now lies in
the fact that it was the immediate
cause of the practical suspension
of Convocation from 1717 till 1852.
When the minds of Churchmen
were in a state of considerable
alarm on the accession of George I.,
an alien in birth, language, and
religion, Benjamin Hoadly, Bishop
of Bangor, published his *Preservative against the Principles and
Practices of the Nonjurors in
Church and State*, in which he
denied the necessity of being in
communion with any visible Church;
and on March 17, 1717, he preached
a sermon reiterating this doctrine,
and making light of religious tests
and ecclesiastical government. A
committee of the Lower House of
Convocation appointed to consider
these utterances reported strongly
against them, but the discussion
aroused the partisanship of Whigs
and Tories, and before the report
could be presented to the Upper
House, Convocation was prorogued.
The report, however, drew from
Dr. Hoadly a dexterous reply; and
a prolonged and bitter controversy
arose, in the course of which over
a hundred publications appeared.
Dr. Sherlock and William Law were
among those who took part in this
Bangorian controversy.

† The late book was *A Plain
Account of the Nature and End
of the Sacrament of the Lord's
Supper*. It gave rise to a wide-
spread controversy at the time,
and then, and since, it has always
been attributed to Bishop Hoadly.
though the authorship was never
openly avowed by him. Law's
reply, called *A Demonstration of
the Gross and Fundamental Errors
of a Plain Account*, etc., was published in 1737.

‡ *Alciphron, or the Minute Philo-*

appearance of the fable of the Bees he drew his pen
against the licentious doctrine that private vices are public
benefits, and morality as well as Religion must joyn in
his applause. Mr. Law's master-work, the *Serious Call,*
is still read as a popular and powerful book of devotion.[25]
His precepts are rigid, but they are founded on the Gospel ;
his satire is sharp, but it is drawn from the knowledge of
human life ; and many of his portraits are not unworthy
of the pen of La Bruyere. If he finds a spark of piety
in his reader's mind, he will soon kindle it to a flame ;
and a Philosopher must allow that he exposes with equal
severity and truth the strange contradiction between the
faith and practise of the Christian World.   [Hell-fire and

---

[25] Dr. Johnson (Life by Bozzy, vol. i. p. 431 [this
should be 341]) styles it " the finest piece of hortatory
Theology in any language "—Would not trust Mrs. Thr.
with it (Letters, vol. ii. p. 214)—hugged it himself
(p. 400).*

sopher, a Platonic dialogue in defence of the Christian religion against the arguments of atheists, sceptics, and fatalists, by Bishop Berkeley, was published in 1732. Warton writes of it, " Alciphron did, indeed, well deserve to be mentioned on this occasion, notwithstanding it has been treated with contempt by a writer much inferior to Berkley in genius, learning, and taste," and adds the following note : " Bishop Hoadley (in letters to Lady Sundon, vol. i. of his works), but Sherlock thought highly of Alciphron, and presented it to Queen Caroline with many encomiums. The Queen was used to be delighted with the conversation of Berkley, and perhaps Hoadley was a little jealous of such a rival."—*Essay on the Genius and Writings of Pope,* ii. 264.

* From Mrs. Thrale to Dr. Johnson. ". . . I fancy there is no comparison between the scholastic learning of the two writers (Law and Watts); but there is prodigious knowledge of the human heart, and perfect acquaintance with common life, in the Serious Call. You used to say you would not trust me with that author upstairs on the dressing-room shelf, yet I now half wish I had never followed any precepts but his."—*Letters to and from the Late Samuel Johnson, LL.D. Published from the original MSS. in her possession by Hester Lynch Piozzi. Lond.,* 1788. Vol. ii. p. 214.

On p. 400 is a letter from Johnson to Miss Boothby, January 8, 1756, in which he writes, " I have returned your *Law,* which, however, I earnestly entreat you to give me ;" but there is no allusion to " hugging it to himself."

eternal damnation are darted from every page of the book; and it is, indeed, somewhat whimsical that the Fanatics who most vehemently inculcate the love of God should be those who despoil him of every amiable attribute.]

CHAPTER II.

I WAS born at Putney in Surry, the twenty-seventh of April. O.S., the eighth of May. N.S., in the year one thousand seven hundred and thirty-seven, within a twelfmonth of my father's marriage with Judith Porten, his first wife. From my birth I have enjoyed the right of Primogeniture; but I was succeeded by five brothers and one sister, all of whom were snatched away in their infancy. [They died so young, and I was myself so young at the time of their deaths, that I could not then feel, nor can I now estimate their loss, the importance of which could only have been ascertained by future contingencies. The shares of fortune to which younger children are reduced by our English laws would have been sufficient, however, to oppress my inheritance; and the compensation of their friendship must have depended on the uncertain event of character and conduct, on the affinity or opposition of our reciprocal sentiments.] My five brothers, whose names may be found in the Parish register of Putney, I shall not pretend to lament; but from my childhood to the present hour I have deeply and sincerely regretted my sister, whose life was somewhat prolonged, and whom I remember to have seen an amiable infant. The relation of a brother and a sister, especially if they do not marry, appears to me of a very singular nature. It is a familiar and tender friendship with a female, much about our own age; an affection perhaps softened by the secret influence of sex, but pure from any mixture of sensual desire, the sole species of Platonic love that can be indulged with truth and without danger.

[About four months before the birth of their eldest son my parents were delivered from a state of servitude, and my father inherited a considerable estate, which was magnified in his own eyes by flattery and hope. The prospect of Spanish gold from our naval contract with the Court of Madrid was suddenly overclouded about three years after my grandfather's decease. The public faith had been pledged for the security of the English merchants; their effects were seized (in 1740) on the first hostilities between the two nations. After the return of peace (in 1749 and 1763), the Contractors or their representatives demanded the restitution of their property with a large claim of damages and interest. But the Catholic Kings absolve themselves from the engagements of their predecessors :[1] the helpless strangers were referred by the ministers to the Judges, and from the Judges to the Ministers, and this antiquated debt has melted away in oblivion and despair. Such a stroke could not have been averted by any foresight or care; but the arts of industry were not devolved from the father to the son, and several undertakings which had been profitable in the hands of the merchant became

---

[1] Ferdinand VI. held a consult of Lawyers and Divines—not obliged to pay former debts—same Moral, continued in fact—Nouv. Voy. en Esp., tom. ii. pp. 30, 31.*

* See Appendix, 4, p. 97.

barren or adverse in those of the gentleman.] At the general election of 1741 Mr. Gibbon and Mr. Delmé stood an expensive and successful contest against Mr. Dummer and Mr. Henly,* afterwards Lord Chancellor and Earl of Northington. The Whig candidates had a majority of the resident voters; but the corporation was firm in the Tory interest: a sudden creation of one hundred and seventy new freemen turned the scale; and a supply was readily obtained of respectable Volunteers who flocked from all parts of England to support the cause of their political friends. The new Parliament opened with the victory of an opposition which was fortified by strong clamour and strange coalitions.[2] From the event of the first divisions, Sir Robert Walpole perceived that he could no longer lead a Majority in the house of Commons, and prudently resigned, after a reign of one and twenty years, the sceptre of the state (1742). But the fall of an unpopular Minister was not succeeded, according to general expectation, by a millennium of happiness and virtue; some Courtiers lost their places, some patriots lost their characters. Lord Orford's offences vanished with his power, and, after a short vibration, the Pelham government was fixed on the old basis of the Whig Aristocracy. In the year 1745 the throne and the constitution were attacked by a rebellion which does

---

[2] Of P. of W. and Jac.—Allowance in [17]37—Mr. Gibbon had been spoken to (Doddington's Diary, p. 444 †)—Was it not Philip Gybbon of Rye—a kinsman?

* For Southampton.

† "A narrative of what passed between the Prince and Mr. Doddington, and afterwards between Sir R. Walpole and Mr. Dodington, upon the resolution of H.R.H. to bring a demand in Parliament for an augmentation of his allowance to £100,000 per annum and for a jointure upon the Princess" (p. 391, ed. 1823).

not reflect much honour on the national spirit, since the English friends of the Pretender wanted courage to joyn his standard, and his enemies (the bulk of the people) allowed him to advance into the heart of the Kingdom." Without daring, perhaps without desiring to aid the rebels, my father invariably adhered to the Tory opposition: in the most critical season, he accepted, for the service of the party, the office of Alderman in the city of London; but the duties were so repugnant to his inclination and habits, that he resigned his Gown at the end of a few months. The second parliament in which he sate * was præmaturely dissolved (1747): and as he was unable or unwilling to maintain a second contest for Southampton, the life of the Senator expired in that dissolution.

[At home my father possessed the inestimable treasure of an amiable and affectionate wife, the constant object during a twelve years' marriage of his tenderness and esteem. My mother's portraits convey some idea of her beauty: the elegance of her manners has been attested by surviving friends; and my aunt Porten could descant for hours on the talents and virtues of her amiable sister. A domestic life would have been the choice and the felicity of my mother, but she vainly attempted to check with a silken rein the passions of an independent husband. The World was open before him: his spirit was lively, his appearance splendid, his aspect chearful, his address polite; he gracefully moved in the highest circles of

---

" Wish for Home—From a Witness that he was advised to march to Oxford—Tory Youths—Fathers would bo forced.

* He had been elected for Petersfield in 1734.

society, and I have heard him boast that he was the only member of Opposition admitted into the old Club at White's, where the first names of the Country were often rejected. Yet such was the pleasing flexibility of his temper, that he could accommodate himself with ease and almost with indifference to every class—to a meeting of Lords or farmers, of Citizens or Foxhunters; and without being admired as a wit, Mr. Gibbon was everywhere beloved as a companion and esteemed as a man. But, in the pursuit of pleasure, his happiness, alas! and his fortune were gradually injured. Œconomy was superseded by fashion; his income proved inadequate to his expence; his house at Putney, in the neighbourhood of London, acquired the dangerous fame of hospitable entertainment; against the more dangerous temptation of play he was not invulnerable, and large sums were silently precipitated into that bottomless pit. Few minds have sufficient ressources to support the weight of idleness; and had he continued to walk in the path of mercantile industry, my father might have been a happier, and his son would be a richer, man.

Of these public and private scenes, and of the first years of my own life, I must be indebted not to memory, but to information. Our fancy may create and describe a perfect Adam, born in the mature vigour of his corporeal and intellectual faculties.

> " As new wak'd from soundest sleep,
> Soft on the flow'ry herb I found me laid
> In balmy sweat, which with his beams the Sun
> Soon dry'd, and on the reaking moisture fed.
> Strait toward Heav'n my wond'ring eyes I turned
> And gaz'd awhile the ample sky, till rais'd
> By quick instinctive motion, up I sprung

> As thitherward endevoring, and upright
> Stood on my feet; about me round I saw
> Hill, dale, and shady woods, and sunny plains,
> And liquid lapse of murm'ring streams; by these
> Creatures that liv'd and mov'd, and walk'd or flew,
> Birds on the branches warbling: all things smil'd;
> With fragrance and with joy my heart o'erflow'd.
> Myself I then perus'd, and limb by limb
> Survey'd, and sometimes went and sometimes ran
> With supple joints, as lively vigor led;
> But who I was, or where, or from what cause,
> Knew not: to speak I try'd and forthwith spake
> My tongue obey'd, and readily could name
> Whate'er I saw." [4]

It is thus that the poet has animated his statue: the Theologian must infuse a miraculous gift of science and language, the Philosopher might allow more time for the gradual exercise of his new senses, but all would agree that the consciousness and memory of Adam might proceed in a regular series from the moment of his birth. Far different is the origin and progress of human nature, and I may confidently apply to myself the common history of the whole species. Decency and ignorance cast a veil over the mystery of generations, but I may relate that after floating nine months in a liquid element, I was painfully transported into the vital air. Of a new born infant it cannot be predicated "he thinks, therefore he *is;*" it can only be affirmed "he suffers, therefore he feels." But in this imperfect state of existence I was still unconscious of myself and of the universe, my eyes were open without the power of vision, and, according to Mr. de Buffon, the

---

[4] Milton, P. L., viii. 253–273, perfectly original—punctuation of fragrance—authority places the comma after "smil'd"—taste might hesitate.

rational soul, that secret and incomprehensible energy, did not manifest its presence till after the fortieth day.[5] During the first year I was below the greatest part of the brute creation, and must inevitably have perished, had I been abandoned to my own care. Three years at least had elapsed before I acquired our peculiar privileges, the facility of erect motion, and the intelligent use of articulate and discriminating sounds. Slow is the growth of the body: that of the mind is still slower: at the age of seven years I had not attained to one half of the strength and proportions of manhood; and could the mental powers be measured with [the] same accuracy, their deficiency would be found far more considerable. The exercise of the understanding combines the past with the present; but the youthful fibres are so tender, the cells are so minute, that the first impressions are obliterated by new images; and I strive without much success to recollect the persons and objects which might appear at the time most forcibly to affect me. The local scenery of my education is, however, before my eyes: my father's contest for Southampton when I must have been between three and four years old, and my childish revenge in shouting, after being whipt, the names of his opponents, is the first event that I seem to remember; but

---

[5] See Buffon, Hist. Nat., tom. ii., iii., suppl. iv.*—more philos. as poet as Milton, tom. ii. pp. 364–370—progress of vision from Cheselden's experience, see Berkely.†

* See Appendix, 5, p. 97.

† Berkeley's *Theory of Vision vindicated and explained* first appeared in *The Daily Post Boy* of September 9, 1732, and was published in a separate form the following year. This is *not* in the Brit. Mus., but a reprint in 1860 gives a facsimile of the title-page of the 1733 edition. At p. 127 reference is made to a case in which Dr. Cheselden couched a boy of thirteen or fourteen. The patient, on seeing for the first time, was unable to judge the distance of objects, but thought they were all close to him.

even that belief may be illusive, and I may only repeat the hearsay of a riper season. In the entire period of ten or twelve years from our birth, our pains and pleasures, our actions and designs, are remotely connected with our present mode of existence ; and, according to a just computation, we should begin to reckon our life from the age of puberty.*]

The death of a new-born child before that of its parents may seem an unnatural, but it is strictly a probable event; since of any given number, the greater part are extinguished before their ninth year, before they possess the faculties of the mind or body. Without accusing the profuse waste or imperfect workmanship of Nature, I shall only observe that this unfavourable chance was multiplied against my infant existence. So feeble was my constitution, so precarious my life, that in the baptism of each of my brothers, my father's prudence successively repeated my Christian name of Edward, that in case of the departure of the eldest son, this patronymic appellation might be still perpetuated in the family.

" Uno avulso non deficit alter."

To preserve and to rear so frail a being, the most tender assiduity was scarcely sufficient, and my mother's attention was somewhat diverted by her frequent pregnancies, by an exclusive passion for her husband, and by the dissipation of the World, in which his taste and

---

* " Tant pour l'esprit que pour le corps, l'enfant n'est rien ou n'est que peu de chose jusqu'à l'âge de puberté ; mais cet âge est l'aurore de nos premiers beaux jours, c'est le moment où toutes les facultés, tant corporelles qu'intellectuelles, commencent à entrer en plein exercise ; où les organes ayant acquis tout leur développement, le sentiment s'épanouit comme une belle fleur, qui bientôt doit produire le fruit précieux de la raison."—Buffon, *Hist. Nat. Supplément*, tome iv. p. 384 (1777).

authority obliged her to mingle. But the maternal office was supplied by my aunt, Mrs. Catherine Porten, at whose name I feel a tear of gratitude trickling down my cheek. A life of celibacy transferred her vacant affection to her sister's first child; my weakness excited her pity; her attachment was fortified by labour and success, and if there are any, as I trust there are some, who rejoyce that I live, to that dear and excellent woman they must hold themselves indebted. Many anxious and solitary days did she consume in the patient tryal of every mode of relief and amusement. Many wakeful nights did she sit by my bedside in trembling expectation that each hour would be my last. [My poor aunt has often told me, with tears in her eyes, how I was nearly starved by a nurse that had lost her milk : how long she herself was apprehensive lest my crazy frame, which is now of common shape, should remain for ever crooked and deformed. From one dangerous malady, the small-pox, I was indeed rescued by the practise of inoculation, which had been recently introduced into England,[6] and was still opposed by medical, Religious, and even political prejudice. But it is only against the smallpox that a preservative has been found : I was successively afflicted by lethargies and feavers; by opposite tendencies to a consumptive and a dropsical habit; by a contraction of

---

[6] First by Lady M. W. M. from C. P.* in 1722—Prince of Wales' post—Q. Caroline—declined, revived about 1740 from America—Kirkpatrick apud Maty, J. B., tom. xiii. pp. 386–391 †—See vol. xiii. pp. 73–77, first in 1727 in Lettres sur les Anglois—loose and lively—Turks never—fate.

* C. P. probably intended for Constantinople, but it was at Adrianople that she first met with the practice, in 1717.
† See Appendix, 6, p. 98.

my nerves, a fistula in my eye, and the bite of a dog most vehemently suspected of madness : and in the list of my sufferings from my birth to the age of puberty few physical ills would be omitted. From Sir Hans Sloane and Dr. Mead, to Ward and the Chevalier Taylor,* every practitioner was called to my aid; the fees of Doctors were swelled by the bills of Apothecaries and Surgeons: there was a time when I swallowed more Physic than food; and my body is still marked with the indelible scars of lancets, issues, and caustics.] Of the various and frequent disorders of my childhood my own recollection is dark; nor do I wish to expatiate on so disgusting a topic. I will not follow the vain example of Cardinal Quirini,[7] who has filled half a volume of his memoirs with medical consultations on his particular case; nor shall I imitate the naked frankness of Montagne, who exposes all the symptoms of his malady, and the operation of each dose of physic on his nerves and bowels.[8] It may not, however, be useless to observe that in this early period the care of my mind was too frequently neglected for that of my health : compassion always suggested an excuse for the indulgence of the master, or the idleness of the pupil; and the chain of

---

[7] Appendix ad L. 1. Part ii. Comment de Rebus Card. A. M. Quirini. Brixiæ, 1750, ad calcem Tom. ii. pp. 145—Some Italian—many German—one Paris—no Dutch or English— Yet Boerhave.

[8] Not in Essais, but in Voyage en Italie, etc., performed in 1580-1, found in the old castle, printed in 1774—Paris in 4to with a very good preface—body rather than soul of Montagne.†

* For an interesting note on these persons, see *Notes and Queries*, Feb. 2, 1889.

† *Journal d'un Voyage en Italie,* par Michel de Montaigne (1774), vol. iii. p. 261. The author enters into the fullest possible details of his maladies and symptoms.

my education was broken as often as I was recalled from the school of learning to the bed of sickness.

As soon as the use of speech had prepared my infant reason for the admission of knowledge, I was taught the arts of reading, writing, and vulgar Arithmetic. So remote is the date, so vague is the memory of their origin in myself, that were not the error corrected by Analogy I should be tempted to conceive them as innate. [In the improved state of society in which I have the good fortune to exist, these attainments are so generally diffused that they no longer constitute the liberal distinctions of Scholars and Gentlemen. The operations of writing and reading must seem, on an abstract view, to require the labour of Genius; to transform articulate sounds into visible signs by the swift and almost spontaneous motion of the hand; to render visible signs into articulate sounds by the voluntary and rapid utterance of the voice. Yet experience has proved that these operations of such apparent difficulty, when they are taught to all may be learned by all, and that the meanest capacity in the most tender age is not inadequate to the task.[9] Between the sister arts there exists, however, a material difference, the one is connected with mental intelligence, the other with manual dexterity. The excellence of reading, if the vocal organ be not defective, the propriety of the cadence, the tones and the pauses, is always in just proportion to the knowledge, taste, and feelings of the reader. But an illiterate scribe may delineate a correct and elegant copy

---

[9] Yet reading art, assurance practise—some authors very good or bad—d'Alembert *—Hatsell.

* This refers to the *Éloge des Académiciens;* cf. Works of d'Alembert. 18 vols. Paris, 1805. Vol. iiL p. 24. The whole essay bears on the subject, but I can find no passage especially applicable.

of penmanship; while the sense and style of the Philosopher or poet are most awkwardly scrawled in such ill-formed and irregular characters that the authors themselves, after a short interval, will be incapable of decyphering them.[10] My own writing is of a middle cast, legible rather than fair; but I may observe that age and long practise, which are often productive of negligence, have rather improved than corrupted my hand. The science of numbers, the third element of our primitive education, may be esteemed the best scale to measure the degrees of the human understanding; a child or a peasant performs with ease and assurance the four first rules of arithmetic; the profound mysteries of Algebra are reserved for the disciples of Newton and Bernouilli.] In my childhood I was praised for the readiness with which I could multiply and divide by memory alone two sums of several figures; such praise encouraged my growing talent, and had I persevered in this line of application, I might have acquired some fame in Mathematical studies.

After this prævious institution at home, or at a day-school at Putney, I was delivered, at the age of seven (April, 1744), into the hands of Mr. John Kirkby, who exercised about eighteen months the office of my domestic Tutor. His own words, which I shall

---

[10] English better than foreigners, present age than last— Compare reformers, etc., in Jortin's Erasmus with our round Robin in Boswell.*

* In John Jortin's *Life of Erasmus*, 1758, there are two plates of specimens of handwriting. Plate I. (p. 629) contains those of Erasmus, Melancthon, Luther, and Œcolampadius; Plate II. (p. 630), Bullinger, Bucer, Tunstal, and Wolsey.

The facsimile of the well-known Round Robin about Johnson's epitaph for the monument of Oliver Goldsmith will be found in Croker's edition of Boswell's *Johnson*.

here transcribe, inspire in his favour a sentiment of pity and esteem. "During my abode in my native County of Cumberland, in quality of an indigent Curate, I used now and then in a summer, when the pleasantness of the season invited, to take a solitary walk to the sea-shore, which lies about two miles from the town where I lived. Here I would amuse myself one while in viewing at large the agreable prospect which surrounded me; and another while (confining my sight to nearer objects), in admiring the vast variety of beautiful shells thrown upon the beach, some of the choicest of which I always picked up to divert my little-ones upon my return. One time among the rest, taking such a journey in my head, I sat down upon the declivity of the beach, with my face to the sea, which was now come up within a few yards of my feet, when immediately the sad thoughts of the wretched condition of my family, and the unsuccessfulness of all endeavours to amend it, came crouding into my mind, which drove me into a deep melancholy, and ever and anon forced tears from my eyes." Distress at last forced him to leave the country; his learning and virtue introduced him to my father, and at Putney he might have found at least a temporary shelter, had not an act of indiscretion again driven him into the World. One day reading prayers in the parish Church, he most unluckily forgot the name of King George; his patron, a loyal subject, dismissed him with some reluctance and a decent reward; and *how* the poor man ended his days I have never [been] able to learn.*

---

* John Kirkby, born 1705, died May 21, 1754. In 1743 he was appointed Rector of Blackmanstone, Romney Marsh, but a work published by him the same year, *A Demonstration from Christian Principles that the Present Regulation of Ecclesiastical Revenues in the*

Mr. John Kirkby is the author of two small Volumes, the Life of Automathes (London, 1745), and an English and Latin Grammar (London, 1746), which as a testimony of gratitude he dedicated (November 5, 1745) to my father. The books are before me : from them the pupil may judge the præceptor, and, upon the whole, the judgement will not be unfavourable. The Grammar is executed with accuracy and skill, and I know not whether any better existed at the time in our language ; but the Life of Automathes aspires to the honours of a Philosophical fiction. It is the story of a youth, the son of a shipwrecked exile, who lives alone on a desert island from infancy to the age of manhood. A Hind is his nurse ; he inherits a cottage with many useful and curious instruments. Some ideas remain of the education of his two first years ; some arts are borrowed from the beavers of a neighbouring lake ; some truths are revealed in supernatural visions. With these helps and his own industry Automathes becomes a self-taught though speechless philosopher, who had investigated with success his own mind, the Natural World, the abstract sciences, and the great principles of morality and Religion. The author is not entitled to the merit of invention, since he has blended the English story of Robinson Crusoe with the Arabian romance of Hai Ebn Yokhdan, which he might read in the Latin version of Pocock.[11]

---

[11] Defoe accused, yet 1 Al. Selkirk returned with the Brit. priv., Oct 1, 1711—accounts of Wood, Rogers, and

Church of England is Contrary to the Design of Christianity, is said to have destroyed his chance of preferment, and to have reduced him to accept the post of tutor to Gibbon, as a means of maintaining himself. Readers of Sir W. Scott's Life will remember that *Automathes* was one of the favourites of his boyish days.

In the Automathes [12] I cannot praise either the depth of thought or elegance of style, but the book is not devoid of entertainment or instruction, and, among several interesting passages, I would select the discovery of fire, which produces by accidental mischief the discovery of conscience.   A man who had thought so much

---

Cooke soon published—substance in Campbell's, vol. i. pp. 150–157—Robinson Crusoe in 1719, publici Juris.* A. S. an hunter—agility, loss of language—R. C. a shepherd, husbandman, etc., small resemblance—Two Vol. may be reduced to 150 pages, leave out Voyages, Cannibals, Spaniards, Religion, etc., those original, man, arts, society, accuracy of fiction too much praised—such an isle would have been a swamp and wilderness—reptiles, mosquitoes, Vines, Sugar canes, goats indigenous in S. A.—Alas! His Cavalier could not deceive Mr. Harte †—Prince Maurice alive in 1635 ‡ (Mem., Vol. ii. p. 62).

[12] Phil. Autodidactus, sive Epistola Abu Jaafir Ebn Tophail de Hai Ebn Yokdhan.   Edw. Pocock the doctor's son, Oxon. 1700, 2nde Edit., B. B. Pocock (T.T.), Le Clerc, B. C.,§ pp. 76–98—master of Averroes who died 1198—Mahometan mystics—Abu Jaafir translated into English by the Quakers —Simon Ockley (1711 in 8°) opposed them with new version and appendix.‖

* *A Cruising Voyage round the World,* . . . by Captain Woodes Rogers. 8vo. London: A. Bell and B. Lintot. 1712. On pp. 124–131 is an account of Alex. Selkirk.

A Voyage to the South Sea and round the World, perform'd in the years 1708, 1709, 1710, *and* 1711, . . . by Captain Edward Cooke. 2 vols., 8vo. London: B. Lintot and R. Gosling. 1712. In chapter x., pp. 105–119, is a description of the island of Juan Fernandez, but there is no mention of Selkirk.

Navigantium atque Itinerantium Bibliotheca, or a Complete Collection of Voyages and Travels, . . . by John Harris. *Now carefully revised and continued down to the present time* [by John Campbell]. 2 vols., folio. London: 1744. In section xvi., pp. 150–181, is an account of the voyage of Captain Woodes Rogers, etc.; on pp. 155–157, of Alexander Selkirk.

Robinson Crusoe was first published on April 25, 1719.

† See Appendix, 7, p. 98.

‡ "I came to the Hague the 8th of March, 1635, having spent three years and a half in Germany, and the greatest part of it in the Swedish army. I spent some time in Holland. . . . There I had the opportunity of seeing the Dutch army and their famous general, Prince Maurice."—*Memoirs of a Cavalier.*   Maurice of Nassau, second son of William the Silent, died at the Hague in April, 1625.

§ I have examined the twenty-eight volumes of the *Bibliothèque Choisie,* but cannot find this reference.   Cf. Memoir E, p. 296.

‖ See Appendix, 8, p. 99.

on the subjects of language and education was surely no ordinary præceptor; my childish years and his hasty departure prevented me from enjoying the full benefit of his lessons, but they enlarged my knowledge of Arithmetic and left a clear impression of the English and Latin Rudiments.

In my ninth year (January, 1746), in a lucid interval of comparative health, my father adopted the convenient and customary mode of English education; and I was sent to Kingston-upon-Thames, to a school of about seventy boys, which was kept by Dr. Woodson * and his assistants. Every time I have since passed over Putney common I have always noticed the spot where my mother, as we drove along in the coach, admonished me that I was now going into the World, and [had] much [to] learn to think and act for myself. The expression may appear ludicrous; yet there is not, in the course of life, a more remarkable change than the removal of a child from the luxury and freedom of a wealthy house to the frugal diet and strict subordination of a school; from the tenderness of parents and the obsequiousness of servants to the rude familiarity of his equals, the insont tyranny of his seniors, and the rod, perhaps, of a cruel and capricious pædagogue. Such hardships may steel the mind and body against the injuries of fortune; but my timid reserve was

---

* Richard Wooddesdon (1704–1774) was a clerk, and subsequently chaplain at Magdalen College, Oxford. He was probably usher to Mr. Hilay at Reading, and between 1732 and 1738 was appointed master of the Free School at Kingston-on-Thames, a post which he held till 1772. Among his pupils were Stevens, the editor of Shakespeare, and Hayley the poet. He was a man of very amiable character; and an account of him, in the *Memoirs of the Life of Gilbert Wakefield*, i. 41, gives several interesting examples of the esteem and affection entertained towards him.—Bloxam's *Magdalen College Register*, i. 136 (1853). It may have been owing to Dr. Wooddesdon's influence that Gibbon was sent to Magdalen College.

astonished by the crowd and tumult of the school; the
want of strength and activity disqualified me for the sports
of the play-field; nor have I forgot how often, in the year
forty-six, I was reviled and buffeted for the sins of my
Tory ancestors.   By the common methods of discipline, at
the expence of many tears and some blood, I purchased the
knowledge of the Latin syntax; and not long since I was
possessed of the dirty volumes of Phædrus and Cornelius
Nepos, which I painfully construed and darkly understood.   The choice of these authors is not injudicious.
The *Lives* of Cornelius Nepos, the friend of Atticus and
Cicero, are composed in the style of the purest age; his
simplicity is elegant, his brevity copious; he exhibits a
series of men and manners; and with such illustrations
as every pedant is not indeed qualified to give, this Classic
biographer may initiate a young Student in the history
of Greece and Rome.   The use of fables or apologues
has been approved in every age, from ancient India to
modern Europe; they convey in familiar images the
truths of morality and prudence, and the most childish
understanding (I advert to the scruples of Rousseau[13]) will
not suppose either that beasts *do* speak, or that men *may*
lye.   A fable represents the genuine characters of animals,
and a skillful master might extract from Pliny and
Buffon some pleasing lessons of Natural history, a science
well adapted to the taste and capacity of children.   The
Latinity of Phædrus is not exempt from an alloy of
the Silver age; but his manner is concise, terse, and

---

[13] Oeuvres de Rousseau, Tom. iv. pp. 157–165; Emile l.
ii.—children do, and do not understand.*

* See Appendix, 9, p. 99.

sententious;[14] the Thracian slave discreetly breathes the spirit of a freeman, and when the text is sound, the style is perspicuous. But his fables, after a long oblivion, were first published by Peter Pithou,[15] from a corrupt manuscript: the labours of fifty Editors confess the defects of the copy, as well as the value of the original; and a schoolboy may have been whipt for misapprehending a passage which Bentley could not restore, and which Burman could not explain.

My studies were too frequently interrupted by sickness; and after a real or nominal residence at Kingston school of near two years, I was finally recalled (December, 1747) by my mother's death, which was occasioned, in her thirty-eighth year, by the consequences of her last labour. [As I had seldom enjoyed the smiles of maternal tenderness she was rather the object of my respect than of my love : some natural tears were soon wiped.] I was too young to feel the importance of my loss, and the image of her person and conversation is faintly imprinted in my memory. The affectionate heart of my aunt, Catherine Porten, bewailed a sister and a friend, but my poor father was inconsolable; and the transport of grief seemed to threaten his life or his

---

[14] See Fabricius, B. L.,* Tom. ii. pp. 24–35, edit. Ernest —Consult prefaces—Burman's quarto.

[15] Pithæus, a scholar, sage, friend in Thuanus, l. cxvii., in Tom. v. pp. 643, 644—Chant du Cygne, published Phædrus and died in 1596.†

[16] Prevot's Marquis—Selima—English translation read and compared at the time.‡

* *Bibliotheca Latina,* by Johann Albert Fabricius (1668-1736). New edition, edited by Ernesti. Leipsic. 3 vols. 1773-4. The whole of chap. iii. is devoted to a consideration of the various editions of the Fables of Phædrus.

† See Appendix, 10, p. 100.

‡ Cf. Memoir A, p. 378.

reason. I can never forget the scene of our first interview, some weeks after the fatal event; the awful silence, the room hung with black, the midday tapers, his sighs and tears, his praises of my mother, a saint in heaven, his solemn adjuration that I would cherish her memory and imitate her virtues; and the fervour with which he kissed and blessed me as the sole surviving pledge of their loves. The storm of passion insensibly subsided into calmer melancholy: [but he persevered in the use of mourning much beyond the term which has been fixed by decency and custom. Three years after my mother's death, his situation is described by Mr. Mallet,[17] who then resided at Putney, and with whose family my father had formed a very intimate connection. In a pleasing little composition entitled the *Wedding-day*, Cupid and Hymen undertake the office of inviting some chosen friends to celebrate the ninth anniversary (October 2, 1750) of the poet's nuptials. Cupid flies eastward to London.

> " His brother too, with sober cheer,
>   For the same end did westward steer;
>   But first a pensive love forlorn,
>   Who three long weeping years has borne
>   His torch revers'd, and all around,
>   Where once it flam'd with cypress bound,
>   Sent off to call a neighbouring friend,
>   On whom the mournful train attend;
>   And bid him, this one day at least,
>   For such a pair, at such a feast,
>   Strip off the sable vest, and wear
>   His once gay look and happier air."]

At a convivial meeting of his friends Mr. Gibbon

---

[17] Mallet, Works in Poets, vol. liii. pp. 184–191.*

* *Cupid and Hymen; or, The Wedding Day.*

might affect or enjoy a gleam of chearfulness; but his plan of happiness was for ever destroyed, and after the loss of his companion he was left alone in a world of which the business and pleasure were to him irksome or insipid. After some unsuccessful tryals he renounced the tumult of London and the hospitality of Putney, and buried himself in the rural or rather rustic solitude of Buriton from which during several years he seldom emerged. [It must not, however, be dissembled that the sorrowful widower was urged to this resolution by the growing perplexity of his affairs. His fortune was impaired; his debts had multiplied, and as long as his son was a minor, he could not disengage his estate from the legal fetters of an entail. Had my mother lived, he must soon have retired into the country, with more comfort indeed, but without the credit of a pious and disinterested motive. Shall I presume to add that a secret inconstancy, which always adhered to his disposition, might impell him at once to sink the man of fashion in the character and occupations of a Hampshire farmer? [18]]

As far back as I can remember, the house, near Putney bridge and churchyard, of my maternal grandfather appears in the light of my proper and native

---

[18] Flatus in Law, pp. 189–195, mem.*

* "Flatus is rich and in health, yet always uneasy and always searching after happiness. Every time you visit him you find some new project in his head; he is eager upon it, as something that is more worth his while, and will do more for him than anything that is already past. Every new thing so seizes him, that if you was to take him from it, he would think himself quite undone. His sanguine temper, and strong passions, promise him so much happiness in everything, that he is always cheated, and is satisfied with nothing."—*Serious Call*, chap. xii.

home. It was there that I was allowed to spend the greatest part of my time, in sickness or in health, during my school-vacations and my parents' residence in London, and finally after my mother's death. Three months after that event, in the spring of 1748, the commercial ruin of her father, Mr. James Porten, was accomplished and declared: he suddenly absconded: but as his effects were not sold, nor the house evacuated till the Christmas following, I enjoyed during the whole year the society of my aunt without much consciousness of her impending fate. I feel a melancholy pleasure in commemorating my obligations to that excellent woman, Mrs. Catherine Porten, the true mother of my mind as well as of my health. Her natural good sense was improved by the perusal of the best books in the English language; and if her reason was sometimes clouded by prejudice, her sentiments were never disguised by hypocrisy or affectation. Her indulgent tenderness, the frankness of her temper, and my innate rising curiosity soon removed all distance between us: like friends of an equal age, we freely conversed on every topic, familiar or abstruse: and it was her delight and reward to observe the first shoots of my young ideas. Pain and languor were often soothed by the voice of instruction and amusement; and to her kind lessons I ascribe my early and invincible love of reading, which I would not exchange for the treasures of India. I should perhaps be astonished were it possible to ascertain the date at which a favourite tale was engraved by frequent repetition in my memory; the cavern of the winds, the palace of Felicity, and the fatal moment, at the end of three months or centuries, when Prince Adolphus is overtaken by Time, who had

worn out so many pair of wings in the pursuit.[19]   Before
I left Kingston school, I was well acquainted with Pope's
Homer and the Arabian Nights-entertainments,[20] two
books which will always please by the moving picture of
human manners and specious miracles. The verses of Pope
accustomed my ear to the sound of poetic harmony; in the
death of Hector and the shipwreck of Ulysses I tasted the
new emotions of terror and pity, and seriously disputed
with my aunt on the vices and virtues of the Heroes of
the Trojan War. From Pope's Homer to Dryden's Virgil
was an easy transition; but I know not how, from some
fault in the author, the translator, or the reader, the pious
Æneas did not so forcibly seize on my imagination, and
I derived more pleasure from Ovid's Metamorphoses,
especially in the fall of Phaëthon, and the speeches of

---

[19] An Episode in Hipp[olytus] of Douglas, I believe by
the Countess d'Anois—foolish novel of love and honour.*

[20] Galland's merit : he chose the best, four Vol. lately in
French, much below, except the Maugreby—he found the
medium between Arab-tongue and French-ear proved by
Richardson (in Arab Grammar)—litteral Version of the best
tale the Spec's glass-merchant Cazotte new translator ingenious and loose : we lose half the pleasure.†

* *Histoire d'Hypolite, Comte de Duglas*, par Mme Catherine La Mothe, Comtesse d'Aulnoy. 1699.

† Antoine Galland (1646–1715), Oriental scholar and numismatist, was a man who attained celebrity by dint of extraordinary energy and perseverance in the face of great obstacles. He was the first to introduce the Arabian Tales, known as the Thousand and One Nights, to European readers. His *Mille et une Nuits, Contes Arabes traduits en français*, appeared in Paris 1704–1708, in 12 vols., 12mo.

Jacques Cazotte, born 1720, was murdered during the Revolution, on September 25, 1792. His career was a very remarkable one; but for the purposes of the present note it is sufficient to record that, in conjunction with an Arab monk, Dom Chavis, he produced a collection of Arabian tales, which formed a continuation of the Thousand and One Nights, and is contained in vols. xxxvii.–xl. of the *Cabinet des Fées*. Dom Chavis, who had but an imperfect knowledge of European languages, in most cases gave the outline of the stories to Cazotte, who rendered them into French. *Maugrabi*, however, is said to be entirely Cazotte's own composition.

Ajax and Ulysses. My grandfather's flight unlocked the door of a tolerable library, and I turned over many English pages of Poetry and romance, of history and travels. Where a title attracted my eye, without fear or awe I snatched the volume from the shelf, and Mrs. Porten, who indulged herself in moral and religious speculation, was more prone to encourage than to check a curiosity above the strength of a boy. This year 1748, the twelfth of my age, I shall note as the most propitious to the growth of my intellectual stature.

[After such satisfaction as could be given to his creditors,] the relicks of my grandfather's fortune afforded a bare annuity for his own maintenance; and his daughter, my worthy aunt, who had already passed her fortieth year, was left naked and destitute. [Her not more wealthy relations were not *absolutely* without bowels; but] her noble spirit scorned a life of obligation and dependence, and after revolving several schemes, she preferred the humble industry of keeping a boarding-house for Westminster school, where she laboriously earned a competence for her old age. This singular opportunity of blending the advantages of private and public education decided my father: after the Christmas holidays, in January, 1749, I accompanied Mrs. Porten to her new house in College street, and was immediately entered in the school, of which Dr. John Nicoll was at time Head-master.[21] At

---

[21] Dr. John Nicoll, 2d or head master 1714–53—third successor of Busby, 1638–95—flogged how many Bishops and Judges (Biogr. Brit., p. 55, new Edit.).*

* John Nicoll, D.D., born in 1683, was appointed second master of Westminster School in 1714, and head-master in 1733. He held this post till 1753, and died in 1765. His name is also spelt "Nichols"

first I was alone; but my aunt's resolution was praised;
her character was esteemed: her friends were numerous
and active: in the course of some years she became
the mother of forty or fifty boys, for the most part of
family and fortune; and as her primitive habitation was
too narrow, she built and occupied a spacious mansion in
Dean's Yard. I shall always be ready to joyn in the
common opinion, that our public schools, which have
produced so many eminent characters, are the best
adapted to the Genius and constitution of the English
people. A boy of spirit may acquire a prævious and
practical experience of the World, and his playfellows
may be the future friends of his heart or his interest.
In a free intercourse with his equals, the habits of truth,
fortitude, and prudence will insensibly be matured; birth
and riches are measured by the standard of personal merit;
and the mimic scene of a rebellion has sometimes * displayed in their true colours the ministers and patriots
of the rising generation. Our seminaries of learning do
not exactly correspond with the precept of a Spartan
King "that the child should be instructed in the arts
which will be useful to the man," [22] since a finished scholar
may emerge from the head of Westminster or Eaton in
total ignorance of the business and conversation of
English Gentlemen in the latter end of the eighteenth

---

[22]

$$E\pi\iota\zeta\eta\tau o\upsilon\nu\tau os \; \delta\epsilon \; \tau\iota\nu os \; \tau\iota\nu a \; \delta\epsilon\iota \; \mu a\nu\theta a\nu\epsilon\iota\nu \; \tau o\upsilon s \; \pi a\iota\delta as,$$
$$T a\upsilon\tau' \; (\epsilon\iota\pi\epsilon\nu) \; o\iota s \; \delta\epsilon \; a\nu\delta\rho\epsilon s \; \gamma\epsilon\nu o\mu\epsilon\nu o\iota \; \chi\rho\eta\sigma o\nu\tau a\iota.$$

Agesilaus.

Apothegmata Græc. Hen. Steph., 1568, p. 306.

by Gibbon and by Cowper, who
was also one of his pupils.

Richard Busby was head-master
1638-1695; Thomas Knipe, 1695-

1711; Robert Freind, 1711-1733;
John Nicoll, 1733-1753.

* This word is scored through in
MS.

century. But these schools may assume the merit of teaching all that they pretend to teach, the Latin and Greek languages : [23] they deposit in the hands of a disciple the keys of two valuable chests ; nor can he complain if they are afterwards lost or neglected by his own fault. The necessity of leading in equal ranks so many unequal powers of capacity and application will prolong to eight or ten years the juvenile studies, which might be dispatched in half that time by the skillful master of a single pupil. Yet even the repetition of exercise and discipline contributes to fix in a vacant mind the verbal science of grammar and prosody ; and the private or voluntary student, who possesses the sense and spirit of the Classics, may offend by a false quantity the scrupulous ear of a well-flogged Critic.[24] For myself, I must be

---

[23] Smith (Wealth, etc., vol. ii. p. 348 *), a fair Judge—how many scholars—English gentry know Latin, should learn more or less Greek—mostly gone by thirty.

[24] Burke's Vectigal †—Sir Grey, Montague, tutti quanti, his superior knowledge.‡

* "In England the public schools are much less corrupted than the universities. In the schools the youth are taught, or at least may be taught, Greek and Latin, that is, everything which the masters pretend to teach, or which it is expected they should teach."—*Wealth of Nations*, ed. Thorold Rogers, ii. 350.

† "Mr. Burke, in the course of some very severe animadversions which he made on Lord North for want of due economy in his management of the public purse, introduced the well-known aphorism, ' Magnum vectigal est parsimonia,' but was guilty of a false quantity by saying ' vectĭgal.' Lord North, while this philippic went on, had been half asleep, and sat heaving backwards and forwards like a great turtle ; but the sound of a false quantity instantly aroused him, and, opening his eyes, he exclaimed in a very marked and distinct manner, ' vectīgal.' ' I thank the noble Lord,' said Burke, with happy adroitness, ' for the correction, the more particularly as it affords me the opportunity of repeating a maxim which he greatly needs to have reiterated upon him.' He then thundered out, ' Magnum vectīgal est-parsimonia.' "—*Recollections of William Wilberforce*, by John S. Harford, pp. 93, 94.

‡ Sir Grey Cooper (1726–1801) was Secretary of Treasury under Lord North, and a Lord of the Treasury in the Coalition Cabinet of North and Fox. His administrative abilities were highly esteemed, and he was considered a

content with a very small share of the civil and litterary fruits of a public school: in the space of two years (1749, 1750), interrupted by danger and debility, I painfully climbed into the third form; and my riper age was left to acquire the beauties of the Latin, and the rudiments of the Greek, tongue. Instead of audaciously mingling in the sports, the quarrels, and the connections of our little World, I was still cherished at home under the maternal wing of my aunt; and my removal from Westminster long preceded the approach of manhood. [In our domestic society I formed, however, an intimate acquaintance with a young nobleman of my own age, and vainly flattered myself that our sentiments would prove as lasting as they seemed to be mutual. On my return from abroad his coldness repelled such faint advances as my pride allowed me to make, and in our different walks of life we gradually became strangers to each other. Yet his private character, for Lord H.* has never affected a public name, leaves me no room to accuse the propriety and merit of my early choice.]

The violence and variety of my complaints, which had excused my frequent absence from Westminster school, at length engaged Mrs. Porten, with the advice of physicians, to conduct me to Bath: at the end of the Michaelmas vacation (1750) she quitted me with reluctance, and I remained several months under the care of a trusty maid-servant. A strange nervous affection, which

---

high authority on financial questions.

Frederic Montagu (1733–1800) was also a Lord of the Treasury, was popular in society, and had literary tastes. Wraxall describes him as "a man of distinguished probity" (*Posthumous Memoirs*, ii. 348).

Lord North and Montagu were educated at Eton. Sir Grey Cooper does not appear to have been at any public school.

* Lionel, Lord Huntingtower, who became fourth Earl of Dysart, died in 1799.

alternately contracted my legs, and produced without any
visible symptoms the most excruciating pain, was in-
effectually opposed by the various methods of bathing
and pumping. From Bath I was transported to Winchester, to the house of a physician; and after the failure
of his medical skill, we had again recourse to the virtues
of the Bath waters. During the intervals of these fits I
moved with my father to Buriton and Putney, and a
short unsuccessful trial was attempted to renew my
attendance at Westminster school. But my infirmities
could not be reconciled with the hours and discipline of
a public seminary; and instead of a domestic tutor, who
might have watched the favourable moments and gently
advanced the progress of my learning, my father was too
easily content with such occasional teachers as the different
places of my residence could supply. I was never forced,
and seldom was I persuaded to admit these lessons; yet
I read with a Clergyman at Bath some odes of Horace,
and several episodes of Virgil, which gave me an imperfect
and transient enjoyment of the Latin Poets. It might
now be apprehended that I should continue for life an
illiterate cripple : but as I approached my sixteenth year,
Nature displayed in my favour her mysterious energies;
my constitution was fortified and fixed, and my disorders,
instead of growing with my growth and strengthening
with my strength, most wonderfully vanished. I have
never possessed or abused the insolence of health; but
since that time few persons have been more exempt from
real or imaginary ills, and till I am admonished by the
Gout the reader shall no more be troubled with
the history of any bodily complaints. My unexpected
recovery again encouraged the hope of my education,

and I was placed at Esher in Surrey, in the house of the Reverend Mr. Philip Francis,[25] in a pleasant spot which promised to unite the various benefits of air, exercise, and study (January, 1752). [Mr. Francis was recommended, I believe, by the Mallets as a scholar and a wit: his two tragedies * have been coldly received, but his version of Demosthenes, which I have not seen, supposes some knowledge of Greek litterature, and he had executed with success and applause the arduous task of a compleat translation of Horace in English verse.† Besides a young Gentleman whose name I do not remember, our family consisted only of myself and his son, who has since been conspicuous in the supreme council of India, from whence he is returned to England with an ample fortune. It was stipulated that his father should always confine himself to a small number; and with so able a præceptor in this private academy, the time which I had lost might have been speedily retrieved. But the experience of a few weeks was sufficient to discover that Mr. Francis's spirit was too lively for his profession; and while he indulged himself in the pleasures of London, his pupils were left idle at Esher in the custody of a Dutch Usher, of low manners and

---

[25] P. Francis an Irishman, died at Bath, 1773—A political writer promoted by Fox; pardoned by Pitt, his son's patron —Biograph. Dramat., fol. i. p. 178.‡

* *Eugenia* (1752) and *Constantine* (1754) "were but coolly received." —*Biogr. Dram.*

† "The lyrical part of Horace never can be perfectly translated: so much of the excellence is in the numbers and expression. Francis has done it the best. I'll take his, five out of six, against them all."—Dr. Johnson.

‡ Rev. Philip Francis (? 1708–1773) was the father of Sir Philip Francis. As private chaplain to Lady Caroline Fox, he taught Charles James Fox to read. His political pamphlets, including his lampoon, *Mr. Pitt's Letter Versified*, were in great part inspired by Lord Holland, through whose influence he became rector of Barrow, in Suffolk, and chaplain to Chelsea Hospital.

contemptible learning. From such careless or unworthy hands I was indignantly rescued : but] my
father's perplexity, rather than his prudence, was urged
to embrace a singular and desperate measure. Without
preparation or delay he carried me to Oxford, and I was
matriculated in the University as a Gentleman Com-
moner of Magdalen College before I accomplished the
fifteenth year of my age (April. 3. 1752).

The curiosity which had been implanted in my infant
mind was still alive and active ; but my reason was not
sufficiently informed to understand the value, or to lament
the loss, of three precious years from my entrance at
Westminster to my admission at Oxford. Instead of
repining at my long and frequent confinement to the
chamber or the couch, I secretly rejoyced in those infirmities which delivered me from the exercises of the
school and the society of my equals. As often as I was
tolerably exempt from danger and pain, reading, free
desultory reading, was the employment and comfort of
my solitary hours : at Westminster my aunt sought only
to amuse and indulge me; in my stations at Bath and
Winchester, at Buriton and Putney, a false compassion
respected my sufferings, and I was allowed, without
controul or advice, to gratify the wanderings of an unripe
taste. My indiscriminate appetite subsided by degrees in
the *Historic* line; and, since Philosophy has exploded all
innate ideas and natural propensities, I must ascribe this
choice to the assiduous perusal of the Universal history
as the octavo Volumes successively appeared. This unequal
work, and a treatise of Hearne, the *Ductor Historicus,**

---

* *Ductor Historicus, or a Short*   Thomas Hearne. 2 vols., 8vo.
System of Universal History, by   1704.

referred and introduced me to the Greek and Roman historians, to as many at least as were accessible to an English reader. All that I could find were greedily devoured, from Littlebury's lame Herodotus, and Spelman's valuable Xenophon, to the pompous folios of Gordon's Tacitus, and a ragged Procopius of the beginning of the last Century. The cheap acquisition of so much knowledge confirmed my dislike to the study of languages, and I argued with Mrs. Porten that, were I master of Greek and Latin, I must interpret to myself in English the thoughts of the Original, and that such extemporary versions must be inferior to the elaborate translations of professed scholars: a silly sophism which could not easily be confuted by a person ignorant of any other language than her own. / From the ancient I leaped to the modern World; many crude lumps of Speed, Rapin, Mezeray, Davila, Machiavel, Father Paul, Bower, etc., passed through me like so many novels, and I swallowed with the same voracious appetite the descriptions of India and China, of Mexico and Peru. [Our family collection was decently furnished; the circulating libraries of London and Bath afforded a rich treasures (*sic*); I borrowed many books, and some I contrived to purchase from my scanty allowance. My father's friends who visited the boy were astonished at finding him surrounded with a heap of folios, of whose titles *they* were ignorant, and on whose contents *he* could pertinently discourse.]

My first introduction to the Historic scenes, which have since engaged so many years of my life, must be ascribed to an accident. In the summer of 1751 I accompanied my father on a visit to Mr. Hoare's, in Wiltshire; but I was less delighted with the beauties of Stourhead than with discovering in the library a common book, the continuation of Echard's Roman history, which is indeed executed with more skill and taste than the prævious work: to me the reigns of the successors of Constantine were absolutely new, and I was immersed in the passage of the Goths over the Danube when the summons of the dinner-bell reluctantly dragged me from my intellectual feast. This transient glance served rather to irritate than to appease my curiosity, and no sooner was I returned to Bath than I procured the second and third Volumes of Howell's history of the World, which exhibit the Byzantine period on a larger scale. Mahomet and his Saracens soon fixed my attention, and some instinct of criticism directed me to the genuine sources. Simon Ockley, an original in every sense, first opened my eyes, and I was led from one book to another till I had ranged round the circle of Oriental history. Before I was sixteen I had exhausted all that could be learned in English of the Arabs and Persians, the Tartars and Turks; and the same ardour urged me to guess at the French of d'Herbelot, and to construe the barbarous Latin of Pocock's Abulpharagius. Such vague and multifarious reading could not teach me to think, to write, or to act; and the only principle that darted a ray of light into the indigested Chaos was an early and rational application to the order of time and place. The maps of Cellarius and Wells imprinted in my mind the picture of ancient Geography; from Strauchius I imbibed the elements of Chronology; the tables of Helvicus and Anderson, the annals of Usher and Prideaux, distinguished the connection of events, and I engraved the multitude of names and dates in a clear and indelible series. But in the discussion of the first ages I overleaped the bounds of modesty and use. In my childish balance I presumed to weigh the systems of Scaliger and Petavius, of Marsham and Newton which I could seldom study in the originals ; [the Dynasties of Assyria and Egypt were my top and cricket-ball ;] and my sleep has been disturbed by the difficulty of reconciling the Septuagint with the Hebrew computation. I arrived at Oxford with a stock of erudition that might have puzzled a Doctor, and a degree of ignorance of which a school boy would have been ashamed.

At the conclusion of this first period of my life, I am tempted to enter a protest against the trite and lavish praise of the happiness of our boyish years, which is echoed with so much affectation in the World. That happiness I have never known, that time I have never regretted ; and were my poor aunt still alive, she would bear testimony to the early and constant uniformity of my sentiments. It will, indeed, be replied that *I* am not a competent Judge ; that pleasure is incompatible with pain, that joy is excluded from sickness ; and that the felicity of a schoolboy consists in the perpetual motion of thoughtless and playful agility, in which I was never qualified to excell. My name, it is most true, could never be enrolled among the sprightly race, the idle progeny of Eton or Westminster, who delight to cleave the water with pliant arm, to urge the flying ball, and to chace the speed of the rolling circle.[26] [But I would ask the warmest and most active Hero of the play-field whether he can seriously compare his childish with his

---

[26] Gray's prospect of Eton College—images extricated from metre—Father Thames at Westminster, instead of margent green, has trading barges and carpenters' yards.

manly enjoyments; whether he does not feel, as the most precious attribute of his existence, the vigorous maturity of sensual and spiritual powers which Nature has reserved for the age of puberty. A state of happiness arising only from the want of foresight and reflection shall never provoke my envy; such degenerate taste would tend to sink us in the scale of beings from a man to a child, a dog and an oyster, till we had reached the confines of brute matter, which cannot suffer, because it cannot feel.] The poet may gaily describe the short hours of recreation; but he forgets the daily, tedious labours of the school, which is approached each morning with anxious and reluctant steps. [Degrees of misery are proportioned to the mind rather than to the object; *parva leves capiunt animos;* and few men, in the tryals of life, have experienced a more painful sensation than the poor schoolboy with an imperfect task, who trembles on the eve of the black Monday. A school is the cavern of fear and sorrow; the mobility of the captive youths is chained to a book and a desk; an inflexible master commands their attention, which every moment is impatient to escape; they labour like the soldiers of Persia under the scourge,[27] and their education is nearly finished before they can apprehend the sense or utility of the harsh lessons which they are forced to repeat.[28] Such

---

[27] Ὑπο μαστιγος, familiar to the readers of Herodotus.

[28] I do not absolutely condemn the rod—use and abuse—had almost extinguished Erasmus (Opp. Tom. i. p. 504)*—horrid cruelty of Dean Colet, founder of St. Paul's (p. 505; Life, p. 175)†—Busby would give 30, 40, 60 lashes to poor *little* boys for trivial offences (Biog. Brit., ii. 53, new edit.).‡

* See Appendix, 11, p. 100.   (not ii.) p. 53 of the new edition
† See Appendix, 12, p. 101.   (1784) of the *Biog. Brit.*, which
‡ The article *Busby* is in vol. iii.   only went to *Fastolf* (vol. v.), and

blind and absolute dependence may be necessary, but can never be delightful : Freedom is the first wish of our heart; freedom is the first blessing of our nature; and, unless we bind ourselves with the voluntary chains of interest or passion, we advance in freedom as we advance in years.]

was never finished. This reference to Busby giving so many lashes to little boys is not, however, in the body of the article, but in a note, and is a quotation from *True and perfect Narrative of the differences between Mr. Busby and Mr. Bagshaw*, published 1659.

·CHAPTER III.

A TRAVELLER who visits Oxford or Cambridge is surprized and edified by the apparent order and tranquillity that prevail in the seats of the English muses.[1] In the most celebrated Universities of Holland, Germany, and Italy, the students, who swarm from different countries, are loosely dispersed in private lodgings at the houses of the burghers: they dress according to their fancy and fortune: and in the intemperate quarrels of youth and wine, their *swords*, though less frequently than of old, are sometimes stained with each other's blood.[2] The use of arms is banished from our English Universities; the

---

[1] Le nombre des Etudians d'Oxford va à 2000. Ils ne portent ni bâton ni epée. Tous portent la robe et le bonnet quarre l'habillement differe suivant le degré et la qualité. . . . Tout et bien reglé dans cette Université: les desordres n'y regnent pas comme dans celles d'Allemagne (Voyage Littéraire en 1733, par M. Jordan (the correspondent of Frederic), pp. 173, 175).

[2] Quarrels of the students—Padua deserted by stranger—unsafe after sunset (Burnet's travels, p. 102)*—At Oxford—North and South, Greeks and Trojans—Duels at Gottingen.

* Bishop Burnet's *Travels through France, Italy, Germany, and Switzerland.* Edin., 1752. P. 101. Letter III. from Florence. "From Vincenza it is eighteen miles to Padua, all like a garden. Here one sees the decays of a vast city, which was once one of the biggest of all Italy. . . . The university here, though so much supported by the Venetians that they pay fifty professors, yet sinks extremely. There are no men of any great fame in it now; and the quarrels among the students have driven away most of the strangers that used to come and study there; for it is not safe to stir abroad here after sunset."

uniform habit of the Academics, the square cap and black gown, is adapted to the civil and even clerical profession; and from the Doctor in Divinity to the under-graduate, the degrees of learning and age are externally distinguished. Instead of being scattered in a town, the students of Oxford and Cambridge are united in Colleges; their maintenance is provided at their own expence or that of the founders; and the stated hours of the hall and chappel represent the discipline of a regular and, as it were, a Religious community. The eyes of the traveller are attracted by the size or beauty of the public edifices; and the principal colleges appear to be so many palaces which a liberal nation has erected and endowed for the habitation of Science. My own introduction to the University of Oxford forms a new æra in my life, and at the distance of forty years I still remember my first emotions of surprize and satisfaction. In my fifteenth year I felt myself suddenly raised from a boy to a man; the persons whom I respected as my superiors in age and Academical rank entertained me with every mark of attention and civility; and my vanity was flattered by the velvet cap and silk gown which discriminate a Gentleman-Commoner from a plebeian student. A decent allowance, more money than a school-boy had ever seen, was at my own disposal, and I might command among the tradesmen of Oxford an indefinite and dangerous latitude of credit. A key was delivered into my hands which gave me the free use of a numerous and learned library; my apartment consisted of three elegant and well-furnished rooms in the new building, a stately pile, of Magdalen College; and the adjacent walks, had they been frequented by Plato's disciples, might have been compared to the Attic shade on the banks of the Ilissus.[3] Such was the fair prospect of my entrance (April. 3: 1752) into the University of Oxford.

A venerable prelate, whose taste and erudition must reflect honour on the society in which they were formed, has drawn a very interesting picture of his Academical life. "I was educated," says Bishop Lowth, "in the *University of Oxford.* I enjoyed all the advantages, both public and private, which that famous seat of learning so largely affords. I spent many years in that illustrious Society, in a well-regulated course of useful discipline and studies, and in the agreeable and improving commerce of Gentlemen and of Scholars; in a society where emulation without envy, ambition without jealousy, contention without animosity, incited industry and awakened genius: where a liberal pursuit of knowledge and a generous freedom of thought was raised, encouraged, and pushed forward, by example, by commendation, and by authority. I breathed the same atmosphere that the HOOKERS, the CHILLINGWORTHS, and the LOCKES had breathed before; whose benevolence and humanity were as extensive as their vast Genius and comprehensive knowledge; who always treated their adversaries with civility and respect; who made candour, moderation, and liberal judgement as much the rule and law as the subject of their discourses. And do you reproach me with my education in This place, and with my relation to This most respectable Body, which I shall always esteem

---

[3] Praised by Hurd (Dialogues, iii. pp. 165–169)—Spartan halls, Attic symposia are or *may be* united.*

* See Appendix, 13, p. 101.

my greatest advantage, and my highest honour."[4]   I transcribe with pleasure this eloquent passage, without examining what benefits or what rewards were derived by Hooker, or Chillingworth, or Locke from their Academical institution; without enquiring whether in this angry controversy the spirit of Lowth himself is purified from the intolerant zeal which Warburton had ascribed to the Genius of the place.[5]   The expression of gratitude is a

---

[4] Letter of a late professor at Oxford (pp. 62–65) by an happy quot. from Clarendon charges W. with having been an attorney's Clerk.*

[5] Idolatry excluded from toleration (pp. 34–51)—and Bengal—the Lingam, Suicide?   Inquisition at Calcutta? Ha![†]

* Robert Lowth (1710–1787), appointed Bishop of St. David's in 1766, but promoted to the see of Oxford the same year, and to that of London in 1777.

The controversy between Lowth and Warburton arose from a passage in Lowth's *Prælectiones*, in which an argument concerning the civil jurisdiction among the Jews involved a question as to the date and authority of the Book of Job (cf. ch. xxxi. 28). The dispute, which was conducted with some asperity by Warburton, extended over ten years. Lowth's *Letter to the Rt. Rev. Author of the Divine Legation of Moses Demonstrated; in answer to the Appendix to the fifth volume of that work, with an Appendix containing a former literary Correspondence by a Late Professor in the University of Oxford*, was published in Oxford, 1765.

The following is the passage in which Lord Clarendon is quoted: "Pray, my Lord, what is it to the purpose where I have been brought up? To have made a proper use of the advantages of a good education is a just praise, but to have overcome the disadvantages of a bad one is a much greater. Had

I not your Lordship's example to justify me, I should think it a piece of extreme impertinence to enquire where *you* were bred, though one might possibly plead as an excuse for it, a natural curiosity to know where and how such a phænomenon was produced. It is commonly said that your Lordship's education was of that particular kind concerning which it is a remark of that great judge of men and manners, Lord Clarendon, that it peculiarly disposes men to be proud, insolent, and pragmatical. 'Colonel Harrison was the son of a butcher, and had been bred up in the place of a clerk to a lawyer; which kind of education introduces men into the language and practice of business; and if it be not resisted by the great ingenuity of the person, inclines young men to more pride than any other kind of breeding, and disposes them to be pragmatical and insolent.' "

† The passage in Lowth's *Letter* here referred to, deals with Warburton's arguments concerning toleration: he had written, "As these patriarchs *did not in facto* (which appears from their history), so they *could not de jure* (which

virtue and a pleasure; a liberal mind will delight to cherish and celebrate the memory of its parents, and the teachers of science are the parents of the mind.[6]   I applaud the filial piety which it is impossible for me to imitate, since I must not confess an imaginary debt to

---

[6] Locke owed no thanks—Student of Christ Church—expelled, never restored after Revol. (Biograph. Brit., vol. v.)—Heads of houses—no public censure—He laughed a good jest, a recommendation, yet was anxious to know (His Works, 4° Edit., Vol. iv. p. 618, 19, in his letters).*

appears from the laws of Nature and Nations) *punish idolatry by the Judge*," and had held that Idolatry was punishable neither by the Law of Nations, nor the Law of Nature. To this Lowth replies: "Granted one nation has no right to punish another Nation for Idolatry, for one nation has no jurisdiction over another nation." . . . "But, 'Idolatry,' you say, 'is not punishable by the Law of Nature.' This is not quite so clear. Idolatry is a crime against the Light of Nature, and therefore against the Law of Nature." After quoting Gal. v. 19, 20, he proceeds to argue that when Idolatry becomes identical with immorality, it is punishable by the Law of Nature. "It is agreed among the most strenuous Advocates of Religious Liberty that Toleration has its proper bounds; and that there are opinions as well as practices, which in a well-regulated free State ought not to be tolerated." After quoting Mr. Locke and Bishop Ellys in support of this contention, he proceeds: "I hope it will not offend your Lordship's toleration if I exclude from Toleration all those who make practices shocking to humanity, and destructive of the human race itself, parts of their religious worship."

The latter part of the note, no doubt, contains Gibbon's memoranda concerning more recent illustrations of the point, especially as regards the Phallic worship and the Brahmanical rite of Suttee. The word *Lingam* or *Linga* in Sanskrit and Hindu signifies a token or badge; thence the symbol of Siva, which is so extensively an object of worship among the Hindus in the form of a cylinder of stone. (On Lingam and Suttee, see Yule's *Glossary of Anglo-Indian Words and Phrases*.)

* In the article in the *Biogr. Brit.*, vol. v. p. 2997, it is stated that on his return to England in 1689, Locke "put in a claim to his student's place at Christ Church, but that society rejected his pretensions, as the proceedings in his deprivation were conformable to their statutes."

Lowth writes to Anthony Collins in 1704, asking him to procure for him a particular account of the proceedings at the meeting of the heads of houses at Oxford, to censure and discourage the reading of his *Essay on Human Understanding*. "When these particulars are obtained," he continues, "it will be fit to consider what use to make of them. In the meantime, I take what has been done as a recommendation of that book to the world, as you do; and I conclude when you and I meet next we shall be merry upon the subject."—Lowth's Works, vol. iv., 4to, pp. 618, 619.

assume the merit of a just or generous retribution. To the University of Oxford *I* acknowledge no obligation; and she will as chearfully renounce me for a son, as I am willing to disclaim her for a mother. I spent fourteen months at Magdalen College; they proved the fourteen months the most idle and unprofitable of my whole life: the reader will pronounce between the school and the scholar; but I cannot affect to believe that Nature had disqualified me for all litterary pursuits. The specious and ready excuse of my tender age, imperfect præparation, and hasty departure may doubtless be alleged, nor do I wish to defraud such excuses of their proper weight. Yet in my sixteenth year I was not devoid of capacity or application; even my childish reading had displayed an early though blind propensity for books, and the shallow flood might have been taught to flow in a deep channel and a clear stream. In the discipline of a well-constituted Academy, under the guidance of skillful and vigilant professors, I should gradually have risen from translations to originals, from the Latin to the Greek Classics, from dead languages to living science; my hours would have been occupied by useful and agreeable studies: the wanderings of fancy would have been restrained, and I should have escaped the temptations of idleness which finally precipitated my departure from Oxford.

Perhaps, in a separate annotation, I may coolly examine the fabulous and real antiquities of our sister Universities, a question which has kindled such fierce and foolish disputes among their fanatic sons. In the mean while, it will be acknowledged that these venerable bodies are sufficiently old to partake of all the prejudices and

infirmities of age. The schools of Oxford and Cambridge
were founded in a dark age of false and barbarous science,
and they are still tainted with the vices of their origin.
Their primitive discipline was adapted to the education
of priests and monks; and the goverment still remains
in the hands of the Clergy, an order of men whose
manners are remote from the present World, and whose
eyes are dazzled by the light of Philosophy. The legal
incorporation of these societies by the charters of Popes
and Kings had given them a monopoly of the public
instruction; and the spirit of monopolists is narrow, lazy,
and oppressive; their work is more costly and less productive than that of independent artists; and the new
improvements so eagerly grasped by the competition of
freedom, are admitted with slow and sullen reluctance in
those proud corporations, above the fear of a rival, and
below the confession of an error. We may scarcely hope
that any reformation will be a voluntary act;[7] and so
deeply are they rooted in law and prejudice, that even
the omnipotence of Parliament would shrink from an
enquiry into the state and abuses of the two Universities.

The use of Academical degrees, as old as the thirteenth
century, is visibly borrowed from the mechanic corporations, in which an apprentice, after serving his time,
obtains a testimonial of his skill, and a license to practise his trade and mystery. It is not my design to
depreciate those honours which could never gratify or
disappoint my ambition; and I should applaud the

---

[7] Lord Townshend wished to reform—severe scheme (B.
B. tom. v. Prideaux (A.A.)—never heard of more. Whiston
(pp. 42–45) Emendenda, always tutors and old fellows.*

* See Appendix, 14, p. 101.

institution, if the degrees of Batchelor or licentiate were bestowed as the reward of manly and successful study; if the name and rank of Doctor or Master were strictly reserved for the professors of science who have approved their title to the public esteem. [The mysterious faculty of Theology must not be scanned by a profane eye, the cloak of reason sits awkwardly on our fashionable Divines,| and in the Ecclesiastical studies of the fathers and councils their modesty will yield to the Catholic universities. Our English civilians and canonists have never been famous; their real business is confined to a small circle; and the double jurisprudence of Rome is overwhelmed by the enormous profession of common lawyers, who, in the pursuit of honours and riches, disdain the mock majesty of our *budge* Doctors.[8] We are justly proud of the skill and learning of our physicians; their skill is acquired in the practise of the hospitals; they seek their learning in London, in Scotland, or on the continent, and few patients would trust their pulse to a medical student if he had passed the fourteen years of his noviciate at Oxford or Cambridge, whose degrees, how-

---

[8] The budge Doctors of the Stoic fur (Comus, 707, and Warton's notes, p. 220)—I do not apply lean and sallow abstinence.*

* "O foolishness of men! that lend their ears
To those Budge Doctors of the Stoick fur,
And fetch their precepts from the Cynick tub,
Praising the lean and sallow Abstinence."
(*Comus*, 723–725.)

Warton's note on this passage is as follows: "Those morose and rigid teachers of abstinence and mortifi-cation, who wear the gown of the Stoic philosophy. *Budge* is fur, antiently an ornament of the scholastic habit. In the more antient colleges of our universities, the annual expenses for furring the robes or liveries of the fellows, appear to have been very considerable. 'The Stoic fur' is as much as if he had said 'the Stoic sect.' But he explains the obsolete word, in which there is a tincture of ridicule, by a very awkward tautology."

ever, are exclusively admitted in the Royal College.
The *Arts* are supposed to include the liberal knowledge
of Philosophy and litterature; but I am informed that
some tattered shreds of the old Logic and Metaphysics
compose the exercises for a Batchelor and Master's degree;
and that modern improvements, instead of introducing
a more rational tryal, have only served to relax the forms
which are now the object of general contempt.[9]]

In all the Universities of Europe except our own,
the languages and sciences are distributed among a
numerous list of effective professors; the students,
according to their taste, their calling, and their diligence,
apply themselves to the proper masters, and in the
annual repetition of public and private lectures, these
masters are assiduously employed.[10] Our curiosity may
inquire what number of professors has been instituted at
Oxford (for I shall now confine myself to my own University), by whom are they appointed, and what may be
the probable chances of merit or incapacity? how many
are stationed to the three faculties, and how many are left
for the liberal Arts? what is the form and what the
substance of their lessons? But all these questions are
silenced by one short and singular answer. "That in the
University of Oxford the greater part of the public professors have for these many years given up altogether even
the pretence of teaching."[11] Incredible as the fact may

---

[9] Here Vicesimus Knox must be used.*
[10] Information from Gottingen—Professors—Lectures, etc.
[11] Smith, W. of N., Vol. ii. L. v. C. 1, P. iii. Article iii.

* This probably refers to *Liberal Education; or, A Practical Treatise on the Methods of acquiring Useful and Polite Learning:* a work first published by Knox in 1781, which passed through ten editions in eight years.

appear, I must rest my belief on the positive and impartial evidence of a [Philosopher *] who had himself resided at Oxford. Dr. Adam Smith assigns as the cause of their indolence that, instead of being paid by voluntary contributions, which would urge them to increase the number, and to deserve the gratitude of their pupills, the Oxford professors are secure in the enjoyment of a fixed stipend, without the necessity of labour, or the apprehension of controul.[12] It has, indeed, been observed, nor is the

---

p. 343—himself a P. at Glasgow—His Theory a small part of his lectures.†

[12] Gray Prof. of modern history at Cambridge, £400 a year (Mem., p. 333), in three years never once read—his remorse—Mason's excuses, pp. 395-399—Never admonished by any superiors.‡

* In Lord Sheffield's edition changed to "a master of moral and political wisdom."

† "In the University of Oxford, the greater part of the public professors have for these many years given up altogether even the pretence of teaching." On this passage, Professor Thorold Rogers, in his edition of the *Wealth of Nations*, makes the following comment. "The condition of Oxford during the seven years in which Adam Smith resided at Balliol College was lower than at any period of its history. . . . The University swarmed with profligates, was a nest of noisy Jacobites, and was at the meanest literary ebb. Its revival hardly commenced till the conclusion of the eighteenth century, when the examinations for degrees became something better than a mere farce."—Vol. ii. p. 346.

‡ Gray writes to Dr. Beattie from Pembroke Hall, October 31, 1768: "We live at so great a distance, that, perhaps, you may not yet have learned, what I flatter myself you will not be displeased to hear: the middle of last summer his Majesty was pleased to appoint me Regius Professor of Modern History in this University; it is the best thing the Crown has to bestow (on a layman) here; the salary is £400 per ann.; but what enhances the value of it to me is, that it was bestowed without being asked" (p. 333).

Mason's comment on this is (p. 395): "This is the last Letter which I have selected for this Section; and I insert it chiefly for the occasion which it affords me of commenting on the latter part of it, where he speaks of his own employment as Professor of Modern History; an office which he had now held nearly three years, and had not begun to execute the duties of it. His health, which was all the time gradually on the decline, and his spirits only supported by the frequent summer excursions, during this period, might, to the candid reader, be a sufficient apology for this omission, or rather procrastination: but there is more to be said in his excuse; and I should ill execute the office I have under-

observation absurd, that except in experimental sciences, which demand a costly apparatus and a dextrous hand, the many valuable treatises that have been published on every subject of learning may now supersede the ancient mode of oral instruction. Were this principle true in its utmost latitude, I should only infer that the offices and salaries which are become useless ought, without delay, to be abolished.[19] But there still remains a material difference between a book and a professor: the hour of the lecture enforces attendance; attention is fixed by the presence, the voice, and the occasional questions of the teacher; the most idle will carry something away; and

---

[19] Dodwell. Præl. Camden—read on the August. hist. 25 lectures only for the authors and private life of Hadrian (Life, vol. 190–217 by Brokesby); must be now worth (since 1722) at least £400 per annum (B. B., p. 168, new edit. *Camden*, Ayliffe, vol. ii. p. 186).*

taken of arranging these papers, with a view of doing honour to his memory, if I did not endeavour to remove every exception that might, with a show of reason, be taken to his conduct in this instance." The remaining pages to 399 are occupied by Mason's attempts to find some other excuse than ill-health. He does not appear to be very successful, and Gray's reasons seem to be principally inability to make up his mind in what form these lectures were to be delivered.

Gray was appointed to the professorship by the Duke of Grafton in 1768. "His salary was £371, out of which he had to provide a French and an Italian teacher. . . . Gray behaved liberally to them; but the habits of the time made lecturing unnecessary."—*Dict. Nat. Biog.*

* Dodwell's *Prælectiones Academicæ in Schola Historices Camdenianâ*, published 1692, were twenty-five in number—six devoted to writers on the Augustan age

generally, and nineteen to Spartian's Life of Hadrian.

Ayliffe's *Antient and Present State of the University of Oxford*, vol. ii. p. 186, gives an account of the founding of the Camden Lectures, from which it appears that in 1622 William Camden, Esq., Clarencieux King-at-Arms, gave the manor of Boxley, in Kent, as a provision for a perpetual Reader in History, "for whose stipend the University now [1714 is the date of Ayliffe's book] receives £140 p. an. But after a certain term of years the Rents and profits of the whole manor, amounting to £400 p. an., devolve to the University, for the use and benefit of this professor. The Charter bears date 1622."

Brokesby, in pp. 190–217 of the Life, merely gives a synopsis of these lectures.

B. B. (iii.), p. 168, new edit., under *Camden*, gives an account of the foundation of this lectureship in much the same terms.

the more diligent will compare the instructions which
they have heard in the school, with the volumes which
they peruse in their chamber. The advice of a skillful
professor will adapt a course of reading to every mind
and every situation; his learning will remove difficulties
and solve objections; his authority will discover, ad-
monish, and at last chastise the negligence of his
disciples; and his vigilant enquiries will ascertain the
steps of their litterary progress. Whatsoever science he
professes, he may illustrate in a series of discourses,
composed in the leisure of his closet, pronounced on
public occasions and finally delivered to the press. I
observe with pleasure that, in the University of Oxford,
Dr. Lowth, with equal eloquence and erudition, has
executed this task, in his incomparable *Prælections* on
the Poetry of the Hebrews.[14]

The College of S! Mary Magdalen [it is vulgarly
pronounced Maudlin] was founded in the fifteenth Century
by a Bishop of Winchester;[15] and now consists of a
President, forty fellows, and a number of inferior students.
It is esteemed one of the largest and most wealthy of
our Academical corporations, which may be compared
to the Benedictine Abbeys of Catholic countries; and
I have loosely heard that the estates belonging to

---

[14] Lowth de sacrâ Hebræorum poesi Prælect. Academ. 1775,
8vo, 3rd edit.; the first in 4to, in 1753. When delivered?
Interesting without Hebrew or faith—good abstract in Blair
(Lectures on Rh., Vol. ii. p. 385–406).*
[15] William Patten of Wainfleet, Lord Chancell.—B. of
Winchester founded Magdalen 1458—merit under James II.,
zeal, privileges. Ayliffe, Hist. of Oxford, Vol. i. p. 342, etc.†

* *Lectures on Rhetoric and Belles Lettres*, by Hugh Blair, D.D., F.R.S. Ed. Lecture XLI. is devoted to the Poetry of the Hebrews.
† See Appendix, 15, p. 102.

Magdalen College, which are leased by those indulgent landlords at small quit-rents and occasional fines, might be raised in the hands of private avarice to an annual revenue of near thirty thousand pounds. Our Colleges are supposed to be schools of science as well as of education, nor is it unreasonable to expect that a body of litterary men, addicted to a life of celibacy, exempt from the care of their own subsistence, and amply provided with books, should devote their leisure to the prosecution of study, and that some effects of their studies should be manifested to the World. The shelves of their library groan under the weight of the Benedictine folios, of the editions of the fathers, and the Collections of the middle ages, which have issued from the single Abbey of St. Germain des Préz at Paris.[16] A composition of Genius must be the offspring of one mind ; but such works of industry as may be divided among many hands, and must be continued during many years are the peculiar province of a laborious community. If I enquire into the manufactures of the monks of Magdalen, if I extend the enquiry to the other Colleges of Oxford and Cambridge, a silent blush, or a scornful frown, will be the only reply. The fellows or monks of my time were decent easy men, who supinely enjoyed the gifts of the founder; their days were filled by a series of uniform employments, the Chappel and the Hall, the Coffee-house and the common room, till they retired, weary and well satisfied, to a long slumber. From the toil of reading or thinking, or writing, they had

---

[16] Lively picture in Hist. de l'Acad., tom. 27. p. 219 (from Quirini's own Comment., tom. i. p. 850—Artificumq. manus inter se operumq. laborem miratur—burnt till extinction more or less.*

* See Appendix, 16, p. 102.

absolved their conscience, and the first shoots of learning and ingenuity withered on the ground without yielding any fruit to the owners or the public. [The only student was a young fellow (a future Bishop) who was deeply immersed in the follies of the Hutchinsonian system; * the only author was an half-starved Chaplain, Ballard † was his name—who begged subscriptions for some Memoirs

---

* This was George Horne (1730–1792). Fellow (1750) and subsequently President (1768) of Magdalen College, Oxford (in which office he was the predecessor of Dr. Routh). In 1781 he was appointed Dean of Canterbury, and in 1790 Bishop of Norwich. His best-known work is his *Commentary on the Psalms* (1771).

He and William Jones of Nayland were the most distinguished adherents of the Hutchinsonian school. Along with a profound reverence for Holy Scriptures, which sometimes led them to be called Methodists, the Hutchinsonians held some eccentric opinions with regard to the origins of the Hebrew language, and were opponents of the Newtonian philosophy. Dr. Horne was the author of several works in defence of these tenets; e.g. *A Fair, Candid, and Impartial Statement of the Case between Sir Isaac Newton and Mr. Hutchinson* (published anonymously, 1753), *A View of Mr. Kennicott's Method of correcting the Hebrew Text* (1760), etc. Horne had been much influenced by the early writings of William Law, and deplored his "falling from the heaven of Christianity into the sink of Paganism, Quakerism, and Socinianism." In 1758 he published his *Cautions to the Readers of Mr. Law, and with very few Varieties to the Readers of Baron Swedenborg,* and *A Letter to a Lady on the subject of Jacob Behmen's Writings.*

"We drank tea with Dr. Horne," writes Boswell in 1776, "late President of Magdalen College and Bishop of Norwich, of whose abilities in different respects the public has eminent proofs, and the esteem annexed to whose character was increased by knowing him personally."

† George Ballard (1706–1755) was not a chaplain, but a choral clerk of Magdalen College. He had a remarkable career; he commenced life as a stay-maker at Campden, co. Gloucester, but displayed an aptitude for scholarship, and especially for Saxon subjects. By the assistance of Dr. Jenner, President of Magdalen, he was appointed to a clerkship in the college, and to the post of one of the Bedells of the University. His health was always infirm, and was much impaired by his close studies, including the transcription of a Saxon Dictionary, which he improved by the addition of nearly 1000 words. He also published, by subscription, his *Memoirs of Several Ladies of Great Britain who have been celebrated for their Writings, or Skill in the Learned Languages, Arts, and Sciences* (1752). This is the book referred to in the text, but Gibbon does not mention the fact that he himself was among the subscribers. Mr. Mores describes Ballard as "a mantua-maker, a person studious in English antiquities, laborious in his pursuits, a Saxonist, and after quitting external ornaments of the sex, a contemplator of their internal qualifications." — Bloxam's *Magdalen Coll. Register,* vol. ii. p. 95 (1857).

concerning the learned ladies of Great Britain.] As a
Gentleman-Commoner, I was sometimes* admitted to the
society of the fellows, and fondly expected that some questions of litterature would be the amusing and instructive
topics of their discourse. Their conversation stagnated in
a round of College business, Tory politics, personal stories,
and private scandal; their dull and deep potations
excused the brisk intemperance of Youth; and their
constitutional toasts were not expressive of the most
lively loyalty for the house of Hanover.[17] A general
election was now approaching; the great Oxfordshire
contest already blazed with all the malevolence of party-
zeal: Magdalen College was devoutly attached to the
Old interest; and the names of Wenman and Dashwood
were more frequently pronounced than those of Cicero
and Chrysostom. The example of the senior fellows
could not inspire the under-graduates with a liberal
spirit, a studious emulation; and I cannot describe, as
I never knew, the discipline of the College. Some
duties may possibly have been imposed on the poor
scholars, whose ambition aspired to the peaceful honours
of a fellowship (" ascribi quietis ordinibus . . . Deorum ");
but no independent members were admitted below the
rank of a Gentleman-Commoner, and our velvet cap was
the cap of liberty. A tradition prevailed that some of
our predecessors had spoken Latin declamations in the
Hall, but of this ancient custom no vestige remained;
the obvious methods of public exercises and examinations
were totally unknown; and I have never heard that

---

[17] Fellow's Journal, *Idler*, No. 33 not by Dr. Johnson—
his awe, nonsense, air ! †

* " Sometimes " in the MS., but   † See Appendix, 17, p. 103.
scored through by Gibbon.

either the President or the Society interfered in the private œconomy of the Tutors and their pupills.

The silence of the Oxford professors, which deprives the Youth of public instruction, is imperfectly supplied by the Tutors, as they are styled, of the several colleges. Instead of confining themselves to a single science which had satisfied the ambition of Burman or Bernouilli, they teach, or promise to teach, either History, or Mathematics, or ancient litterature, or moral philosophy; and as it is possible that they may be defective in all, it is highly probable that of some they will be ignorant. They are paid, indeed, by private contributions, but their appointment depends on the head of the house; their diligence is voluntary, and will consequently be languid, while the pupills themselves and their parents are not indulged in the liberty of choice or change. The first Tutor into whose hands I was resigned, appears to have been one of the best of the tribe : Dr. Waldegrave was a learned and pious man, of a mild disposition, strict morals, and abstemious life, who seldom mingled in the politics or the jollity of the College.* But his knowledge of the World was confined to the University; his learning was of the last, rather than the present age; his temper was indolent; his faculties, which were not of the first-rate, had been relaxed by the climate; and he was satisfied, like his fellows, with the slight and superficial discharge of an important trust. As soon as my tutor had sounded the insufficiency of his disciple in school-learning, he proposed

---

* Thomas Waldegrave, born 1721; entered Lincoln College, 1728; Fellow of Magdalen, 1733; D.D., 1747; was Dean and Bursar of the college. In July, 1752, he was presented to the college living of Washington, in Sussex, where he died, 1784. His *Annotationes in Platonis Opera* he describes as "the *oblivia vitæ* after the death of a friend, and that friend a wife."

that we should read every morning from ten to eleven the comedies of Terence. The sum of my improvement in the University of Oxford is confined to three or four Latin plays; and even the study of an elegant Classic which might have been illustrated by a comparison of ancient and modern theatres, was reduced to a dry and literal interpretation of the Author's text. During the first weeks I constantly attended these lessons in my tutor's room; but as they appeared equally devoid of profit and pleasure, I was once tempted to try the experiment of a formal apology. The apology was accepted with a smile. I repeated the offence with less ceremony; the excuse was admitted with the same indulgence: the slightest motive of lazyness or indisposition, the most trifling avocation at home or abroad, was allowed as a worthy impediment, nor did my tutor appear conscious of my absence or neglect. Had the hour of lecture been constantly filled, a single hour was a small portion of my Academic leisure. No plan of study was recommended for my use; no exercises were prescribed for his inspection; and at the most precious season of Youth, whole days and weeks were suffered to elapse without labour or amusement, without advice or account. I should have listened to the voice of reason and of my tutor: his mild behaviour had gained my confidence; I preferred his society to that of the younger students,* and in our evening walks to the top of Heddington hill we freely conversed on a variety of subjects. Since the days of Pocock and Hyde, Oriental

---

* "Mr. Finden, an ancient Fellow of Magdalen College, and a contemporary of Gibbon, told me that his superior abilities were known to many, but that the gentlemen-commoners, of which number Gibbon was one, were disposed to laugh at his peculiarities: and were once informed by Finden, rather coarsely, but with some humour, that, if their heads were entirely scooped, Gibbon had brains sufficient to supply them all."—From Dr. Routh.—MILMAN.

learning has always been the pride of Oxford, and I once expressed an inclination to study Arabic. His prudence discouraged this childish fancy; but he neglected the fair occasion of directing the ardour of a curious mind. During my absence in the summer vacation, Dr. Waldegrave accepted a college living at Washington, in Sussex, and on my return I no longer found him at Oxford. From that time I have lost sight of my first tutor; but at the end of thirty years (1781) he was still alive, and the practise of exercise and temperance had entitled him to an healthy old age.

The long recess between the Trinity and Michaelmas terms empties the Colleges of Oxford as well as the courts of Westminster. I spent at my father's house at Buriton in Hampshire, the two months of August and September, [which, in the year 1752, were curtailed, to my great surprize, of eleven days by the alteration of the style.] It is whimsical enough that as soon as I left Magdalen college my taste for books began to revive, but it was the same blind and boyish taste for the pursuit of exotic history. Unprovided with original learning, unformed in the habits of thinking, unskilled in the arts of composition, I resolved—to write a book. The title of this first Essay, *the Age of Sesostris*, was perhaps suggested by Voltaire's Age of Louis XIV., which was new and popular; but my sole object was to investigate the probable date of the life and reign of the Conqueror of Asia. I was then enamoured of Sir John Marsham's Canon Chronicus,[18] an elaborate work of whose merits

---

[18] Best edit. London, 1672, in folio—Hebrew Chronology.*

* Sir John Marsham (1602–1685) wrote *Chronicus Canon Ægyptiacus, Ebraicus, Græcus, et Disquisitiones.* —See Hallam's *Lit.*, iv. 191, 8vo ed.

and defects I was not yet qualified to judge. According to his specious, though narrow plan, I settled my Hero about the time of Solomon, in the tenth Century before the Christian Æra. It was therefore incumbent on me, unless I would adopt Sir Isaac Newton's shorter Chronology, to remove a formidable objection; and my solution, for a youth of fifteen is not devoid of ingenuity. In his version of the sacred books, Manetho the High priest has identified Sethosis or Sesostris with the elder brother of Danaus, who landed in Greece, according to the Parian marble fifteen hundred and ten years before Christ.[19] But in my supposition the High priest is guilty of a voluntary error : flattery is the prolific parent of falsehood; [and falsehood, I will now add, is not incompatible with the sacerdotal Character.] Manetho's history of Egypt is dedicated to Ptolemy Philadelphus, who derived a fabulous or illegitimate pedigree from the Macedonian Kings of the race of Hercules.[20] Danaus is the ancestor of Hercules; and after the failure of the elder branch, his descendants, the Ptolemies are the sole representatives of the Royal family, and may claim by inheritance the Kingdom which they hold by conquest. Such were my juvenile discoveries; at a riper age I no longer presume to connect the Greek,

---

[19] Fragments to Joseph. contra Apion. in L. i. C. 15. Tom. ii. p. 447.* Edit. Havercamp, real loss, see Fabricius and Gerard Voscius.†

[20] Quidam Phillippo genitum esse credebant certum pellice ejus ortum constabat Q. C., L. ix. C. 8, cum not Freinshein.

* See Appendix, 18, p. 103.

† Jean Albert Fabricius (1668–1736) wrote an appendix to the Works of Josephus, which is printed in Havercamp's edition.

In a letter (in French), printed in this edition, Manasseh ben Israel writes to M. Arnauld, "Touchant Flave Josephe escrit en hebreu plusieurs en doutent, et entre autres le très docte & célèbre Gerard Vossius."

the Jewish, and the Egyptian antiquities which are lost in a distant cloud; nor is this the only instance in which the belief and knowledge of the child are superseded by the more rational ignorance of the man. During my stay at Buriton my infant labour was diligently prosecuted, without much interruption from company or country diversions; and I already heard the music of public applause. The discovery of my own weakness was the first symptoms of taste: on my return to Oxford the Age of Sesostris was wisely relinquished; but the imperfect sheets remained twenty years at the bottom of a drawer, till in a general clearance of papers (November, 1772) they were committed to the flames.

After the departure of Dr. Waldegrave, I was transferred with the rest of his live stock to a senior fellow, whose literary [and moral] character did not command the respect of the College. Dr. [Winchester *] well remembered that he had a salary to receive, and only forgot that he had a duty to perform. Instead of guiding the studies and watching over the behaviour of his disciple, I was never summoned to attend even the ceremony of a lecture; and except one voluntary visit to his rooms, during the eight months of his titular office, the tutor and pupill lived in the same College as strangers to each other. The want of experience, of advice, and of occupation soon betrayed me into some improprieties of

---

* Thomas Winchester (1713–1780) was in succession chorister, clerk, demy, and Fellow of Magdalen College. In 1749 he became Rector of Horsington, co. Lincoln, and in 1760 of Appleton, co. Bucks. A man of sound and good, if not brilliant, talents, and a staunch supporter of the Church of England, he took an active, if not a very prominent, part in the religious controversies of his time, especially in opposition to *The Confessional* by Archdeacon Blackburne, and *Pietas Oxoniensis* by Sir Richard Hill, Bart. For a full account of him, see the Register of the Members of Magdalen College, Oxford, by John Rouse Bloxam, D.D., vol. i. p. 150, *et sqq.*, 1853.

conduct, ill-chosen company, late hours, and inconsiderate expence. My growing debts might be secret, but my frequent absence was visible and scandalous; and a tour to Bath, a visit into Buckinghamshire, and four excursions to London in the same winter, were costly and dangerous frolicks. They were, indeed, without a meaning, as without an excuse: the irksomeness of a cloystered life repeatedly tempted me to wander; but my chief pleasure was that of travelling; and I was too young and bashful to enjoy, like a manly Oxonian in town, the taverns and bagnios of Covent Garden.[21] In all these excursions I eloped from Oxford; I returned to College; in a few days I eloped again, as if I had been an independent stranger in a hired lodging, without once hearing the voice of admonition, without once feeling the hand of controul. Yet my time was lost, my expences were multiplied, my behaviour abroad was unknown; folly as well as vice should have awakened the attention of my superiors, and my tender years would have justified a more than ordinary degree of restraint and discipline.

---

[21] See Conoisseur No. XI. worked up in Colman's farce—Pallas quas condidit arces ipsa colat, good.*

* *Connoisseur*, No. XI.: "On the Excursions of Young Academics to London."

—— *Pallas quas condidit arces Ipsa colat.*—VIRG.

"Let Pallas dwell in towers herself has raised."

"The principal character in Steele's comedy of the *Lying Lover* is young Bookwit, an Oxonian, who at once throws off the habit and manners of an academic, and assumes the dress, air, and conversation of a man of the town.

... By a review I have lately made of the people in this great metropolis, as Censor, I find that the town swarms with bookwits. The playhouses, parks, taverns, and coffee-houses are thronged with them. ... The whole time these lettered beaux remain in London is spent in a continual round of diversion. Their sphere, indeed, is somewhat confined; for they generally eat, drink, and sleep within the precincts of Covent Garden."

It might at least be expected that an Ecclesiastical school should inculcate the orthodox principles of Religion. But our venerable Mother had contrived to unite the opposite extremes of bigotry and indifference : an heretic or unbeliever was a monster in her eyes; but she was always, or often, or sometimes remiss in the spiritual education of her own children. According to the statutes of the University, every student, before he is matriculated, must subscribe his assent to the thirty-nine articles of the Church of England, which are signed by more than read, and read by more than believe them. My insufficient age excused me, however, from the immediate performance of this legal ceremony ; and the Vice-Chancellor directed me to return, so soon as I should have accomplished my fifteenth year, recommending me in the mean while to the instruction of my College. My College forgot to instruct, I forgot to return, and was myself forgotten by the first Magistrate of the University. Without a single lecture, either public or private, either Christian or protestant, without any Academical subscription, without any episcopal confirmation, I was left, by the dim light of my Catechism, to grope my way to the Chappel and communion-table, where I was admitted without a question how far or by what means I might be qualified to receive the sacrament. Such almost incredible neglect was productive of the worst mischiefs.[22] From my childhood I had been fond

---

[22] Ignorance, religious, of under graduates, who are soon ordained—complaint of Dr. Prideaux—Dr. Busby offered to endow two Catechists—rejected by both Univers.—Confessional, p. 435–440.*

* *The Confessional, or a Full and Free Inquiry into the Right, Utility, Edification and Success of Establishing Systematical Confes-*

of Religious disputation; my poor aunt has been often puzzled by my objections to the mysteries which she strove to believe; nor had the elastic spring been totally broken by the weight of the Atmosphere of Oxford. The blind activity of idleness urged me to advance without armour into the dangerous mazes of controversy, and at the age of sixteen I bewildered myself in the errors of the Church of Rome.

The progress of my conversion may tend to illustrate, at least, the history of my own mind. It was not long since Dr. Middleton's * free inquiry had sounded an alarm in the Theological World; much ink and much gall had been spilt in the defence of the primitive miracles; and the two dullest of their champions were crowned with Academic honours by the University of Oxford. The name of Middleton was unpopular, and his proscription very naturally tempted me to peruse his writings and those of his antagonists.† His bold criticism, which approaches the precipice of infidelity, produced on my

---

sions of *Faith and Doctrine in Protestant Churches.* Published 1770. Pp. 435–440. The author of this work, which was published anonymously, was the Rev. Francis Blackburne, Archdeacon of Cleveland.

Dr. Prideaux complains that "young men frequently come to the university without any knowledge or tincture of religion at all, and have little opportunity of improving themselves at all."—*Life of Dr. Prideaux,* p. 91 (1748).

"Dr. Busby offered to endow two catechetical lectures . . . provided the undergraduates should be obliged to attend, and none of them be admitted to the degree of Bachelor of Arts till after having been examined by the Catechist as

to their knowledge in the doctrines and precepts of the Christian religion. But this condition being rejected by *both* universities, the benefaction was rejected therewith, and the Church has ever since suffered for the want of it."—*Life of Dr. Prideaux,* p. 92.

* Conyers Middleton (1683–1750), the opponent of Bentley. His *Letter to Waterland* (1731) impugning the historical accuracy of some of the books of the Old Testament, and his *Free Enquiry into the Miraculous Powers which are supposed to have subsisted in the Christian Church* (1749), an attack on the miracles of the early Christian Church, gave rise to prolonged and bitter controversy.

† Dr. Dodwell and Dr. Church.

mind a singular effect; and had I persevered in the communion of Rome, I should now apply to my own fortune the prediction of the Sibyll.

> " Via prima salutis,
> Quod minimum reris, Graiâ pandetur ab Urbe."

The elegance of style and freedom of argument were repelled by a shield of prejudice. I still revered the characters, or rather the names, of the Saints and fathers whom Dr. Middleton exposes, nor could he destroy my implicit belief that the gift of miraculous powers was continued in the Church during the first four or five Centuries of Christianity. But I was unable to resist the weight of historical evidence, that within the same period most of the leading doctrines of Popery were already introduced in Theory and practise; nor was my conclusion absurd, that Miracles are the test of truth, and that the Church must be orthodox and pure, which was so often approved by the visible interposition of the Deity. The marvellous tales, which are so boldly attested by the Basils and Chrysostoms, the Austins and Jeroms, compelled me to embrace the superior merits of Celibacy, the institution of the monastic life, the use of the sign of the cross, of holy oil, and even of images, the invocation of Saints, the worship of relicks, the rudiments of purgatory in prayers for the dead, and the tremendous mystery of the sacrifice of the body and blood of Christ, which insensibly swelled into the prodigy of Transubstantiation. In these dispositions, and already more than half a convert, I formed an unluckly (*sic*) intimacy with a young Gentleman of our College [whose name I shall spare]. With a character less resolute Mr. ——* had

---

* Molesworth.

imbibed the same Religious opinions, and some Popish books, I know not through what channel, were conveyed into his possession. I read, I applauded, I believed; the English translations of two famous works of Bossuet, Bishop of Meaux, the Exposition of the Catholic doctrine, and the history of the Protestant variations, atchieved my conversion, and I surely fell by a noble hand. I have since examined the originals with a more discerning eye, and shall not hesitate to pronounce that Bossuet is, indeed, a master of all the weapons of controversy. In the Exposition, a specious Apology, the Orator assumes, with consummate art, the tone of candour and simplicity, and the ten-horned Monster is transformed at his magic touch into the milk-white hind, who must be loved as soon as she is seen. In the history, a bold and well-aimed attack, he displays with an happy mixture of narrative and argument, the faults and follies, the changes and contradictions of our first Reformers, whose Variations (as he dextrously contends) are the mark of heretical error, while the perpetual Unity of the Catholic Church is the sign and test of infallible truth. To my actual feelings it seems incredible that I could ever believe that I believed in Transubstantion!* But my conqueror oppressed me with the sacramental words, "Hoc est corpus meum," and dashed against each other the figurative half-meanings of the Protestant sects; every objection was resolved into Omnipotence, and after repeating at St. Mary's the Athanasian creed, I humbly acquiesced in the Mystery of the real presence.

---

* The word is generally spelt thus throughout the autobiographies by Gibbon.

> " To take up half on trust, and half to try,
> Name it not faith, but bungling bigotry.
> Both knave and fool the merchant we may call,
> To pay great sums and to compound the small ;
> For who would break with Heaven, and would not break for all ? " *

No sooner had I settled my new Religion, than I resolved to profess myself a Catholic. Youth is sincere and impetuous, and a momentary glow of Enthusiasm had raised me above all temporal considerations.

By the keen protestants who would gladly retaliate the example of persecution, a clamour is raised of the encrease of popery, and they are always loud to declaim against the toleration of priests and Jesuits who pervert so many of his Majesty's subjects from their Religion and Allegiance. On the present occasion, the fall of one or more of her sons directed this clamour against the University ; and it was confidently affirmed that Popish missionaries were suffered, under various disguises, to introduce themselves into the Colleges of Oxford. But [the love of † truth and justice enjoyns] me to declare that, as far as relates to myself, this assertion is false, and that I never conversed with a priest, or even with a papist, till my resolution from books was absolutely fixed. In my last excursion to London I addressed myself to a Roman Catholic bookseller in Russel-street, ‡ Covent Garden, who recommended me to a priest of whose name and order I am at present ignorant.§ In our first interview

---

* *The Hind and the Panther,* i. 141.

† " Justice obliges me " in Lord Sheffield's edition.

‡ Mr. Lewis.

§ His name was Baker, a Jesuit, and one of the chaplains of the Sardinian Ambassador. Mr. Gibbon's conversion made some noise ; and Mr. Lewis, the Roman Catholic bookseller of Russell Street, Covent Garden, was summoned before the Privy Council and interrogated on the subject. This was communicated by Mr. Lewis's son, 1814.— LORD SHEFFIELD.

he soon discovered that persuasion was needless, and, after sounding the motives and merits of my conversion, he consented to admit me into the pale of the Church; and at his feet on the eighth of June, 1753, I solemnly, though privately, abjured the errors of heresy. The seduction of an English Youth of family and fortune was an act of as much danger as glory; but he bravely overlooked the danger, of which I was not then sufficiently informed. "Where a person is reconciled to the see of Rome, or procures others to be reconciled, the offence," says Blackstone, "amounts to High-treason." And if the humanity of the age would prevent the execution of this sanguinary statute, there were other laws, of a less odious cast, which condemned the priest to perpetual imprisonment, and transferred the proselyte's estate to his nearest relation. An elaborate controversial Epistle, approved by my director and addressed to my father, announced and justified the step which I had taken. My father was neither a bigot nor a philosopher, but his affection deplored the loss of an only son, and his good sense was astonished at my strange departure from the Religion of my Country. In the first sally of passion he divulged a secret, which prudence might have suppressed, and the gates of Magdalen College were for ever shut against my return. Many years afterwards, when the name of Gibbon was become as notorious as that of Middleton, it was industriously whispered at Oxford that the historian had formerly "turned Papist." My character stood exposed to the reproach of inconstancy, and this invidious topic would have been handled without mercy by my opponents, could they have separated my cause from that of the University. For my own part, I am proud of an honest sacrifice of interest to conscience; I can never blush if my tender mind was entangled in the sophistry that seduced the acute and manly understandings of CHILLINGWORTH and BAYLE, who afterwards emerged from superstition to scepticism.

While Charles the First governed England, and was himself governed by a Catholic Queen, it cannot be denied that the Missionaries of Rome laboured with impunity and success in the Court, the country, and even the Universities.   One of the sheep—

> " Whom the grim Wolf, with privy paw,
>   Daily devours apace, and nothing said "— *

is Mr. William Chillingworth, master of arts, and fellow of Trinity College, who, at the ripe age of twenty-eight years, was persuaded to elope from Oxford to the English seminary of Douay, in Flanders. Some disputes with Fisher, a subtle Jesuit, might first awaken him from the prejudices of education; but he yielded to his own victorious argument, "That there must be somewhere an infallible judge, and that the Church of Rome is the only Christian society which either does or can pretend to that character." After a short tryal of a few months, Mr. Chillingworth was again tormented by religious scruples; he returned home, resumed his studies, unravelled his mistakes, and delivered his mind from the yoke of authority and superstition. His new creed was built on the principle that the Bible is our sole judge, and private reason our sole interpreter; and he ably maintains this principle in the Religion of a protestant, a book (1634) which, after startling the Doctors of Oxford, is still

---

* Milton's *Lycidas*.

esteemed the most solid defence of the Reformation. The learning, the virtue, the recent merits of the author entitled him to fair preferment; but the slave had now broke his fetters, and the more he weighed the less was he disposed to subscribe the thirty-nine articles of the Church of England. In a private letter he declares with all the energy of language that he could not subscribe them without subscribing his own damnation, and that if ever he should depart from this immoveable resolution, he would allow his friends to think him a madman or an atheist. As the letter is without a date, we cannot ascertain the number of weeks or months that elapsed between this passionate abhorrence and the Salisbury register, which is still extant, "Ego Gulielmus Chillingworth, . . . omnibus hisce articulis et singulis in iisdem contentis, volens et ex animo subscribo, et consensum meum iisdem præbeo. 20 die Julii, 1638." But, alas! "the Chancellor and prebendary of Sarum soon deviated from his own subscription; as he more deeply scrutinized the article of the Trinity, neither Scripture nor the primitive fathers could long uphold his orthodox belief, and he could not but confess that the doctrine of Arius is either a truth, or at least no damnable heresy." From this middle region of the air, the descent of his reason would naturally rest on the firmer ground of the Socinians; and, if we may credit a doubtful story and the popular opinion, his anxious enquiries at last subsided in Philosophic indifference. So conspicuous, however, were the candour of his Nature and the innocence of his heart, that this apparent levity did not affect the reputation of Chillingworth. His frequent changes proceeded from too nice an inquisition into truth. His doubts grew out of himself; he assisted them with all the strength of his reason; he was then too hard for himself; but finding as little quiet and repose in those victories, he quickly recovered by a new appeal to his own judgement, so that in all his sallies and retreats he was, in fact, his own convert.

Bayle was the son of a Calvinist minister in a remote province of France, at the foot of the Pyrenees. For the benefit of education, the Protestants were tempted to risk their children in the Catholic Universities; and in the twenty second year of his age, young Bayle was seduced by the arts and arguments of the Jesuits of Thoulouse. He remained about seventeen months (19th March, 1669—19th August, 1670) in their hands, a voluntary captive; and a letter to his parents, which the new convert composed or subscribed (15th April, 1670,) is darkly tinged with the spirit of Popery. But Nature had designed him to think as he pleased, and to speak as he thought : his piety was offended by the excessive worship of creatures; and the study of physics convinced him of the impossibility of Transubstantion, which is abundantly refuted by the testimony of our senses. His return to the communion of a falling sect was a bold and disinterested step, that exposed him to the rigour of the laws, and a speedy flight to Geneva protected him from the resentment of his spiritual tyrants, unconscious as they were of the full value of the prize which they had lost. Had Bayle adhered to the Catholic Church, had he embraced the Ecclesiastical profession, the Genius and favour of such a proselyte might have aspired to wealth and honours in his native country; but the Hypocrite would have found less happiness in the comforts of a

benefice or the dignity of a mitre than he enjoyed at
Rotterdam in a private state of exile, indigence, and
freedom.   Without a country, or a patron, or a prejudice,
he claimed the liberty, and subsisted by the labours, of
his pen : the inequality of his voluminous works is
explained and excused by his alternately writing for
himself, for the booksellers, and for posterity ; and if a
severe critic would reduce him to a single folio, that
relick, like the books of the Sybill, would become still
more valuable.   A calm and lofty spectator of the Religious tempest, the Philosopher of Rotterdam condemned
with equal firmness the persecution of Lewis XIV. and
the Republican maxims of the Calvinists, their vain
prophecies and the intolerant bigotry which sometimes
vexed his solitary retreat.   In reviewing the controversies
of the times, he turned against each other the arguments
of the disputants : successively wielding the arms of the
Catholics and protestants, he proves that neither the way
of authority nor the way of examination can afford the
multitude any test of Religious truth ; and dexterously
concludes, that custom and education must be the sole
grounds of popular belief.   The ancient paradox of
Plutarch, that Atheism is less pernicious than superstition,
acquires a tenfold vigour when it is adorned with the
colours of his wit, and pointed with the acuteness of his
logic.   His critical Dictionary is a vast repository of facts
and opinions ; and he balances the *false* Religions in his
sceptical scales till the opposite quantities (if I may use
the language of · Algebra) annihilate each other.   The
wonderful power, which he so boldly exercised of assem-
bling doubts and objections had tempted him jocosely to
assume the title of the νεφεληγερετα Ζευς—the cloud-

compelling Jove; and in a conversation with the ingenious Abbé (afterwards Cardinal) de Polignac, he freely disclosed his universal Pyrrhonism. "I am most truly," said Bayle, "a protestant; for I protest indifferently against all Systems and all Sects."

The Academical resentment which I may possibly have provoked will prudently spare this plain narrative of my studies, or rather of my idleness; and of the unfortunate event which shortened the term of my residence at Oxford. But it may be suggested that my father was unluckly in the choice of a society and the chance of a tutor. It will perhaps be asserted that in the lapse of forty years many improvements have taken place in the College and the University. I am not unwilling to believe that some Tutors might have been found more active than Dr. Waldegrave, and less contemptible than Dr. [Winchester.] [About the same time, and in the same walk, a Bentham was still treading in the footsteps of a Burton, whose maxims he had adopted, and whose life he has published. The Biographer, indeed, preferred the school logic to the new Philosophy, Burger's dicius to Locke; and the Hero appears in his own writings a stiff and conceited Pedant. Yet even these men, according to the measure of their capacity, might be diligent and useful; and it is recorded of Burton that he taught his pupils what he knew, some Latin, some Greek, some Ethics and Metaphysics, referring them to proper masters for the languages and sciences of which he was ignorant.] At a more recent period many students have been attracted by the merit and reputation of Sir William Scott,* then a tutor in University College, and now conspicuous in the

---

* Afterwards Lord Stowell.

profession of the Civil law: my personal acquaintance with that Gentleman has inspired me with a just esteem for his abilities and knowledge; and I am assured that his Lectures on history would compose, were they given to the public, a most valuable treatise. Under the auspices [of the present Archbishop of York, Dr. Markham, himself an eminent scholar,*] a more regular discipline has been introduced, as I am told, at Christ Church: a course of Classical and philosophical studies is proposed and even pursued in that numerous seminary: Learning has been made a duty, a pleasure and even a fashion; and several young Gentlemen who do honour to the College in which they have been educated. According to the will of the Donor, the profits of the second part of Lord Clarendon's history has been applied to the establishment of a riding-school, that the polite exercises might be taught, I know not with what success, in the University. The Vinerian professorship is of far more serious importance; the laws of his country are the first science of an Englishman of rank and fortune, who is called to be a Magistrate, and may hope to be a Legislator. This judicious institution was coldly entertained by the graver Doctors, who complained—I have heard the complaint—that it would take the young people from their books; but Mr. Viner's benefaction is not unprofitable, since it has at least produced the excellent commentaries of Sir William Blackstone. [The manners and opinions of our Universities must follow at a distance the progressive motion of the age; and some prejudices, which reason could not subdue, have been slowly obliterated by time. The last generation of Jacobites is extinct; "the right Divine of Kings

---

* In Lord Sheffield's edition, " of the late Deans."

to govern wrong " is now exploded, even at Oxford; and the remains of Tory principles are rather salutary than hurtful, at a time when the Constitution has nothing to fear from the prerogative of the Crown, and can only be injured by popular innovation. But the inveterate evils which are derived from their birth and character must still cleave to our Ecclesiastical corporations: the fashion of the present day is not propitious, in England, to discipline and œconomy; and even the exceptionable mode of foreign education has been lately preferred by the highest and most respectable authority in the Kingdom. I shall only add that Cambridge appears to have been less deeply infected than her sister with the vices of the Cloyster; her loyalty to the house of Hanover is of a more early date, and the name and philosophy of her immortal Newton were first honoured in his native Academy.]

APPENDIX TO MEMOIR F.

1. (p. 1.) The river Rother "on its Kent side has Newenden, which I am almost perswaded was the haven so long sought for, called by the *Notitia, Anderida.*" After describing how the place had been taken, and the inhabitants had been put to the sword by Hengist and Ælla, he continues: "For many ages after (as Huntingdon tells us) there appeared nothing but ruins; till under Edward the first, the Friars Carmelites, just come from Mount Carmel in Palestine, and desiring solitary places above all others, had a little Monastery built here at the charge of *Thomas Albuger*, Knight; upon which a town presently sprung up, and with respect to the *old* one that had been demolished, began to be called *Newenden*, i.e. *a new town in a Valley. . . .*" Lower down the river, near its mouth, is *Apuldore*, which "in the time of the Saxons, An. 894, stood at the mouth of the river *Limene*, as their Chronicle tells us. . . . Now if the sea came so lately as An. 894 to the town of *Apledore*, in all probability five hundred years before, in the Romans' time, it might come as far as *Newenden*, the place of the city and Castle of *Anderida*, erected here by the Romans to repel the Saxon Rovers; the sea here in all ages having retired by degrees."—Camden's *Britannia*, edited by Edmund Gibson, D.D., Bishop of London, 2nd edit., vol. i. p. 258.

2. (p. 5.) "Cette dame etait ce qu'on appelle proprement une beauté Angloise; pétrie de lys et de roses, de neige et de lait quant aux couleurs; faite de cire, à l'égard des bras et des mains, de la gorge et des pieds: mais tout cela sans âme et sans air. . . . La Nature en avoit fait une poupée dès son enfance; et poupée jusqu'à la mort resta la blanche Wetenhall. M. de Wetenhall avoit étudié pour être d'église; mais son frère aîné s'étant laissé mourir dans le temps que celui-ci finissoit ses études, au lieu de prendre les ordres il prit le chemin d'Angleterre, et Mademoiselle Bedingfield, dont nous parlons, pour femme. . . . Et comme Hamilton la regardoit avec une attention qui paroissoit assez tendre elle regardoit Hamilton comme un homme assez propre au petits projets dont elle étoit convenue avec sa conscience. . . . Milord Muskerry avoit à deux ou trois petits milles de Tunbridge une belle maison, appelée Summerhill. Mlle. Hamilton après avoir passé huit ou dix jours à Peckham ne put se dispenser d'y venir demeurer pendant le reste du voyage. Elle obtint du Seigneur Wetenhall que madame sa femme y vint aussi: et quittant le triste Peckham et son ennuyeux seigneur, cette petite cour fut établié à Summerhill."—Œuvres de Grammont. 3 Vols. 1805. (Vol. i. pp. 336–341, 345.)

3. (p. 15.) "Après la mort de Vital Michieli, second du nom, qui fut tué le propre jour de Pasques, ce peuple lassé de la longue domination de ses Ducs reprit le Gouvernement, et continua pourtant d'élire un prince pour donner plus de crédit aux afaires; mais il resserra son pouvoir à un point, qu'il ne lui laissa presque plus rien que le titre et la presséance. Et tout se faisoit alors par le Grand Conseil qui étoit composé de 470 citoiens, nommés par 12 electeurs, tirés des six quartiers de la Ville et les 470 se changoient tous les ans le jour de Saint Michel, afin de contenter tout le monde à son tour. Ce qui dura jusques au tems du Duc Pierre Gradenigue Second qui reforma le Grand Conseil en 1298, en faisant passer dans le Conseil de Quarante qu'ils appellent *Quarantania Criminale*, une nouvelle ordonnance dont la teneur étoit que tous ceux qui dans cette année-la composoient le corps du Grand Conseil . . . en fussent, eux et leurs descendans en perpétuité. . . . Ce changement produisit, comme il est ordinaire dans toutes les mutations des Etats, la fameuse conjuration des Quirins des Tiepoles et de quelques autres familles anciennes qui furent exclues totalement.

"Venise a donc été gouverné par les Conseils et les Tribuns dans son enfance. . . . Le peuple l'aiant retirée de la tutele des ducs, prit la conduite de sa jeunesse. . . . Sa virilité a commencé sous les nobles, et a duré depuis la Reformation du Gouvernement, qu'ils appellent *Il Serrar di Consiglio* par où finit la Démocratie. . . . Quoiqu'il soit, Venise a cet avantage de s'être maintenue plus long-tems que toutes les plus fameuses Republiques de l'Antiquité."—*Hist. du Gouv. de Venise*, par le Sieur Amelot de la Houssaye (1677), pp. 3, 4, 6.

---

4. (p. 29.) "Phillippe V. laissa, comme nous l'avons dit, des dettes pour la valeur de quarante-cinq millions de piastres (plus de cent soixante-huit millions de livres tournois). A sa mort, Ferdinand VI., son fils & son successeur, Prince équitable & pieux, effrayé d'un fardeau si énorme, flottant entre la crainte de le faire supporter à l'Etat & le scrupule de frustrer ses créanciers de leurs droits, assembla un Junte composée d'Evêques, de Ministres & de gens de loi, & lui proposa cette question singulière: Si un Roi est ténu d'acquitter les dettes de son prédécesseur? Croira-t-on qu'elle fut decidée à la négative par la pluralité, sous prétexte que l'Etat était un patrimoine dont le Souverain n'étoit que l'ususruitier, & ne répondoit que de ses propres engagemens? Cette décision, contre laquelle réclamoient à l'envi l'équité, la raison & la politique, tranquillisa la conscience du Monarque, & légitima à ses yeux ce qui étoit une véritable banqueroute. Le payement des dettes de L'Espagne fut donc entièrement suspendu."— Bourgoanne (or Burgoing), *Etat de l'Espagne*, vol. ii. p. 30.

---

5. (p. 34.) "C'est par le toucher seul que nous pouvons acquérir des connoissances complètes et réelles, c'est ce sens qui rectifie tous les autres sens dont les effets ne seroient que des illusions et ne produiroient que des erreurs dans notre esprit, si le toucher ne nous apprenait à juger. Mais comment se fait le développement de ce sens important? comment nos premières connoissances arrivent-elles à notre ame? n'avons-nous pas oublié tout ce qui s'est passé dans les ténèbres de notre enfance? comment retrouverons-nous la première trace de nos pensées? n'y a-t-il pas même de la témérite à vouloir remonter jusque-là? Si la chose étoit moins importante, on auroit raison de nous

blâmer; mais elle est peut-être, plus que toute autre, digne de nous occuper, et ne sait-on pas qu'on doit faire des efforts toutes les fois qu'on veut atteindre à quelque grand objet?

"J'imagine donc un homme tel qu'on peut croire qu'étoit le premier homme au moment de la création, c'est-à-dire, un homme dont le corps et les organes seroient parfaitement formés, mais qui s'eveilleroit tout neuf pour lui-même et pour tout ce qui l'environne. Quels seroient ses premiers mouvemens, ses premières sensations, ses premiers jugemens! Si cet homme vouloit nous faire l'histoire de ses pre- mières pensées, qu'auroit-il à nous dire? quelle seroit cette histoire? Je ne puis me dispenser de la faire parler lui-même, afin d'en rendre les faits plus sensibles: ce recit philosophique, qui sera court, ne sera pas une digression inutile."— Buffon, *Histoire Naturelle*, tome iii. p. 363 (1750).

The foregoing sentences, to- gether with the description of the awakening sensations which follows them, but which is too long for quotation here, is apparently the passage which Gibbon intended to compare with the above lines of Milton. Cf. Gibbon's own note 68 to Memoir E.

---

6. (p. 36.) *Journal Britannique*, par M. Maty, Docteur en Philo- sophie et en Médecine, et membre de la Société Royale de Londres. 12mo. Hague, 1754.

Mois de mars et d'avril, 1754.

The Analysis of Inoculation: comprising the History, Theory, and Practice of it; with an occasional consideration of the most remarkable appearances in the Small-pox, by J. Kirkpatrick, M.D. London, 1754.

In the course of a long review of this work, Dr. Maty writes: "Ce n'est pas à l'industrie humaine que Mr. Kirkpatrick paroit disposé à rapporter dans sa iv. section la première découverte de l'inocula- tion. Les nations ignorantes de l'Asie de qui nous tenons cette operation en ignorent l'inventeur et la date. Pylarini, Médecin Italien, qui se trouvoit à Con- stantinople en 1701 paroit y avoir observé le premier cette méthode artificielle dont après avoir verifié les circonstances et les succès, il fit l'essai sur quatre enfans d'un Grec de ses amis. . . . Un memoire Manuscript du feu Chevalier Hans Sloane, que Mr. Ranby, a com- muniqué à notre auteur, nous apprend que ce fut en consequence d'une lettre que ce Chevalier avoit écrite à Mr. Sherard, Consul de la Nation en Turquie, que la relation de Pylarini fut composée et envoyée à la Société Royale. Cette informa- tion eut été negligée, si Mme Mon- taigu épouse de l'Ambassadeur de ce nom à Constantinople n'y avoit fait inoculer en 1717 son propre fils agé de six ans. . . . Cette dame a l'honneur d'avoir introduit cette pratique en Angleterre: *Dux fœmina facti*."

---

7. (p. 42.) Gustavus Adolphus, during his campaign in 1732, had to throw his troops across the Lech, in face of Tully's army, which occu- pied a strong position on the oppo- site bank. Dr. Walter Harte, in his *Life of Gustavus Adolphus*, writes: "The construction and fixing of the bridge appeared more difficult to his majesty than the fighting part. He greatly disliked the in- equality of the banks in respect of height, which rendered a bridge of boats or pontons inconvenient, if not entirely useless; and he like- wise knew that the bed of the river was a sort of cone inverted: which intelligence he procured by various artifices, one in particular extremely curious; nevertheless I shall decline relating it, having some doubts concerning the authen-

ticity of the narrative." To this is added the following footnote: "It is to be seen in the *Memoirs of a Cavalier*, 8vo, printed at Leeds in Yorkshire, about the year 1740." —*A History of Gustavus Adolphus, King of Sweden*, etc., by the Rev. Walter Harte, M.A. Third edition. 2 vols. 8vo. 1807.

Defoe, in his *Memoirs of a Cavalier*, relates that when Gustavus Adolphus wished to ascertain the depth of the river, one of his soldiers, a sergeant of dragoons, volunteered for the task, and going down to the Lech, disguised as a boor, and carrying a long pole, entered into conversation with the soldiers on the other bank, pretending that he wished to cross over, and asking for their assistance. In the end he thus obtained all the information he required, and returned to the Swedish camp in safety.

---

8. (p. 42.) "Tho' he had been father of nine children, we have only an account of his eldest son, Edward Pococke, who, under the doctor's direction, published in 1671, 4to, with a Latin translation, an Arabic piece, intitled Philosophus Autodidactus Sive Epistola Abu Jaafir Ebn Tophail de Hai Ebn Yokdhan. In qua ostenditur quomodo ex inferiorum contemplatione ad superiorum notitiam ratio humana ascendere possit. The design of the author, who was a Mahometan philosopher, is to shew by an ingenious fiction how human reason, by observation and experience, without any assistance, may arrive at the knowledge of natural things, and from thence rise to supernatural; particularly the knowledge of God and of a future state. . . .

"The language concerning an extraordinary union and intimate conjunction with God, obtained by a steady looking upon Him, without the help of any external means, is evidently the principle of the Quietist; and this principle induced the Quakers to translate the book into English, seeing there was something in it which favoured their enthusiastic notions; and to prevent any such mischief thereby, Simon Ockley, M.A., Vicar of Swavesey, in Cambridgeshire, gave a new translation in 1711, 8vo, under the title, *The Improvement of human Reason, exhibited in the Life of Hai Ebn Yokdhan*, etc., with an appendix in which the possibility of man's attaining the true knowledge of God and things necessary to salvation without *instruction* is briefly considered.

"It appears from the introduction and several passages in the original book that the author of it, Abu Jaafir Ebn Tophail, had imbibed this notion; and it was in order to describe the nature of the mystical union, as well as to recommend the means of attaining it, that he undertook the treatise. He also declares this was the true, though mystical, sense of the philosophy of Averröes, Avicen, Amerpace, Algazali, Alpharabius, and the best Mahometan philosophers, who were all of them, therefore, what he calls mystics. . . .

"Dr. Pococke tells he has good reason to think the author was contemporary with Averröes, who died very old, Anno Heg. 595, or Anno Dom. 1198."—*Biogr. Brit.*, s.v. "Pococke."

---

9. (p. 44.) " Emile n'apprendra jamais rien par cœur, pas même des fables, pas même celles de La Fontaine, toutes naïves, toutes charmantes qu'elles sont ; car les mots des fables ne sont pas plus les fables que les mots de l'histoire ne sont l'histoire. Comment peut-on s'aveugler assez pour appeler les fables la morale des enfants, sans songer que l'apologue, en les amusant les abuse ; que, séduits

par la mensonge, ils laissent échapper la verité, et que ce qu'on fait pour leur rendre l'instruction agréable les empêche d'en profiter? Les fables peuvent instruire les hommes; mais il faut dire la verité nue aux enfants; sitot qu'on la couvre d'un voile, ils ne se donnent plus la peine de le lever. On fait apprendre les fables de La Fontaine à tous les enfants, et il n'y en a pas un seul qui les entende. Quand ils les entendroient, ce serait encore pis; car la morale en est tellement mêlée et si disproportiounée à leur âge, qu'elle les porteroit plus au vice qu'à la vertu. Ce sont encore là, direz vous, des paradoxes. Soit; mais voyons si ce sont des vérités, etc., etc."—*Œuvres de Rousseau*, vol. viii. p. 165. Paris. 20 vols. 1826.

---

10. (p. 45.) " Amico arcta mecum necessitudine conjuncto, quod inscripta mihi ipsius quædam ad æternitatem victura monumenta testantur, alteram uberibus lachrimis deflendum cogor adjungere, Petrum Pithœum Augustobonæ Tricassium natum, familia nobili ex inferiore Neustria oriundum, virum nostra ætate maximum, sive probitatem morum et veram nec fucatam pietatem, sive ingenium excellens, exactamque et omnium rerum quas perspectas habuit, habuit autem plus quam alius quisquam multis retro sæculis, reconditam cognitionem, et tum iu suis tum in alienis cernendis acre et ab omni livore purum judicium, spectes . . . in literarum studiis sic versatus est, ut, assidue exquirendo et scrutando bibliothecas, antiquorum scripta vel a mendis vel ab interitu vindicaret, vel alios, quos in ea re aliquid posse judicabit, exhortando, impellendo atque juvando, nullo tempore non aliquid moveret ac promoveret; sub ipsum vitae exitum beati Hilarii fragmentis historicis, et Phædri Augusti liberti fabulis publicatis."—De Thou (J. A.), *Historia Sui Temporis*, vol. v.

Gibbon regarded De Thou as "one of his masters." See Memoir B, p. 104.

---

11. (p. 60.) " Ne parentes quidem recte possunt educare liberos, si tantum metuantur. Prima cura est amari, paulatim succedit non terror, sed liberalis quædam reverentia, quæ plus habet ponderis quam metus.

" Quam igitur belle prospicitur his pueris, qui vix dum quadrimi mittuntur in ludum literarium, ubi præsidet præceptor ignotus, agrestis, ac moribus parum sobriis, interdum ne cerebri quidem sani, frequenter lunaticus, aut morbo comitiali obnoxius, aut lepræ, quam nunc vulgus scabiem Gallicam appellat. Neminem enim hodie tam abjectum, tam inutilem, tam nullius rei videmus, quem vulgus non existimet idoneum moderando ludo literario. Atque illi se regnum nactos rati, mirum quam ferociant, quod habeant imperium, non in belluas, ut inquit Comicus, sed in eam ætatem, quam oportebat omni lenitate foveri. Dicas non esse scholam, sed carnificinam, præter crepitum ferularum, præter virgarum strepitum, præter ejulatus ac singultus, præter atroces minas nihil illic auditur. Quid aliud hinc discant pueri, quam odisse literas? Hoc odium ubi semel insedit teneris animis, etiam grandes facti abhorrent a studiis. . . .

" Gallis literatoribus secundum Scotos nihil est plagosius. Hi moniti respondere solent; eam Nationem, quemadmodum de Phrygia dictum est, nonnihil plagis emendari. Hoc au verum sit, alii viderint, fateor tamen nonnihil in Natione discriminis esse, sed multo magis in singulorem ingeniorum proprietate: Quosdam occidas potius quam verberibus emendes; at eosdem benevolentia blandisq; monitis ducas quocunq; velis. Hac indole fateor me puerum fuisse, quum Præceptor, cui præ cæteris eram charus, quod diceret se nescio quid magnæ Spei de me concipere, magis advigilaret, velletque tandem experiri quam essem virgarum patiens; objecit commissum, de quo nec somniaram unquam, ac cæcidit—Ea res omnem studiorum amorem mihi excussit; adeoq; dejecit puerilem animum, ut minimum abfuerit quin dolore contabescerem. Jam hinc mihi conjecta, vir egregie, quam multa fælicissima ingenia perdant isti Carnifices indocti; sed doctrinæ persuasione tumidi, morosi, vinolenti, truces, & vel animi gratia cædunt; nimirum ingenio tam truculento, ut ex alieno cruciatu capiant voluptatem. Hoc genus homines lamios aut carnifices esse decuit, non pueritiæ formatores. Nec ulli crudelius excarnificant pueros quam qui nihil habent quod illos doceant. Hi quid agant in Scolis, nisi ut plagis & jurgiis diem extrahant."—Desiderius Erasmus, *Pueros de virtutem ac Literas liberaliter Instituendos.* Opera. Lugd., 1703, fol. 504.

---

12. (p. 60.) "Under these two excellent Masters of Paul's School; if there was any fault in the Management of it, it was in the Practice of too much severity, owing a little to the Roughness of that Age, and to the established Customs of Cruelty. Somewhat, too, may be attributed to that austere temper of the Founder, D. Colet; who verily thought, there was a Necessity of harsh Discipline to humble the Spirit of Boys, to inure them to Hardship and prepare them for Mortifications and other Sufferings and Afflictions in the World."—Knights, *Life of John Colet*, p. 173.

---

13. (p. 64.) Dialogue VIII., "On the Uses of Foreign Travel." In this dialogue Mr. Locke is represented as defending the English mode of education as practised at the universities, against Lord Shaftesbury, who is an advocate of the advantages of foreign travel. The passage referred to is this—

"Mr. Locke. All this, my Lord, is very well; yet, setting aside a certain colouring of expression which takes and amuses the imagination, I see but little to admire in this picture; certainly not enough to make one regret the want of the original, and seriously to prefer this easy manner of breeding to that stricter form which prevails in our own universities: where the day begins and ends with religious offices; where the diligence of the youth is quickened and relieved, in turn, by stated hours of study and recreation; where temperance and sobriety are even *convivial* virtues; and the two extremes of a festive jollity and unsocial gloom are happily tempered by the decencies of a *common table*; where, in a word, the discipline of Spartan HALLS and the civility of Athenian BANQUETS are, or may be, united."

---

14. (p. 68.) *Biogr. Brit.*, ed. 1760, *s.v.* Prideaux (Dr. Humphrey), p. 3434, note AA.

Having finished this work (*Directions to Churchwardens*), he (Prideaux) went on with his *Connection of the History of the Old and New Testament*, which he had begun immediately upon dropping the designed *History of Appropriations.*

The note on this passage states that "while he was thus engaged, Charles, Lord Viscount Townsend, one of the Principal Secrataries (*sic*) of State to King George the First, meditating a design to introduce a kind of Reformation in the English Universities, consulted our Dean, who thereupon drew up the plan for that purpose, and sent to his Lordship, under the title of

'Articles for the Reformation of the two Universities.'" [Then follows the proposed scheme, under 68 heads or articles.] " No doubt can be made of the Dean's good intention in these articles ; but whoever knows anything of the state of the Universities, need not be told that the scheme is absolutely impracticable. As an argument that proves too much, proves nothing ; so a scheme that aims at too much loseth everything."

A corresponding sketch was drawn for Cambridge by Mr. W. Whiston, under the title of "Emendanda in Academia."—*Memoirs of the Life of Mr. Whiston*, p. 42, *et sqq.*, 2nd ed., 1753.

---

15. (p. 73.) "William Patten, the Founder of this College, was born at Wainfleet in Lincolnshire, where liv'd his Father, Richard Patten, and his Mother Margery, Daughter of Richard Brereton, Knight, his Father and Mother being both descended from antient Families in their respective Counties, had, besides William, two other Sons, the one named John, a Graduate in this University, and afterwards Archdeacon of Surrey, and (as some say) Dean of Chichester; and Richard of Basclow in Derbyshire. William, surnamed Wainfleet, from the place of his birth, according to the custom of the monks in those Times, was for the first Part of his Education sent to Wickham-School near Winchester, and from thence remov'd to Oxford, tho' to what College some have doubted, but most probably to New-College, as Tradition has deliv'r' it down; others say to Merton, and that he was either Chaplain or Post-Master therein. He stay'd not long in Oxford after he was promoted to the Degree of a Bachelor in Divinity, (a Degree in that Age not so common as in the Present) but was made chief Master of Winchester-School, (which is a vehement Presumption that he was a Fellow of Wickham's College in Oxford, it being a Post of good Reputation and Profit, and never given to any other than a Wickhamist) ,wherein he continued for twelve years together, and was then advanc'd by his good Patron K. Henry VI., to be Provost of Eaton College; and lastly, on the 30th July, 1447, he was created Bishop of Winchester, over which he presided 39 years, in which time he was for 9 years Lord High Chancellor of England, viz. from the 11th of October, 1449, to 7th July, 1458, quitting this Office a little before the Battle of Northampton. He stuck close to the Interest of his aforesaid Patron, so that he was frown'd upon by King Edward IV., and in the employments of Bishop and Chancellor (as premised) he amassed together Money enough to attempt great Designs, and by some publick Work of Charity to perpetuate his name to after Ages; and to this End he first built a Hall, and then a College at Oxford, dedicating both of them to St. Mary Magdalen; of which in their proper Order."— Ayliffe, *State of the University of Oxford*, p. 342.

---

16. (p. 74.) " Il arriva à Paris au mois de mai 1711 ; & pour choisir un séjour favorable tout à la fois à sa piété & à sa curiosité, il logea à St. Germain-des-Prés. Ce que sent Énée dans Virgile [" Artificumque manus inter se operumque laborem Miratur."—*Æneid*, l. 1, v. 455], lorsque plein du dessein de bâtir une grande ville, il arrive à Carthage, & qu'il considère avec transport tant de bras en mouvement, tant de beaux édifices qui s'élèvent ; le P. Quirini le sentit en entrant dans cette illustre Abbaye: on y travailloit alors aux annales des Bénédictins, à une traduction françoise du nouveau Testament, à un apparat de

la bibliothèque des Pères, a l'histoire de Paris, à la colloction des Decrétales, au glossaire de Du Cauge, à des éditions d'Origène, de St. Basile, de St. Cyrille, & le P. Bandury rassembloit toutes les pièces de son Empire Oriental." —*Académie Royale : Des Inscrip-*

tions et Belles Lettres, tom. 27, p. 219.

The page of Quirini's *Commentarii de Rebus Pertinentibus ad Ang. Mar. S. R. E. Cardinalem Quirinum* is 85 of the 1849 edition, and is merely a plain account of his stay in Paris.

---

17. (p. 76.) No. 33, Saturday, Dec. 2, 1758, contains *The Journal of a Senior Fellow or Genuine Idler just transmitted from Cambridge by a facetious correspondent.* It professes to set forth day by day and hour by hour the trivial and selfish pursuits in which the said Fellow passed his time. In his concluding remarks the author writes—

"I hope it will not be concluded from this specimen of academic life, that I have attempted to decry our Universities. If literature is not the essential requisite of the modern academic, I am yet persuaded that Cambridge and Oxford, however degenerated, surpass the fashionable *academies* of our metropolis and the *gymnasia* of foreign countries. . . . There is at least one very powerful incentive to learning; I mean the GENIUS *of the place.* . . . English Universities render their students virtuous at least, by excluding all opportunities of vice; and by teaching them the principles of the Church of England, confirm them in those of true Christianity."

---

18. (p. 80.) " Multoque post tempore, Armaïs, qui in Ægypto fuerat relictus, omnia contra quam frater monuerat ne faceret, sine timore faciebat. Nam & reginæ vini inferebat, aliisque concubinis ad libitum misceri non cessabat: persuasusque ab amicis corona utebatur, & contra fratrem insurgebat. Is vero qui constitutus erat super sacra Ægyptiaca codicillos Sethosi misit, eum de omnibus certiorem faciens, quodque frater ipsius Armaïs contra eum bellum movebat. Illico igitur Pelusium reversus est, & proprium tenuit regnum. Provincia vero ex ejus nomine appellata est Ægyptus, dicit enim quod Sethosis quidem Ægyptus vocabatur, Armaïs autem frater ejus Danaus.

" 16. Atque hæc quidem Manetho. Ergo si tempus ad initam annorum istorum rationem exigemus, constabit omnino, quos Pastores ipsi vocabant, majores nostros, annis ante tribus nonaginta supra trecentos, ubi ex Ægypto migrassent regionem illam insedisse, quam Danaus Argos venisset, qui tamen ab Argivis pro antiquissimo celebratur. Ita duo nobis eaque sane præcipua, hoc Manethonis quod Ægyptiarum literarum fidem sequitur, testimonio confecta sunt: alterum eos in Ægyptum aliunde profectos esse; alterum indidem ipsos alio commigrasse, quod etiam posterius adeo vetustum, ut Trojana tempora annis prope mille antecederet. Ista vero quaë Manetho non ex literis Ægyptiacis, sed (sicut ipse professus est) ab incertis auctoribus memorata, adjecit, postea particulatim excutiam, ea mendacia esse ostendens sine verisimilitudine conficta."—*Flavii Josephi quæ reperiri potuerunt opera omnia. . . . Collegit, disposuit, et post Jo. Hudsonum . . . recensuit Sigebertus Havercampus.* 2 vols., folio, 1726.

MY OWN LIFE.*

A sincere and simple narrative of my own life may amuse some of my leisure hours, but it will expose me, and perhaps with justice, to the imputation of vanity. Yet I may judge, from the experience both of past and of the present times, that the public is always curious to *know* the men who have left behind them any image of their minds : the most scanty accounts are compiled with diligence and perused with eagerness ; and the student of every class may derive a lesson or an example from the lives most similar to his own. [The author of an important and successful work may hope without presumption that he is not totally indifferent to his numerous readers:] my name may hereafter be placed among the thousand articles of a Biographia Britannica, and I must be conscious that no one is so well qualified as myself to describe the series of my thoughts and actions. The authority of my masters, of the grave Thuanus and the philosophic Hume, might be sufficient to justify my design ; but it would not be difficult to produce a long list of ancients and moderns who, in various forms, have exhibited their own portraits. Such portraits are often the most interesting, and sometimes the only interesting, parts of their

---

* Memoir B, from his birth till the eve of his journey into Italy in 1764.

writings; and, if they be sincere, we seldom complain of the minuteness or prolixity of these personal memorials. The lives of the younger Pliny, of Petrarch, and of Erasmus are expressed in the Epistles which they themselves have given to the World; the Essays of Montagne and Sir William Temple bring us home to the houses and bosoms of the authors; we smile without contempt at the headstrong passions of Benvenuto Cellini, and the gay follies of Colley Cibber. The confessions of St. Austin and Rousseau disclose the secrets of the human heart; the Commentaries of the learned Huet have survived his Evangelical demonstration; and the Memoirs of Goldoni are more truly dramatic than his Italian comedies. The Heretic and the Churchman are strongly marked in the characters and fortunes of Whiston and Bishop Newton; and even the dullness of Michael de Marolles and Antony Wood acquires some value from the faithful representation of men and manners. That I am the equal or superior of some of these Biographers the efforts of modesty or affectation cannot force me to dissemble.

I was born at Putney, in the County of Surrey, the twenty-seventh of April, OS., (the eighth of May, NS.), in the year one thousand seven hundred and thirty-seven; the first child of the marriage of Edward Gibbon, Esq., and of Judith Porten. My lot might have been that of a slave, a savage, or a peasant; nor can I reflect without pleasure on the bounty of Nature, which cast my birth in a free and civilized country, in an age of science and Philosophy, in a family of honourable rank, and decently endowed with the gifts of fortune.

[Of this family the primitive seat was in the County of Kent. It is proved by authentic records that as early as the year 1326 the Gibbons were possessed of lands in the parish of Rolvenden, and it should seem that their ancient patrimony, without much encrease or diminution, is still in the hands of the elder branch. They are distinguished by the title of Esquire, at a time when it was less promiscuously bestowed; and I continue to bear the Armorial coat, the ancient symbol of their gentility: "A Lyon rampant, gardant, between three scallop-shells, Argent on a field Azure." The use of these arms about the time of Queen Elizabeth is attested by the whimsical revenge of Edmond Gibbon, Esq.: instead of the three scallop-shells, he substituted, for himself only, three Ogresses, and these female monsters were designed to represent his three kinswomen, against whom he had maintained a lawsuit for the patronage of the free school of Benenden, a foundation of their common ancestors. In the beginning of the seventeenth Century a younger branch of the Gibbons, from which I descend, migrated from the country to the city, from a rural to a commercial life; nor am I ashamed of an useful profession which has been long since ennobled by the national good sense and the example of the most ancient gentry of England. It would be as easy as it might be tedious to enumerate our various marriages, both in Kent and in London, with the most respectable families—the Hextalls, the Ellenbriggs, the Calverleys, the Phillips of Tenterden, the Berkleys of Beauston, the Whetnalls of East Peckham and of Cheshire, the Edgars of Suffolk, and the Cromers of Surrey, whose progenitor, William Cromer (in the years 1413 and 1424), was twice Lord Mayor of the City of London. By the females, I draw my pedigree from the Lord Say and Sele, who was Lord High Treasurer of

England under the reign of Henry the Sixth: he fell a sacrifice to the blind fury of Jack Cade and his Kentish Insurgents; and if Shakespeare be a faithful historian, a man of letters may be proud of his connection with the Patron and Martyr of learning. But in the male line I can discover only two persons who have left any monument more conspicuous than a gravestone in a parish church.

I. In the year 1340, John Gibbon was *Marmorarius* or Architect (the office of an Esquire), in the service of Edward the Third; he built Queensborough Castle, and the royal grant of the profits of the passage between Sandwich and Stoner, in the Isle of Thanet, is not the reward of a vulgar mechanick.

II. John Gibbon, the brother, as it should appear, of my great-grandfather Matthew, has exhibited the proofs of his lively wit and extensive reading, which are not, indeed, without some alloy of prejudice and enthusiasm. He was born in 1629, and died at the age of ninety, after having filled near fifty years the station in the College of Heralds of Blue-mantle Poursuivant at Arms. I cannot forbear to relate that in a voyage to Virginia in 1659, he recognized, at a War-dance of the Indians, the colours and symbols of his art which were painted on their naked bodies; nor will I suppress his whimsical conclusion, "that Heraldry is engrafted naturally into the sense of human race." He published at London, in 1682, his *Introductio ad Latinam Blazoniam*, an English text besprinkled with Latin sentences and verses of his own composition; and in this small but elaborate treatise, he claims the invention of expressing the language of Heraldry in a Classical idiom. But this domestic record, which illustrates the antiquity of his name and blood, was lost in his own family, till, about two years ago, it was sent me, by a singular chance, from Wolfenbuttel in Germany to Lausanne in Switzerland. The science of hereditary distinctions is favourable to Monarchy, and Blue-mantle, like the rest of his kindred, was a zealous Tory both in Church and State.

My grandfather, Edward Gibbon, a man of sense and business, was of some note in the political as well as the commercial World, and under Lord Oxford's * administration he exercised the office of one of the Commissioners of the Customs near four years, till the death of Queen Anne. Before he was elected a Director of the South Sea Company (1716) he had acquired, chiefly by his own industry, a fortune of sixty thousand pounds; but in the calamitous year *twenty* he suffered with his brethren, without a tryal, by an arbitrary bill of pains and penalties. Of the mischiefs or merits of the South Sea Scheme, I am neither a competent nor an unbyassed judge; but if the national calamity was contrived by the fraud of the Directors, I fear that my grandfather's abilities will not leave him the apology of ignorance or error. Whatever might be his guilt, it could neither be proved by evidence nor punished by law; the proceedings of the house of Commons are stained with personal and party malice, and few will be found, in these days of moderation and justice, to applaud an act of parliamentary tyranny which was not excused by the defence of the public safety. After the Directors had delivered on oath the amount of their respective

* Robert Harley, Chancellor of the Exchequer 1710; created Earl of Oxford, and became Lord Treasurer 1711; dismissed from office 1714.

fortunes, the measure of their future allowances was determined not by any judicial enquiry, but by hasty and capricious votes on the character and conduct of each individual. My grandfather had estimated his property at the ample sum of one hundred and six thousand five hundred and forty-three pounds five shillings and six-pence; and when the question was put whether fifteen or ten thousand pounds should be assigned to Mr. Gibbon, it was carried without a division for the smaller allowance. By his skill and industry this remnant was again multi-plied; it is suspected that he had found means to elude the impending stroke by prævious settlements and secret conveyance, and at the time of his death (at Christmas, 1736) he could not be less opulent than he had been before the South Sea Calamity. Besides his landed Estates in Hampshire and Buckinghamshire, besides large sums which were employed in trade or vested in stock, he had purchased a spacious house and gardens at Putney, in Surry, where he lived with decent hospitality and a respectable character. His wife, my grandmother, was of the name of Acton, an ancient and honourable name in Shropshire; and he had given his sister to Sir Whit-more Acton, the head of the family, and father of Sir Richard, the present baronet. A younger branch is settled abroad, and it is with pleasure that I acknow-ledge for my cousin the Chevalier or General Acton, the favourite minister of the King of the two Sicilies. By my grandfather's last Will, his two daughters were enriched at the expence of his son, to whose marriage he was not perfectly reconciled. Of my two aunts, Catherine became the wife of Mr. Edward Elliston, an East India Captain; their daughter and heiress,

Catherine, was married in the year 1756 to Edward Eliot, Esq. (now Lord Eliot), of Port Eliot, in the county of Cornwall, and their three sons are my nearest relations on the father's side. A life of devotion and celibacy was the choice of my aunt, Mrs. Hester Gibbon,* who, at the age of eighty-five, still resides in a hermitage at Cliffe, in Northamptonshire, having survived many years her spiritual guide and faithful companion, Mr. William Law. In his *Serious Call*, the characters of Flavia and Miranda, of the profane and the pious sister, are admirably drawn by a writer of Genius who had studied and renounced the World.

The same Mr. William Law was domestic tutor to my father, who was born in the year 1707. His education was liberal, at Westminster School, and at Emanuel College in the University of Cambridge; and he was afterwards permitted to visit Paris, and some parts of France and Italy. On his return home the gay youth despised the mercantile profession of his ancestors, and after his father's death he enjoyed, and perhaps abused, the gifts of independence and fortune. He was twice chosen a Member of Parliament, at the general elections of 1734 and 1740 : at the former he obtained an easy seat for the borough of Petersfield, and at the latter he prevailed after a sharp and expensive contest for the town and county of Southampton. The principles of his family, and the memory of his father's wrongs, engaged him in a strenuous, though silent, opposition against Sir Robert Walpole : my father steadily adhered to the party of the Tories, or Country Gentlemen; with

---

* She died in 1790, aged eighty-six; was buried beside Wm. Law, who died April 9, 1761.

them he gave many a vote, and with them he drank
many a bottle. He loved and married* a young lady
of the neighbourhood, Miss Judith Porten; but in his
father's eyes the deficiency of fortune was not compensated by the superior qualifications of beauty, virtue,
and understanding. By her he had seven children, six
sons and a daughter, all of whom, except myself, died
in their infancy. After an happy union of ten years,
she was snatched away by an untimely death : his affliction was deep and permanent, and he soon retired to his
estate at Buriton, in Hampshire, from the business and
pleasures of the World. Although I retain a faint remembrance of her person, I have never known in its full
extent the inestimable blessing of a mother. But her
loss was amply supplied by her sister, my aunt, Mrs.
Catherine Porten, to whose tender care I owe the preservation of my infancy and the first dawnings of my
reason, and at whose name I feel a tear of gratitude
trickling down my cheek. Their common father, Mr.
James Porten of Putney, was a merchant of doubtful
credit, which soon ended in a Bankruptcy. His son,
Sir Stanier Porten, is still alive, and barely alive : merit
and industry could alone raise him to the honourable
stations of Consul-General in Spain, Secretary to the
Embassy at Paris, Under-Secretary of State, and Commissioner of the Excise, which he has successively filled.

According to the calculations of Monsieur de Buffon,
about half the infants that are born are cut off in
their infancy, before they have completed their eighth
year; and the chances that I should not live to

---

* In 1736.

compose this narrative were, at the time of my birth, in the proportion of above three to one. Such may be the general probabilities of human life, but the ordinary dangers of infancy were multiplied far beyond this measure by my personal infirmities; and so little hope did my parents entertain, that after bestowing at my baptism the favourite appellation of Edward, they provided a substitute, in case of my departure, by successively adding it to the Christian names of my younger brothers. My poor Aunt Porten has often told me, with tears in her eyes, how I was almost starved by a nurse who had lost her milk, and how long she trembled lest my crazy frame, which is now of the common shape, should be for ever crooked and deformed. From one dangerous malady, the small-pox, I was indeed rescued by the practice of inoculation, which had been recently introduced into England, and was still opposed by Theological, medical, and even political prejudice. But it is only against the small-pox that a preservative has been found : and I could recapitulate from memory or hearsay almost every disease which afflicted my childhood—feavers and lethargies, a fistula in the eye, a tendency to a dropsical and consumptive habit, a contraction of the nerves, with a variety of nameless disorders; and, as if Nature was not sufficient without the concurrence of accident, I was once bit by a dog most vehemently suspected of madness. From Sloane and Mead to Ward and the Chevalier Taylor, every practitioner was alternately summoned : the fees of Doctors were swelled by the bills of Apothecaries and Surgeons; there was a time when I swallowed almost as much physick as food, and my body is still marked with the scars of bleeding, issues, and caustics. From these ills and from these remedies I have wonderfully escaped. Instead of growing with my growth and strengthening with my strength, my complaints, as I advanced to the age of puberty, insensibly disappeared. I have never known the insolence of active and vigorous health; but my constitution has ripened to a sound and temperate maturity, and since the age of fifteen I have seldom required the serious advice of a Physician.

The first moment of animal life may be dated from the first pulsation of the heart in the human fœtus; but the nine months which we pass in a dark and watery prison, and the first years after we have seen the light and breathed the air of this world, must be substracted from the period of our rational existence. When I strive to ascend into the night and oblivion of infancy, the most early circumstance which I can connect with any known æra is my father's contest and election for Southampton. At that time (1740) I was about three years of age: I had already acquired the familiar use of my mother-tongue, and I was soon instructed in the elements of reading and writing, which in this age of learning are almost as universal as those of language. In the seventh year of my age, after some lessons at a day-school at Putney, I was delivered to the care of a domestic tutor. His name was Mr. John Kirkby, his profession Ecclesiastical, his principles those of a Non-juror, and it was on his omission of the prayer for the Royal family that loyalty or prudence obliged my father to dismiss him from his house. A child is incapable of estimating the learning and genius of his præceptor; but at the end of four and forty years, I can discern them in his writings, and these writings were peculiarly adapted to the task of education.

In the year 1745 he published *Automathes*, a Philosophical romance, in which the self-taught Philosopher grows to manhood, virtue, and science on a desert island; and in the month of November of the same year, he dedicated to my father, as a testimony of gratitude, his treatise on the English and Latin Grammar. Besides the rudiments of the two languages, I imbibed with ease the rules of simple and compound Arithmetic; my ready skill in numbers and calculations was applauded, and had I cultivated the early taste, the author of history might have been lost in the Mathematician.

After this short tryal of domestic tuition my father adopted the easy and customary mode of education, and in a lucid interval of health I was sent to a school at Kingston, consisting of about seventy scholars, under the care of Dr. Woodson * and his assistants. As often as I have since passed over Putney Common, I have always noticed the spot where my mother, as we drove along in the coach, exhorted me to remember that I was going into the world, and must learn to think and act for myself. The expression may appear burlesque, but there is not in the course of life a more remarkable change than the removal of a child (I was then about eight years old) from the freedom and luxury of a wealthy house to the frugal diet and strict subordination of a school; from the tenderness of parents and the obsequiousness of servants to the rude familiarity of his equals, the insolent tyranny of his seniors, and the rod, perhaps, of a cruel

---

* Richard Wooddesdon; see note, p. 43.

and capricious pædagogue. Such hardships may be useful to steel the mind and body against the assaults of fortune, but I shall never regret the boyish felicity which those may praise who are dissatisfied with the present hour. Of a timid and reserved disposition, *I* was astonished by the crowd and tumult of the new scene; my want of strength and activity disabled me from joyning in the sports of the play-field; nor have I forgot how often, in the year forty-five, I was reviled and buffetted for the sins of my Tory ancestors. By the common methods of discipline, at the expence of many tears and some blood, I purchased the knowledge of the Latin syntax. Not long since I was still possessed of the dirty Volumes of Phædrus, Ovid, and Cornelius Nepos, which I painfully construed and darkly understood; they might have suggested the most pleasing lessons of taste, mythology, and history, which a rational teacher would have adapted to the capacity of a child.

From Kingston I was recalled on my mother's death; nor would my father have entertained a thought of a public school, unless he could have placed me under the watchful and affectionate eye of my aunt, Mrs. Porten. Her father's bankrupcy left her destitute of fortune, and her noble spirit, scorning a life of obligation and dependence, preferred the obscure industry of keeping a boarding-house at Westminster, where she laboriously earned a competency for her old age. In her house in College Street and at the adjacent school I passed two years and a half—from January, 1748, to August, 1750—nor could I rise to the third form without improving my acquaintance with the Latin Classics. But my studies were interrupted by long and frequent illness; the labour of

two masters (Drs. Nichols and Johnson *) and of half a
dozen Ushers was inadequate to the instruction of five
hundred boys, and the slow march of public exercises
must be proportioned to the lowest degree of ability and
application. From this seminary, which has produced
so many eminent persons, I was unfortunately removed
before my style or my ear could be formed by the habits
of Latin composition in prose and verse; before I could
taste the beauties of eloquence and poetry; before I had
entered on the rudiments of the Greek language, and
before my childish intimacies had ripened into serious
and solid friendships. The care of my education became
subordinate to that of my health; during two years
(1750–1752) I was moved by my father from place to
place. I spent many months at Bath and Winchester
for the benefit of the waters or of medical advice; all
study was often interdicted, nor could I derive much
knowledge from the rare and occasional lessons of such
teachers as could be found on the spot. During the
months of February and March, 1751, I resided at Esher,
in Surry, in the house of the Reverend Mr. Philip
Francis; and the translator of Horace might have
taught me to relish the Latin poets, had not my friends
discovered in a few weeks that he preferred the pleasures
of London to the instruction of his pupils. At length,
as my puerile disorders appeared to abate, my father was
persuaded to place me, without sufficient preparation,

---

* For John Nicoll, see note, p. 50.
James Johnson became second
master in 1733, and resigned the
post in 1748, on being appointed
chaplain to George II., whom he
accompanied to Hanover. He
afterwards was Bishop of Gloucester (1752), and subsequently of
Worcester (1759), and died from
the effects of a fall from his horse
in 1774.

at Magdalen College, in the University of Oxford, where I was matriculated as a Gentleman-Commoner on the third of April, 1752, before I had compleated the fifteenth year of my Age.

It is on the tender and vacant mind that the first characters of science and language are most deeply engraved; and I am often conscious that the defects of my first education have not been perfectly supplied by the voluntary labour of my riper years. Yet, in my progress from infancy to the age of puberty, the faculties of memory and reason were insensibly fortified, my stock of ideas was encreased, and I soon discovered the spirit of enquiry and the love of books to which I owe the happiness of my life. My aunt, Mrs. Porten, whom I must always mention with respectfull gratitude, possessed a clear and manly understanding, and her natural taste was improved by the perusal of the best authors in the English language. In sickness or in health I was often resigned to her care, and my long vacations from school were chiefly passed in her father's house near the bridge and churchyard at Putney. She was truly my mother, she became my friend: all distance and reserve were banished between us; we freely conversed on the most familiar or abstruse subjects, and it was her delight and reward to observe the first shoots of my childish fancy. During many hours, as she sat anxious and watchful by my bedside, have I listened to the books which she read and the stories which she related; and a favourite tale from the English translation of Hippolitus, Earl of Douglas, is still present to my memory: the cavern of the winds, the palace of felicity, and the fatal moment, at the end of three months, or three Centuries, in which Prince Adolphus is overtaken by old time, who had worn out so many pairs of wings in the fruitless chase. I soon tasted the Arabian nights entertainments—a book of all ages, since in my present maturity I can revolve without contempt that pleasing medley of Oriental manners and supernatural fictions. But it is in rude ages and to youthful minds that the marvellous is most attractive: the decoration of the imaginary world is more splendid, its events more interesting, its laws more—more consonant to justice and virtue, and our ignorance is easily reconciled to the violation of probability and truth. From these tales I rose to the father of poetry, but I could only embrace the phantom of Homer; nor was I then capable of discerning that Pope's translation is a portrait endowed with every merit, except likeness to the original. His elegant and sonorous verse I repeated with emphasis, and retained without labour. I was delighted with the exploits of the Iliad, and the adventures of the Odyssey; the Heroes of the Trojan war soon became my intimate acquaintance, and I often disputed with my aunt on the characters of Hector and Achilles. From Pope's Homer to Dryden's Virgil was an easy transition; but I know not how, by the fault of the author or the translator or the reader, the pious Æneas less forcibly seized on my imagination; and I could read with more pleasure some parts of the Metamorphoses, the fall of Phaëthon, and the speeches of Ajax and Ulysses in the old version of Sandys's Ovid. Our English writers of poetry, Romances, history, and travels were my daily and indiscriminate food; my aunt's partiality encouraged me to open the works of philosophy and divinity least adapted to the capacity of a child, but I was either too young or too old to partake of her enthusiasm for the Characteristics of Shaftsbury. During the nine months (from March to December, 1747) between my grandfather's absconding and the sale of his effects, I rioted without controul in his library, which had been hitherto locked, and I should distinguish this period, the eleventh year of my age, by the plentiful nourishment and rapid growth of my mind.

Yet my reason was not sufficiently informed to understand the value and regret the loss of the four succeeding years (1748–1752), from my first introduction at Westminster to my settlement at Oxford. Instead of repining at my long and frequent confinement to the chamber or the couch, I secretly rejoyced in the infirmities which delivered me from the exercises of the school, and the society of my equals. As often as I was tolerably exempt from pain and danger, reading—free desultory reading—was the occupation and comfort of my solitary hours, and my father's acquaintance who visited the child were astonished at finding him surrounded with an heap of folios of whose names *they* were often ignorant, and on whose contents *he* could pertinently descant. During the first years of this period, I still enjoyed the conversation of my indulgent aunt, and in my subsequent stations at Bath and Winchester, at Putney and Buriton, a false compassion respected my sufferings, and I was left to gratify my unripe taste without the discipline of a master, or even the advice of a learned friend. By degrees the wanderings of my fancy subsided in the historic line, and as the doctrine of innate ideas is no longer fashionable, I must ascribe this choice to the assiduous perusal of the Universal history as the separate Volumes successively appeared. From the references in that unequal collection, and from an useful treatise, the Ductor Historicus of Hearne, I obtained some knowledge of the Greek and Latin Historians. As many as were accessible to an English student I endeavoured to procure, and all were devoured in their turns—from Littlebury's lame Herodotus, and Spelman's valuable Xenophon, to the pompous folios of Gordon's Tacitus, and a ragged Procopius of the beginning of the last Century. The cheap attainment of so much learning confirmed my dislike to the study of language, and I represented to my aunt that, were I master of Latin and Greek, I must interpret to myself in English the thoughts of the original, and that such hasty extemporary versions would be probably inferior to the elaborate translations of professed scholars: a feeble sophism, but which could not be easily refuted by a person ignorant of any language but her own. My litterary wants began to multiply; the circulating libraries of London and Bath were exhausted by my importunate demands, and my expences in books surpassed the measure of my scanty allowance. Of my eagerness to explore any new path of history, I recollect a singular example.

In the year 1751 my father carried me to Mr. Hoare's seat, in Wiltshire; but I was much less delighted with the beauties of Stourhead than with the accident of finding in the library a volume of Echard's continuation, which gave me the first notions of the passage of the Goths into the Roman Empire. Nor was I satisfied till I had obtained from the second part of Howell's History of the World a more compleat knowledge of that memorable event which, at the end of thirty years, I was destined to relate.

From ancient I descended to modern times, many crude lumps of Speed, Rapin, Mezeray, Davila, Machiavel, Father Paul, Bower, etc., passed through me like so many Novels; my curiosity was not limited to Europe, and I swallowed with the same voracious appetite the description of China and the Indies, the American Decads of Herrera, the artful missions of the Jesuits, and the simple traditions of the Incas, so pompously styled the Royal Commentaries of Peru. But I must applaud the reason or instinct which led me to seek and to find the genuine monuments of Eastern history; before the age of sixteen I was master of all the *English* materials, which I have since employed in the chapters of the Persians and Arabians, the Tartars and Turks, and the consciousness of their defects urged me to guess at the French of d'Herbelot, and to construe the barbarous Latin of Pocock's Abulpharagius. Such vague and multifarious reading, which could not teach me to think or to act, was enlightened, however, by an early and constant attachment to the order of time and place. The Geography and maps of Wells and Cellarius fixed in my mind the picture of the ancient World. From the introduction of Strauchius I imbibed the principles of Chronology; in the annals of Usher and Prideaux I distinguished the series and connection of events; and the multitude of dates and æras soon arranged themselves in my memory in a regular and permanent system. But in the discussion of the first ages I overstepped the boundaries of modesty and use. Scaliger and Petavius, Marsham and Newton, I alternately presumed to weigh in my childish balance; the dynasties of Egypt and Assyria were my top and cricket-ball, and my sleep was often disturbed by the difficulty of reconciling the Hebrew with the Septuagint computation. I arrived at Oxford with a stock of Erudition which might have puzzled a Doctor, and a degree of ignorance of which a schoolboy would have been ashamed. To complete this account of my puerile studies, I shall here observe that I soon attempted and soon abandoned two litterary projects far above my strength: a critical enquiry into the age of Sesostris, and the paralel lives of the Emperor Aurelian and Selim the Turkish Sultan, who, in their cruelty, valour, and Syrian Victories, may indeed support some kind of resemblance.

I entered on my new life at Magdalen College, in the University of Oxford, with surprize and satisfaction. These sentiments were naturally produced by my sudden promotion, before the age of fifteen, to the rank of a man; the general civility with which I was treated; the silk gown and velvet cap of a Gentleman-Commoner; a decent allowance in my own disposal with a loose and dangerous credit; an elegant apartment of three rooms in the new buildings; the beauty of the walks and public edifices; and the key of the College library, which I might use or abuse without much interruption from the fellows of the Society. I may wish that the fruits of my noviciate had corresponded with this flattering appearance, and that I could now proclaim my gratitude in the well-chosen words of Dr. Lowth, the late Bishop of London—

"I was educated in the University of Oxford. I enjoyed all the advantages, both public and private, which that famous seat of learning so largely affords.

I spent many happy years in that illustrious society, in a well-regulated course of useful discipline and studies, and in the agreeable and improving commerce of Gentlemen and scholars; in a society where emulation without envy, ambition without jealousy, contention without animosity, incited industry and awakened Genius; where a liberal pursuit of knowledge and a generous freedom of thought was raised, encouraged, and pushed forward, by example, by commendation, and by authority. I breathed the same atmosphere that the *Hookers*, the Chillingworths, and the Lockes had breathed before," etc.

It may indeed be observed that the Atmosphere of Oxford did not agree with Mr. Locke's constitution, and that the Philosopher justly despised the Academical bigots who expelled his person and condemned his principles.* For me the University will as gladly renounce me for her son as I shall disclaim her for my mother, since I am compelled to acknowledge that the fourteen months which I spent in Magdalen College were totally lost for every purpose of study or improvement. If I am reminded that my tender years, my short residence, and my imperfect præparation could not derive much benefit from the institution of that learned body, I am willing that such reasons should operate with their proper weight. Yet I may affirm that, at the age of fifteen, I was not destitute of capacity and application; that even my

---

* The subject of the expulsion of Locke has been set at rest by the publication of Lord Grenville;[1] who, anxious as he might be to uphold the character of the University, would have disdained the attainment even of this object by the slightest compromise of truth and justice. The disgraceful act was not that of the University, but of the servile Head of a College in obedience to an arbitrary Court.—MILMAN.

---

[1] *Oxford and Locke*, by Lord Grenville, 1829.

childish reading had proved an early though blind propensity to books and learning, and that the shallow flood might have easily been taught to flow in a deep and regular channel. In the discipline of a well-constituted society, and under the guidance of a skillful teacher, my youthful ardour would have been encouraged and directed. I should gradually have risen from translations to originals, from the Latin to the Greek Classics, from dead languages to living science; and the six years which my father had allotted for my Academical education might have been successfully employed in the labour of learning. When I reflect, indeed, on the advantages which I gained in a liberal acquaintance with the nations, the manners, and the idiom of Europe, I must rather rejoyce than repine at my early deliverance from the habits and prejudices of an English Cloyster. But instead of speculating on what *might* have been the colour of my life and opinions, I shall now state with simple sincerity the result of my personal experience of Magdalen College in the university of Oxford.

The elegant Dissertations of Lowth on the Hebrew poetry, and the useful commentaries of Blackstone on the laws of England, were first delivered in the form of Academical lectures. But the assertion of Mr. Adam Smith is generally true, that in the University " of Oxford the greater part of the public professors for these many years past have given up altogether even the pretence of teaching." Instead of a course of lectures by the masters of each particular science to a great number of disciples, the task of instruction is abandoned to the College-Tutors, who teach, or undertake to teach, the whole circle, at least, of elementary knowledge in separate lessons to their private pupils. The first Tutor to whose care I was resigned appears to have been one of the best of the Tribe. Dr. Waldegrave was a learned and pious man, of strict morals, and a mild disposition, who seldom mingled either in the business or the jollity of the College. He soon gained my regard and confidence; I preferred his company to that of the younger students, and in our evening walks to the top of Heddington hill, we freely conversed on a variety of topics. But this respectable tutor was a stranger to the polite or philosophic world: his temper was indolent; his faculties, which were not of the first-rate, had been relaxed by the climate; and he was content, like the rest of his fellows, with a slight and superficial performance of an important trust. No plan of study was formed; no litterary exercises were prescribed; he suffered me to waste my leisure without account or advice; his morning lessons were confined to the space of a single hour, and that hour was filled by an easy task for the master and the pupil. We read together the Comedies of Terence; the whole sum of my improvement at Oxford may be reduced to the perusal of two or three Latin plays; and even this employment, which might have been productive of so much Philosophical reflection and critical remark, consisted only of a cold, dry interpretation of the text and metre. During the first weeks I regularly attended these lessons in my tutor's room, but as they were equally devoid of profit and pleasure, I was once tempted to make the experiment of a formal apology. The apology was accepted with a smile. I repeated the offence with less ceremony; the excuse was accepted with the same indulgence. The slightest motive of lazyness or indisposition, the most trifling avocation at home or abroad, was a sufficient obstacle; my visits became rare and occasional, nor did my tutor appear conscious of my absence or neglect. Before my return to Oxford, after spending the vacation in Hampshire, Dr. Waldegrave was removed to a College-living; but I was transferred, with the rest of his pupils, to his Academical heir, a Dr. Winchester, whose only science was supposed to be that of a broker and salesman. From my own experience I am not, indeed, qualified to represent his character; his person I scarcely knew, and in the eight months for which he demanded a salary I never received a word of lesson or advice from the Director of my studies. The defects of private tuition might have been supplied by public discipline and example; but the example of the old Monks (I mean the fellows) was not likely to incite the emulation and diligence of the novices and undergraduates. The forty principal members of our opulent foundation, who had been amply endowed with the means of study and subsistence, were content to slumber in the supine enjoyment of these benefits; they had absolved themselves from the labour of reading, or thinking, or writing, and the first shoots of learning or genius rotted on the ground without producing any fruits either for the owners or the public. Their conversations, to which I have sometimes listened in the common room, stagnated within the narrow circle of College business and Tory politics; their deep and dull compotations left them no right to blame the warmer intemperance of youth, and their constitutional toasts were not expressive of the most sincere loyalty to the house of Hanover. The discipline of the society I neither felt nor observed; a tradition still remained that Latin declamations had been spoken by the Gentlemen-Commoners in the Hall; but in my time the custom was abolished: the obvious methods of rewards and censures, of exercises and examinations, were unknown; nor could I learn that the conduct of Tutors and pupils had ever awakened the attention of the President. For my own part, the want of occupation and experience soon led me into some irregularities of bad company, late hours, and improper expence. My debts might be secret, my absence was visible: a tour into Buckinghamshire, an excursion to Bath, four excursions to London, were idle and dangerous follies; and my tender years might have justified a more than ordinary restraint. Yet I eloped from Oxford, I returned; I again eloped in a few days, as if I had been an independent stranger in a hired lodging, without once hearing the voice of admonition, or once feeling the hand of controul. I am told, and I am willing to believe, that since the year fifty-three some reformation has taken place. The essential vices of the University are, however, inherent to its dark Antiquity, to the spirit of an Ecclesiastical corporation, to the fixed salaries of the professors, and to the lazy opulence of the Colleges, which I flatter by comparing them to so many Abbeys of Benedictine monks.

It might at least be expected that an Ecclesiastical school should have diligently inculcated on the minds of youth the study of Religion, and the arguments that establish the truth of the Christian and pro-testant Systems. But the University of Oxford had contrived to unite the opposite extremes of bigotry and indifference. According to her statutes, every student, on his matriculation, subscribes, either with or without reading them, the thirty-nine articles of the Church of England; but this ceremony was postponed on account of my age, and the Vice-Chancellor directed me to return so soon as I had accomplished my fifteenth year, referring me in the mean while to the Religious instructions of my College. My College forgot to instruct; I forgot to return, and was myself forgotten by the Vice-Chancellor; and thus, without signing any symbol of faith, without being sanctifyed by any rites of confirmation, I groped my way by the light of my Catechism to the Chappel and the Communion table. Like most children who are born with any natural sense, I had formerly puzzled my aunt by my questions and objections on the mysteries of Religion, and the heavy atmosphere of Oxford had not totally broken the elasticity of my mind. Without guide or preparation, my idle curiosity was unluckily directed to the study of the disputes between the Protestants and the Papists; and I soon persuaded myself that victory and salvation were on the side of the Church of Rome. The University of Oxford, which has suffered some reproach from my short apostacy, was insulted by the false supposition that some Jesuits, some Romish Wolves must have been permitted to steal into the fold and to devour the lambs while the shepherd was asleep. In truth and justice, I must affirm that I never conversed at Oxford with a priest or even with a Catholic, till my resolution was irrevocably fixed; and it was fixed by some books of controversy, the first of which I borrowed from a young Gentleman of the College who secretly inclined to the same opinions. I read till my ignorance was entangled in the net of texts of scripture and passages of the Fathers. The hard doctrine of transubstantion (*sic*) was smoothed by the protestant belief in the mystery of the trinity: the vices of the Reformation were triumphantly urged, and I yielded to the specious argument that a wise legislator would provide a supreme and visible Judge for the interpretation of his laws.   If I now smile or blush at the recollection of my folly, I may derive some countenance from the example of Chillingworth and Bayle, who, at a riper age, were seduced by similar sophistry to embrace the same system of superstition.   I may claim the merit of treading in their footsteps, when, after a transient delusion, they broke their fetters and resumed the command of their captive reason.   But, in their return to the Religion of their fathers, my two predecessors were carried beyond the term from whence they had departed. It was with deep reluctance that Chillingworth subscribed the thirty-nine articles, several parts of which he disbelieved; his acute understanding was repeatedly vanquished by itself, and his last opinions were most probably those of an Arian or Socinian.   The free and comprehensive Genius of Bayle balanced the Religions of the Earth in the scales of his sceptical philosophy, till the adverse quantities, if I may use the language of Algebra, had annihilated each other.

No sooner was my reason subdued than I resolved to approve my faith by my works, and to enter without delay into the pale of the Church of Rome.   In my last excursion to London, I addressed myself to a Catholic bookseller in Russell street, Covent Garden; he recommended me to a priest of whose name and order I am at present ignorant, and by *his* exhortations I was confirmed in my pious design.   The conversion of a young Englishman of family and fortune could not fail of making much noise, and might be attended with some danger; but his zeal overlooked these worldly considerations, and at his feet, on the eighth of June, 1753, I solemnly, though privately, abjured the errors of heresy. In the sacrifice of this world to the next, I might affect the glory of a Confessor; but I must freely acknowledge that the sincere change of my speculative opinions was not inflamed by any lively sense of devotion or enthusiasm, and that in the giddyness of my age I had not seriously weighed the temporal consequences of this rash step. The intelligence, which I imparted to my father in an elaborate controversial Epistle, struck him with astonishment and grief: he was neither a bigot nor a philosopher; but his affection deplored the loss of an only son, and his good-sense could not understand or excuse my strange departure from the Religion of my Country.] After carrying me to Putney, to the house of his friend Mr. Mallet, by whose philosophy I was rather scandalized than reclaimed, it was necessary to form a new plan of education, and to devise some method which, if possible, might effect the cure of my spiritual malady.

[The gates of Oxford were shut against my return; in every part of England I might be accessible to the seductions of my new friends, and] after much debate it was determined, from the advice and personal experience of Mr. Eliot (now Lord Eliot *), to fix me, during some years, at Lausanne in Switzerland. Mr. Frey, a Swiss Gentleman of Basil, undertook the conduct of the journey: we left London the 19th of June,

---

* Edward Eliot, Esq., M.P. for Cornwall, born 1727; was elevated to the peerage as the first Baron Eliot of St. Germans, 1784; died 1804. His wife was Gibbon's cousin, Catherine Elliston.

crossed the sea from Dover to Calais, travelled post through several provinces of France, by the direct road of St. Quentin, Rheims, Langres, and Besançon, and arrived the 30th of June at Lausanne, where I was immediately settled under the roof and tuition of Mr. Pavilliard, a Calvinist Minister.

The first marks of my father's displeasure rather astonished than afflicted me: when he threatened to banish and disown and disinherit a rebellious son, I cherished a secret hope that he would not be able or willing to effect his menaces, and the pride of conscience encouraged me to sustain the honourable and important part which I was now acting. My spirits were raised and kept alive by the rapid motion of the journey, the new and various scenes of the continent, and the civility of Mr. Frey, a man of sense, and who was not ignorant of books or the World. But after he had resigned me into Pavilliard's hands, and I was fixed in my new habitation, I had leisure to contemplate the strange and melancholy prospect. My first complaint arose from my ignorance of the language. In my childhood I had once studied the French Grammar, and I could imperfectly understand the easy prose of a familiar subject. But when I was thus suddenly cast on a foreign land, I found myself deprived of the use of speech and of hearing; and during some weeks, incapable not only of enjoying the pleasures of conversation, but even of asking or answering a question in the common intercourse of life. To an home-bred Englishman every object, every custom was offensive, but the native of any country might have been disgusted with the general aspect of his lodging and entertainment.

[The Minister's wife, Madame Pavilliard, governed our

domestic œconomy : I now speak of her without resentment, but in sober truth she was ugly, dirty, proud, ill-
tempered and covetous. Our hours, of twelve for dinner,
of seven for supper, were arbitrary, though inconvenient
customs ; the appetite of a young man might have overlooked the badness of the materials and cookery, but his
appetite was far from being satisfied with the scantiness
of our daily meals, and more than one sense was offended
by the appearance of the table which during eight successive days was regularly covered with the same linnen.]
I had now exchanged my elegant apartment in Magdalen College for a narrow, gloomy street, the most un-
frequented of an unhandsome town ; for an old inconvenient house, and for a small chamber ill-contrived and
ill-furnished, which on the approach of winter, instead of
a companionable fire, must be warmed by the dull invisible
heat of a stove. From a man I was again degraded to
the dependence of a schoolboy. Mr. Pavilliard managed
my expences, which had been reduced to a diminutive
scale : I received a small monthly allowance for my
pocket-money ; and, helpless and awkward as I have ever
been, I no longer enjoyed the indispensable comfort of a
servant. My condition seemed as destitute of hope as it
was devoid of pleasure : I was separated for an indefinite,
which appeared an infinite, term, from my native Country ;
and I had lost all connection with my Catholic friends.
I have since reflected with surprize, that, as the Romish
Clergy of every part of Europe maintain a close correspondence with each other, they never attempted by
letters or messages, to rescue me from the hands of the
heretics, or at least to confirm my zeal and constancy in
the profession of the faith.—Such was my first introduction

to Lausanne, a place where I spent near five years with pleasure and profit, which I afterwards revisited without compulsion, and which I have finally selected as the most grateful retreat for the decline of my life.

But it is the peculiar felicity of youth, that the most unpleasing objects and events seldom make a deep or lasting impression. At the flexible age of sixteen I soon learned to endure and gradually to adopt the new forms of arbitrary manners: the real hardships of my situation, [the house, the table and the mistress] were alleviated by time; [and to this coarse and scanty fare I am perhaps indebted for the establishment of my constitution.] Had I been sent abroad in a more splendid style such as the fortune and bounty of my father might have supplied, I might have returned home with the same stock of language and science as our countrymen usually import from the continent. An exile and a prisoner as I was, their example betrayed me into some irregularities of wine, of play, and of idle excursions; but I soon felt the impossibility of associating with them on equal terms, and after the departure of my first acquaintance I held a cold and civil correspondence with their successors. This seclusion from English society was attended with the most solid benefits. In the *pays de Vaud* the French language is used with less imperfection than in most of the distant provinces of France: in Pavilliard's family necessity compelled me to listen and to speak; and if I was at first disheartened by the apparent slowness, in a few months I was astonished by the rapidity of my progress. My pronunciation was formed by the constant repetition of the same sounds; the variety of words and idioms, the rules of grammar and distinctions of genders, were impressed in my memory: ease and freedom were obtained by practise, correctness and elegance by labour; and before I was recalled home, French, in which I spontaneously thought, was more familiar than English to my ear, my tongue, and my pen. The first effect of this opening knowledge was the revival of my love of reading, which had been chilled at Oxford; and I soon turned over, without much choice, almost all the French books in my tutor's library. Even these amusements were productive of real advantage; my taste and judgement were now somewhat riper: I was introduced to a new mode of style and litterature: by the comparison of manners and opinions, my views were enlarged, my prejudices were corrected, and a copious voluntary abstract of the *Histoire de l'Eglise et de l'Empire*, by le Sueur, may be placed in a middle line between my childish and my manly studies. As soon as I was able to converse with the natives, I began to feel some satisfaction in their company; my awkward timidity was polished and emboldened, and I frequented for the first time assemblies of men and women. The acquaintance of the Pavilliards prepared me by degrees for more elegant society. I was received with kindness and indulgence in the best families of Lausanne; and it was in one of these that I formed an intimate, lasting connection with Mr. Deyverdun, a young man of an amiable temper and excellent understanding. In the arts of fencing and dancing small indeed was my proficiency, and some expensive months were idly wasted in the riding-school. My unfitness to bodily exercise reconciled me to a sedentary life, and the horse, the favourite of my countrymen, never contributed to the pleasures of my youth.

My obligations to the lessons of Mr. Pavilliard gratitude will not suffer me to forget: [but truth compells me to own, that my best præceptor was not himself eminent for genius or learning. Even the real measure of his talents was under-rated in the public opinion: the soft credulity of his temper exposed him to frequent imposition; and his want of eloquence and memory in the pulpit disqualified him for the most popular duty of his office. But] he was endowed with a clear head and a warm heart; his innate benevolence had asswaged the spirit of the Church; he was rational because he was moderate; in the course of his studies he had acquired a just though superficial knowledge of most branches of litterature; by long practise he was skilled in the arts of teaching; and he laboured with assiduous patience to know the character, gain the affection, and open the mind of his English pupil. As soon as we began to understand each other, he gently led me into the path of instruction: I consented with pleasure that a portion of the morning hours should be consecrated to a plan of modern history and Geography, and to the critical perusal of the French and Latin Classics, and at each step I felt myself invigorated by the habits of application and method.

The principles of philosophy were associated with the examples of taste; and by a singular chance, the book, as well as the man, which contributed the most effectually to my education, has a stronger claim on my gratitude than on my admiration. Mr. de Crousaz,* the adversary

---

* Jean Pierre de Crousaz, born at Lausanne, 1663; Professor of Philosophy and Mathematics at Groningen, 1724; Professor of Philosophy, Lausanne, 1737; where he died, 1748.

of Bayle and Pope, is not distinguished by lively fancy
or profound reflexion; and even in his own country, at
the end of a few years, his name and writings are almost
obliterated. But his philosophy had been formed in the
school of Locke, his Divinity in that of Limborch and
Le Clerc; in a long and laborious life, several generations
of pupils were taught to think, and even to write; his
lessons rescued the Academy of Lausanne from Calvinistic
prejudice, and he had the rare merit of diffusing a more
liberal spirit among the Clergy and people of the Pays
de Vaud. His System of Logic, which in the last editions
has swelled to six tedious and prolix volumes, may be
praised as a clear and methodical abridgement of the art
of reasoning, from our simple ideas to the most complex
operations of the human understanding. This system
I studied, and meditated, and abstracted, till I have
obtained the free command of an universal instrument,
which I soon presumed to exercise on my catholic
opinions. Pavilliard was not unmindful that his first
task, his most important duty, was to reclaim me from
the errors of Popery. The intermixture of sects has
rendered the Swiss Clergy acute and learned on the
topics of controversy; and I have some of his letters in
which he celebrates the dexterity of this attack, and my
gradual concessions after a firm and well-managed
defence.* I was willing, and I am now willing, to allow
him an handsome share of the honour of my conversion;

---

* M. Pavilliard has described to
me the astonishment with which
he gazed on Mr. Gibbon standing
before him: a thin little figure,
with a large head, disputing and
urging, with the greatest ability,
all the best arguments that had
ever been used in favour of popery.
Mr. Gibbon many years ago became
very fat and corpulent, but he had
uncommonly small bones, and was
very slightly made.—SHEFFIELD.

yet I must observe that it was principally effected by my private reflexions, and I still remember my solitary transport at the discovery of a philosophical argument against the doctrine of transubstantian (*sic*): *that* the text of scripture, which seems to inculcate the real presence, is attested only by a single sense—our sight; while the real presence itself is disproved by three of our senses— the sight, the touch, and the taste. The various articles of the Romish creed disappeared like a dream, and after a full conviction, on Christmas Day 1754, I received the sacrament in the Church of Lausanne. It was here that I suspended my Religious enquiries, acquiescing with implicit belief in the tenets and mysteries which are adopted by the general consent of Catholics and Protestants.

Such, from my arrival at Lausanne during the first eighteen or twenty months (July, 1753—March, 1755) were my useful studies, the foundation of all my future improvements. [But in the life of every man of letters, there is an æra, from a level, from whence he soars with his own wings to his proper height, and the most important part of his education is that which he bestows on himself.] My worthy tutor had the good sense and modesty to discern how far he could be useful: as soon as he felt that I advanced beyond his speed and measure, he wisely left me to my Genius; and the hours. of lesson were soon lost in the voluntary labour of the whole morning, and sometimes of the whole day. The desire of prolonging my time gradually confirmed the salutary habit of early rising, to which I have always adhered, with some regard to seasons and situations; but it is happy for my eyes and my health that my temperate

ardour has never been seduced to trespass on the hours
of the night. During the last three years of my residence
at Lausanne I may assume the merit of serious and solid
application, but I am tempted to distinguish the last
eight months of the year 1755 as the period of the most
extraordinary diligence and rapid progress. In my
French and Latin translations I adopted an excellent
method, which, from my own success, I would recommend
to the imitation of students. I chose some Classic writer,
such as Cicero and Vertot, the most approved for purity
and elegance of style. I translated, for instance, an
Epistle of Cicero into French, and, after throwing it aside
till the words and phrases were obliterated from my
memory, I re-translated my French into such Latin as
I could find, and then compared each sentence of my
imperfect version with the ease, the grace, the propriety
of the Roman Orator. A similar experiment was made
on some pages of the Revolutions of Vertot; I turned
them into Latin, re-turned them after a sufficient interval into my own French, and again scrutinized the
resemblance or dissimilitude of the copy and the original.
By degrees I was less ashamed, by degrees I was more
satisfied with myself; and I persevered in the practise of
these double translations, which filled several books, till
I had acquired the knowledge of both idioms, and the
command at least of a correct style. This useful exercise
of writing was accompanied and succeeded by the more
pleasing occupation of reading the best authors. Dr.
Middleton's history, which I then appreciated above its
true value, naturally directed me to the writings of Cicero.
The most perfect editions, that of Olivet, which may
adorn the shelves of the rich, that of Ernesti, which should

lie on the table of the learned, were not in my power.
For the familar Epistles I used the text and English
Commentary of Bishop Ross; but my general Edition was
that of Verbruggius, published at Amsterdam in two
large Volumes in folio, with an indifferent choice of
various notes. I read with application and pleasure *all*
the Epistles, *all* the Orations, and the most important
treatises of Rhetoric and Philosophy; and as I read, I
applauded the observation of Quintilian, that every student
may judge of his own proficiency by the satisfaction
which he receives from the Roman Orator. Cicero in
Latin and Xenophon in Greek, are, indeed, the two
ancients whom I would first propose to a liberal scholar,
not only for the merit of their style and sentiments, but
for the admirable lessons which may be applied almost
to every situation of public and private life. Cicero's
Epistles may in particular afford the models of every
form of correspondence, from the careless effusions of
tenderness and friendship, to the well-guarded declaration
of discreet and dignified resentment. After finishing
this great Author, a library of eloquence and reason, I
formed a more extensive plan of reviewing the Latin
Classics, under the four divisions of (1) Historians,
(2) Poets, (3) Orators, and (4) Philosophers, in a
Chronological series, from the days of Plautus and
Salust to the decline of the language and Empire of
Rome; and this plan, in the last twenty-seven months
of my residence at Lausanne (January, 1756—April,
1758), I *nearly* accomplished. Nor was this review,
however rapid, either hasty or superficial. I indulged
myself in a second and even a third perusal of Terence,
Virgil, Horace, Tacitus, etc., and studied to imbibe the

sense and spirit most congenial to my own. I never suffered a difficult or corrupt passage to escape, till I had viewed it in every light of which it was susceptible. Though often disappointed, I always consulted the most learned or ingenious commentators, Torrentius and Dacier on Horace, Catrou and Servius on Virgil, Lipsius on Tacitus, Meziriac on Ovid, etc.; and in the ardour of my enquiries I embraced a large circle of historical and critical erudition. My abstracts of each book were made in the French language; my observations often branched into particular Essays; and I can still read, without contempt, a dissertation of eight folio pages on eight lines (287–294) of the fourth Georgic of Virgil. Mr. Deyverdun, my friend, whose name will be frequently repeated, had joyned with equal zeal, though not with equal perseverance, in the same undertaking. To him every thought, every composition, was instantly communicated; with him I enjoyed the benefits of a free conversation on the topics of our common studies.

But it is scarcely possible for a mind endowed with any active curiosity to be long conversant with the Latin Classics without aspiring to know the Greek originals whom they celebrate as their masters, and of whom they so warmly recommend the study and imitation.

"Vos exemplaria Græca
Nocturnâ versate manu, versate diurnâ."

It was now that I regretted the early years which had been wasted in sickness, or idleness, or more idle reading; that I condemned the perverse method of our schoolmasters, who, by first teaching the mother-language, might descend with so much ease and perspicuity to the origin and etymology of a derivative idiom.

In the nineteenth year of my age I determined to supply this defect, and the lessons of Pavilliard again contributed to smooth the entrance of the way, the Greek Alphabet, the grammar, and the pronunciation according to the French accent. [As he had possessed only such a stock as was requisite for an Ecclesiastic, our first book was St. John's Gospel, and should probably have construed the whole of the new testament, had I not represented the absurdity of adhering to the corrupt dialect of the Hellenist Jews.] At my earnest request we presumed to open the Iliad, and I had the pleasure of beholding, though darkly and through a glass, the true image of Homer, whom I had long since admired in an English dress. After my tutor [conscious of his inability] had left me to myself, I worked my way through about half the Iliad, and afterwards interpreted alone a large portion of Xenophon and Herodotus. But my ardour, destitute of aid and emulation, was gradually cooled, and, from the barren task of searching words in a lexicon, I withdrew to the free and familiar conversation of Virgil and Tacitus. Yet in my residence at Lausanne I had laid a solid foundation, which enabled me in a more propitious season to prosecute the study of Grecian litterature.

From a blind idea of the usefullness of such abstract science, my father had been desirous, and even pressing, that I should devote some time to the Mathematics; nor could I refuse to comply with so reasonable a wish. During two winters I attended the private lectures of Mr. de Traytorrens, who explained the Elements of Algebra and Geometry as far as the Conic sections of the Marquis de l'Hopital, and appeared satisfied with my diligence and improvement. But as my childish

propensity for numbers and calculations was totally
extinct, I was content to receive the passive impression
of my professor's lectures, without any active exercise of
my own powers: as soon as I understood the principles,
I relinquished for ever the pursuit of the Mathematics;
nor can I lament that I desisted before my mind was
hardened by the habit of rigid demonstration, so destructive of the finer feelings of moral evidence, which must,
however, determine the actions and opinions of our lives.
I listened with more pleasure to the proposal of studying
the law of Nature and Nations, which was taught in the
academy of Lausanne by Mr. Vicat, a professor of some
learning and reputation. But, instead of attending his
public or private course, I preferred in my closet the
lessons of his masters and my own reason. Without being
disgusted by [the pedantry of] Grotius, or [the prolixity
of] Puffendorf, I studied in their writings the duties of a
man, the rights of a Citizen, the theory of Justice (it is
alas! a theory), and the laws of peace and war, which have
had some influence on the practise of modern Europe.
My fatigues were alleviated by the good sense of their
commentator Barbeyrac: Locke's treatise of Government
instructed me in the knowledge of Whig principles, which
are rather founded in reason than in experience; but my
delight was in the frequent perusal of Montesquiou, whose
energy of style and boldness of hypothesis were powerful
to awaken and stimulate the Genius of the Age. The logic
of de Crousaz had prepared me to engage with his master
Locke and his antagonist Bayle, of whom the former may
be used as a bridle, and the latter as a bridle * to the
curiosity of a young philosopher. According to the

---

* "Spur" in Memoir C, p. 234.

nature of their respective works, the schools of argument and objection, I carefully went through the Essay on human understanding, and occasionally consulted the most interesting articles of the Philosophic dictionary. In the infancy of my reason I turned over, as an idle amusement, the most serious and important treatise: in its maturity the most trifling performance could exercise my taste or judgement; and more than once I have been led by a novel into a deep and instructive train of thinking. But I cannot forbear to mention three particular books, since they may have remotely contributed to form the historian of the Roman Empire. 1. From the provincial letters of Pascal, which almost every year I have perused with new pleasure, I learned to manage the weapon of grave and temperate irony, even on subjects of Ecclesiastical solemnity. 2. The life of Julian, by the Abbé de la Bleterie, first introduced me to the man and the times; and I should be glad to recover my first essay on the truth of the miracle which stopped the rebuilding of the temple of Jerusalem. 3. In Giannone's Civil history of Naples I observed with a critical eye the progress and abuse of Sacerdotal power, and the Re-volutions of Italy in the darker ages. This various reading, which I now conducted with [skill and] discretion, was digested, according to the precept and model of Mr. Locke, into a large Commonplace-book; a practise, however, which I do not strenuously recommend. The action of the pen will doubtless imprint an idea on the mind as well as on the paper; but I much question whether the benefits of this laborious method are adequate to the waste of time, and I must agree with Dr. Johnson *

---

* *Idler*, No. 74.

"that what is twice read is commonly better remembered than what is transcribed."

During two years, if I forget some boyish excursions of a day or a week, I was fixed at Lausanne; but at the end of the third summer my father consented that I should make the tour of Switzerland with Pavilliard, and our short absence of one month (September 21^{rst}— October 20th, 1755) was a reward and relaxation of my assiduous studies. The fashion of climbing the mountains and viewing the *Glaciers* had not yet been introduced by foreign travellers, who seek the sublime beauties of Nature. But the political face of the Country is not less diversified by the forms and spirit of so many various Republics, from the jealous government of the *few* to the licentious freedom of the *many*. I contemplated with pleasure the new prospects of men and manners; though my conversation with the natives would have been more free and instructive, had I possessed the German as well as the French language. We passed through most of the principal towns of Switzerland—Neufchâtel, Bienne, Soleurre, Arau, Baden, Zurich, Basil, and Bern : in every place we visited the Churches, arsenals, libraries, and all the most eminent persons; and after my return I digested my notes in fourteen or fifteen sheets of a French journal, which I dispatched to my father as a proof that my time and his money had not been mispent. Had I found this journal among his papers, I might be tempted to select some passages; but I will not transcribe the printed accounts, and it may be sufficient to notice a remarkable spot, which left a deep and lasting impression on my memory. From Zurich we proceeded [on a pilgrimage not of devotion, but of curiosity] to the Benedictine

Abbey of Einsidlen, more commonly styled our Lady of the Hermits. I was astonished by the profuse ostentation of riches in the poorest corner of Europe : amidst a savage scene of woods and mountains, a palace appears to have been erected by Magic; and it *was* erected by the potent magic of Religion. A crowd of palmers and votaries was prostrate before the Altar : the title and worship of the Mother of God provoked my indignation; and the lively naked image of superstition suggested to me, as in the same place it had done to Zuinglius, the most pressing argument for the reformation of the Church. About two years after this tour, I passed at Geneva an useful and agreable month; but this excursion, and some short visits in the Pays de Vaud, did not materially interrupt my studious and sedentary life at Lausanne.

My thirst of improvement, and the languid state of science at Lausanne, soon prompted me to solicit a litterary correspondence with several men of learning, whom I had not an opportunity of personally consulting.

1. In the perusal of Livy (xxx. 44) I had been stopped by a sentence in a speech of Hannibal,* which cannot be reconciled by any torture with his character or argument. The commentators dissemble or confess their perplexity : it occurred to me that the change of a single letter by substituting *Otio* instead of *Odio* might restore a clear and consistent sense ; but I wished to weigh my emendation in scales less partial than my own. I addressed myself to Mr. Crevier,† the successor of Rollin,

---

* "Tunc flesso decuit, quum adempta nobis arma, incensæ naves, interdictum externis bellis, illo enim vulnere concidimus. Nec esse in vos *odio* vestro consultum ab Romanis credatis."

† Jean Baptiste Louis Crevier (1693-1765), Professor of Rhetoric at the College of Beauvais.

and a Professor in the University of Paris, who had published a large and valuable Edition of Livy : his answer was speedy and polite ; he praised my ingenuity, and adopted my conjecture, [which I must still applaud as easy and happy.] 2. I maintained a Latin correspondence, at first anonymous, and afterwards in my own name, with Professor Breitinger,* of Zurich, the learned Editor of a Septuagint Bible : in our frequent letters we discussed many questions of antiquity, many passages of the Latin Classics. I proposed my interpretations and amendments : his censures, for he did not spare my boldness of conjecture, were sharp and strong ; and I was encouraged by the consciousness of my strength, when I could stand in free debate against a critic of such eminence and erudition. 3. I corresponded on similar topics with the celebrated Professor Matthew Gesner,† of the University of Gottingen, and he accepted as courteously as the two former the invitation of an unknown Youth. But his abilities might possibly be decayed ; his elaborate letters were feeble and prolix ; and when I asked his proper direction, the vain old man covered half a sheet of paper with the foolish enumeration of his titles and offices. 4. These professors of Paris, Zurich, and Gottingen were strangers whom I presumed to address on the credit of their name ; but Mr. Allamand,‡ Minister at Bex, was

---

* Johann Jacob Breitinger, born at Zurich, 1701 ; Professor of Hebrew and Greek ; died 1776.

† Johann Matthias Gesner (1691–1761), Professor of Eloquence and Poetry, Göttingen.

‡ This writer is scarcely known except by this mention of him; he was Protestant minister at Bex, and published anonymously, in 1745, *Une Lettre sur les assemblées des religionnaires en Languedoc, ecrite à un gentilhomme protestant de cette province,* par M. D. L., F. D. M. (Rotterdam on title-page).

my personal friend, with whom I maintained a more free and interesting correspondence. He was a master of language, of science, and, above all, of dispute; and his acute and flexible logic could support with equal address, and perhaps with equal indifference, the adverse sides of every possible question. His spirit was active, but his pen had been indolent. Mr. Allamand had exposed himself to much scandal and reproach by an anonymous letter (1745) to the Protestants of France, in which he labours to persuade them that *public* worship is the exclusive right and duty of the State, and that their numerous assemblies of dissenters and rebels are not authorized by the law or the Gospel. His style is animated, his arguments are specious; and if the papist may seem to lurk under the mask of a protestant, the philosopher is concealed under the disguise of a papist. After some tryals in France and Holland, which were defeated by his fortune or his character, a Genius that might have enlightened or deluded the World was buried in a Country living, unknown to fame and discontented with mankind. "Est sacrificulus in pago et rusticos decipit." As often as private or Ecclesiastical business called him to Lausanne, I enjoyed the pleasure and benefit of his conversation, and we were mutually flattered by our attention to each other. Our correspondence in his absence chiefly turned on Locke's Metaphysics, which he attacked and I defended; the origin of ideas, the principles of evidence, and the doctrine of liberty.

"And found no end, in wandering mazes lost."

By fencing with so skilfull a master, I acquired some dexterity in the use of my philosophic weapons; but I was still the slave of education and prejudice; he had some measures to keep; and I much suspect that he never shewed me the true colours of his secret scepticism.

Before I was recalled from Switzerland I had the satisfaction of seeing the most extraordinary man of the age—a poet, an historian, a Philosopher, who has filled thirty quartos, of prose and verse, with his various productions, often excellent and always entertaining : need I add the name of Voltaire ? After forfeiting, by his own misconduct, the friendship of the first of Kings, he retired, at the age of sixty, with a plentiful fortune, to a free and beautiful country, and resided two winters (1757 and 1758) in the town or neighbourhood of Lausanne. My desire of beholding Voltaire, whom I then rated above his real magnitude, was easily gratified : he received me with civility as an English youth ; but I cannot boast of any peculiar notice or distinction—"Virgilium vidi tantum." The Ode which [he] composed on his first arrival on the banks of the Leman Lake—

"O Maison d'Aristippe !   O Jardin d'Epicure ! " etc.

had been imparted as a secret to the Gentleman by whom I was introduced : he allowed me to read it twice ; I knew it by heart ; and, as my discretion was not equal to my memory, the author was soon displeased by the circulation of a copy. In writing this trivial anecdote, I wished to observe whether my memory was impaired, and I have the comfort of finding that every line of the poem is still engraved in fresh and indelible characters. The highest gratification which I derived from Voltaire's residence at Lausanne was the uncommon circumstance of hearing a great poet declaim his own productions on the stage. He had formed a troop of Gentlemen and Ladies, some of whom were not destitute of talents : a decent theatre was framed at Monrepos, a country house at the end of a suburb; dresses and scenes were provided at the expence of the actors, and the author directed the rehearsals with the zeal and attention of paternal love. In two successive winters his tragedies of Zayre, Alzire, Zulime, and his sentimental comedy of the Enfant prodigue were played at the Theatre of Monrepos, [but it was not without much reluctance and ill-humour that the envious bard allowed the representation of the Iphigenie of Racine. The parts of the young and fair were distorted by his fat and ugly niece, Madame Denys, who could not, like our admirable Pritchard, make the spectators forget the defects of her age and person.] For himself Voltaire reserved the characters best adapted to his years—Lusignan, Alvarez, Benassar, Euphemon; his declamation was fashioned to the pomp and cadence of the old stage, and he expressed the enthusiasm of poetry rather than the feelings of Nature. My ardour, which soon became conspicuous, seldom failed of procuring me a ticket; the habits of pleasure fortified my taste for the French theatre, and that taste has perhaps abated my idolatry for the Gigantic Genius of Shakespeare, which is inculcated from our infancy as the first duty of an Englishman. The wit and philosophy of Voltaire, his table and theatre, refined in a visible degree the manners of Lausanne; and, however addicted to study, I enjoyed my share of the amusements of Society. After the representations of Montrepos I sometimes supped with the Actors: I was now familiar in some, and acquainted in many, houses; and my evenings were generally devoted to cards and conversation, either in private parties or numerous assemblies.

I hesitate, from the apprehension of ridicule, when I approach the delicate subject of my early love. By this word I do not mean the polite attention of the gallantry, without hope or design, which has originated from the spirit of chivalry, and is interwoven with the texture of French manners. [I do not confine myself to the grosser appetite which our pride may affect to disdain, because it has been implanted by Nature in the whole animal creation, "Amor omnibus idem." The discovery of a sixth sense, the first consciousness of manhood, is a very interesting moment of our lives; but it less properly belongs to the memoirs of an individual, than to the natural history of the species.] I understand by this passion the union of desire, friendship, and tenderness, which is inflamed by a single female, which prefers her to the rest of her sex, and which seeks her possession as the supreme or the sole happiness of our being. I need not blush at recollecting the object of my choice; and though my love was disappointed of success, I am rather proud that I was once capable of feeling such a pure and exalted sentiment. The personal attractions of Mademoiselle Susanne Curchod were embellished by the virtues and talents of the mind. Her fortune was humble, but her family was respectable : her mother, a native of France, had preferred her religion to her country; the profession of her father did not extinguish the moderation and philosophy of his temper, and he lived content with a small salary and laborious duty in the obscure lot of Minister of Crassy, in the mountains that separate the pays de Vaud from the County of Burgundy. In the solitude of a sequestered village he bestowed a liberal, and even learned, education on his only daughter; she

surpassed his hopes by her proficiency in the sciences
and languages; and in her short visits to some relations
at Lausanne, the wit and beauty and erudition of Mademoiselle Curchod were the theme of universal applause.
The report of such a prodigy awakened by (*sic*) curiosity;
I saw and loved. I found her learned without pedantry,
lively in conversation, pure in sentiment, and elegant
in manners; and the first sudden emotion was fortified
by the habits and knowledge of a more familiar acquaintance. She permitted me to make her two or three visits
at her father's house: I passed some happy days in the
mountains of Burgundy; and her parents honourably
encouraged a connection [which might raise their daughter
above want and dependence]. In a calm retirement the
gay vanity of youth no longer fluttered in her bosom;
she listened to the voice of truth and passion, and I
might presume to hope that I had made some impression
on a virtuous heart. At Crassy and Lausanne I indulged
my dream of felicity; but, on my return to England, I
soon discovered that my father would not hear of this
strange alliance, and that, without his consent, I was
myself destitute and helpless. After a painful struggle
I yielded to my fate; the remedies of absence and time
were at length effectual, and my love subsided in friendship and esteem. The minister of Crassy soon afterwards
died; his stipend died with him: his daughter retired
to Geneva, where, by teaching young ladies, she earned
a hard subsistence for herself and her mother; but in
her lowest distress she maintained a spotless reputation
and a dignified behaviour. [The Dutchess of Grafton
(now Lady Ossory) has often told me that she had nearly
engaged Mademoiselle Curchod as a Governess, and her

declining a life of servitude was most probably blamed by the wisdom of her short-sighted friends.] A rich banker of Paris, a citizen of Geneva, had the good-fortune and good sense to discover and possess this inestimable treasure; and in the capital of taste and luxury she resisted the temptations of wealth, as she had sustained the hardships of indigence. The Genius of her husband has exalted him to the most conspicuous station in Europe: in every change of prosperity and disgrace he has re-clined on the bosom of a faithful friend; and Mademoiselle Curchod is now the wife of Mr. Necker the Minister, and perhaps the legislator, of the French Monarchy.

[Such as I am, in Genius or learning or manners, I owe my creation to Lausanne: it was in that school, that the statue was discovered in the block of marble; and my own religious folly, my father's blind resolution, produced the effects of the most deliberate wisdom.] One mis-chief, however, and in the eyes of my countrymen a serious and irreperable mischief, was derived from the success of my Swiss education: I had ceased to be an Englishman. At the flexible period of youth, from the age of sixteen to twenty-one, my opinions, habits, and sentiments were cast in a foreign mould: the faint and distant remembrance of England was almost obliterated; my native language was grown less familiar; and I should have chearfully accepted the offer of a moderate independent fortune on the terms of perpetual exile. By the good sense and temper of Pavilliard my yoke was insensibly lightened; he left me master of my time and actions; but he could neither change my situation nor encrease my allowance, and with the pro-gress of my years and reason I impatiently sighed for the moment of my deliverance. At length, in the spring of the year one thousand seven hundred and fifty-eight, my father signified his permission and his pleasure that I should immediately return home. We were then in the midst of a war; the resentment of the French at our taking their ships without a declaration had rendered that polite nation somewhat peevish and difficult: they denied a passage to English travellers; and the road through Germany was circuitous, toilsome, and perhaps, in the neighbourhood of the armies, exposed to some danger. In this perplexity, two Swiss officers of my acquaintance in the Dutch service, who were returning to their garrisons, offered to conduct me through France as one of their companions; nor did we sufficiently reflect that my borrowed name and regimentals might have been considered, in case of a discovery, in a very serious light. I took my leave of Lausanne on the 11th of April, 1758, with a mixture of joy and regret, in the firm resolution of revisiting, as a man, the persons and places which had been so dear to my youth. We travelled slowly, but pleasantly, in a hired coach, over the hills of Franche-comté and the fertile province of Lorraine, and passed, without accident or enquiry, through several fortified towns of the French frontier: from thence we entered the wild Ardennes of the Austrian dutchy of Luxemburgh; and, after crossing the Meuse at Liege, we traversed the heaths of Brabant, and reached, on the fifteenth day, our Dutch garrison, Bois le Duc. In our passage through Nancy my eye was gratified by the aspect of a regular and beautiful City, the work of Stanislaus, who, after the storms of Polish royalty, reposed in the love and

gratitude of his new subjects of Lorraine. In our halt
at Maestricht I visited Mr. de Beaufort, a learned Critic,
who was known to me by his specious arguments against
the five first Centuries of the Roman history. After dropping my regimental companions, I stepped aside to visit
Rotterdam and the Hague. I wished to have observed
a country, the monument of freedom and industry; but
my days were numbered, and a longer delay would have
been ungraceful : I hastened to embark at the Brill, landed
the next day at Harwich, and proceeded to London,
where my father awaited my arrival. The whole term of
my first absence from England was four years, ten months,
and fifteen days.

In the prayers of the Church our personal concerns
are judiciously reduced to the threefold distinction of
mind, body, and *estate.* The sentiments of the mind
excite and exercise our social sympathy : the review of
my moral and litterary character is the most interesting
to myself and to the public ; and I may expatiate without
reproach on my private studies, since they have produced
the public writings which can alone entitle me to the
esteem and friendship of my readers. [The pains and
pleasures of the body, how important soever to ourselves,
are an indelicate topic of conversation. I shall not follow
the vain example of Cardinal Quirini, who has filled half
a volume of his memoirs with medical consultations on
his own particular case. I shall not imitate the naked
frankness of Montaigne who exposes the most disgusting
symptoms of his malady, and marks the operation of each
remedy on his nerves and bowels.] The experience of the
World inculcates a discreet reserve on the subject of our
estate ; and we soon learn that a free disclosure of our riches

or poverty, would provoke the malice of envy, or encourage the insolence of contempt. [Yet I am tempted to glance in a few words on the state of my private circumstances, as I am persuaded that had I been more indigent or more wealthy, I should not have possessed the leisure or the perseverance to prepare and execute my voluminous history. My father's impatience for my return to England was not wholly of the desinterested kind. I have already hinted that he had been impoverished by his two sisters, and that his gay character and mode of life were less adapted to the acquisition than the expenditure of wealth. A large and legitimate debt for the supply of naval stores was lost by the injustice of the Court of Spain : his elegant hospitality at Putney exceeded the measure of his income; the honour of being chosen a Member of the Old club at White's had been dearly paid, and a more pernicious species of gaming, the contest for Southampton, exhausted his sickly finances. His retirement into Hampshire on my mother's death was coloured by a pious motive; some years of solitude allowed him to breathe; but it was only by his son's majority that he could be restored to the command of an entailed estate. The time of my recall had been so nicely computed that I arrived in London three days before I was of age : the priests and the altar had been prepared, and the victim was unconscious of the impending stroke. According to the forms and fictions of our law, I levied a fine and suffered a recovery : the entail was cut off; a sum of ten thousand pounds was raised on mort[g]age for my father's use, and he repaid the obligation by settling on me an annuity for life of three hundred pounds a year. My submission at the time was blind and almost involuntary; but it has been justified by duty and interest to my cooler thoughts, and I could only regret that the receipt of some appropriated fund was not given into my own hands. My annuity, though somewhat more valuable thirty years ago, was, however, inadequate to the style of a young Englishman of fashion in the most wealthy Metropolis of Europe; but I was rich in my indifference, or, more properly, my aversion for the active and costly pleasures of my age and country. Some arrears, especially my bookseller's bill, were occasionally discharged; and the extraordinaries of my travels into France and Italy amounted, by prævious agreement, to the sum of twelve hundred pounds. But the ordinary scale of my expence was proportioned to my ordinary revenue; my desires were regulated by temper as much as by philosophy; and as soon as my purse was empty I had the courage to retire into Hampshire, where I found in my father's house a liberal maintenance, and in my own studies an inexhaustible source of amusement. With a credit which might have been largely abused I may assume the singular merit, that I never lost or borrowed twenty pounds in the twelve years which elapsed between my return from Switzerland and my father's death.]

The only person in England whom I was impatient to see was my aunt Porten, the affectionate guardian of my tender years. I hastened to her house in College Street, Westminster, and the evening was spent in the effusions of joy and confidence. It was not without some awe and apprehension that I approached the presence of my father. My infancy, to speak the truth, had been neglected at home; the severity of his look and language

at our last parting still dwelt on my memory; nor could
I form any notion of *his* character, or *my* probable reception.   They were both more agreable than I could
expect.   The domestic discipline of our ancestors has
been relaxed by the philosophy and softness of the age ;
and if my father remembered that he had trembled before
a stern parent, it was only to adopt with his own son an
opposite mode of behaviour.   He received me as a man
and a friend; all constraint was banished at our first
interview, and we ever afterwards continued on the same
terms of easy and equal politeness: he applauded the
success of my education ; every word and action was
expressive of the most cordial affection ; and our lives
would have passed without a cloud, if his œconomy had
been equal to his fortune, or if his fortune had been
equal to his desires.   During my absence he had married
his second wife, Miss Dorothea Patton, who was introduced to me with the most unfavourable prejudice : I
considered his second marriage as an act of displeasure,
[and the rival who had usurped my mother's bed appeared in the light of a personal and domestic enemy.
I will not say that I was apprehensive of the bowl or
dagger, or that I had then weighed the sentence of
Euripides—

> Εχθρα γαρ επιουσα μητρυια τεκνοις
> Τοις προσθ' εχιδνης ουδεν ηπιοτερα.*

But I well knew that the *odium novercale* was proverbial
in the language of antiquity; the Latin poets always
couple with the name of stepmother the hateful epithets

---

* ['Εχθρὰ γὰρ ἡ 'πιουσα μητρυιὰ τέκνοις
Τοῖς προσθ', εχιδνης οὐδέν ἠπιοτέρα.]
Eurip. *Alc.* 310.

of *crudelis*, sœva, scelerata ; and on the road I had often
repeated the line of Virgil—

"Est mihi namque domi pater, est injusta noverca."]

But the injustice was in my own fancy, and the
imaginary monster was an amiable and deserving woman.
I could not be mistaken in the first view of her understanding, her knowledge, and the elegant spirit of her
conversation : her polite welcome, and her assiduous care
to study and gratify my wishes, announced at least that
the surface would be smooth ; and my suspicions of art
and falsehood were gradually dispelled by the full
discovery of her warm and exquisite sensibility. After
some reserve on my side, our minds associated in confidence and friendship ; and as Mrs. Gibbon had neither
children nor the hopes of children, we more easily adopted
the tender names and genuine characters of mother and
of son. By the indulgence of these parents, I was left at
liberty to consult my taste or reason in the choice of
place, of company, and of amusements, and my excursions
were only bounded by the limits of the island and the
measure of my income. Some faint efforts were made
to procure me an employment of Secretary to a foreign
Embassy ; and I listened to a scheme which would again
have transported me to the Continent. Mrs. Gibbon,
with seeming wisdom, exhorted me to take chambers in
the Temple, and devote my leisure to the study of the
Law. I cannot repent of having neglected her advice ;
few men, without the spur of necessity, have resolution to
force their way through the thorns and thickets of that
gloomy labyrinth. Nature had not endowed me with the
bold and ready eloquence which makes itself heard amidst
the tumult of the bar—

[Vincentem strepitus, et natum rebus agendis.]

and I should probably have been diverted from the labours of litterature, without acquiring the fame or fortune of a successful pleader. I had no need to call to my aid the regular duties of a profession; every day, every hour, was agreeably filled; nor have I known, like so many of my countrymen, the tediousness of an idle life.

Of the two years (May 1758—May 1760) between my return to England and the embodying the Hampshire militia, I passed about nine months in London and the remainder in the country. The metropolis affords many amusements which are open to all; it is itself an astonishing and perpetual spectacle to the curious eye; and each taste, each sense, may be gratified by the variety of objects that will occur in the long circuit of a morning walk. I assiduously frequented the Theatres at a very prosperous æra of the stage, when a constellation of excellent actors, both in tragedy and comedy, was eclipsed by the meridian brightness of Garrick, in the maturity of his judgement and vigour of his performance. The pleasures of a town life, [the daily round from the tavern to the play, from the play to the coffee-house, from the coffee-house to the ——] are within the reach of every man who is regardless of his health, his money, and his company. By the contagion of example I was sometimes seduced; but the better habits which I had formed at Lausanne induced me to seek a more elegant and rational society; and if my search was less easy and successful than I might have hoped, I shall at present impute the failure to the disadvantages of my situation and character. Had the rank and fortune of my parents given them an annual establishment in London, their own house would have introduced me to a numerous and polite circle of acquaintance. But my father's taste had always preferred the highest and the lowest company, for which he was equally qualified; and after a twelve years' retirement he was no longer in the memory of the great with whom he had associated. I found myself a stranger in the midst of a vast and unknown city, and at my entrance into life I was reduced to some dull family parties, and some scattered connections which were not such as I should have chosen for myself. The most useful friends of my father were the Mallets: they received me with civility and kindness, at first on his account, and afterwards on my own; and (if I may use Lord Chesterfield's word) I was soon *domesticated* in their house. Mr. Mallet, a name among the English poets, is praised by an unforgiving enemy for the ease and elegance of his conversation, and [whatsoever might be the defects of] his wife, [she] was not destitute of wit or learning. By his assistance I was introduced to Lady Hervey,* the mother of the present Earl of Bristol: her age and infirmities confined her at home; her dinners were select; in the evening her house was open to the best company of both sexes and all nations; nor was I displeased at her preference and even affectation of the manners, the language, and the litterature of France. But my progress in the English World was in general left to my own efforts, and those efforts were languid and slow. I had not been endowed by art or Nature with those happy gifts of confidence

---

* Mary Lepell, wife of John, Lord Hervey.

and address which ¡unlock every door and every bosom;
nor would it be reasonable to complain of the just
consequences of my sickly childhood, foreign education,
and reserved temper. While coaches were rattling
through Bond Street, I have passed many a solitary
evening in my lodging with my books: my studies
were sometimes interrupted by a sigh which I breathed
towards Lausanne; and on the approach of spring I
withdrew without reluctance from the noisy and expensive
scene of crowds without company, and dissipation without
pleasure. In each of the twenty-five years of my
acquaintance with London (1758–1783) the prospect
gradually brightened; and this unfavourable picture
most properly belongs to the first period after my return
from Switzerland.

My father's residence in Hampshire, where I have
passed many light, and some heavy hours, was at Buriton,
near Petersfield, one mile from the Portsmouth road, and
at the easy distance of fifty-eight miles from London.
An old mansion, in a state of decay, had been converted
into the fashion and convenience of a modern house; and
if strangers had nothing to see, the inhabitants had little
to desire. The spot was not happily chosen, at the end
of the village and the bottom of the hill; but the aspect
of the adjacent grounds was various and chearful: the
downs commanded a noble prospect, and the long hanging woods in sight of the house could not perhaps
have been improved by art or expence. My father
kept in his own hands the whole of his estate, and
even rented some additional land; and whatsoever
might be the balance of profit and loss, the farms supplied him with amusement and plenty. The produce

maintained a number of men and horses, which were multiplied by the intermixture of domestic and rural servants; and in the intervals of labour, the favourite team, an handsome set of bays or greys, was harnessed to the coach. The œconomy of the house was regulated by the taste and prudence of Mrs. Gibbon; she prided herself in the elegance of her occasional dinners; and from the uncleanly avarice of Madame Pavilliard, I was suddenly transported to the daily neatness and luxury of an English table. Our immediate neighbourhood was rare and rustic; but from the verge of our hills, as far as Chichester and Goodwood, the western district of Sussex was interspersed with noble seats and hospitable families, with whom we cultivated a friendly, and might have enjoyed a very frequent, intercourse. As my stay at Buriton was always voluntary, I was received and dismissed with smiles; but the comforts of my retire- ment did not depend on the ordinary pleasures of the Country. My father could never inspire me with his love and knowledge of farming. [When he galloped away on a fleet hunter to follow the Duke of Richmond's foxhounds, I saw him depart without a wish to join in the sport; and in the command of an ample manour, I valued the supply of the kitchen much more than the exercise of the field.] I never handled a gun, I seldom mounted an horse; and my philosophic walks were soon terminated by a shady bench, where I was long detained by the sedentary amusement of reading or meditation. At home I occupied a pleasant and spacious apartment; the library on the same floor was soon considered as my peculiar domain, and I might say with truth that I was never less alone than when

by myself. My sole complaint, which I piously suppressed, arose from the kind restraint imposed on the
freedom of my time. By the habit of early rising I
always secured a sacred portion of the day, and many
scattered moments were stolen and employed by my
studious industry. But the family hours of breakfast, of
dinner, of tea, and of supper were regular and long: after
breakfast Mrs. Gibbon expected my company in her
dressing-room; after tea my father claimed my conversation and the perusal of the newspapers; and in the
midst of an interesting work I was often called down
to receive the visit of some idle neighbours. Their
dinners and visits required, in due season, a similar return;
and I dreaded the period of the full moon, which was
usually reserved for our more distant excursions. I
could not refuse attending my father, in the summer
of 1759, to the races at Stockbridge, Reading, and
Odiham, where he had entered a horse for the hunter's
plate; and I was not displeased with the sight of our
Olympic games, the beauty of the spot, the fleetness
of the horses, and the gay tumult of the numerous
spectators. As soon as the Militia business was agitated,
many days were tediously consumed in meetings of
Deputy-Lieutenants at Petersfield, Alton, and Winchester. In the close of the same year, 1759, Sir
Simeon (then Mr.) Stewart attempted an unsuccessful
contest for the county of Southampton, against Mr.
Legge, Chancellor of the Exchequer: a well-known
contest, in which Lord Bute's influence was first exerted
and censured. Our canvass at Portsmouth and Gosport
lasted several days; but the interruption of my studies
was compensated in some degree by the spectacle of

English manners, and the acquisition of some practical knowledge.

If in a more domestic or more dissipated scene my application was somewhat relaxed, the love of knowledge was inflamed and gratified by the command of books, and I compared the poverty of Lausanne with the plenty of London. My father's study at Buriton was stuffed with much trash of the last age, with much High-church Divinity and politics, which have long since gone to their proper place: yet it contained some valuable Editions of the Classics and the fathers, the choice, as it should seem, of Mr. Law; and many English publications of the times had been occasionally added. From this slender beginning I have gradually formed a numerous and Select library, the foundation of my works, and the best comfort of my life both at home and abroad. On the receipt of the first quarter, a large share of my allowance was appropriated to my literary wants. I cannot forget the joy with which I exchanged a banknote of twenty pounds for the twenty volumes of the Memoirs of the Academy of Inscriptions; nor would it have been easy, by any other expenditure of the same sum, to have procured so large and lasting a fund of rational amusement. At a time when I most assiduously frequented this school of ancient litterature, I thus expressed my opinion of a learned and various Collection, which since the year 1759 has been doubled in magnitude though not equally in merit: "Une de ces sociétés, qui ont mieux immortalisé Louis XIV. qu'une ambition souvent pernicieuse aux hommes, commençoit déjà ces recherches qui réunissent la justesse de l'esprit, l'aménité, et l'érudition: où l'on voit tant de découvertes, et quelquefois, ce qui ne cède qu'à peine aux decouvertes, une *ignorance* modeste et *savante*." The review of my library must be reserved for the period of its maturity; but in this place I may allow myself to observe that I am not conscious of having ever bought a book from a motive of ostentation; that every volume, before it was deposited on the shelf, was either read or sufficiently examined, and that I soon adopted the tolerating maxim of the elder Pliny, "Nullum esse librum tam malum ut non ex aliquâ parte prodesset." I could not yet find leisure or courage to renew the pursuit of the Greek language except by reading the lessons of the old and new testament every Sunday, when I attended the family to Church. The series of my Latin authors was less strenuously completed; but the acquisition, by inheritance or purchase, of the best editions of Cicero, Quintilian, Livy, Tacitus, Ovid, etc., afforded a fair opportunity, which I seldom neglected. I persevered in the useful methods of abstracts and observation, and a single example may suffice of a note which had almost swelled into a work. The solution of a passage of Livy (xxxviii. 38) involved me in the dry and dark treatises of Greaves, Arbuthnot, Hooper, Bernard, Eissenschmidt, Gronovius, La Barre, Freret, etc.; and in my French Essay (c. xx.) I ridiculously send the reader to my own *manuscript* remarks on the weights, coins, and measures of the ancients, which were abruptly terminated by the Militia drum.

As I am now entering on a more ample field of society and study, I can only hope to avoid a vain and prolix garrulity by overlooking the vulgar crowd of my acquaintance, and confining myself to such intimate

friends, among books and men, as are best entitled to
my notice by their own merit and reputation, or by the
deep impression which they have left on my mind.
Yet I will embrace this occasion of recommending to
the young student a practise which about this time I
adopted myself. After glancing my eye over the
design and order of a new book, I suspended the
perusal till I had finished the task of self-examination;
till I had revolved, in a solitary walk, all that I knew,
or believed, or had thought on the subject of the whole
work, or of some particular chapter. I was then qualified
to discern how much the author added to my original
stock and I was sometimes satisfied by the agreement,
I was sometimes armed by the opposition of our ideas.
The favourite companions of my leisure were our English
writers since the Revolution; they breathe the spirit of
reason and liberty, and they most seasonably contributed
to restore the purity of my own language, which had been
corrupted by the long use of a foreign Idiom. By the
judicious advice of Mr. Mallet, I was directed to the
writings of Swift and Addison : wit and simplicity are
their common attributes; but the style of Swift is supported by manly original vigour; that of Addison is
adorned by the female graces of elegance and mildness;
and the contrast of too coarse or too thin a texture is
visible even in the defects of these celebrated authors.
The old reproach, that no British altars had been raised
to the muse of history, was recently disproved by the
first performances of Robertson and Hume, the histories
of Scotland and of the Stuarts. I will assume the presumption to say that I was not unworthy to read them;
nor will I disguise my different feelings in the repeated

perusals. The perfect composition, the nervous language, the well-turned periods of Dr. Robertson, inflamed me to the ambitious hope that I might one day tread in his footsteps: the calm philosophy, the careless inimitable beauties of his friend and rival, often forced me to close the volume with a mixed sensation of delight and despair.

The design of my first work, the Essay on the study of litterature, was suggested by a refinement of vanity, the desire of justifying and praising the object of a favourite pursuit. In France, to which my ideas were confined, the learning and language of Greece and Rome were neglected by a philosophic age. The guardian of those studies, the Academy of Inscriptions, was degraded to the lowest rank among the three Royal societies of Paris: the new appellation of *Erudits* was contemptuously applied to the successors of Lipsius and Casaubon; and I was provoked to hear (see Mr. d'Alembert's Discours preliminaire à l'Encyclopedie) that the exercise of the memory, their sole merit, had been superseded by the nobler faculties of the imagination and the judgement. I was ambitious of proving, by my own example as well as by my precepts, that all the faculties of the mind may be exercised and displayed by [the] study of ancient litterature; I began to select and adorn the various proofs and illustrations which had offered themselves in reading the classics, and the first pages or chapters of my Essay were composed before my departure from Lausanne. The hurry of the journey, and of the first weeks of my English life, suspended all thoughts of serious application; but my object was ever before my eyes, and no more than ten days, from the first to the eleventh of July, were suffered to elapse after my summer establishment at Buriton. My Essay was finished in about six weeks, and as soon as a fair copy had been transcribed by one of the French prisoners at Petersfield, I looked round for a critic and a judge of my first performance. A writer can seldom be content with the doubtful recompense of solitary approbation, but a youth ignorant of the World and of himself must desire to weigh his talents in some scales less partial than his own : my conduct was natural, my motive laudable, my choice of Dr. Maty * judicious and fortunate. By descent and education, Dr. Maty, though born in Holland, might be considered as a Frenchman ; but he was fixed in London by the practise of physic, and an office in the British Musæum. His reputation was justly founded on the eighteen Volumes of the *Journal Britannique*, which he had supported, almost alone, with perseverance and success. This humble though useful labour, which had once been dignified by the Genius of Bayle and the learning of Le Clerc, was not disgraced by the taste, the knowledge, and the judgement of Maty : he exhibits a candid and pleasing view of the state of litterature in England during a period of six years (January, 1750—December, 1755); and, far different from his angry son, he handles the rod of criticism with the tenderness and reluctance of a parent. The author of the *Journal Britannique* sometimes aspires to the character of a Poet and philosopher : his style is pure and elegant, and in his virtues or even his defects he may be ranked as one of the last disciples of the school of Fontenelle. His answer to my first letter was

---

* Matthew Maty, M.D. (1718-1776), under-librarian (1753) and librarian (1772) of the British Museum.

prompt and polite : after a careful examination he returned my Manuscript, with some animadversion and much applause; and when I visited London, in the ensuing winter, we discussed the design and execution in several free and familiar conversations. In a short excursion to Buriton I reviewed my Essay, according to his friendly advice; and after suppressing a third, adding a third, and altering a third, I consummated my first labour by a short preface, which is dated February 3ᵈ, 1759. Yet I still shrunk from the press with the terrors of virgin modesty : the manuscript was safely deposited in my desk; and as my attention was engaged by new objects, the delay might have been prolonged till I had fulfilled the precept of Horace, ."nonumque prematur in annum." Father Sirmond, a learned Jesuit, was still more rigid, since he advised a young friend to expect the mature age of fifty before he gave himself or his writings to the public (Olivet, Histoire de l'Académie Françoise, tom. ii. p. 143). The counsel was singular, but it is still more singular that it should have been approved by the example of the author. Sirmond was himself fifty-five years of age when he published (in 1614) his first work, an Edition of Sidonius Apollinaris, with many valuable annotations. (See his life, before the great Edition of his works in five volumes in folio, Paris, 1696, e Typographiâ Regiâ.)

Two years elapsed in silence; but in the spring of 1761 I yielded to the authority of a parent, and complyed, like a pious son, with the wish of my own heart. My private resolves were influenced by the state of Europe. About this time the belligerent powers had made and accepted overtures of peace : our English

plenipotentiaries were named to assist at the Congress of
Augsburg, which never met; I wished to attend them as
a Gentleman or a secretary, and my father fondly believed
that the proof of some litterary talents might introduce
me to public notice and second the recommendations of
my friends.   After a last revisal I consulted with Mr.
Mallet and Dr. Maty, who approved the design and promoted the execution.   Mr. Mallet, after hearing me read
my manuscript, received it from my hands, and delivered it
into those of Becket, with whom he made an agreement
in my name: an easy agreement; I required only a
certain number of copies, and, without transferring my
property, I devolved on the bookseller the charges and
profits of the Edition. Dr. Maty undertook, in my absence,
to correct the sheets: he inserted, without my knowledge,
an elegant and flattering Epistle to the Author: which
is composed, however, with so much art that, in case
of a defeat, his favourable report might have been
ascribed to the indulgence of a friend for the rash
attempt of a *young English Gentleman*. The work was
printed and published under the title of *Essai sur
l'étude de la littérature, à Londres, chez T. Becket et
P. A. de Hondt*. 1761, in a small Volume in duodecimo.
My dedication to my father, a proper and pious address,
was composed the 28th of May: Dr. Maty's letter is dated
the 16th of June; and I received the first copy (June the
23rd) at Alresford, two days before I marched with the
Hampshire militia. Some weeks afterwards, on the same
ground, I presented my book to the late Duke of York, who
breakfasted in Colonel Pitt's tent; [and as the regiment
was just returned from a field-day, the author appeared
before his Royal Highness, somewhat disordered with

sweat and dust, in the Cap, dress, and acoutrements of a Captain of Grenadiers.] By my father's direction and Mallet's advice, a number of copies were given to several [of their acquaintance and my own; to the Duke of Richmond, the Marquis of Caernarvon, the Earls of Litchfield, Waldegrave, Egremont, Shelburne, Bute, Hardwicke, Bath, Granville, and Chesterfield, Lady Hervey, Sir Joseph Yorke, Sir Matthew Fetherstone, Messieurs Walpole, Scott, Wray, etc.] : two books were sent to the Count de Caylus, and the Dutchess d'Aiguillon, at Paris; I had reserved twenty for my friends at Lausanne, as the first fruits of my education and a grateful token of my remembrance; and on all these persons I levied an unavoidable tax of civility and compliment. It is not surprizing that a work, of which the style and sentiments were so totally foreign, should have been more successful abroad than at home. I was delighted by the copious extracts, the warm commendations, and the flattering predictions of the Journals of France and Holland; and the next year (1762) a new Edition (I believe at Geneva) extended the fame, or at least the circulation, of the work. In England it was received with cold indifference, little read, and speedily forgotten; a small impression was slowly dispersed; the bookseller murmured, and the author (had his feelings been more exquisite) might have wept over the blunders and the baldness of the English translation. The publication of my History fifteen years afterwards revived the memory of my first performance, and the Essay was eagerly sought in the shops. But I refused the permission which Becket solicited of reprinting it: the public curiosity was imperfectly satisfied by a pyrated copy of the booksellers of Dublin; and when a copy of the original edition has been discovered in a sale, the primitive value of half a crown has risen to the fanciful price of a Guinea or thirty shillings. Such is the power of a name.

I have expatiated on the [loss of my litterary maidenhead]; a memorable æra in the life of a student, when he ventures to reveal the measure of his mind. His hopes and fears are multiplied by the idea of self-importance, and he believes for a while that the eyes of mankind are fixed on his person and performance. Whatsoever may be my present reputation, it no longer rests on the merit of this first Essay; and at the end of twenty-eight years I may appreciate my juvenile work with the impartiality, and almost with the indifference, of a stranger. In his answer to Lady Hervey, the Count de Caylus admires, or affects to admire, "les livres sans nombre que Mr. Gibbon a lus et très bien lus." But, alas! my stock of erudition at that time was scanty and superficial; and if I allow myself the liberty of naming the Greek masters, my genuine and personal acquaintance was confined to the Latin Classics. The most serious defect of my Essay is a kind of obscurity and abruptness, which always fatigues, and may often elude, the attention of the reader. Instead of a precise and proper definition, the title itself, the sense of the word *Litterature* is loosely and variously applied: a number of remarks and examples, historical, critical, philosophical, are heaped on each other without method or connection; and, if we except some introductory pages, all the remaining chapters might indifferently be reversed or transposed. The obscurity of many passages is often affected, brevis

esse laboro, obscurus fio ; the desire of expressing perhaps a common idea with sententious and oracular
brevity : alas, how fatal has been the imitation of
Montesquieu !   But this obscurity sometimes proceeds
from a mixture of light and darkness in the author's
mind ; from a partial ray which strikes upon an angle,
instead of spreading itself over the surface of an object.
After this fair confession I shall presume to say that the
Essay does credit to a young writer of two and twenty
years of age, who had read with taste, who thinks with
freedom, and who writes in a foreign language with spirit
and elegance.   The defence of the early History of Rome
and the new Chronology of Sir Isaac Newton form a
specious argument.   The patriotic and political design of
the Georgics is happily conceived ; and any probable
conjecture which tends to raise the dignity of the poet
and the poem deserves to be adopted without a rigid
scrutiny.   Some dawning of a philosophic spirit en-
lightens the general remarks on the study of history and
of man.   I am not displeased with the enquiry into the
origin and nature of the Gods of Polytheism.   [In a
riper season of judgement and knowledge, I am tempted to
review the curious question whether those fabulous Deities
were mortal men or allegorical beings : perhaps the two
systems might be blended in one ; perhaps the distance
between them is in a great measure verbal and apparent.
In the rapid course of this narrative I have only time
to scatter two or three hasty observations.   *That* in the
perusal of Homer a naturalist would pronounce his Gods
and men to be of the same species, since they were
capable of engendering together a fruitful progeny.   *That*
before the Reformation St. Francis and the Virgin Mary

had almost attained a similar Apotheosis; and that the
Saints and Angels, so different in their origin, were wor-
shipped with the same rites, by the same nations. *That*
the current of superstition and science flowed from India
to Egypt, from Egypt to Greece and Italy; and that
the incarnations of the Cœlestial Deities, so darkly
shadowed in our fragments of Egyptian theology, are
copiously explained in the sacred books of the Hindoos.
Fifteen centuries before Christ, the great Osiris, the
invisible agent of the Universe, was born or manifested
at Thebes, in Bœotia, under the name of Bacchus; the
idea of Bishen is a metaphysical abstraction; the adventures of Kishen, his perfect image, are those of a man
who lived and died about five thousand years ago in the
neighbourhood of Delhi.]   Upon the whole, I may apply
to the first labour of my pen the speech of a far superior
Artist when he surveyed the first productions of his
pencil.   After viewing some portraits which he had
painted in his youth, my friend Sir Joshua Reynolds
acknowledged to me that he was rather humbled than
flattered by the comparison with his present works; and
that, after so much time and study, he had conceived
his improvement to be much greater than he found it
to have been.*

---

* The intelligent modern reader
will be inclined to adopt Gibbon's
estimate of his early work. Its
faults are very clearly indicated;
it is a collection of shrewd and
acute observations, without order
or connection. The defence of the
early History of Rome and of
Newton's Chronology are not more
than specious; there is ingenuity,
but little more, in the theory about
the Georgics; and Gibbon, in his
maturer judgment, might have
smiled at his attributing the thirty
years' quiet of the turbulent vete-
rans who composed the military
colonies to the pacific influence of
Virgil's poetry. No subject has
been pursued with greater erudition and variety of opinion by
Continental scholars than the
origin of polytheism. Gibbon's
theory was far advanced beyond
his age, and might suggest something like an amicable compromise
between the Symbolists and Anti-

At Lausanne I composed the first chapters of my Essay in French, the familiar language of my conversation and studies, in which it was easier for me to write than in my mother-tongue. After my return to England I continued the same practise, without any affectation, or design of repudiating (as Dr. Bentley would say) my vernacular idiom. But I should have escaped some Anti-gallican clamour had I been content with the more natural character of an English author; I should have been more consistent had I rejected Mallet's [foolish] advice of prefixing an English dedication to a French book; a confusion of tongues which seemed to accuse the ignorance of my patron. The use of a foreign dialect might be excused by the hope of being employed as a negociator, by the desire of being generally understood on the continent; but my true motive was doubtless the ambition of new and singular fame, an Englishman claiming a place among the writers of France. The Latin tongue had been consecrated by the service of the Church; it was refined by the imitation of the ancients; and in the XVth and XVIth Centuries the scholars of Europe enjoyed the advantage, which they have gradually resigned, of conversing and writing in a common and learned idiom. As that idiom was no longer in any country the vulgar speech, they all stood on a level with each other; yet a citizen of old Rome might have smiled at the best Latinity of the Germans and Britons, and we may learn from the *Ciceronianus* of Erasmus how difficult it was found to steer a middle course between pedantry

---

Symbolists of Germany, the respective schools of Creuzer and Voss. The essay is to be found in the fourth volume of the miscellaneous works.—MILMAN.

and barbarism. The Romans themselves had sometimes attempted a more perilous task, of writing in a living language, and appealing to the taste and judgement of the natives. The vanity of Tully was doubly interested in the *Greek* memoirs of his own Consulship; and if he modestly supposes that some Latinisms might be detected in his style, he is confident of his own skill in the art of Isocrates and Aristotle, and he requests his friend Atticus to disperse the copies of his work at Athens and in the other cities of Greece (*ad Atticum*, i. 19, ii. 1). But it must not be forgot that, from infancy to manhood, Cicero and his contemporaries had read and declaimed and composed with equal diligence in both languages, and that he was not allowed to frequent a Latin school till he had imbibed the lessons of the Greek Grammarians and Rhetoricians. In modern times the language of France has been diffused by the merit of her writers, the social manners of the natives, the influence of the Monarchy, and the exile of the protestants: several foreigners have seized the opportunity of speaking to Europe in this common dialect, and Germany may plead the authority of Leibnitz and Frederic, of the first of her philosophers and the greatest of her Kings. The just pride and laudable prejudice of England has restrained the communication of idioms; and, of all the nations on this side of the Alps, my countrymen are the least practised and least perfect in the exercise of the French tongue. By Sir William Temple and Lord Chesterfield it was only used on occasions of civility and business, and their printed letters will not be quoted as models of composition. Lord Bolingbroke may have published in French a sketch of his reflections on exile; but his reputation now reposes on the address of Voltaire, "Docte sermones utriusque linguæ;" and, by his English dedication to Queen Caroline, and his Essay on Epic poetry, it should seem that Voltaire himself wished to deserve a return of the same compliment. The exception of Count Hamilton cannot fairly be urged; though an Irishman by birth, he was educated in France from his childhood: yet I *am* surprized that a long residence in England, and the habits of domestic conversation, did not affect the ease and purity of his inimitable style; and I regret the omission of his English verses, which might have afforded an amusing object of comparison. I might therefore assume the "primus ego in patriam meam," etc.; but with what success I have explored this untrodden path must be left to the decision of my French readers. Dr. Maty, who might himself be questioned as a foreigner, has secured his retreat at my expence. "Je ne crois pas que vous vous piquiez d'être moins facile à reconnoitre pour un Anglois que Lucullus pour un Romain." My friends at Paris have been more indulgent: they received me as a conntryman, or at least as a provincial; but they were friends and Parisians. The defects which Maty insinuates, "ces traits saillans, ces figures hardies, ce sacrifice de la regle au sentiment, et de la cadence à la force," are the faults of the youth rather than of the stranger; and after the long and laborious exercise of my own language, I am conscious that my French style has been ripened and improved.

I have already hinted that the publication of my Essay was delayed till I had embraced the military profession. I shall now amuse myself with the recollection of an active scene which bears no affinity to any other period of my studious and social life. [From the general idea of a militia, I shall descend to the militia of England in the war before the last; to the state of the Regiment in which I served, and to the influence of that service on my personal situation and character.

The defence of the state may be imposed on the body of the people, or it may be delegated to a select number of mercenaries; the exercise of arms may be an occasional duty or a separate trade, and it is this difference which forms the distinction between a militia and a standing army. Since the union of England and Scotland, the public safety has never been attacked, and has seldom been threatened by a foreign invader; but the sea was long the sole safeguard of our isle. If the reign of the Tudors or the Stuarts was often signalized by the valour of our soldiers and sailors, they were dismissed at the end of the campaign or the expedition for which they had been levied. The national spirit at home had subsided in the peaceful occupations of trade, manufactures, and husbandry, and if the obsolete forms of a militia were preserved, their discipline in the last age was less the object of confidence than of ridicule.

> " The country rings around with loud alarms,
> And raw in fields the rude Militia swarms :
> Mouths without hands maintained at vast expence,
> In peace a charge, in war a weak defence.
> Stout once a month they march, a blust'ring band,
> And ever but in times of need at hand.
> This was the morn when, issuing on the guard,
> Drawn up in rank and file they stood prepar'd,
> Of seeming arms to make a short essay;
> Then hasten to be drunk—the business of the day." *

---

* Dryden, *Cymon and Iphigenia*.

The impotence of such unworthy soldiers was supplied from the æra of the restoration by the establishment of a body of mercenaries: the conclusion of each war encreased the numbers that were kept on foot, and although their progress was checked by the jealousy of opposition, time and necessity reconciled, or at least accustomed, a free country to the annual perpetuity of a standing army. The zeal of our patriots, both in and out of Parliament (I cannot add, both in and out of office), complained that the sword had been stolen from the hands of the people. They appealed to the victorious example of the Greeks and Romans, among whom every citizen was a soldier; and they applauded the happiness and independence of Switzerland, which, in the midst of the great monarchies of Europe, is sufficiently defended by a constitutional and effective militia. But their enthusiasm overlooked the modern changes in the art of war, and the insuperable difference of government and manners. The liberty of the Swiss is maintained by the concurrence of political causes: the superior discipline of their militia arises from the numerous intermixture of Officers and soldiers whose youth has been trained in foreign service; and the annual exercise of a few days is the *sole* tax which is imposed on a martial people, consisting for the most part of shepherds and husbandmen. In the primitive ages of Greece and Rome, a war was determined by a battle, and a battle was decided by the personal qualities of strength, courage, and dexterity which every citizen derived from his domestic education. The public quarrel was his own; he had himself voted in the assembly of the people; and the private passions of the majority had pronounced the general decree of the Republic. On the event of the contest each freeman had staked his fortune and family, his liberty and life ; and if the enemy prevailed, he must expect to share in the common calamity of the ruin or servitude of his native city. By such irresistible motives were the first Greeks and Romans summoned to the field ; but when the art was improved, when the war was protracted, their militia was transformed into a standing army, or their freedom was oppressed by the more regular forces of an ambitious neighbour.

Two disgraceful events, the progress in the year forty-five of some naked highlanders, the invitation of the Hessians and Hanoverians in fifty-six, had betrayed and insulted the weakness of an unarmed people. The country Gentlemen of England unanimously demanded the establishment of a militia ; a patriot was expected—

> " Otia qui rumpet patriæ, residesque movebit
> ——————— in arma viros." *

and the merit of the plan, or at least of the execution, was assumed by Mr. Pitt, who was then in the full splendour of his popularity and power. In the new model the choice of the officers was founded on the most constutional (*sic*) principle, since they were all obliged, from the Colonel to the Ensign, to prove a certain qualification, to give a landed security to the country, which entrusted them for her defence with the use of arms. But in the first steps of this institution the legislators of the Militia despaired of imitating the practise of Switzerland. Instead of summoning to the standard *all* the inhabitants

---

* " Otia qui rumpet patriæ residesque movebit
  Tullus in arma viros, et jam desueta triumphis
  Agmina."

(Virg. Æn. vi. 814).

of the Kingdom who were not disabled by age, or excused
by some indispensable avocation, they directed that a
moderate proportion should be chosen by lot for the term
of three years, at the end of which their places were to
be supplied by a new and similar ballot. Every man
who was drawn had the option of serving in person, of
finding a substitute, or of paying ten pounds; and, in
a country already burthened, this honourable duty was
degraded into an additional tax.   It is reported that the
subjects of Queen Elizabeth amounted to 1,172,674 men
able to bear arms (Hume's History of England, vol. v.
p. 482 of the last octavo edition); and if in the war
before the last many active and vigorous hands were
employed in the fleet and army, the difference must have
been amply compensated by the general encrease of popu-
lation, and we may smile at this mighty effort which
reduced the national defence to the puny establishment
of thirty-two thousand men.   The Sunday afternoons had
first been appointed for their exercise, but superstition
clamoured against the profanation of the sabbath, and a
useful day was substracted from the labour of the week.
Whatever was the day, such rare and superficial practise
could never have entitled them to the character of
soldiers.   But the King was invested with the power of
calling the Militia into actual service on the event or the
danger of rebellion or invasion; and in the year 1759
the British Islands were seriously threatened by the
armaments of France.   At this crisis the national spirit
most gloriously disproved the charge of effeminacy which,
in a popular Estimate, had been imputed to the times; a
martial enthusiasm seemed to have pervaded the land, and
a constitutional army was formed under the command of

the nobility and gentry of England. After the naval victory of Sir Edward Hawke * (November 20th, 1759), the danger no longer subsisted; yet, instead of disbanding the first regiments of militia, the remainder was embodied the ensuing year, and public unanimity applauded their illegal continuance in the field till the end of the War. In this new mode of service they were subject, like the regulars, to martial law: they received the same advantages of pay and cloathing, and the families, at least of the principals, were maintained at the charge of the parish. At a distance from their respective counties these provincial corps were stationed, and removed, and encamped by the command of the Secretary at War: the officers and men were trained in the habits of subordination, nor is it surprizing that some regiments should have assumed the discipline and appearance of veteran troops. With the skill they soon imbibed the spirit of mercenaries, the character of a militia was lost; and, under that specious name, the crown had acquired a second army more costly and less useful than the first. The most beneficial effect of this institution was to eradicate among the Country gentlemen the relicks of Tory, or rather of Jacobite prejudice. The accession of a British king reconciled them to the government, and even to the court; but they have been since accused of transferring their passive loyalty from the Stuarts to the family of Brunswick; and I have heard Mr. Burke exclaim in the house of Commons, "They have changed the Idol, but they have preserved the Idolatry."

By the general ardour of the times, my father, a

---

* His victory over De Conflans, near Quiberon.

new Cincinnatus, was drawn from the plough: his authority and advice prevailed on me to relinquish my studies; a general meeting was held at Winchester; and before we knew the consequences of an irretrievable step, we accepted (June 12th, 1759) our respective commissions of Major and Captain in the South battalion of the Hampshire. The proportion of the County of Southampton had been fixed at nine hundred and sixty men, who were divided into the two regiments of the North and South, each consisting of eight companies. By the special exemption of the isle of Wight *we* lost a company; our Colonel resigned, and we were reduced to the legal definition of an independent battalion, of a Lieutenant-Colonel Commandant (Sir Thomas Worsley, Baronet *), a Major, five Captains, seven lieutenants, seven Ensigns, twenty-one Serjeants, fourteen drummers, and four hundred and twenty rank and file. I will not renew our prolix and passionate dispute with the Duke of Bolton, our Lord-Lieutenant, which at that time appeared to me an object of the most serious importance: by the interpretation of an act of parliament, we contested his right of naming himself Colonel of the two Battalions; after the final decision of the Attorney-general and Secretary at War, his poor revenge was confined to the use and abuse of his power, in the choice of an Adjutant and the promotion of officers. In the year 1759 our ballot was slowly compleated, and as the fear of an invasion passed away, we began to hope, my father and myself, that our campaigns would extend no farther than Petersfield and Alton, the seat of our

---

* Of Pilewell, Hants, and Appuldurcombe, Isle of Wight. He died in 1768.

particular companies. We were undeceived by the king's sign-manual for our embodying, which was issued May 10th, 1760. It was too late to retreat; it was too soon to repent: the Battalion on the 4th of June assembled at Winchester, from whence, in about a fortnight, we were removed, at our own request, for the benefit of a foreign education. In a new-raised Militia the neighbourhood of home was always found inconvenient to the officers and mischievous to the men.

The battalion continued in actual service above two years and a half, from May 10, 1760, to December 23, 1762. In this period of a military life I have neither sieges nor battles to relate; but, like my brother Major Sturgeon, I shall describe our marches and counter-marches as they are faithfully recorded in my own journal or commentary of the times. i. Our first and most agreeable station was at Blandford, in Dorsetshire, where we enjoyed about two months (June 17—August 23) the beauty of the country, the hospitality of the neighbouring gentlemen, the novelty of command and exercise, and the consciousness of our daily and rapid improvements. ii. From this school we were led against the enemy, a body of French three thousand two hundred strong, who had occupied Portchester castle, near Portsmouth: it must not, indeed, be dissembled that our enemies were naked, unarmed prisoners, the object of pity rather than of terror; their misery was somewhat alleviated by public and private bounty, but their sufferings exhibited the evils of war, and their noisy spirits the character of the nation. During the months of September, October, and November, 1760, we performed this disagreable duty by large detachments of a Captain, four subalterns, and two hundred and thirty men, at first from Hilsea barracks, and afterwards from our quarters at Titchfield and Fareham. The barracks within the Portsmouth lines are a square of low, ill-built huts, in a damp and dreary situation: on this unwholsome spot we lost many men by feavers and the small-pox; and our dispute with the Duke of Bolton, which produced a series of arrests, memorials, and court-martials, was not less pernicious to the discipline than to the peace of the regiment. iii. Rejoycing in our escape from this sink of distemper and discord, we performed with alacrity a long march (December 1–11) to Cranbrook, in the Weald of Kent, where we had been sent to guard eighteen hundred French prisoners at Sissinghurst. The inconceivable dirtyness of the season, the country, and the spot aggravated the hardships of a duty too heavy for our numbers; but these hardships were of short duration, and before the end of the month we were relieved by the interest of our Tory friends under the new reign. iv. At Dover, in the space of five months, we began to breathe (December 27, 1760—May 31, 1761); for the men the quarters were healthy and plentiful, and our dull leisure was enlivened by the society of the fourteenth Regiment in the castle, and some sea-parties in the spring. Our persecutions were at an end: the command was settled; we smiled at our own prowess, as we exercised each morning in sight of the French coast; and before we left Dover we had recovered the union and discipline which we possessed at our departure from Blandford. v. In the summer of 1761 a camp was formed near Winchester, in which we solicited and obtained a place. Our march from Dover to Alton, in Hampshire, was a pleasant walk

(June 1–12): I was appointed Captain of the new company of Grenadiers, and, with proper cloathing and acoutrements, we assumed somewhat of the appearance of regular troops. The four months (June 25—October 21) of this encampment were the most splendid and useful period of our military life. Our establishment amounted to near five thousand men—the thirty-fourth Regiment of foot, and six militia corps, the Wiltshire, Dorsetshire, South Hampshire, Berkshire, and the North and South Gloucestershire. The regulars were satisfied with their ideal pre-eminence; the Gloucestershire, Berkshire, and Dorsetshire approached by successive steps the superior merit of the Wiltshire, the pride and pattern of the Militia—an active, steady, well-appointed regiment of eight hundred men, which had been formed by the strict and skilfull discipline of their Colonel, Lord Bruce.[*] At our entrance into camp we were indisputably the last and worst; but we were excited by a generous shame—

"Extremos pudeat rediisse"—

and such was our indefatigable labour that, in the general reviews, the South Hampshire were rather a credit than a disgrace to the line. A friendly emulation, ready to teach and eager to learn, assisted our mutual progress; but the great evolutions, the exercise of acting and moving as an army which constitutes the best lessons of a camp, never entered the thoughts of the Earl of Effingham,[†] our drowzy General. vi. The Devizes, our

---

[*] Thomas Bruce Brudenell, born 1730, succeeded his uncle as second Baron Bruce of Tottenham, 1747. The earldom of Ailesbury, which had become extinct on the death of his predecessor, the third earl, in 1747, was revived in his favour in the same year. Died 1814.

[†] Thomas Howard, second Earl of Effingham, succeeded his father 1743; died 1763. His wife, Elizabeth Beckford, was a sister of the author of *Vathek*.

winter quarters during four months (October 23, 1761—February 28, 1762), are a populous town, full of disorder and disease: the men who were allowed to work earned too much money, and their drunken quarrels with the townsmen and Colonel Barré's black musqueteers * were painfully repressed by the sharp sentences of one and twenty Court-martials. The Devizes afforded, however, a great number of fine young recruits, whom we enlisted from the Regimental stock-purse without much regard to the forms or the spirit of the Militia laws. vii. After a short march and halt at Salisbury, we paid a second visit of ten weeks (March 9—May 31) to our old friends at Blandford, where, in that garden of England, we again experienced the warm and constant hospitality of the natives. The spring was favourable to our military exercise, and the Dorsetshire Gentlemen, who had cherished our infancy now applauded a Regiment in appearance and discipline, not inferior to their own. viii. The necessity of discharging a great number of men, whose term of three years was expired, forbade our encampment in the summer of 1762, and the colours were stationed at Southampton in the last six or seven months (June—December) of our actual service. But after so long an indulgence we could not complain that, during many of the first and last weeks of this period, a detachment almost equal to the whole was required to guard the French prisoners at Forton and Fareham. The operation of the ballot was slow and tedious. In the months of August and September our life at Southampton was, indeed, gay and busy; the battalion had

---

* The 106th Regiment, raised in 1761 and disbanded shortly after the peace; it was commanded by Colonel Isaac Barré.

been renewed in youth and vigour, and so rapid was the improvement that, had the militia lasted another year, we should not have yielded to the most perfect of our brethren. The prelinaries (*sic*) of peace and the suspension of arms determined our fate : we were dismissed with the thanks of the king and parliament, and on the 23rd of December, 1762, the companies were disembodyed at their respective homes. The officers possessed of property rejoiced in their freedom ; those who had none lamented the loss of their pay and profession ; but it was found by experience that the greatest part of the men were rather civilized than corrupted by the habits of military subordination.]

A young mind, unless it be of a cold and languid temper, is dazzled even by the play of arms ; and in the first sallies of my enthusiasm I had seriously wished and tryed to embrace the regular profession of a soldier. The military feaver was cooled by the enjoyment of our mimic Bellona, who gradually unveiled her naked deformity. How often did I sigh for my true situation of a private gentleman and a man of letters : how often did I repeat the complaints of Cicero "Clitellæ bovi sunt impositæ. Est incredibile quam me negotii tædeat. Ille cursus animi et industriæ meæ præclarâ operâ cessat. Lucem, *libros,* urbem, domum, vos desidero. Sed feram ut potero, sit modo annuum ; Si prorogatur, actum est." * From a service without danger I might indeed have

---

* "Est incredibilo quam me negotii tædeat. Non habet satis magnum campum, ille tibi non ignotus cursus animi et industriæ meæ præclara opera cessat. . . . Denique hæc non desidero ; lucem, forum, urbem, domum, vos desidero. Sed feram ut potero ; sit modo annuum. Si prorogatur actum est . . . clitellæ bovi sunt impositæ, Cillane, non est nostrum onus."— *Epist. ad Atticum,* lib. v. 15.

retired without disgrace ; but as often as I hinted a wish of resigning, my fetters were riveted by [my father's authority, the entreaties of Sir Thomas Worsley, and some regard for the wellfare of a corps of which I was the principal support. My proper province was the care of my own, and afterwards of the Grenadier, company : but, with the rank of first captain, I possessed the confidence, and supplied the place of the Colonel and Major. In their presence or in their absence I acted as the commanding officer : every memorial and letter relative to our disputes was the work of my pen ; the detachments or court-martials of any delicacy or importance were my extraordinary duties ; and to supersede the Duke of Bolton's adjutant, I always exercised the Battalion in the field. Sir Thomas Worsley was an easy good-humoured man fond of the table and of his bed ; our conferences were marked by every stroke of the midnight and morning hours, and the same drum which invited him to rest has often summoned me to the parade. His example encouraged the daily practise of hard and even excessive drinking which has sown in my constitution the seeds of the gout]. The loss of so many busy and idle hours was not compensated by any elegant pleasure ; and my temper was insensibly soured by the society of our rustic officers [who were alike deficient in the knowledge of scholars, and the manners of gentlemen]. In every state there exists, however, a balance of good and evil. The habits of a sedentary life were usefully broken by the duties of an active profession : in the healthful exercise of the field I hunted with a battalion instead of a pack, and at that time I was ready, at any hour of the day or night, to fly from quarters to London, from London to quarters, on the slightest call of private or regimental business. But my principal obligation to the militia was the making me an Englishman and a soldier. After my foreign education, with my reserved temper, I should long have continued a stranger in my native country, had I not been shaken in this various scene of new faces and new friends; had not experience forced me to feel the characters of our leading men, the state of parties, the forms of office, and the operation of our civil and military system. In this peaceful service I imbibed the rudiments of the language and science of tactics, which opened a new field of study and observation. I diligently read and meditated the *Memoires Militaires* of Quintus Icilius (Mr. Guichardt *), the only writer who has united the merits of a professor and a veteran. The discipline and evolutions of a modern battalion gave me a clearer notion of the Phalanx and the Legions, and the Captain of the Hampshire grenadiers (the reader may smile) has not been useless to the historian of the Roman Empire.

When I complain of the loss of time, justice to myself and to the Militia must throw the greatest part of that reproach on the first seven or eight months, while I was

---

* Charles Theophilus Guischardt (or Guichard), a member of a French refugee family, was born in Magdeburg in 1724 or 1725: he was destined for the Protestant ministry, but following his natural bent, he became a soldier, and served in the Dutch army.

After the treaty of Aix-la-Chapelle in 1748, he employed his leisure in writing his *Mémoires militaires sur les Grecs et les Romains.* He subsequently translated the *Military Institutions* of Onosauder, Arrian's *Tactics,* and Hirtius' Analysis of Cæsar's campaigns in Africa. When Frederic the Great was in Silesia in 1757, he summoned Guischardt to Breslau, and was much attracted by him. He asked him on one occasion whom he considered the best of Cæsar's aides-de-camp. "Quintus Icilius," replied Guischardt. "Then," said Frederic, "you shall be my Quintus Icilius"—a sobriquet which he thenceforward assumed. He rose to the rank of colonel in the King's service, and in 1773 brought out an enlarged edition of his work, and died in 1775.

obliged to learn as well as to teach. The dissipation of Blandford and the disputes of Portsmouth consumed the hours which were not employed in the field; and amid the perpetual hurry of an Inn, a barrack, or a guard-room, all litterary ideas were banished from my mind. After this long fast, the longest which I have ever known, I once more tasted at Dover the pleasures of reading and thinking, and the hungry appetite with which I opened a volume of Tully's philosophical works is still present to my memory. The last review of my Essay before its publication had prompted me to investigate the *Nature of the Gods:* my enquiries led me to the Histoire Critique du Manicheisme of Beausobre, who discusses many deep questions of Pagan and Christian Theology; and from this rich treasury of facts and opinions I deduced my own consequences, beyond the holy circle of the Author. After this recovery I never relapsed into indolence; and my example might prove that in the life most adverse to study some hours may be stolen, some minutes may be snatched: amidst the tumult of Winchester camp I sometimes thought and read in my tent; in the more settled quarters of the Devizes, Blandford, and Southampton I always secured a separate lodging and the necessary books; and in the summer of 1762, while the new militia was raising, I enjoyed at Buriton two or three months of litterary repose. In forming a new plan of study, I hesitated between the Mathematics and the Greek language, both of which I had neglected since my return from Lausanne. I consulted a learned and friendly Mathematician, Mr. George Scott, a pupil of de Moivre, and his map of a country which I have never explored may perhaps be more serviceable to others. As soon as

I had given the preference to Greek, the example of
Scaliger and my own reason determined me on the choice
of Homer, the Father of poetry and the bible of the
ancients; but Scaliger ran through the Iliad in one and
twenty days, and I was not dissatisfied with my own
diligence for performing the same labour in an equal
number of weeks. After the first difficulties were sur-
mounted, the language of Nature and harmony soon
became easy and familiar, and each day I sailed on the
Ocean with a brisker gale and a more steady course.

> Εν δ' ανεμος πρησεν μεσον ιστιον, αμφι δε κυμα
> Στειρη πορφυρεον μεγαλ' ιαχε, νηος ιουσης :
> 'Η δ' εθεεν κατα κυμα διαπρησσουσα κελευθα.*

In the study of a poet who has since become the
most intimate of my friends, I successively applied many
passages and fragments of Greek writers, and among these
I shall notice a life of Homer, in the Opuscula Mytho-
logica of Gale, several books of the Geography of Strabo,
and the entire treatises of Longinus, which, from the title
and the style, is equally worthy of the epithet of *Sublime.*
My grammatical skill was improved, my vocabulary was
enlarged, and in the militia I acquired a just and indelible
knowledge of the first of languages. On every march, in
every journey, Horace was always in my pocket and often
in my hand; but I should not mention his two critical
Epistles, the amusement of a morning, had they not been
accompanied by the elaborate commentary of Dr. Hurd,
now Bishop of Worcester. On the interesting subjects of
composition and imitation of Epic and Dramatic poetry,
I presumed to think for myself; and fifty close-written

---

* 'Εν δ'ανεμος πρῆσε μέσον ἱστίον, ἀμφὶ δὲ κῦμα
Στείρη πορφύρεον μεγάλ' ἰάχε, νηὸς ἰούσης ·
'Η δ'έθεε κατὰ κῦμα διαπρήσσουσα κέλευθον.
(Iliad, i. 481.)

pages in folio could scarcely comprize my full and free discussion of the sense of the master and the pedantry of the servant.

After his oracle Dr. Johnson, my friend Sir Joshua Reynolds denies all original Genius, any natural propensity of the mind to one art or science rather than another. Without engaging in a metaphysical or rather verbal dispute, I *know*, by experience, that from my early youth I aspired to the character of an historian. While I served in the Militia, before and after the publication of my Essay, this idea ripened in my mind; nor can I paint in more lively colours the feelings of the moment than by transcribing some passages, under their respective dates, from a Journal which I kept at that time.

BURITON, APRIL 14, 1761.

(*In a short excursion from Dover.*)

"Having thought of several subjects for an historical composition, I chose the expedition of Charles VIII. of France into Italy. I read two Memoirs of Mr. de Foncemagne in the Academy of Inscriptions (Tom. xvii. pp. 539–607), and abstracted them. I likewise finished this day a dissertation, in which I examined the right of Charles VIII. to the crown of Naples, and the rival claims of the houses of Anjou and Arragon. It consists of ten folio pages, besides large notes."

BURITON, AUGUST 4, 1761.

(*In a week's excursion from Winchester camp.*)

"After having long revolved subjects for my intended historical Essay, I renounced my first thought of the

o

expedition of Charles VIII. as too remote from us, and rather an introduction to great events than great and important [in itself.   I successively chose and rejected the Crusade of Richard the First, the Barons' Wars against John and Henry III., the history of Edward the black Prince, the lives and comparison of Henry V. and the Emperor Titus, the life of Sir Philip Sidney, or of the Marquis of Montrose.   At length I have fixed on Sir Walter Raleigh for my Hero.   His eventful story is varied by the characters of the soldier and sailor, the courtier and historian; and it may afford such a fund of materials as I desire, which have not yet been properly manufactured.   At present I cannot attempt the execution of this work.   Free leisure, and the opportunity of consulting many books, both printed and manuscript, are as necessary as they are impossible to be attained in my present way of life.   However, to acquire a general insight into my subject and ressources, I read the life of Sir Walter Raleigh by Dr. Birch, his copious article in the General Dictionary by the same hand, and the reigns of Queen Elizabeth and James the First in Hume's History of England."

BURITON, JANUARY, 1762.

(In a month's absence from the Devizes.)

"During this interval of repose I again turned my thoughts to Sir Walter Raleigh, and looked more closely into my materials.   I read the two volumes in quarto of the Bacon papers, published by Dr. Birch; the Fragmenta Regalia of Sir Robert Naunton; Mallet's life of Lord Bacon, and the political treatises of that great man in the first Volume of his works, with many of his letters in the second; Sir William Monson's Naval tracts; and the elaborate life of Sir Walter Raleigh, which Mr. Oldys has prefixed to the best edition of his history of the World. My subject opens upon me, and in general improves on a nearer prospect."

BURITON, JULY 26, 1762.

(*During my summer residence.*)

"I am afraid of being reduced to drop my Hero; but my time has not, however, been lost in the research of his story, and of a memorable æra of our English annals. The life of Sir Walter Raleigh by Oldys is a very poor performance; a servile panegyric, or flat Apology, tediously minute, and composed in a dull and affected style. Yet the author was a man of diligence and learning, who had read every thing relative to his object, and whose ample collections are arranged with perspicuity and method. Except some anecdotes lately revealed in the Sidney and Bacon Papers, I know not what I should be able to add. My ambition (exclusive of the uncertain merit of style and sentiment) must be confined to the hope of giving a good abridgement of Oldys. I have even the disappointment of finding some parts of this copious work very dry and barren, and these parts are unluckily some of the most cha-racteristic: Raleigh's colony of Virginia, his quarrels with Essex, the true secret of his conspiracy, and, above all, the detail of his private life, the most essential and important to a Biographer. My best ressource would be in the circumjacent history of the

times, and perhaps in some digressions artfully introduced, like the fortunes of the Peripatetic philosophy
in the portrait of Lord Bacon. But the reigns of
Elizabeth and James I. are the period of English
history which has been the most variously illustrated;
and what new lights could I reflect on a subject which
has exercised the accurate industry of *Birch*, the lively
and curious acuteness of *Walpole*, the critical spirit of
Hurd, the vigorous sense of *Mallet* and *Robertson*, and
the impartial philosophy of *Hume*. Could I even sur-
mount these obstacles, I should shrink with terror from
the modern history of England, where every character
is a problem, and every reader a friend or an enemy;
where a writer is supposed to hoist a flag of party, and
is devoted to damnation by the adverse faction. Such
would be *my* reception at home; and abroad, the historian of Raleigh must encounter an indifference far more
bitter than censure or reproach. The events of his life
are interesting; but his character is ambiguous, his actions
are obscure, his writings are English, and his fame is confined to the narrow limits of our language and our island.
I must embrace a safer and more extensive theme.

"There is one which I should prefer to all others,
The History of the Liberty of the Swiss, of that independence which a brave people rescued from the house of
Austria, defended against a Dauphin of France, and
finally sealed with the blood of Charles of Burgundy.
From such a theme, so full of public spirit, of military
glory, of examples of virtue, of lessons of government,
the dullest stranger would catch fire: what might not
I hope, whose talents, whatsoever they may be, would
be inflamed by the zeal of patriotism? But the materials

of this history are inaccessible to me, fast locked in the obscurity of an old barbarous German dialect, of which I am totally ignorant, and which I cannot resolve to learn for this sole and peculiar purpose.

"I have another subject in view, which is the contrast of the former history: the one a poor, warlike, virtuous Republic, which emerges into glory and freedom; the other a Commonwealth, soft, opulent, and corrupt, which, by just degrees, is precipitated from the abuse to the loss of her liberty: both lessons are, perhaps, equally instructive. This second subject is, *The history of the Republic of Florence, under the house of Medicis:* a period of one hundred and fifty years, which rises or descends from the dregs of the Florentine democracy to the title and dominion of Cosmo de Medicis in the Grand Duchy of Tuscany. I might deduce a chain of revolutions not unworthy of the pen of Vertot; singular men and singular events; the Medicis four times expelled, and as often recalled; and the Genius of freedom reluctantly yielding to the arms of Charles V. and the policy of Cosmo. The character and fate of Savanarola, and the revival of arts and letters in Italy, will be essentially connected with the elevation of the family and the fall of the Republic. The Medicis ('stirps quasi fataliter nata ad instauranda vel fovenda studia.' Lipsius ad Germanos et Gallos, Epist. vii.) were illustrated by the patronage of learning, and enthusiasm was the most formidable weapon of their adversaries. On this splendid subject I shall most probably fix; but *when,* or *where,* or *how* will it be executed? I behold in a dark and doubtful perspective

'Res altâ terrâ, et caligine mersas.'"

The youthful habits of the language and manners of France had left in my mind an ardent desire of revisiting the continent on a larger and more liberal plan. According to the law of custom, and perhaps of reason, foreign travel completes the education of an English Gentleman: my father had consented to my wish, but I was detained above four years by my rash engagement in the militia. I eagerly grasped the first moments of freedom: three or four weeks in Hampshire and London were employed in the preparations of my journey, and the farewell visits of friendship and civility; my last act in town was to applaud Mallet's new tragedy of Elvira; a post-chaise conveyed me to Dover, the packet to Boulogne, and such was my diligence that I reached Paris on the 28th of January, 1763, only thirty-six days after the disbanding of the Militia. Two or three years were loosely defined for the term of my absence; and I was left at liberty to spend that time in such places and in such a manner as was most agreable to my taste and judgement.

In this first visit I passed three months and a half (January 28—May 9) at Paris, and a much longer space might have been agreably filled without any intercourse with the natives. At home we are content to move in the daily round of pleasure and business; and a scene which is always present is supposed to be within our knowledge, or at least within our power. But in a foreign country curiosity is our business and our pleasure; and the traveller, conscious of his ignorance and covetous of his time, is diligent in the search and the view of every object that can deserve his attention. I devoted many hours of the morning to the circuit of Paris and the neighbourhood, to the visit of churches and palaces conspicuous by their architecture, to the royal manufactures, collections of books and pictures, and all the various treasures of art, of learning, and of luxury. An Englishman may hear without reluctance that in these curious and costly articles Paris is superior to London, since the opulence of the French capital arises from the defects of the government and Religion. In the absence of Lewis XIV. and his successors, the Louvre has been left unfinished; but the millions which have been lavished on the sands of Versailles and the morass of Marli could not be supplied by the legal allowance of a British King. The splendour of the French nobles is confined to their town residence; that of the English is more usefully distributed in their country seats; and we should be astonished at our own riches, if the labours of architecture, the spoils of Italy and Greece, which are now scattered from Inverary to Wilton, were accumulated in a few streets between Marybone and Westminster. All superfluous ornament is rejected by the cold frugality of the Protestants; but the Catholic superstition, which is always the enemy of reason, is often the parent of taste; the wealthy communities of priests and monks expend their revenues in stately edifices, and the parish Church of St. Sulpice, one of the noblest structures in Paris, was built and adorned by the private industry of a late Curate. In this outset, and still more in the sequel of my tour, my eye was amused; but the pleasing vision cannot be fixed by the pen; the particular images are darkly seen through the medium of five and twenty years, and the narrative of my life must not degenerate into a book of travels.

But the principal end of my journey was to enjoy the society of a polished and amiable people, in whose favour I was strongly prejudiced; and to converse with some authors, whose conversation, as I fondly imagined, must be far more pleasing and instructive than their writings. The moment was happily chosen. At the close of a successful war, the British name was respected on the continent.

> "Clarum et venerabile nomen
> Gentibus."

Our opinions, our fashions, even our games, were adopted in France; a ray of national glory illuminated each individual, and every Englishman was supposed to be born a patriot and a philosopher. For myself, I carried a personal recommendation; my name and my Essay were already known; the compliment of writing in the French language entitled me to some returns of civility and gratitude. I was considered as a man of letters, [or rather as a gentleman] who wrote for his amusement: [my appearance, dress, and equipage distinguished me from the tribe of authors who, even at Paris, are secretly envied and despised by those who possess the advantages of birth, fortune.] Before my departure I had obtained from the Duke de Nivernois, Lady Hervey, the Mallets, Mr. Walpole, etc., many letters of recommendation to their private or litterary friends. Of these epistles the reception and success was determined by the character and situation of the persons by whom and to whom they were addressed; the seed was sometimes cast on a barren rock, and it sometimes multiplied an hundred fold in the production of new shoots, spreading branches, and exquisite fruit. But, upon the whole, I had reason to praise the national urbanity, which from the court has diffused its gentle influence to the shop, the cottage, and the schools. Of the men of Genius of the age, Montesquieu and Fontenelle were no more; Voltaire resided on his own estate near Geneva; Rousseau in the preceding year had been driven from his hermitage of Montmorency; and I blush at my neglecting to seek, in this journey, the acquaintance of Buffon. Among the men of letters whom I saw, d'Alembert and Diderot held the foremost rank in merit, or at least in fame: [these two associates were the elements of water and fire; but the eruption was clouded with smoke, and the stream, though devoid of grace, was limpid and copious.] I shall content myself with enumerating the well-known names of the Count de Caylus,* of the Abbés de la Bleterie,† Barthelemy,‡ Raynal, § Arnaud, ‖ of Messieurs de la Condamine,¶ Duclos,** de Ste. Palaye,†† de

---

* Anne-Claude-Philippe, Comte de Caylus (1692–1765), au artist and archæologist, and patron of the arts: he travelled in the East, and bequeathed some valuable collections to the Bibliothèque du Roi.

† J. B. Réné de la Bletterie (1696–1772) translated Tacitus, and wrote lives of Julian the Apostate and of the Emperor Jovian.

‡ Jean Jacques Barthélemy (1716–1795), author of *Voyage du Jeune Anacharsis en Grèce*, and of several archæological papers.

§ Guillaume T. F. Raynal (1713–1796) threw up his orders to join the Encyclopedists; became editor of the *Mercure*, and in 1770 published his famous *Histoire philosophique des deux Indes*. Late in life he formally renounced his republican opinions.

‖ François Arnaud (1721–1784) was for a time Abbot of Grandchamp: he was a man of consider-

able ability, but of no great industry, and his works were mostly of a fugitive character. He wrote a *Lettre sur la musique au Comte de Caylus*, and was jointly with M. Suard editor of *l'Histoire ancienne des peuples de l'Europe par du Buat*.

¶ Charles Marie de la Condamine (1701–1774), traveller and mathematician; wrote *Relation d'un voyage dans l'intérieur de l'Amerique méridionale* and *Histoire des Pyramides de Quito*.

** Charles Pineau Du Clos (1704–1722) wrote a history of the reigns of Louis XI., and Louis XIV. and XV.; a novel, *Acajou et Zirphile*, and *Considérations sur les mœurs*.

†† Jean Baptiste de la Curne de Ste. Palaye (1697–1781), author of *Mémoires sur l'ancienne Chevalerie* and *Histoire des Troubadours*.

Bougainville,* Caperonnier,† de Guignes,‡ Suard,§ etc., without attempting to discriminate the shades of their characters, or the degrees of our connection.   Alone, in a morning visit, I commonly found the wits and authors of Paris less vain, and more reasonable, than in the circles of their equals, with whom they mingle

---

* Jean Pierre de Bougainville (1722–1763), brother of the famous traveller, was secretary of the Académie des Inscriptions, and author of *Parallèle de l'Expedition d'Alexandre dans les Indes avec cette de Thamas Kouli-Khan*.

† Jean Capperonnier (1716–1775) was professor of Greek, and afterwards librarian of the Bibliothèque du Roi in Paris.   He edited several classical authors, as well as Joinville's *Histoire de St. Louis*.

‡ Joseph de Guignes (1721–1800), an Orientalist, and author of several learned works on the Huns, Turks, and Tartars : he was made a member of the Royal Society in 1752.

§ Jean Baptiste Antoine Suard (1733–1817) was secretary of the Académie Française. He translated into French Robertson's *History of America, Charles V.*, and Cook's *Voyages;* wrote *Lettres sur Gluck et Piccini*, etc.

In an article in the *Quarterly Review* (No. 100), by Dean Milman, the following passage from M. Suard's description of Gibbon at this time is quoted :—

"As to his manners in society, without doubt the agreeableness (*amabilité*) of Gibbon was neither that yielding and retiring complaisance, nor that modesty which is forgetful of self; but his vanity (*amour-propre*) never showed itself in an offensive manner : anxious to succeed and to please, he wished to command attention, and obtained it without difficulty by a conversation animated, sprightly, and full of matter : all that was dictatorial (*tranchant*) in his tone betrayed not so much that desire of domineering over others, which is always offensive, as confidence in himself; and that confidence was justified both by his powers and by his success.   Notwithstanding this, his conversation never carried one away (*n'entrainait jamais*); its fault was a kind of arrangement, which never permitted him to say anything unless well. This fault might be attributed to the difficulty of speaking a foreign language, had not his friend, Lord Sheffield, who defends him from this suspicion of study in his conversation, admitted at the least that before he wrote a note or a letter he arranged completely in his mind what he wished to express. He appears, indeed, always to have written thus. Dr. Gregory, in his *Letters on Literature*, says that Gibbon composed as he was walking up and down his room, and that he never wrote a sentence without having perfectly formed and arranged it in his head. Besides, French was at least as familiar to him as English; his residence at Lausanne, where he spoke it exclusively, had made it for some time his habitual language; and one would not have supposed that he had ever spoken any other, if he had not been betrayed by a very strong accent, by certain *tics* of pronunciation, certain sharp tones, which, to ears accustomed from infancy to softer inflexions of voice, marred the pleasure which was felt in listening to him."

in the houses of the rich. Four days in the week I had a place, without invitation, at the hospitable tables of Mesdames Geoffrin * and du Bocage, † of the celebrated Helvetius,‡ and of the Baron d'Olbach : § in these *Symposia* the pleasures of the table were improved by lively and liberal conversation ; the company was select, though various and voluntary, [and each unbidden guest might mutter a proud, an ungrateful sentence.

Αυτοματοι δ'αγαθοι δειλων επι δαιτας ιασιν. ‖

---

* Marie Thérèse Rodet (1699–1777) was married, at the age of fifteen, to M. Geoffrin, a colonel in the Paris militia. She was early left a widow, and for many years maintained one of the most remarkable salons in Paris. It was said that no stranger who had not been present at these gatherings had seen Paris. Without any cultivated education herself, she supplied the want by her remarkable tact, combined with an unusual benevolence of disposition. She held two dinners a week, for literary men and artists respectively, and was always ready out of her limited means to assist those who were in difficulties.

Stanislas Poniatowski, when he succeeded to the throne of Poland, never forgot his obligations to Madame Geoffrin, and she paid him a visit in Warsaw in her sixty-eighth year. On her way thither she received a remarkable welcome at the court of the Emperor of Austria.

Her manners were brusque and *naïve*, and it is this which probably gave offence to Gibbon.

† Marie Anne Le Page, the wife of Fiquet du Boccage (1710–1802), was a woman of a very cultivated mind, who, as a leader of society and a poetess, won her way to the first rank.

Her first success was in gaining the prize at the Académie at Rouen with her poem, *Prix alternatif entre les belles-lettres et les Sciences.* Her *Mort d'Abel* was an attempt to imitate the style of Milton. Chief among her other works are *Les Amazones* and *La Columbiade.* When she was received by Voltaire at Ferney, he placed a laurel wreath on her head.

‡ Claude Adrien Helvetius (1715–1771): his work, *de l'Esprit,* in which his materialistic philosophy is set forth, was condemned by the Sorbonne, the Pope, and the Parliament, and was publicly burnt, 1759. He was also the author of *l'Homme, le Bonheur,* and some poems.

§ Paul Thiry, Baron d'Holbach (1723–1789), wrote, among many other works, his *Système de la Nature* (1770), in which he states the arguments for materialism. He married Mdlle. d'Aine ; and, on her death, married, with the sanction of the Pope, her sister. Rousseau speaks of him as " un fils de parvenu, qui jouissait d'une assez grande fortune dont il usait noblement, recevant chez lui des gens de lettres, et par son savoir et ses connaissances tenant bien sa place au milieu d'eux."

‖ 'Αυτόματοι δ'ἀγαθοὶ δειλῶν ἐπὶ δαῖτας ἴασι.

(Eupolis, χρυσουν γένος.)

Yet I was often disgusted with the capricious tyranny of Madame Geoffrin, nor could I approve the intolerant zeal of the philosophers and Encyclopædists the friends of d'Olbach and Helvetius; they laughed at the scepticism of Hume, preached the tenets of Atheism with the bigotry of dogmatists, and damned all believers with ridicule and contempt.] The society of Madame du Bocage was more soft and moderate than that of her rivals, and the evening conversations of Mr. de Foncemagne * were supported by the good sense and learning of the principal members of the Academy of inscriptions. The Opera and the Italians I occasionally visited; but the French theatre, both in tragedy and comedy, was my daily and favourite amusement. Two famous actresses then divided the public applause: for my own part, I preferred the consummate art of the Clairon to the intemperate sallies of the Dumesnil, which were extolled by her admirers as the genuine voice of nature and passion. [I have reserved for the last the most pleasing connection which I formed at Paris—the acquisition of a female friend, by whom I was sure of being received every evening with the smile of confidence and joy. I delivered a letter from Mrs. Mallet to Madame Bontems,† who had distinguished herself by a translation of Thomson's Seasons into French

---

* Etienne Laurcault de Foncemagne (1694–1779) wrote several papers on primitive historical subjects in *Journal* of the Académie des Inscriptions, but his chief literary achievement was his controversy with Voltaire concerning the *Testament Politique du Cardinal de Richelleu*, the genuineness of which he maintained with success.

He was a brilliant conversationalist, and a man of a most benevolent disposition.

† Marie Jeanne de Chatillon, wife of Pierre Henri Bontemps, paymaster of the forces in Paris, was born in 1718, and died in 1768. Garrick, as well as Gibbon, frequented her salon.

prose : at our first interview we felt a sympathy which banished all reserve, and opened our bosoms to each other. In every light, in every attitude, Madame B. was a sensible and amiable Companion, an author careless of litterary honours, a devotee untainted with Religious gall. She managed a small income with elegant economy : her apartment on the Quai des Theatins commanded the river, the bridges, and the Louvre; her familiar suppers were adorned with freedom and taste; and I attended her in my carriage to the houses of her acquaintance, to the sermons of the most popular preachers, and in pleasant excursions to St. Denys, St. Germain, and Versailles. In the middle season of life, her beauty was still an object of desire : the Marquis de Mirabeau, a celebrated name, was neither her first nor her last lover; but if her heart was tender, if her passions were warm, a veil of decency was cast over her frailties.] Fourteen weeks insensibly stole away : but had I been rich and independent, I should have prolonged, and perhaps have fixed, my residence at Paris.

Between the expensive style of Paris and of Italy it was prudent to interpose some months of tranquil simplicity, and at the thoughts of Lausanne I again lived in the pleasures and studies of my early youth. Shaping my course through Dijon and Besançon, in the last of which places I was kindly entertained by my cousin Acton, I arrived in the month of May, 1763, on the banks of the Leman lake. It had been my intention to pass the Alps in the autumn; but such are the simple attractions of the place that the annual circle was almost revolved before my departure from Lausanne in the ensuing spring. An absence of five years had not made much alteration in manners, or even in persons: my old friends of both sexes hailed my voluntary return—the most genuine proof of my attachment: they had been flattered by the present of my book, the produce of their soil; and the good Pavilliard shed tears of joy as he embraced a pupil [with whose success his vanity as well as friendship might be delighted *]. To my old list I added some new acquaintance [who in my former residence had not been on the spot, or in my way], and among the strangers I shall distinguish Prince Lewis of Wirtemberg,† the brother of the reigning Duke, at whose country-house near Lausanne I frequently dined. A wandering meteor, and at length a falling star, his light and ambitious spirit had successively dropt from the firmament of Prussia, of France, and of Austria; and his faults, which he styled his misfortunes, had driven him into philosophic exile in the Pays de Vaud. He could now moralize on the vanity of the World, the equality of mankind, and the happiness of a private station: his address was affable and polite, and, as he had shone in courts and armies, his memory could supply, and his eloquence could adorn, a copious fund of interesting anecdotes. His first enthusiasm was that of charity and agriculture; but the Sage gradually lapsed in the Saint, and Prince Lewis of Wirtemberg is now buried in an hermitage near Mayence, in the last stage of mystic devotion. By some ecclesiastical quarrel Voltaire had

---

* Lord Sheffield's edition, "whose literary merit he might fairly impute to his own labour."

† Ludwig Eugene of Wurtemburg (1731–1795) was a lieut.-general in the service of the French king, and distinguished himself in the Seven Years' War. He succeeded to the duchy on the death of his brother Charles in 1793, and joined the coalition against France in the following year.

been provoked to withdraw himself from Lausanne: but the theatre which he had founded, the Actors whom he had formed, survived the loss of their master; and recent from Paris, I assisted with pleasure at the representation of several tragedies and comedies. I shall not descend to specify particular names and characters; but I cannot forget a private institution which will display the innocent freedom of Swiss manners. My favourite society had assumed, from the age of its members, the proud denomination of the spring (*la societé du printems*). It consisted of fifteen or twenty young unmarried Ladies, of genteel though not of the very first families; the eldest perhaps about twenty; all agreable, several handsome, and two or three of exquisite beauty. At each other's houses they assembled almost every day: without the controul or even the presence of a mother or an aunt, they were trusted to their own prudence among a crowd of young men of every nation in Europe. They laughed, they sung, they danced, they played at cards, they acted comedies; but in the midst of this careless gayety they respected themselves, and were respected by the men: the invisible line between liberty and licentiousness was never transgressed by a gesture, a word, or a look, and their virgin chastity was never sullied by the breath of scandal or suspicion. After tasting the luxury of England and Paris, I could not have returned with patience to the table and table-cloth of Madame Pavilliard, nor was her husband offended that I now entered myself as a *pensionaire*, or boarder, in the more elegant house of Mr. de Mescry, which may be entitled to a short remembrance, as it has stood above twenty years, perhaps, without a paralel in Europe. The house in which we lodged was spacious and convenient, in the best street, and commanding from behind a noble prospect over the country and the lake. Our table was served with neatness and plenty ; the boarders were numerous; we had the liberty of inviting any guests at a stated price; and in the summer the scene was occasionally transferred to a pleasant Villa about a league from Lausanne. The characters of the master and mistress were happily suited to each other and to their situation. At the age of seventy-five, Madame de Mesery, who has survived her husband, is still a graceful, I had almost said a handsome, woman : she was alike qualified to preside in her kitchen and her drawing-room; and such was the equal propriety of her conduct, that, of two or three hundred foreigners, none ever failed in respect, none could complain of her neglect, and none could ever boast of her favour. Mesery himself, of the noble family of de Crousaz, was a man of the World, a jovial companion, whose easy manners and natural sallies maintained the chearfulness of his house. His wit could laugh at his own ignorance : he disguised, by an air of profusion, a strict attention to his interest; and in [the exercise of a mean trade] he appeared like a nobleman who spent his fortune and entertained his friends. In this agreable family I resided near eleven months (May 1763—April 1764) ; [but the habits of the militia and the example of my countrymen betrayed me into some riotous acts of intemperance, and before my departure I had deservedly forfeited the public opinion which had been acquired by the virtues of my better days.] Yet in this second visit to Lausanne, among a crowd of my English companions, I knew and esteemed Mr. Holroyd [late Captain in the Royal

Forresters], and our mutual attachment was renewed and fortified in the subsequent stages of our Italian journey. Our lives are in the power of chance, and a slight variation, on either side, in time or place, might have deprived me of a friend whose activity in the ardour of youth was always prompted by a benevolent heart, and directed by a strong understanding.

If my studies at Paris had been confined to the study of the World, three or four months would not have been unprofitably spent. My visits, however superficial, to the cabinet of medals and the public libraries opened a new field of enquiry; and the view of so many Manuscripts of different ages and characters induced me to consult the two great Benedictine Works, the *Diplomatica* of Mabillon, and the *Palæographia* of Montfaucon. I studied the theory without attaining the practise of the art; nor should I complain of the intricacy of Greek abbreviations and Gothic alphabets, since every day, in a familiar language, I am at a loss to decypher the Hieroglyphics of a female note. In a tranquil scene, which revived the memory of my first studies, idleness would have been less pardonable: the public libraries of Lausanne and Geneva liberally supplied me with books, and if many hours were lost in dissipation, many more were employed in litterary labour. In the country, Horace and Virgil, Juvenal and Ovid, were my assiduous companions; but in town I formed and executed a plan of study for the use of my Transalpine expedition: the topography of old Rome, the ancient Geography of Italy, and the science of medals. 1. I diligently read, almost always with my pen in my hand, the elaborate treatises of Nardini, Donatus, etc., which fill the

fourth Volume of the Roman Antiquities of Grævius.
2. I next undertook and finished the *Italia Antiqua*
of Cluverius, a learned native of Prussia, who had
measured, on foot, every spot, and has compiled and
digested every passage of the ancient writers.   These
passages in Greek or Latin I perused in the text of
Cluverius, in two folio Volumes; but I separately read
the descriptions of Italy by Strabo, Pliny, and Pom-
ponius Mela, the Catalogues of the Epic poets, the Itine-
raries of Wesseling's Antoninus, and the coasting
Voyage of Rutilius Numatianus; and I studied two
kindred subjects in the Mesures Itineraires of d'Anville
and the copious work of Bergier, *Histoire des grands
Chemins de l'Empire Romain.*   From these materials I
formed a table of roads and distances reduced to our
English measure; filled a folio commonplace-book with
my collections and remarks on the Geography of Italy,
and inserted in my journal many long and learned notes
on the *Insulæ* and populousness of Rome, the Social War,
the passage of the Alps by Hannibal, etc. 3. After
glancing my eye over Addison's agreable Dialogues,
I more seriously read the great work of Ezechiel
Spanheim, de præstantiâ et usû Numismatum, and
applied with him the medals of the Kings and Emperors,
the families and colonies, to the illustration of ancient
history.   And thus was I armed for my Italian journey.

MEMOIRS OF THE LIFE AND WRITINGS OF EDWARD GIBBON.*

[I was born the twenty-seventh of April, O.S. (the eighth of May, N.S.), in the year one thousand seven hundred and thirty-seven, the first child of the marriage of Edward Gibbon, Esqre, and of Judith Porten, his first wife. The place of my nativity is Putney, in the county of Surry, a pleasant village on the banks of the Thames, about four miles from London. My lot in this World might have been that of a savage, a slave, or a peasant; and I must applaud the felicity of my fate, which has cast my birth in an age of science and Philosophy, in a free and civilized country, in a family of honourable rank, and decently endowed with the gifts of fortune.

Of this family, the primitive seat was in the county of Kent. It is proved by authentic records that, as early as the year 1326, the Gibbons were possessed of lands in the parish of Rolvenden, and it should seem that their ancient patrimony, without much encrease or diminution, is still in the hands of the elder branch. They are distinguished by the title of *Esquire*, at a time when

---

* Memoir C (written about 1789); from his birth till 1772, when, two years after his father's death, he let the farm of Buriton, and removed to London.

it was less promiscuously bestowed; and I continue to bear the armorial coat, the ancient symbol of their gentility: "A Lyon, rampant, gardant, between three scallop-shells, Argent on a field Azure." The use of these arms in the reign of Queen Elizabeth is attested by the whimsical revenge of Edmond Gibbon, Esqre. Instead of the three scallop-shells, he substituted, during his own life, three Ogresses; and these female monsters denoted his three kinswomen, against whom he had maintained a lawsuit for the patronage of the free school of Benenden, a foundation of their common ancestors. In the beginning of the seventeenth century, a younger branch of the Gibbons, from which I descend, migrated from the country to the city, from a rural to a commercial life; nor am I ashamed of their mercantile profession, which has long since been ennobled by the example of our most ancient gentry and the good sense of the English nation. It would be as easy as it might be tedious to recapitulate our various inter-marriages, both in Kent and in London, with the most respectable families—the Hextalls, the Ellenbrigs, the Calverleys, the Philips of Tenterden, the Berkleys of Beauston, the Whetnalls of East Peckham and of Cheshire, the Edgars of Suffolk, and the Cromers of Surry, whose progenitor, William Cromer (in the years 1413 and 1424), was twice Lord Mayor of the City of London. By the females I draw my pedigree from the Lord Say and Seale, who, under the reign of Henry the sixth, was Lord High Treasurer of England. That Minister fell a victim to the blind rage of Jack Cade and his Kentish insurgents; and if Shakespeare be a faithful historian, a man of letters may be proud of his descent from the patron and martyr of learning. But in the male line I can discover only two persons of my name, who have left any memorial of themselves more conspicuous than a gravestone in a parish church. i. In the year 1340, John Gibbon was *Marmorarius*, or Architect (the office of an esquire in the service of Edward the Third). He built Queensborough castle, an important fortress for the defence of the Kingdom; and the Royal grant of the toll of the passage between Sandwich and Stonar, in the Isle of Thanet, is not the reward of a vulgar Mechanick. ii. Another John Gibbon, the brother, as it should appear, of my great-grandfather Matthew, has exhibited the proofs of his lively wit and extensive reading, which are not, indeed, without some alloy of prejudice, enthusiasm, and vanity; since he considered Heraldry as the first of arts, and himself as the first of Heralds. He was born in the year 1629, and died in a very advanced age, after exercising near fifty years the office of Bluemantle Poursuivant at arms in the Heralds' College. In his youth he had been a soldier and a traveller; at a war-dance of the Indians of Virginia he recognized the colours and symbols of his art, which were emblazoned on their naked bodies, and the reader will smile at his conclusion "that Heraldry is ingrafted naturally into the sense of human race." In the year 1682 he published at London his *Introductio ad Latinam Blazoniam*, in 12°, an English text interspersed with Latin sentences and verses of his own composition; and in this small but elaborate treatise he claims the invention of expressing the terms of Heraldry in a classical idiom. But this domestic record, which illustrates the antiquity of his name and blood, was lost in his own family till, about three years ago, a singular chance transmitted a copy of his work from Wolfenbuttel in Germany to Lausanne in Switzerland. The science of hereditary distinctions is favourable to Monarchy, and Blue-mantle, like the rest of his kindred, was a zealous Tory both in Church and State. Many of his letters are still preserved in the college; nor will it be thought singular that the same mind should be addicted to the congenial studies of Heraldry and Astrology.

My grandfather, Edward Gibbon, was of some note in the commercial and even the political World. In the four last years of Queen Anne (1710–1714) he exercised the office of one of the Commissioners of the Customs; the Ministers often consulted him on subjects of trade and finances, which he understood, according to the testimony of Lord Bolingbroke, as deeply as any man in England. Before he was chosen a director of the South Sea Company (in 1716), he had acquired a fortune of sixty thousand pounds; but, in the calamitous year twenty, he suffered with his brethren by an arbitrary bill of pains and penalties, against which they were not allowed to be heard by their council. Of the merits and mischiefs of the South Sea Scheme, I am neither a competent nor a disinterested judge; but if the public ruin was contrived by the directors, I fear that my grandfather's abilities will not leave him the Apology of ignorance or error. Whatever might be his guilt, it could neither be proved by evidence nor punished by law; the proceedings of the house of commons were stained with personal and party malice, and few will be found, in these days of moderation, to applaud an act of parliamentary tyranny which could not be excused by the defence of the national safety. The directors were compelled to deliver on oath the value of their respective estates, and the poor allowances which were left for their support were determined, not by a judicial enquiry, but by hasty and passionate votes on the character and conduct of each individual. Some part of my grandfather's fortune was legally and, perhaps, honestly secured by prævious settlements and conveyances: he acknowledged the ample sum of one hundred and six thousand five hundred and forty-three pounds five shillings and sixpence; and when the question was put whether fifteen or ten thousand pounds should be assigned to Mr. Gibbon, it was carried, without a division, for the smaller allowance. His conscience had sullenly submitted to the new oaths of allegiance; but the avowal of Tory and the suspicion of Jacobite principles exposed him to the resentment of a Whig majority. They could not, however, strip him of his credit and experience; he rose with fresh vigour from his fall, and the wealth of which he died possessed could not be inferior to the property of which he had been so unjustly despoiled. Besides his landed estates in Buckinghamshire and Hampshire, besides large sums either employed in trade or vested in the funds, he had purchased a spacious house and gardens at Putney, in Surrey, where he lived with decent hospitality and a respectable character. A stern, sensible countenance is impressed on his portraits: as the wisest, the richest, or the oldest, he became the oracle of his neighbours; and while he ruled his family with a rod of iron, he was approached with awe by those who might have smiled at his frowns.

His wife, my grandmother, was of the name of Acton, an ancient and honourable name in Shropshire: his sister married Sir Whitmore Acton, the head of the family, and father of Sir Richard, the present Baronet. A younger branch has settled abroad, and it is with pleasure that I acknowledge for my cousin the Chevalier or General Acton, the favourite Minister of the King of the two Sicilies.

My grandfather died about Christmas, 1736, and his last will enriched, at the expence of his only son, his two daughters, Catherine and Hester. The former married Captain Edward Elliston, in the service of the East India Company; and Catherine, their only daughter, is now Lady Eliot. Mrs. Hester Gibbon, who has preferred a life of celibacy and devotion, still inhabits, at the age of eighty-five, a small hermitage in Northampton-shire. Her spiritual guide and faithful companion was Mr. William Law, a Nonjuror, a Wit, and a Saint, who seems to have believed all that he professed, and to have practised all that he enjoyned. His controversial tracts, however lively or acute, are buried with those of his antagonists; but his invective against the Stage is sometimes quoted for the extravagance of his zeal, and his *Serious Call* is a powerful and popular book of devotion. Under the names of Flavia and Miranda he has described my two aunts, the Heathen and the Christian sister.

My father, Edward Gibbon, born in the year 1707, was introduced into the World with the advantage of Academical institution, foreign travel, and a seat in Parliament; but had he been confined, like his ancestors, to a mercantile counter, his life might have been happier, and

my situation would be more opulent. Under the tuition
of Mr. William Law, he was removed from Westminster
School to Emanuel College at Cambridge, and his education was finished by a tour to Paris and the provinces of
France. On his return home he was chosen to serve in
Parliament for the borough of Petersfield (in 1734), and
at the next general election (in 1741) he stood a warm
and successful contest for the town of Southampton. In
the great opposition to Sir Robert Walpole, he appeared
a strenuous though a silent patriot. With the Tories he
gave many a vote, with them he drank many a bottle;
and the interest of his party engaged him to assume for
a while an Alderman's gown in the city of London. After
his father's death he moved with ease and spirit in the
polite circles of the metropolis; in the old club at
White's he had the advantage of losing his money in the
best company, and the expence of his house and equipage
was regulated by the law of fashion rather than by that
of œconomy. His early connection with my mother was
formed by the intercourse of the neighbouring families:
friendship was kindled into love, and love was justified
by esteem.

> " Notitiam primosque gradus vicinia fecit:
>   Tempore crevit amor; tædæ quoque jure coissent,
>   Sed vetuere patres: quod non potuere vetare
>   Ex æquo captis ardebant mentibus ambo."

Such is the beginning of a love tale at Babylon or at
Putney; but in the case of my parents the resistance was
not equal on both sides, and Mr. James Porten, a merchant
of slender fortune and sinking credit, would have gladly
accepted an alliance which could be displeasing only to
his more wealthy and ambitious neighbour. The harsh

commands of my grandfather were eluded by the secret correspondence and stolen interviews of the lovers, and he at length pronounced a reluctant and ungracious consent to their union. His aversion was subdued by the soft dexterity of my mother; and, had he lived to embrace her first child, it is probable that a will which had been signed in anger would have been cancelled by affection. Her beauty was adorned with the solid and pleasing accomplishments of the mind; and my father's constancy was rewarded by ten years of domestic felicity. It could be interrupted only by her untimely death, after she had given him six sons and one daughter, all of whom, except myself, died in their infancy. I was too young to know the value or to feel the loss of my mother; but the image of my father's grief is deeply imprinted in my memory, and his long mourning has been celebrated by Mr. Mallet in an elegant poem on the anniversary of his own nuptials—

> " But first a pensive love forlorn,
>   Who three long weeping years has borne
>   His torch revers'd, and all around,
>   Where once it flam'd with cypress bound,
>   Sent off, to call a neighbouring friend,
>   On whom the mournful train attend :
>   And bid him, this one day at least,
>   For such a pair, at such a feast,
>   Strip off the sable veil, and wear
>   His once gay look and happier air."

But the sorrowful widower soon withdrew from the gay and busy scenes of the World, and his prudent retreat from London and Putney to his farm at Buriton, in Hampshire, was ennobled by the pious motive of conjugal affliction.

According to the calculations of Monsieur de Buffon,

half the number of new-born children are cut off before they have compleated their eighth year; and the chances that I should not live to compose this narrative were, at the time of my birth, in the proportion of three to one. Such may be the general probabilities of human life; but the ordinary dangers of childhood were multiplied far beyond this measure by my personal infirmities. So little hope did my parents entertain, that, after bestowing at my baptism the favourite appellation of Edward, they provided a substitute, in case of my departure, by successively joyning the same addition to the Christian names of my younger brothers. A numerous acquaintance and encreasing family engrossed the time, and divided the attention of Mrs. Gibbon: her heart was solely devoted to her husband; and my infancy might have been fatally neglected, had I not found a second mother in her maiden sister, Mrs. Catherine Porten, at whose name I feel a tear of gratitude trickling down my cheek. My poor aunt has often told me, with tears in her eyes, how nearly I was starved by a nurse who had lost her milk, and how long she trembled lest my crazy frame, which is now of the common shape, should be for ever crooked and deformed. From one dangerous malady, the small-pox, I was indeed rescued by the practise of inoculation, which had been lately introduced into England, and was still opposed by Theological, medical, and even political prejudice. But it is only against the small-pox that a preservative has been found; and I could recapitulate from memory or hearsay almost every disease which afflicted my tender years—feavers and lethargies, a fistula in the eye, a tendency to a consumptive and to a dropsical habit, a contraction of the nerves, with a variety of nameless disorders. And, as if the plagues of nature were not sufficient without the concurrence of accident, I was once bit by a dog most vehemently suspected of madness. From Sloane and Mead to Ward and the Chevalier Taylor, every practitioner, both regular and empiric, was alternately summoned; the fees of Doctors were swelled by the bills of Apothecaries and Surgeons; there was a time when I swallowed almost as much physic as food, and my body is still marked with the scars of bleedings, issues, and caustics. From these ills and from these remedies I have wonderfully escaped. Instead of growing with my growth and strengthening with my strength, my complaints, as I approached the age of puberty, have insensibly vanished. I have never known the insolence of active and vigorous health; but my constitution has gradually ripened to a sound and temperate maturity, and since the age of fifteen I have seldom required the serious advice of a physician. Of my bodily state thus much may suffice. Such objects can only be interesting to the reader as far as they have influenced the choice or the studies of a litterary life; nor shall I imitate the example of Montagne, who in his Essays, and more especially in his travels, has filled whole pages with the changes of disease and the operations of medecine.

In the first period of life the use of speech and the rudiments of reading and writing soon distinguished me from a brute and a savage. About the seventh year of my age (1744) I was placed under the care of a domestic tutor, Mr. John Kirkby, a learned and pious Nonjuror. He is the author of an English grammar, which he gratefully dedicated to my father (November, 1745); and of the life of Automathes (London, 1745), a moral romance, which blends the Arabian fable of a self-taught philosopher with the English adventures of Robinson Crusoe. Mr. Kirkby appears to have been qualified for the task of education, but his public refusal to name King George in the prayers of the Church obliged my father to dismiss him before I could imbibe either science or prejudice from his lessons. In a lucid interval of health, when I was eight years of age, I was removed from the indulgence and luxury of a private family to the tumult, the discipline, and the hardships of a school at Kingston of about seventy boys. Under the rod of Dr. Woodson I learned the rules of the Latin grammar; and not many years ago I was master of the dirty and dog's-eared copies of Cornelius Nepos, Phædrus, and Ovid's Epistles, which I painfully construed and darkly understood. From Kingston School I was recalled by frequent relapses of illness, and finally by my mother's death (1747): my grandfather, Mr. James Porten, became a bankrupt; and his daughter, my aunt Catherine, scorning a life of dependence, preferred the humble industry of keeping a boarding-house in College Street, near Westminster school. This singular union of private care and public institution tempted my father, and I continued near two years (from Christmas, 1748, to August, 1750) an effective or nominal disciple of the great seminary of the English Youth. Under the discipline of Dr. Nichols, or rather of his inferior ushers, I was permitted to crawl as high as the third form: but my progress was checked by various and repeated malady; and, as I was taken away in the beginning of my fourteenth year, I could not be indebted to Westminster School for the Classical learning, the knowledge of the World, and the early friendships, which are celebrated as the peculiar merits of this mode of education. During the two following years (1750–1752) I was moved by my father from place to place, and I spent many months at Bath and at Winchester for the benefit of the waters or of medical advice; the prosecution of my studies was often interdicted, nor could I derive much improvement from the rare and occasional lessons of such teachers as could be procured on the spot. In the months of February and March, 1751, I resided at Esher, in Surrey, in the house of the Reverend Mr. Philip Francis; and] the translator of Horace might have taught me to relish the Latin poets, had not my friends discovered in a few weeks that he preferred the pleasures of London to the instruction of his pupils. [At length, as my puerile disorders appeared to abate, my father was persuaded to place me, without sufficient preparation, at Magdalen College, in the University of Oxford, where I was matriculated as a Gentleman-Commoner on the third of April, 1752, before I had compleated the fifteenth year of my age.

The defects of my scholastic education have not perhaps been perfectly supplied by the voluntary labours of my riper years; but, with the encrease of my strength and stature, the faculties of the mind were gradually expanded, and I soon discovered the spirit of enquiry and the love of books to which I owe the happiness of my life. This early taste was encouraged and cultivated by my aunt, Mrs. Catherine Porten, who was endowed with a sound understanding and a competent share of English litterature. My long vacations from Kingston and Westminster school were chiefly spent in her house. She became the mother of my mind as well as of my health : all distance was banished between us ; we freely conversed on the most familiar and abstruse topics, and it was her delight and reward to applaud the shoots of my childish fancy. The Arabian nights entertainments, and the English translation of the Iliad and the Odyssey, are the two first books of which I retain a distinct and pleasing idea. My imagination was enchanted with the perpetual mixture of supernatural and human agents : the harmonious verses of Pope fixed themselves in my memory ; and before I was ten years old I disputed with my aunt about the story of the marvellous lamp, and the characters of Achilles and Ulysses. Books of fiction were my first and favourite amusement ; but in the nine months (from March to December, 1748) between my grandfather Porten's absconding and the sale of his effects, his study-door was unlocked : I glanced my eye over the shelves, and, as often as a title or subject allured my curiosity, I presumed to open the volume, without any just measure of the relative powers of the writer and the reader. My judgement was not sufficiently formed to estimate the value or to regret the loss of the four succeeding years from my first introduction to Westminster till my settlement in Magdalen College. Instead of repining at my long and frequent confinement to the chamber and the couch, I secretly rejoyced in the infirmities which delivered me from the exercises of the school and the society of my equals. As often as I was exempt from pain and danger, reading—free desultory reading—was the occupation and comfort of my solitary hours ; and my father's acquaintance, who visited the child, were astonished at finding him surrounded with an heap of folios, of whose names *they* were ignorant, and on whose contents *he* could pertinently descant. Without the discipline of a master or the advice of a friend, the early bent of my mind was directed to histories of all ages and nations, and to Voyages and travels into all the countries of the globe. The circulating libraries of London and Bath were greedily ransacked; and I devoured the translations of the Greek and Latin Authors, from Littlebury's lame Herodotus, and Spelman's valuable Xenophon, to Gordon's pompous Tacitus, and a ragged Procopius of the beginning of the last century. My curiosity was stimulated by the remoteness of time and place; and while I had a superficial knowledge of the modern transactions of Europe, I was familiarly conversant with the Arabian Caliphs, the Khans of Tartary, the out-lying Empires (as Sir William Temple styles them) of China and Peru, and the dark and doubtful Dynasties of Assyria and Egypt. Such vague multifarious reading could neither teach me to think nor to act, and the only principle which darted some rays of light into the rude and undigested Chaos was the instinctive love and accurate study of ancient Geography and Chronology. I arrived at Oxford with a stock of Erudition that might have puzzled a' Doctor, and a degree of ignorance of which a school-boy would have been ashamed. My first litterary attempts were a new plan of Chronological tables, the paralel lives of Aurelian and Selim, and a critical enquiry into the age of Sesostris.

The stately buildings of Oxford, and especially of Magdalen College, excite the admiration of a stranger; the apparent decencies of habit and order solicit his reverence: and the cloysters, the walks, and the libraries are appropriated to the use of a studious and contemplative life. I was delighted with the novelty of the scene; my dress and rank of a gentleman-commoner, a competent allowance, and a spacious apartment elated my childish vanity with the idea of manly independence. But I must blush for myself or for my teachers, when I declare that, of all the years of my life, the fourteen months which I spent at Oxford were most compleatly lost for every purpose of improvement; and the University will not be ambitious of a son who disclaims all sense of filial piety and gratitude. I am willing to make every reasonable abatement for my tender age, insufficient preparation, and short residence. Yet I must confess the presumptuous belief that neither my temper nor my talents were averse to the lessons of science; that the discipline of well-regulated studies might have inflamed the ardour and restrained the wanderings of youth; and that some share of reproach will adhere to the Academical institution which could damp every spark of industry in a curious and active mind. A master of moral and political wisdom has observed that "in the University of Oxford the greater part of the public professors, for these many years past, have given up altogether even the pretence of teaching" (Riches of nations, Vol. ii. p. 343); and this melancholy truth, which sounds almost incredible in foreign Academies, is not disproved by the rare and honourable exceptions of Blackstone and Lowth. The silence of the professors is imperfectly supplied by the College tutors who instruct, or promise to instruct, their pupils in language and science. My first tutor, Dr. Waldegrave, was one of the best of the tribe; we read, in two or three months, two

or three comedies of Terence; he gave me every morning
an hour at his chambers; but my absence was excused
on the slightest pretence, and I soon discovered that
my attendance and my apologies were equally superfluous. His successor, Dr. Winchester, never deserved
the annual stipend of twenty Guineas by a single word
of instruction, of enquiry, or of advice. I compliment
our English *Fellows* when I compare them to the Monks
of a Benedictine Abbey. Instead of animating the
under-graduates by the example of diligence, they
enjoyed in tranquil indolence the benefactions of the
founder, and their slumbers were seldom disturbed by
the labour of writing, of reading, or thinking. Their
discourse in the common room, to which I was sometimes
admitted, stagnated in the narrow circle of college
business and Tory politicks; their deep and dull compotations left them no right to censure the warmer
intemperance of youth; and their constitutional toasts
were not expressive of the most sincere loyalty to the
house of Hanover. I have heard that Latin declamations were formerly pronounced by the Gentlemen-commoners in the hall; but in my time the silk gown and
velvet cap were sacred from all duty of exercise or
examination. Idleness and inexperience soon led me
into some disorders of late hours, bad company, and
improper expence: my debts might be secret, my
absence was notorious; a tour into Buckinghamshire,
an excursion to Bath, four excursions to London, were
costly and dangerous follies; and my childish years
might have justified a more than ordinary restraint.
Yet I eloped from Oxford, I returned; I again eloped
in a few days; as if I had been an independent stranger

in an hired lodging, without once hearing the voice of admonition or once feeling the hand of controul. Such was my Academical life. I shall rejoyce to hear that any reformation has been since introduced into the University or the College.

In religious matters the University of Oxford united the extremes of bigotry and indifference. As I had not compleated, at the time of my matriculation, the fifteenth year of my age, I was excused from the legal obligation of subscribing the thirty-nine articles of the Church of England; but my Academical teachers were as careless of spiritual as of litterary instruction, and I groped my way to the chappel and the communion-table by the dim light of my catechism. Religion had often been the theme of my infant curiosity; the shrewdness of my questions and objections had sometimes puzzled my pious aunt; nor had the dull atmosphere of Oxford compleatly broken the elasticity of my mind. Some Popish books unluckily fell into my hands: I was bewildered in the maze of controversy, and my understanding was oppressed by their specious arguments, till I believed that I believed in the stupendous mysteries and infallible authority of the Catholic Church. As the University has suffered some reproach on my account, truth and justice oblige me to declare that such books were the sole instruments of my conversion, and that I never saw any emissary of Rome within the precincts of Oxford. But no sooner had I resolved to save my soul at the expence of my fortune, than I eloped to London and addressed myself to Mr. Lewis a Popish bookseller in Russel street, who introduced me to a priest, perhaps a Jesuit, of his acquaintance.

That zealous missionary exposed his life to the rigour of our intolerant laws; and on the eighth of June, 1753, I solemnly, though privately, abjured at his feet the errors of heresy. My father was neither a philosopher nor a bigot, but he deplored the loss of an only son; and his good sense could not understand or excuse my strange departure from the Religion of my Country. The gates of Oxford were shut against my return; no place in England was thought safe and convenient; and by the advice of his friends, the Protestant city of Lausanne in Switzerland was chosen for my exile and education. This plan, which was immediately executed, has been attended with the most salutary effects; but I have since reflected with surprize, that the neighbouring priests of France and Savoy, who must have corresponded with their English brethren, should have made no attempts, by letters or messages, to rescue me from the hands of the heretics, or at least to confirm my zeal and constancy in the profession of the faith. My pride was perhaps offended by their neglect; the Calvinist Minister in whose house I lived acquired my confidence and softened my prejudices; the fervour of enthusiasm subsided; and my growing reason was gradually invigorated by age, study, and liberal conversation. After an obstinate dispute and a serious enquiry, I sincerely confessed that the doctrine and worship of the Protestants are most agreable to sense and scripture, and my father rejoyced to hear that on Christmas Day, 1754, I received the sacrament in the Cathedral of Lausanne. In either step, of my error and my repentance, I honestly obeyed the dictates of conscience, and should I be taxed with levity and rashness,

I can plead the respectable examples of Chillingworth
and Bayle. At a riper age, their acute understandings
were deceived by the same arguments, and their spirit,
like my own, emerged from the servitude of superstition.

After passing the sea for the first time between Dover
and Calais, I followed the direct road through Picardy,
Champagne, and Franchecomté, and arrived, on the 30th
of June, 1753, at Lausanne, where my companion, Mr.
Frey, delivered his charge into the house and the hands
of Mr. Pavillard, a Calvinist minister, to whose tuition I
was entrusted. I beheld with surprize and aversion the
first aspect of a place in which I have spent the five
most interesting years of my youth, which I afterwards
freely revisited, and which I have finally chosen as the
most grateful retreat for the decline of life. Ignorant
of the language and manners, I felt myself suddenly
deprived of the use of hearing and speech, and condemned to a solitary and hopeless exile in a new World.
My father's indignation had dismissed my servant, stinted
my expence, and reduced me from the liberty of a man
to the dependance of a schoolboy. My gay apartments
in Magdalen College were exchanged for a small ill-
furnished room in the most dreary street of an unhandsome town; and, on the approach of winter, the dull
invisible heat of a stove succeeded to the chearful blaze
of a companionable fire. Our coarse and scanty meals,
which were served at noon and at seven in the evening,
could neither provoke nor satisfy the appetite; and more
than one sense was offended by the appearance of the
table, as it was covered eight successive days with
the same linnen. The vulgar and sordid œconomy of the
house in which I lodged and boarded may be chiefly

ascribed to the temper of Madame Pavillard, the minister's wife: I now can speak of her without resentment; but, in sober truth, she was ugly, dirty, proud, ill-natured, and covetous. Her husband, Mr. Pavillard, deserves a far different character; he is entitled to my gratitude; but gratitude must not persuade me that the true author of my education was himself eminent for Genius or learning. Even the real value of his abilities was under-rated in the public opinion; the soft credulity of his virtue exposed him to frequent imposition, and the want of eloquence and memory in the pulpit disqualified him for the most popular duty of his office. But he was endowed with a clear head and a warm heart; his innate benevolence had asswaged the proud prejudice of a Churchman, and his opinions were rational because his temper was moderate. In the course of his Academical studies he had acquired a just, though superficial knowledge; by long practise he was skilled in the arts of teaching; and he laboured with assiduous patience to discern the character, to gain the confidence, and to open the mind of his English disciple. As soon as we began to understand each other, he tempted me from the blind and undistinguishing love of reading into a path of useful instruction. I consented with pleasure that a portion of the morning hours should be consecrated to the perusal of the French and Latin Classics, to the principles of logic, and to a series of the modern history and geography of Europe; and at each step I felt myself invigorated by the practise and success of methodical application. His prudence repressed and dissembled some youthful sallies; and as soon as I was confirmed in the habits of industry and temperance, he gave the reins into my own hands. His favourable report of my behaviour and progress gradually obtained some latitude of action and expence, and he wished to alleviate the hardships of my lodging and entertainment. These hardships were made tolerable by custom, and I was insensibly reconciled to the place, to the people, and to myself. The lively and flexible character of youth forgets the past, enjoys the present, and anticipates the future.

Every man who rises above the common level has received two educations: the first from his teachers; the second, more personal and important, from himself. He will not, like the fanatics of the last age, define the moment of grace; but he cannot forget the æra of his life in which his mind has expanded to its proper form and dimensions. My worthy tutor had the good sense and modesty to discern how far he could be useful; as soon as he felt that I advanced beyond his speed and measure, he left me to the impulse of my Genius; and the hours of lecture were lost in the voluntary labours of the morning, and often of the whole day. The desire of prolonging my time gradually confirmed the habit of early rising, to which I have always adhered with some regard to seasons and situations; but it is happy for my eyes and health that my temperate ardour has never been seduced to trespass on the hours of the night. During the three last years of my residence at Lausanne, from the spring of 1755 to the spring of 1758, I may assume the merit of spontaneous and solid industry; the three interesting languages, the French, the Latin, and the Greek, were the first objects of my application, and I always associated the studies of Philosophy with those of litterature.

In the Pays de Vaud, of which Lausanne is the

principal town, the French language is used with less corruption than in many of the provinces of France. In Pavillard's family I was compelled to listen, to ask, and to converse, and in a few months I was astonished at my rapid success. My pronunciation was formed by the repetition of the same sounds; my vocabulary was multiplied; a free and elegant use of the idiom was obtained by practise; propriety and correctness were acquired by labour; and before I left Switzerland, French, in which I naturally thought, was more familiar than English to my ear, my tongue, and my pen. A dead language can only be studied in the Closet; but in my French and Latin versions the two dialects were made subservient to each other by a method which I would strenuously recommend to the imitation of every student. In some Classic of approved purity—in Tully or Vertot, for instance—I chose some pages which I translated into the opposite language. My translation I threw aside till the words and sentences were obliterated from my memory. I then returned it into the primitive idiom, critically compared the defects of my copy with the native graces of the original, and persevered in this useful labour till, after filling several volumes with these double versions, I had attained the theory and practise of French and Latin composition. The perusal of the Roman Classics was at once my exercise and reward. Dr. Middleton's history, which I then esteemed above its value, directed me to the writings of Cicero, and I read with application and pleasure *all* his Epistles, *all* his orations, and his most valuable treatises of Rhetoric and Philosophy. I tasted the beauties of language, I breathed the spirit of freedom, and I imbibed from his precepts and examples the public and private sense of a man. After finishing the works of Tully, a library of eloquence and reason, I entered on the general study of the Latin Classics, under the four divisions of (1) Historians, (2) Poets, (3) Orators, and (4) Philosophers, from the days of Plautus and Sallust to the decline of the language and Empire of Rome; and this plan, in the last twenty-seven months of my residence at Lausanne (January, 1756—April, 1758), I nearly accomplished. Nor was this review, however rapid, either hasty or superficial. I indulged myself in a second or even a third perusal of the best authors; I never suffered a difficult or corrupt passage to escape me till I had examined it in every light, with my own glasses and those of the most approved commentators: in the ardour of my enquiries I embraced a large scope of critical and historical erudition, and my various abstracts, observations, and Essays were diligently composed in the French language. From I (*sic*) knowledge of the Latin Imitations, I aspired to the Greek Originals, and in the nineteenth year of my age I resolved to supply the defect of my first education. The lessons of Pavillard again contributed to smooth the entrance of the way, and he led me through the Alphabet, the Grammar, and the Gospel, to the utmost limits of his own progress. As soon as my tutor left me to myself, I presumed to open the Iliad, which I already knew in an English dress, and afterwards interpreted by my own labour a large portion of Xenophon and Herodotus. My ardour, destitute of aid and emulation, was insensibly cooled; but at Lausanne I had laid a solid foundation, which enabled me in a more propitious season to prosecute the study of Grecian litterature.

The first text of my philosophical studies, the book which taught me the use and conduct of my understanding, was the Logic of Mr. de Crousaz, a native and Professor of Lausanne, who died about five years before my arrival. His reputation is already faded; but his moderate and methodical writings were useful in their day to form the reason, the taste, and even the style of his countrymen; and he rescued the clergy of the Pays de Vaud from the heavy and intolerant yoke of the theology of Calvin. After I had transfused into my own mind the principles of Crousaz, as soon as I possessed some dexterity in the use of the weapons of arguments, I ventured to engage with his adversary Bayle, and his master Locke, the former of whom may be applied as a spur, and the latter as a bridle to the curiosity of a young philosopher. I carefully meditated the Essay on the Human Understanding, and I freely revolved the most interesting articles of the Critical dictionary. The law of Nature and Nations was taught with some reputation by Professor Vicat; but instead of following his public or private course, I preferred the solitary lessons of *his* masters, and my own reason. Without being disgusted by the pedantry of Grotius or the prolixity of Puffendorf, I investigated in their systems the rights of a man, the duties of a Citizen, the Theory of justice, and the laws of peace and war, which have had some influence on the modern practise of Europe. My fatigues were alleviated by the good sense and learning of their commentator Barbeyrac; but my delight was in the frequent enjoyment of the *Esprit des loix*, an immortal work which was then in the freshness of fame, and which has powerfully agitated the Genius of the Age. In compliance with my father's desire, some time was devoted to the Mathematics; during two successive winters (1757 and 1758) I devoured without much appetite the Elements of Algebra and Geometry, as far as the conic sections of the Marquis de l'Hôpital, and my Professor, Mr. de Traytorrens, was satisfied with my diligence and improvement. From these serious and scientific pursuits I derived a maturity of judgement, a philosophic spirit, of more value than the sciences themselves; and my lighter and more desultory reading was now conducted with taste and discretion. I could extract and digest the nutritive particles of every species of litterary food: a novel has often suggested a train of moral or metaphysical thinking; and it may not be impertinent to recollect that Pascal and Gianone first accustomed me to the use of irony and criticism on subjects of Ecclesiastical gravity. A copious choice of facts and opinions was arranged, according to the precept and method of Mr. Locke, in a folio commonplace-book; the action of the pen will doubtless leave a mark on the memory as well as on the paper, but I much question whether the encrease of knowledge affords a compensation for the waste of time. The languid state of learning in the Academy and town of Lausanne compelled me to seek at a distance more instructive conversation. I solicited and maintained a correspondence of Classic litterature with Messieurs Crevier, Breitinger, and Gesner, three celebrated professors of Paris, Zurich, and Gottingen. I had formed a personal intimacy with the minister, Allamand of Bex, a man of Genius, worthy of a greater theatre. In our letters we debated the darkest and most important questions of Metaphysics; but as I was entangled by prejudice, and he was restrained by prudence, I suspect that he never shewed the true colours of his secret scepticism.

In the exercises of the body, which have been reduced to a polite art, I was less successful than in those of the mind. A skillful fencing-master could never communicate to my arm the dextrous management of a foil or sword ; and once, in a boyish quarrel, my awkwardness was punished by the loss of some drops of blood. My total want of an ear and taste for music disqualified me for the profession of a dancer: I attempted with indifferent grace to walk a minuet, but I have never been able to unravel the mazes of a country dance. The Manage or Riding-house, then flourished under the care of Mr. de Mesery, a Gentleman of Lausanne ; but he could not be proud of such a disciple as myself, and after the fruitless expence and labour of five months, I gladly withdrew from his Equestrian school without an hope of being ever promoted to the use of stirrups or spurs. This unfitness for bodily exercise reconciled me, however, to a sedentary life ; and many precious hours were employed in my closet which at the same age are wasted on horseback by the strenuous idleness of my countrymen. During an active period of five years, from sixteen to twenty-one, I was generally confined to the precincts of Lausanne, as much by my own choice as by my father's command. A month's tour with Pavillard (September 21— October 20, 1755) was a practical lecture on the Geography and governments of Switzerland. Without climbing the mountains or exploring the *Glaciers* (which were not yet famous or fashionable), we travelled slowly in a coach through the principal towns, Neufchâtel, Bienne, Soleurre, Arau, Baden, Zurich, Basil, and Bern, and visited in every place the persons and things best worthy of our attention. At the rich Abbey of Einsidlen, the Swiss Loretto, I viewed with the contempt of a protestant and a philosopher the Idolatrous worship of our Lady of the Hermits; and a French journal of fifteen or sixteen sheets might satisfy my father that neither *my* time nor *his* allowance had been mispent. In the autumn, before my return to England, I was permitted to spend a pleasant and rational month (September, 1757) at Geneva.

My application to books was serious and severe; but my temper was never that of a recluse student, and the Swiss subjects of the Pays de Vaud are educated in the manners as well as in the language of France. As soon as I was able to converse with the natives, I began to find some amusement and improvement in their company: my awkward timidity was emboldened by degrees, and I frequented for the first time assemblies of men and women. In the eyes of a traveller the inhabitants of Lausanne may appear nearly on a level; but in their private life a line of separation is drawn between the noble and the plebeian families, and the prejudice which has been mollified by reason and riches then subsisted in its ancient vigour. But every society was accessible to a young Englishman, and from the humble kindred and acquaintance of the Pavillards I was gradually introduced into more elegant circles. My long residence and decent behaviour naturalized me in the place: in the families of the first rank I was received with kindness and indulgence: my afternoons were filled by frequent and almost daily engagements to numerous or select parties of cards or conversation; and my choice of good company was the best preservative against the ignoble vices and follies of youth. Lausanne is not sufficiently wealthy or populous to support a regular stage; but my love of the French Drama was gratified by a very singular event: a succession of Tragedies and comedies—Zayre, Alzire, l'Enfant prodigue, Zulime, Iphigenie, etc.—was acted on a private theatre by a company of Gentlemen and Ladies, and their great leader, Voltaire himself, declaimed his own verses with the enthusiasm of an author. From the smiles and frowns of a King, the poet had escaped to a land of freedom, and his letters (Correspondance Generale, tom. iv., v.) celebrate with lavish praise the climate, the prospects, and the trouts of the lake, the politeness of the people, the talents of his actors, and the taste of his audience, which he prefers without hesitation to the *parterre* of Paris. I was introduced, without being known, to that extraordinary man, "Virgilium vidi tantum:" he reigned two winters at Lausanne by the double influence of his wit and fortune (in 1757 and 1758), and the Clergy was scandalized by the visible progress of luxury and Deism.

I should be ashamed if the warm season of youth had passed away without any sense of friendship or love; and in the choice of their objects I may applaud the discernment of my head or heart. Mr. George Deyverdun, of Lausanne, was a young Gentleman of high honour and quick feelings, of an elegant taste and a liberal understanding: he became the companion of my studies and pleasures; every idea, every sentiment, was poured into each other's bosom; and our schemes of ambition or retirement always terminated in the prospect of our final and inseparable union. The beauty of Mademoiselle Curchod, the daughter of a country clergyman, was adorned with science and virtue : she listened to the tenderness which she had inspired ; but the romantic hopes of youth and passion were crushed, on my return, by the prejudice or prudence of an English parent. I sighed as a lover, I obeyed as a son ; my wound was insensibly healed by time, absence, and the habits of a new life ; and my cure was accelerated by a faithful report of the tranquillity and chearfulness of the Lady herself. Her equal behaviour under the tryals of indigence and prosperity has displayed the firmness of her character. A citizen of Geneva, a rich banker of Paris, made himself happy by rewarding her merit ; the genius of her husband has raised him to a perilous eminence ; and Madame Necker now divides and alleviates the cares of the first minister of the finances of France.

Whatsoever have been the fruits of my education, they must be ascribed to the fortunate shipwreck which cast me on the shores of the Leman lake. I have sometimes applied to my own fate the verses of Pindar, which remind an Olympic champion that his victory was the consequence of his exile ; and that at home, like a domestic fowl, his days might have rolled away inactive or inglorious.

> . . . ἤτοι καὶ τεά κεν,
> Ἐνδομάχας ἀτ' ἀλέκτωρ,
> Συγγόνω παρ' ἑστία
> Ἀκλεης τιμὰ κατεφυλλοροησε . . .
> Εἰ μη στάσις ἀντιάνειρα
> . . . ἀμερσε πάτρας.
>
> (*Olymp.* xii.)

If my childish revolt against the Religion of my country had not stripped me in time of my Academic gown, the five important years, so liberally improved in the studies and conversation of Lausanne, would have been steeped in port and prejudice among the monks of Oxford. Had the fatigue of idleness compelled me to read, the path of learning would not have been enlightened by a ray of philosophic freedom. I should have grown to manhood ignorant of the life and language of Europe, and my knowledge of the World would have been confined to an English Cloyster. Had I obtained a more early deliverance from the regions of sloth and pedantry, had I been sent abroad with the indulgence which the favour and fortune of my father might have allowed, I should probably have herded with the young travellers of my own nation, and my attainments in language and manners and science would have been such as they usually import from the continent. But my religious error fixed me at Lausanne, in a state of banishment and disgrace: the rigid course of discipline and abstinence to which I was condemned invigorated the constitution of my mind and body; poverty and pride estranged me from my countrymen: I was reduced to seek my amusement in myself and my books; and in the society of the natives, who considered me as their fellow-citizen, I insensibly lost the prejudices of an Englishman. My friends may indeed complain that this foreign education has eradicated the love and preference of my native country; my mother-tongue was grown less familiar, and I had few objects to remember and fewer to regret in the British islands. If I was impatient of my situation, it was rather as a prisoner than as an exile; and I should gladly have accepted a small independent estate on the easy terms of passing my life in Switzerland with the two persons who possessed the different affections of my heart.

At length, in the spring of the year 1758, my father signified his permission and his pleasure that I should immediately return home. The jealousy of war prohibited my passage through France, but I assumed the name and dress of a Swiss Officer in the Dutch service, without sufficient reflection on the danger of a discovery and the guilt of a disguise. I took my leave of Lausanne on the 11th of April, with a mixture of joy and grief, and expressed my sincere resolution of visiting, as a man, the persons and places which had been so dear to my youth. My Journey was slow and pleasant, through the provinces of Franche-Comté, Lorraine, Luxembourg, and Liege. After dropping my two military companions at their garrisons of Maestricht and Bois-le-Duc, I indulged myself in a short visit to the Hague and Rotterdam, embarked at the Brill, and landed in England on the 4th of May, 1758, after an absence of four years, ten months, and fifteen days.

Section II.

At the age of twenty-one I returned as a stranger, with a prejudice rather adverse than favourable to my native country. My aunt, Mrs. Catherine Porten, still kept a boarding-house at Westminster; and the nurse of my infancy, the friend of my youth, was the only person in England of whom I had cherished a tender remembrance, whose kind embraces I was impatient to seek. Of my father's character I had little knowledge; my infancy had seldom been favoured with his smiles. I could not forget the severity of his look and language at our last parting; his letters to Lausanne had been few, brief, and imperious; and in the relation between us, I saw nothing but authority on his side and dependence on mine. About three years before my return from Switzerland he had engaged in a second marriage with Mrs. Dorothea Patton, a lady of forty years of age, of a respectable family and a moderate fortune. This step might be interpreted as an act of his displeasure, and, without knowing her, I was disposed to hate the rival of my mother and the enemy of her son. My favourite Classics might teach me to dread the bowl or dagger of a stepmother. Euripides has observed that a second wife is more cruel than a viper to the children of a former bed, and on the road I had often muttered the line of Virgil—

" Est mihi namque domi pater, est injusta noverca."

But my fears and prejudice were removed by her presence, and this viper appeared to be a woman of polished manners, an excellent understanding, and an amiable character. Her behaviour at our first meeting assured me that the surface would be smooth, and the suspicion of artifice was gradually dispelled by the discovery of her warm and exquisite sensibility. After some reserve on my side, our minds associated in confidence and friendship; and as Mrs. Gibbon had neither children, nor hopes of children of her own, we more easily adopted the tender names and genuine sentiments of mother and of son. By her mediation, perhaps, my father was prepared to receive me as a man and a friend. The rigour of parental discipline has been relaxed by the philosophy and softness of the age, and if he remembered how he had himself trembled in the presence of a stern father, it was only to adopt a more liberal and indulgent mode of behaviour. All constraint was banished on our first interview, and we continued to live on the same terms of easy and equal politeness. He applauded the success of my education; every word and action was expressive of the most cordial affection, and our serene friendship would never have been darkened by a cloud if his fortune had been adequate to his wishes, or if his œconomy had always been proportioned to his fortune. Some years of retirement in Hampshire had allowed him to breathe, but it was only with the legal consent of his son that he could break the fetters of an entail, and alleviate in some degree the weight of his incumbrances. The time of my recall had been so nicely computed that I arrived in London three days before I was of age, and my blind submission to the sacrifice which he required has been justified by the more enlightened sense of duty and prudence. According to the forms and fictions of our law, I levied a fine, I suffered a recovery; the entail was cut off; a sum of ten thousand pounds was raised on mortgage for my father's use, and he acknowledged the obligation by settling on me for life an annuity of three hundred pounds a year. During the seven years (1758–1760, 1765–1770) which I divided between London and Buriton, my ordinary expences were reduced to this moderate stipend; the extraordinaries of the Militia and my travels (1760–1765) were defrayed, the former by my pay of Captain, the latter by a stipulated supply of twelve hundred pounds, and I may claim the singular merit of never having borrowed a shilling during the whole term of my filial dependence. From the fashionable follies of English youth, the vanity of dress, the mischief of play, and the impulse of perpetual

motion, I was saved by temper as well as by œconomy;
and with the private establishment of a lodging, a servant,
and a chair, my amusements were simple, and my appetites moderate. As soon as my purse was emptied by
the unavoidable charges of a town life, I retired without
a murmur to the shelter of domestic hospitality, and all
circulation was suspended for some months; like those
animals who repose in a torpid state, without any occasion
to exhaust or renovate their vital juices.

Of the two years between my return to England and
the embodying of the Hampshire militia (May, 1758—
May, 1760), I passed about ten months in London. The
metropolis affords many amusements, which are open to
all: it is itself a perpetual and astonishing spectacle to
the curious eye; and each taste, every sense, may be
gratified by the variety of objects that will occur in the
long circuit of a morning walk. I assiduously frequented
the Theatres at a very propitious æra, when a constellation of excellent actors, both in tragedy and comedy, was
eclipsed by the meridian brightness of Garrick, in the
maturity of his judgement and the vigour of his performance. The pleasures of a town life, the daily round
from the tavern to the play, from the play to the coffee-
house, from the Coffee-house to the Bagnio, are within
the reach of every man who is regardless of his money,
his health, and his company; nor will I deny that, by
the contagion of example, I was sometimes seduced. The
better habits which I had formed at Lausanne induced
me to seek a more rational and elegant society; but
my search was not easy or successful, and the first tryal
of a capital did not correspond with the gay pictures
of my fancy. I had promised myself the pleasure of

conversing with every man of litterary fame; but our most eminent authors were remote in Scotland, or scattered in the country, or buried in the Universities, or busy in their callings, or unsocial in their tempers, or in a station too high or too low to meet the approaches of a solitary youth. Had the rank and fortune of my parents given them an annual establishment in town, their house would have introduced me to an encreasing circle of their equals; but my father had always delighted in a club of peers or of farmers, for which he was equally qualified; and, after a twelve years' retirement, he was no longer in the memory of the great with whom he had associated. I found myself a foreigner in a vast and unknown city, and at my entrance into life I was reduced to some dull family parties, to some old Tories of the Cocoa-tree, and to some casual connections, such as my taste and esteem would never have selected. The most useful of my father's friends were the Mallets; they entertained me with civility and kindness, at first on his, and afterwards on my own account; and I was soon (if I may use Lord Chesterfield's word) *domesticated* in the family. Mr. Mallet himself, a name among the English poets, is praised by an unforgiving enemy (Dr. Johnson) for the ease and elegance of his conversation; and his wife, what- soever might be her faults, was not deficient in wit or knowledge. By his assistance I was introduced to Lady Hervey, the mother of the present Earl of Bristol, who had established a French house in St. James's place. At an advanced period of life, she was distinguished by her taste and politeness; her dinners were select: every evening her drawing-room was filled by a succession of the best company of both sexes and all nations; nor was

I displeased at her preference and even affectation of the
books, the language, and manners of the Continent. But
my progress in the English World was in general left to
my own efforts, and those efforts were languid and slow.
I was not endowed by Nature or art with those happy
gifts of confidence and address which unlock every door
and every bosom : it would be unreasonable to complain
of the just consequences of my sickly childhood, foreign
education, and reserved disposition; but, amidst the
crowds of London, I often breathed a sigh towards the
society of Lausanne.]

My father's residence in Hampshire, where I have
passed many light, and some heavy hours, was at Buriton,
near Petersfield, one mile from the Portsmouth road, and
at the easy distance of fifty-eight miles from London.
An old mansion, in a state of decay, had been converted
into the fashion and convenience of a modern house, of
which I occupied the most agreable apartment; and if
strangers had nothing to see, the inhabitants had little to
desire. The spot was not happily chosen, at the end of
the village and the bottom of the hill : but the aspect
of the adjacent grounds was various and chearful; the
downs commanded the prospect of the sea, and the long
hanging woods in sight of the house could not perhaps
have been improved by art or expence. My father kept
in his own hands the whole of his estate, and even
rented some additional land; and whatsoever might be
the balance of profit and loss, the farm supplied him
with amusement and plenty. With the produce he
maintained a number of men and horses, which were
multiplied by the intermixture of domestic and rural
servants; and in the intervals of labour, the favourite

team, an handsome set of bays or greys, was harnessed to
the coach. The œconomy of the house was regulated by
the taste and prudence of Mrs. Gibbon, who prided herself
in the elegance of her occasional dinners, and from the
dirty * avarice of Madame Pavillard I was transported
to the neatness and luxury of an English table. Our
immediate neighbourhood was rare and rustic; but from
the verge of our hills, as far as Chichester and Goodwood,
the western district of Sussex was filled with noble seats
and hospitable families, with whom we maintained a
friendly, and might have enjoyed a frequent, intercourse.
But the comforts of my retirement did not depend on
the ordinary pleasures of the country. [The science of
farming could never be adapted to my understanding ;
and, in the command of an ample manor, I valued the
supply of the table rather than the exercise of the field.]
I never handled a gun, I seldom mounted an horse, and
my walks were soon terminated by [some shady bench of
philosophic contemplation. When my father galloped
away on a fleet hunter to meet the Duke of Richmond's
foxhounds, I saw him depart without the wish or idea
of following his footsteps. Yet I was sometimes obliged
to accompany him to the provincial assemblies of races,
assizes, and balls. After the militia business began to
be agitated, many tedious days were consumed at Petersfield, Alton, and Winchester, in our meetings of Justices
and Deputy-Lieutenants. In the contest for Hampshire
in 1759 between Stuart and Legge, we supported the
former candidate with some trouble and expence ; and I
had an opportunity of observing in his train the politics

* " Uncleanly " in Lord Sheffield's edition.

and humours of an English canvass. From these excursions I always returned with pleasure to my home at Buriton: a domestic bond of affection and confidence is the purest blessing of life; and, as my stay was voluntary, I was received and dismissed with smiles.

The love of learning was so deeply implanted in my mind, as an amusement and even as a passion, that it could no longer be eradicated by any change of place or circumstances. In some respects my removal from Switzerland to England was not unfavourable to the progress of my studies. The library at Buriton was my first inheritance and peculiar domain. It] was stuffed with much trash of the last age, with much High Church divinity and politics, which have long since gone to their proper place; but it contained some valuable Editions of the Classics and Fathers, the choice, as it should seem, of Mr. Law, and many English publications of the times had been occasionally added. [The right of alienating or purchasing I was allowed to exercise without much controul or much assistance; my bookseller's bill was a weighty though pleasant article of expence; and the annual sales in London afforded a plentiful feast, at which my litterary hunger was provoked and gratified. The critical review of my library may be reserved for the season of its maturity; after observing in this place that I have never purchased a book from a motive of ostentation, that every volume was read or examined before it was deposited on the shelf; and that I soon adopted the tolerating maxim of the elder Pliny, "Nullum esse librum tam malum, ut non ex aliquâ parte prodesset."

After my library, I must not forget an occasional place of weekly study, the parish Church, which I frequented commonly twice every Sunday, in conformity with the pious or decent custom of the family. I deposited in our pew the octavo Volumes of Grabe's Septuagint, and a Greek Testament of a convenient edition; and in the lessons, Gospels, and Epistles of the morning and evening service, I accompanied the reader in the original text, or the most ancient version of the Bible. Nor was the use of this study confined to words alone : during the psalms, at least, and the sermon I revolved the sense of the chapters which I had read and heard; and the doubts, alas! or objections that invincibly rushed on my mind were almost always multiplied by the learned expositors whom I consulted on my return home. Of these Ecclesiastical meditations few were transcribed, and still fewer have been preserved; but I find among my papers a polite and elaborate reply from Dr. Hurd (now Bishop of Worcester), to whom I had addressed, without my name, a critical disquisition on the sixth Chapter of the book of Daniel. Since my escape from Popery I had humbly acquiesced in the common creed of the Protestant Churches; but in the latter end of the year 1759 the famous treatise of Grotius (de veritate Religionis Christianæ) first engaged me in a regular tryal of the evidence of Christianity. By every possible light that reason and history can afford, I have repeatedly viewed the important subject; nor was it my fault if I said with Montesquieu, "Je lis pour m'edifier mais cette lecture produit souvent en moi un effet tout contraire," since I am conscious to myself that the love of truth and the spirit of freedom directed my search. The most accurate philosophers and the most orthodox Divines will perhaps agree that the belief of miracles and mysteries cannot be supported on the brittle basis, the distant report, of human testimony, and that the faith as well as the virtue of a Christian must be formed and fortified by the inspiration of Grace.

In the pregnant state of a young mind, the ideas which reading and meditation have generated are impatient to deliver themselves on paper. Among the works of my leisure, I had planned and undertaken a more elaborate composition; and the French language was used without affectation, as most easy and familiar to my pen. I was animated by the desire of vindicating a favourite study from the unjust contempt of the French philosophers, who had degraded Scholars or *Erudits* among the lowest mechanics of science. I was ambitious to prove, by my example as well as by my arguments, that all the nobler faculties, as well as the memory, might be employed and displayed in the study of ancient litterature. I had began to select and adorn the various proofs and illustrations which had offered themselves in the perusal of the Classics, and some pages or chapters of my Essay were finished before my departure from Lausanne. The hurry of the journey and the novelty of the English World suspended my application, but the] object was ever before my eyes; and no more than ten days (from the first to the eleventh of July, 1758) were suffered to elapse after my summer establishment at Buriton. My Essay was compleated in about six weeks; and as soon as a fair copy had been transcribed by one of the French prisoners at Petersfield, I looked round for a critic and a judge of my first performance. [An author is seldom content with the doubtful reward of self-approbation; but a youth, ignorant of mankind and of himself, may reasonably] desire to weigh his talents in some scales less partial than his own. [My choice of Dr. Maty was judicious and fortunate. By descent and education he was a Frenchman: the eighteen Volumes (1750-1755) of his *Journal Britannique* are a fair monument of a learned and liberal mind; and in the delicacy of his taste and philosophy, that ingenious physician might be considered as the last disciple of the school of Fontenelle. His answer to the first letter of a stranger was prompt and polite; and after a careful examination, he returned my manuscript with some animadversion and much applause. In the ensuing winter, when I visited my Judge at the British Musæum, we discussed the design and execution in several free and familiar conversations. In a short excursion to Buriton I reviewed my Essay according to his friendly advice: a third was suppressed; a third was added; a third was altered. After marking the date (February 3ᵈ 1759) by a short preface, the Manuscript was deposited in my bureau. I still shrunk from the press with the terrors of virgin modesty, and the nine years of Horace might have slipped away before I could have resolved to encounter the public eye. My hours were agreably spent among the Latin and English classics; and the perfect recovery of my own language was the serious and laudable object of my diligence. By the wise counsel of Mr. Mallet, himself no contemptible writer, I studied, in the prose of Swift and Addison, the purity, the grace, the idiom, of the English style; and my emulation was kindled by the recent histories of Hume and Robertson; far distant as I was from the presumptuous hope that *my* name might one day be ranked with those celebrated names. In my first Essay I had gathered some of the flowers, in my second I would have removed some of the thorns, of litterature. A passage of Livy (xxxviii. 38) involved me in the dry and dark treatises of Greaves, Arbuthnot, Hooper, Bernard, Eisenschmidt, la Barre, Freret, Gronovius, etc., and in my French work (c. xx.) I absurdly send my reader to my own manuscript remarks on the measures, weights, and coins of the ancients. This important subject, an abstruse and technical language, is connected with the Geography, history, and œconomy of Greece and Rome; but my half-finished researches were abruptly terminated by the sound of the Militia drum.]

In the outset of a glorious war the English people had been defended and (*sic*) the aid of German mercenaries. A national Militia has been the cry of every patriot since the Revolution ; and this measure, both in parliament and in the field, was supported by the Country Gentlemen or Tories, who insensibly transferred their loyalty to the house of Hanover. In the act of offering our names and receiving our commissions, as Major and Captain in the Hampshire Regiment (June 12, 1759), we had not supposed that we should be dragged away, my father from his farm, myself from my books, and condemned more than two years and a half (May 10, 1760—December 23, 1762) to a wandering life of military servitude. But a weekly or monthly exercise of thirty thousand provincials would have left them useless and ridiculous ; and after the pretence of an invasion had vanished, the popularity of Mr. Pitt gave a sanction to the illegal step of keeping them till the end of the War under arms, in constant pay and duty, and at a distance from their respective homes. When the king's order for our embodying came down, it was too late to retreat and too soon to repent. The south battalion of the Hampshire militia was a small independent corps of four hundred and seventy-six, officers and men, commanded by Lieutenant-Colonel Sir Thomas Worsley, who, after a prolix and passionate contest, delivered us from the tyranny of the Lord Lieutenant, the Duke of Bolton. My proper station, as first Captain, was at the head of my own, and afterwards of the Grenadier company; but in the absence, or even in the presence, of the two field-Officers, I was entrusted by my friend and my father with the effective labour of dictating the orders and exercising the battalion. With the help of an original journal, I could write the history of my bloodless and inglorious campaigns; but as these events have lost much of their importance in my own eyes, they shall be dispatched in a few words. From Winchester, the first place of assembly (June 4, 1760), we were removed, at our own request, for the benefit of a foreign education. By the arbitrary, and often capricious orders of the War Office, the Battalion successively marched to the pleasant and hospitable Blandford (June 17); to Hilsea barracks, a seat of disease and discord (September 1); to Cranbrook in the Weald of Kent (December 11); to the sea-coast of Dover (December 27); to Winchester camp (June 25, 1761); to the populous and disorderly town of the Devizes (October 23); to Salisbury (February 28, 1762); to our beloved Blandford a second time (March 9); and finally to the fashionable resort of Southampton (June 2), where the colours were fixed till our final dissolution (December 23). On the beach at Dover we had exercised in sight of the Gallic shores; [but the only occasion where we saw the face of an enemy was in our duty at Porchester castle and Sissinghurst, which were occupied by above five thousand Frenchman. These enemies, it is true, were naked, unarmed prisoners: they were relieved by public and private bounty; but their distress exhibited the calamities of War: and their joyous noise the vivacity of the nation.] But the most splendid and useful scene of our life, was a four months encampment on Winchester down, under the command of the Earl of Effingham. Our army consisted of the thirty-fourth Regiment of foot and six Militia corps, [the Wiltshire, Dorsetshire, Berkshire, North and South Glostershire, and South Hampshire, amounting to five thousand men; and the discipline of the Wiltshire claimed a pre-eminence which was not disputed by the regulars themselves.] The consciousness of our defects was stimulated by friendly emulation: we improved our time and opportunities in morning and evening field-days, and in the general reviews the South Hampshire were rather a credit than a disgrace to the line. In our subsequent quarters of the Devizes and Blandford we advanced with a quick step in our military studies; the ballot of the ensuing summer renewed our vigour and youth; and had the Militia subsisted another year, we might have contested the prize with the most perfect of our brethren.

[My first work, the *Essai sur l'etude de la Litterature*, was published in the year 1761, during the service of the Militia. If I had yielded to the impulse of youthful vanity, if I had given my Manuscript to the World, because I was tired of keeping it in my closet, the venial sin might be honestly confessed, and would be easily pardoned. But I can affirm, in truth and conscience, that it was forced from my reluctant hands by the advice and authority of my father. He was himself impatient to enjoy the glory of his son; and he fondly conceived that the success of a Classical performance in the French language might recommend the author to some honourable employment in the approaching congress of Augsburgh, which indeed was refused to the pacific wishes of Europe. After a last revisal I anxiously consulted my two Judges, Mr. Mallet and Dr. Maty : they approved the design and promoted the execution. The præposterous mixture of an English dedication was enjoyned by Mr. Mallet; and he delivered the Manuscript to Becket, a bookseller, who undertook the impression in a small volume in duodecimo, on the easy terms of supplying me with a certain number of copies. Dr. Maty engaged, in my absence,. to correct the sheets ; and it was without my knowledge that he inserted an elegant and flattering Epistle—so prudent, however, that, in case of a defeat, he might excuse his friendly indulgence to a *young English Gentleman.* I received the first copy at Alresford (June 23, 1761) two days before I marched into camp. Some weeks afterwards, on the same ground, I presented my book to the late Duke of York ; and as the Battalion was returning from a field-day, the author, somewhat disfigured with sweat and dust, appeared before his Royal Highness in the cap, dress, and accoutrements of a grenadier. According to my father's and Mallet's directions, my litterary gifts were distributed to several eminent characters in England and France. I had reserved for my friends at Lausanne some tokens of my gratitude and affection ; and from these correspondents I reaped a sure harvest of civility and praise. It is not surprizing that a work, in language and manner so totally foreign, should have been more favourably entertained abroad than at home : I was delighted with the copious extracts, warm applause, and fair predictions of the Journals of Holland and Paris; and a new edition (I believe of Geneva) diffused its fame, or at least its circulation, on the Continent. In Britain it was treated with cold indifference, little read, and speedily forgotten; the bookseller murmured that a small impression was slowly dispersed, and the author (had his feelings been more exquisite) might have wept over the baldness and blunder of his English translation. Fifteen years afterwards (such is the power of a name), the first Volume of my history revived the memory of my Essay on the study of literature : the shops were eagerly searched; and when the book occurs in an auction, the fanciful price is raised from half a crown to a Guinea or thirty shillings. The public curiosity was gratified in some degree by a pyrated Edition at Dublin. But, as I was proprietor of the copy, I denied Becket the permission, which he solicited, of reprinting it; and my denial was the effect of pride rather than modesty. Yet, in a cool, impartial perusal, near thirty years after the first effusion, I am less ashamed than I might have expected of this juvenile treatise. The want of order and perspicuity, the ardour of style and the affectation of wit (Œuvres de Rousseau, tom. xxxiii. p. 88), are the errors of an ambitious youth. But the substance is the fruit of sound though superficial reading and thinking; the spirit is liberal; and my Essay contains the seeds of some ideas, especially on the Polytheism of the ancients, which might deserve the illustrations of a riper judgement. The merit of language still remains, and that merit is singular : the examples of Count Hamilton and the

Chevalier Ramsay are inadequate, and I may esteem myself the first British writer who has aspired to the purity and elegance of a French style.*

In the narrative of my litterary life, the first seven or eight months of the Militia must be thrown aside as an absolute blank. My hours were miserably wasted in the exercises of the field or of the bottle, in the contemptible details and disputes of the Battalion. In the tumultuous hurry of an Inn, a barrack, or a guard-room, I was alike destitute of leisure and of books; but no sooner had we reached the quiet solitude of Dover, than my mind resumed its elasticity, and I can remember the pleasure with which I opened a volume of Tully's philosophical works, and afterwards followed my enquiries into the Critical history of Manicheism, by the moderate and sagacious Beausobre. After this recovery I never relapsed into indolence, and my example might prove that, in the life most adverse to study, some hours may be stolen, some minutes may be snatched. Amidst the agitation of a camp, I sometimes thought and read in my tent, and in the more settled quarters of the Devizes, Blandford, and Southampton, I always secured a separate lodging and sufficient books. In the Militia I confirmed and much improved my knowledge of the Greek language. Reason and the practise of Scaliger directed me to Homer, the father of poetry, the bible of the ancients. *He* ran through the Iliad in twenty-one days; but *I* was

---

* Two modern writers of imagination, Mr. Beckford and the late Mr. Hope, originally wrote, the one *Vathek*, the other *Anastasius*, in French; but perhaps the most extraordinary effort of composition in a foreign language by an Englishman is the translation of Hudibras by Mr. Townley.—MILMAN.

To these may be added the late Lord Stanhope's *Histoire des Princes de Condé*.

not dissatisfied with my own diligence, which accomplished the same task in as many weeks. From the Iliad, I proceeded with ease and delight to the Odyssey; the simple prose of Strabo and the sublime figures of Longinus enlarged my sphere of Geography and Criticism; and in a dissertation of thirty folio pages, I weighed in my own scales the Epistles of Horace and the Commentary of Hurd. The daily occupations of the Militia introduced me to the science of Tactics, which opened a new field of reading and remark. The narratives and precepts of Polybius and Cæsar, of Arrian and Onosander, were consulted in the original text, and elucidated by their best interpreter, Mr. Guichardt, who alone has applied the learning of a Professor and the experience of a Prussian veteran to the military system of the ancients. A familiar view of the discipline and evolutions of a modern battalion gave me a clearer notion of the Phalanx and the Legion; and the Captain of the Hampshire Grenadiers (the reader may smile) has not been useless to the historian of the decline and fall of the Roman Empire. After the publication of my Essay, I revolved the plan of a second work; and a secret Genius might whisper in my ear that my talents were best qualified to excell in the line of historical composition. The ages of the World and the climates of the Globe were open to my choice, and many names and subjects which had dazzled my eyes were successively proscribed by my cooler meditation: the Expedition of Charles VIII. into Italy; the Crusade of Richard I.; the Wars of the Barons till the establishment of Magna Charta; the exploits of the Black Prince; the parallel characters of the Emperor Titus and Henry V.; and the lives of Sir Philip Sydney and Sir Walter

Raleigh. The history of the origin and establishment of the liberty of the Swiss, and the Revolutions of the Republic of Florence under the family of Medicis, sustained the most rigorous scrutiny; and I long hesitated between these interesting themes. My short excursions to Buriton were commonly employed in these preparatory tryals, and the trains of reading, of thinking, and sometimes of writing into which I was led, left me no room to repine at the loss of time or the failure of the experiment. But I was soon called away from my library to the battalion; and these historical projects were finally suspended by the long interruption of my travels.

That, in the Militia, a sedentary life was broken by some salutary exercise of the mind and body, I shall not deny. My active duties forced me from the closet into the field: I hunted with a battalion instead of a pack; and at any hour of the day or night I was ready to fly from quarters to London, from London to quarters, on the slightest call of business or amusement. A quick and various succession of new scenes and new faces emboldened the reserve of a foreigner and a student; and I became familiar with the government and manners, the interests and characters, of the English world. But these casual benefits bore no proportion to the loss of time, of temper, and of health. Our Colonel, Sir Thomas Worsley, was an easy, good-humoured man, fond of my company, of his bottle, and bed: our customary sittings were marked by every stroke of the midnight and morning hours, and the same drum which invited him to rest has often summoned me to the parade. His example encouraged in the Hampshire militia the vice of drinking; and those acts (let me confess), those habits of intemperance, have sown in my constitution the seeds of the gout. My philosophy was sowred by the ignorance and vulgarity of our rustic officers; and my passions were heated by our regimental disputes, in which my pen was too often degraded to the ungrateful task of writing letters and memorials against the claims and injuries of the Duke of Bolton.] A youth of any spirit is fired even by the play of arms, and in the first sallies of my enthusiasm I had seriously attempted to embrace the regular profession of a soldier. But this military feaver was cooled by the enjoyment of our mimic Bellona, who soon unveiled to my eyes her naked deformity. And often did I sigh for my proper station in society and letters! How often (a proud comparison) did I repeat the complaint of Cicero in the command of a provincial army—"Clitellæ bovi sunt impositæ. Est incredibile quam me negotii tædeat. . . . Ille cursus animi et industriæ meæ præclarâ operâ cessat. Lucem, libros, urbem domum, vos desidero. Sed feram ut potero, sit modo annuum. Si prorogatum actum est." From a service without danger I might, indeed, have retired without disgrace : but as often as I hinted a wish of resigning, my fetters were rivetted by the friendly entreaties of the Colonel, the parental authority of the Major, and my own regard for the honour and wellfare of the Battalion. When I felt that my personal escape was impracticable, I bowed my neck to the yoke ; my servitude was protracted far beyond the annual patience of Cicero, and it was not till after the preliminaries of peace that I received my discharge, from the act of Government which disembodied the Militia.

[As soon as I was restored to the freedom of an English Gentleman, I resolved, with my father's consent, to execute the plan of foreign travel, which had been suspended above four years by the general war, and my particular engagements. Two or three years were loosely defined for my tour of France and Italy: the measure of my extraordinary expence had been already fixed; the choice of place and distribution of time were left to my own judgement; and such was my eagerness, that in forty days I had shifted the scene from a guard-room at Gosport to an Hôtel in the Fauxbourg St. Germain at Paris, where I resided (January 28—May 9, 1763) between three and four months.

The moment was happily chosen. At the end of a successful war the British name was respected on the continent—

> "Clarum et venerabile nomen
> Gentibus."

Our opinions, our fashions, and even our games, were adopted in France; and every Englishman was supposed to be born a patriot and a philosopher. I had provided myself, before my departure, with honourable and effective recommendations. My Essay entitled me to a favourable reception; and the style of my appearance and equipage distinguished me from the hungry authors who, even at Paris, are secretly envied and despised. In the worlds of fashion and of science the national urbanity surpassed my sanguine expectation. I listened to the oracles of d'Alembert and Diderot, who reigned at the head of the *Encyclopedie* and the philosophic sect. I shall be content to enumerate the well-known names of the Count de Caylus, of the Abbés de la Bleterie, Barthelemy, Raynal, Arnaud, of Messieurs de la Conda-mine, Duclos, de Bougainville, de Ste. Palaye, de Guignes,

Caperonnier, Suard, etc., without attempting to discriminate the shades of their characters or the degrees of our acquaintance. Four times a week I might seat myself, without invitation, at the hospitable and elegant tables of Mesdames Geoffrin and du Bocage, of the celebrated Helvetius, and of Baron d'Holbach. These Symposia were enlivened by the free conflict of wit and knowledge: the company was select, though various and voluntary, and each unbidden guest might mutter to himself—

Αὐτομάτοι δ' ἀγάθοι δείλων ἐπὶ δαῖτας ἴασιν.*

But I was often disgusted by the capricious tyranny of Madame Geoffrin; nor could I approve the intolerant zeal of the friends of d'Holbach and Helvetius, who preached the tenets of scepticism with the bigotry of dogmatists, and rashly pronounced that every man must be either an Atheist or a fool. The society of Madame du Bocage was more soft and moderate, and the evening conversations of Mr. de Foncemagne were supported by the erudition and good sense of the principal members of the Academy of Inscriptions. The Opera and the Italians I occasionally visited; but the French Theatre, both in Tragedy and Comedy, was my daily and favourite amusement. Two rival Actresses divided the public applause; but I will confess that the consummate art of the Clairon was more agreable to my taste then the intemperate though powerful sallies of the Dumesnil. In the course of my morning excursions I explored every object of curiosity in the City and Country; the palaces, churches, and convents,

---

* Written without accent or breathing.

the libraries, manufactures, and galleries of pictures. The treasures of the Royal library I would have gladly transported to London; but, as an Englishman, I beheld without envy the rich ornaments of Paris, which has devoured a kingdom; I darted a contemptuous look on the stately monuments of superstition, and I viewed with horror the prodigies of Versailles and Marly, which have been cemented with the blood of the people. I have reserved for the last the most exquisite blessing of life —a female friend who received me every evening with the smile of confidence and joy. Madame B[ontemps] was an author without vanity, a devotee without gall: she managed a small income with œconomy and taste; in the middle season of life, her beauty was an object of desire, and if her heart was tender, if her passions were warm, decency and gratitude should cast a veil over her frailties. Fourteen weeks stole away in the enchantment of Paris; and had I been independent and rich, I should have prolonged, and perhaps perpetuated, my stay.

It had been my first design to advance from the metropolis into the southern provinces of France; but I was diverted from this long and costly circuit by the recent expences of Paris, and the ancient love of Lausanne. Shaping my course through Dijon and Besançon, I arrived, in the month of May, 1763, on the delightful banks of the Leman Lake; and such were the simple attractions of the spot, that the summer was lost in the autumn and succeeding winter, before I could resolve to pass the Alps. An absence of five years had not produced much alteration in manners or even in persons. My old friends of both sexes hailed my return—the most genuine proof of my attachment: they had been flattered by the gift of my book, the growth of their soil; and Pavillard shed tears of joy in embracing a pupil whose litterary merit he might fairly impute to his own labours. After a taste of English and Parisian luxury, it was impossible that I could reconcile myself to his wife's œconomy; nor were they offended at my entering myself as a *Pensionaire*, or boarder, in the family of Monsieur and Madame de Mesery. A style of elegant hospitality and polite freedom was maintained by the various talents of the Gentleman and Lady: their apartments in town and country were spacious and elegant, and their whole establishment stood for many years unparaleled in Europe. The most numerous of their guests were the English: and I will not deny that the contagion of my countrymen and the habits of the militia seduced me into some intemperance and riot, which might have been more excusable in my first residence at Lausanne. As a youth I had courted the grave and instructive conversation of my elders; as a man I was most amused in a young society, which had assumed the proud though fading denomination of the *Spring* (*la société du printems*). It consisted of fifteen or twenty unmarried women, all agreeable, some handsome, and two sisters of exquisite beauty. Under the guard of their own prudence, they assembled almost every day at each other's houses, which, in the absence of their mothers, were open to the young men of every nation. They laughed, they sung, they danced, they played at cards, they acted dramatic pieces; but in the midst of this careless gayety they respected themselves and were respected by the men: the invisible line between liberty and licentiousness was never transgressed by a gesture, a word, or a look, and their virgin chastity was never sullied by the breath of scandal—a singular institution, expressive of the innocent simplicity of Swiss manners! Some Ecclesiastical quarrel had provoked Voltaire to retire to his castle of Ferney, where I again visited the poet and the actor without seeking his more intimate acquaintance, to which I now might have pleaded a better title. But the Theatre which he had founded, the disciples whom he had formed at Lausanne, survived the loss of their master; and recent from Paris, I assisted with pleasure at the representation of several tragedies and comedies on their humble stage. In my ancient school I still found motives and moments of application. My studies were chiefly preparations for my Classic tour—the Latin poets and historians, the science of Manuscripts, medals, and inscriptions, the rules of Architecture, the Topography and antiquities of Rome, the Geography of Italy, and the military roads which pervaded the Empire of the Cæsars. Perhaps I might boast that few travellers more compleatly armed and instructed have ever followed the footsteps of Hannibal. As soon as the return of spring had unlocked the mountains, I departed from Lausanne (April 18, 1764) with an English companion (Mr., afterwards Sir William Guise), whose partnership divided and alleviated the expences of the Journey.]

I shall advance with rapid brevity in the narrative of my Italian tour, in which somewhat more than a year (April, 1764—May, 1765) was agreeably employed. Content with tracing my line of march, and slightly touching on my personal feelings, I shall wave the minute investigation of the scenes which have been viewed by thousands,

and described by hundreds of our modern travellers.
Rome is the great object of our pilgrimage, and i. The
Journey. ii. The residence, and iii. The return will form
the most proper and perspicuous division. i. I climbed
Mount Cenis, and descended into the plain of Piedmont,
not on the back of an Elephant, but on a light osier seat,
in the hands of the dextrous and intrepid chairmen of
the Alps. The architecture and government of Turin
presented the same aspect of tame and tiresome uniformity, but the Court was regulated with decent and
splendid œconomy; and I was introduced to his Sardinian
Majesty, Charles Emanuel,* who, after the incomparable
Frederic, held the second rank (*proximus longo tamen
intervallo*) among the Kings of Europe. The size and
populousness of Milan could not surprize an inhabitant
of London; [the Dome or Cathedral is an unfinished
monument of Gothic superstition and wealth:] but the
fancy is amused by a visit to the Boromean islands,
an enchanted palace, a work of the fairies in the
midst of a lake encompassed with mountains, and far
removed from the haunts of men. I was less amused
by the marble palaces of Genoa, than by the recent
memorials of her deliverance (in December, 1746) from
the Austrian tyranny: and I took a military survey
of every scene of action within the inclosure of her
double walls. My steps were detained at Parma and
Modena by the precious relics of the Farnese and Este
collections; but, alas! the far greater part had been
already transported, by inheritance or purchase, to Naples

---

* Charles Emanuel III., King
of Sardinia, born 1701; succeeded
his father, 1730; defeated the Aus-
trians at Guastalla, 1734; was defeated by the French and Spaniards
at Coni, 1744; died 1773.

and Dresden. By the road of Bologna and the Apenine
I at last reached Florence, where I reposed from June
to September, during the heat of the summer months.
In the gallery, and especially in the *Tribune*, I first
acknowledged, at the feet of the Venus of Medicis, that
the chissel may dispute the pre-eminence with the pencil—
a truth in the fine arts which cannot, on this side of the
Alps, be felt or understood. At home I had taken some
lessons of Italian ; on the spot I read with a learned
native the Classics of the Tuscan idiom; but the short-
ness of my time, and the use of the French language,
prevented my acquiring any facility of speaking ; and I
was a silent spectator in the conversations of our envoy,
Sir Horace Mann, whose most serious business was that
of entertaining the English at his hospitable table.
After leaving Florence I compared the solitude of Pisa
with the industry of Lucca and Leghorn, and continued
my journey through Sienna to Rome, where I arrived
in the beginning of October. ii. My temper is not very
susceptible of enthusiasm, and the enthusiasm which I
do not feel I have ever scorned to affect. But at the
distance of twenty-five years I can neither forget nor
express the strong emotions which agitated my mind
as I first approached and entered the *eternal City*. After
a sleepless night, I trod with a lofty step the ruins of the
Forum ; each memorable spot where Romulus *stood*, or
Tully spoke, or Cæsar fell, was at once present to my eye ;
and several days of intoxication were lost or enjoyed before
I could descend to a cool and minute investigation. My
guide was Mr. Byers,* a Scotch antiquary of experience

---

* James Byres, of Tonley, in   forty years in Rome in the study
Aberdeenshire (1733–1817), spent   of archæology and in collecting

and taste; but in the daily labour of eighteen weeks the powers of attention were sometimes fatigued, till I was myself qualified, in a last review, to select and study the capital works of ancient and modern art. Six weeks were borrowed for my tour of Naples, the most populous of cities relative to its size, whose luxurious inhabitants seem to dwell on the confines of paradise and hell-fire. I was presented to the boy-King * by our new Envoy, Sir William Hamilton, who, wisely diverting his correspondence from the Secretary of State to the Royal society and British Musæum, has elucidated a country of such inestimable value to the Naturalist and Antiquarian. On my return I fondly embraced, for the last time, the miracles of Rome; but I departed without kissing the feet of Rezzonico (Clement XIII.), who neither possessed the wit of his predecessor Lambertini, nor the virtues of his successor Ganganelli. iii. In my pilgrimage from Rome to Loretto I again crossed the Apennine: from the coast of the Adriatic I traversed a fruitful and populous country, which would alone disprove the paradox of Montesquieu that modern Italy is a desert. Without adopting the exclusive prejudice of the natives, I sincerely admired the paintings of the Bologna school. I hastened to escape from the sad solitude of Ferrara, which in the age of Cæsar was still more desolate. The spectacle of Venice afforded some hours of astonishment [and some days of disgust]; the university of Padua is

---

antiquities. At one time he possessed the Portland Vase, which he sold to Sir William Hamilton. Sir James Hall alludes to the great influence exercised by him in educating the classical taste of his countrymen.

* Ferdinand IV., born 1751; succeeded to the kingdom of the Two Sicilies on the accession of his father, Carlos III., to the throne of Spain, 1759; died 1825.

a dying taper; but Verona still boasts her amphitheatre, and his native Vicenza is adorned by the classic architecture of Palladio. The road of Lombardy and Piedmont (did Montesquieu find them without inhabitants?) led me back to Milan, Turin, and the passage of Mount Cenis, where I again crossed the Alps in my way to Lyons.

The use of foreign travel has been often debated as a general question, but the conclusion must be finally applied to the character and circumstances of each individual. With the education of boys, *where* or *how* they may pass over some juvenile years with the least mischief to themselves or others, I have no concern. But after supposing the prævious and indispensable requisites of age, judgement, a competent knowledge of men and books, and a freedom from domestic prejudices, I will briefly describe the qualifications which I deem most essential to a traveller. He should be endowed with an active, indefatigable vigour of mind and body, which can seize every mode of conveyance, and support with a careless smile every hardship of the road, the weather, or the Inn. [It must stimulate him with a restless curiosity, impatient of ease, covetous of time, and fearless of danger; which drives him forth, at any hour of the day or night, to brave the flood, to climb the mountain, or to fathom the mine on the most doubtful promise of entertainment or instruction. The arts of common life are not studied in the closet; with a copious stock of classical and historical learning, my traveller must blend the practical knowledge of husbandry and manufactures; he should be a Chymist, a botanist, and a master of mechanics. A musical ear will multiply the pleasures of his Italian tour; but a correct and exquisite eye, which commands the landskip of a country, discerns the merit of a picture, and measures the proportions of a building, is more closely connected with the finer feelings of the mind, and the fleeting image shall be fixed and realized by the dexterity of the pencil. I have reserved for the last a virtue which borders on a vice; the flexible temper which can assimilate itself to every tone of society from the court to the cottage; the happy flow of spirits which can amuse and be amused in every company and situation. With the advantage of an independent fortune and the ready use of national and provincial idioms, the traveller should unite the pleasing aspect and decent familiarity which makes every stranger an acquaintance, and the art of conversing with ignorance and dulness on some topic of local or professional infor-mation.] The benefits of foreign travel will correspond with the degrees of these [various] qualifications, but in this sketch [of ideal perfection] those to whom I am known will not accuse me of framing my own panygeric. [Yet the historian of the decline and fall must not regret his time or expence, since it was the view of Italy and Rome which determined the choice of the subject. In my Journal the place and moment of conception are recorded; the fifteenth of October, 1764, in the close of evening, as I sat musing in the Church of the Zoccolanti or Franciscan fryars, while they were singing Vespers in the Temple of Jupiter on the ruins of the Capitol.] But my original plan was circumscribed to the decay of the City rather than of the Empire; and though my reading and reflections began to point towards that object, some years elapsed, and several avocations intervened, before I was seriously engaged in the execution of that laborious work.

I had not totally renounced the southern provinces of France, but the letters which I found at Lyons were expressive of some impatience, [the measure of absence and expence was filled;] Rome and Italy had satiated my curious appetite, and [the excessive heat of the weather decided the sage resolution of turning my face to the north, and seeking] the peaceful retreat of my family and books. After an happy fortnight, [I tore myself from the embraces of *] Paris, embarked at Calais, again landed at Dover, after an interval of two years and five months, and hastily drove through the summer dust and solitude of London. [On the 25th of June, 1765, I reached the rural mansion of my parents, to whom I was endeared by my long absence and chearful submission.

After my first (1758) and my second return to England (1765), the forms of the pictures were nearly the same: but the colours had been darkened by time;] and the five years and a half between my travels and my father's death (1770) are the portion of my life which I passed with the least enjoyment, and which I remember with the least satisfaction. [I have nothing to change (for there was not any change) in the annual distribution of my summers and winters, between my domestic residence in Hampshire and a casual lodging at the west end of the town; though once, from the tryal of some months, I was tempted to substitute the tranquil dissipation of Bath instead of the smoke, the expence, and the tumult of the Metropolis, fumum, et opes, strepitumque

---

* "Reluctantly left" in Lord Sheffield's edition.

Romæ.] Every spring I attended the monthly meeting and exercise of the militia at Southampton; and, by the resignation of my father and the death of Sir Thomas Worsley, I was successively promoted to the rank of Major and Lieutenant-Colonel-Commandant. [Under the care (may I presume to say?) of a veteran officer, the south Battalion of the Hampshire militia acquired the degree of skill and discipline which was compatible with the brevity of time and the looseness of peaceful subordination;] but I was each year more disgusted with the Inn, the wine, the company, and the tiresome repetition of annual attendance and daily exercise. At home, the œconomy of the family and farm still maintained the same creditable appearance. [I was received, entertained, and dismissed with similar kindness and indulgence :] my connection with Mrs. Gibbon was mellowed into a warm and solid attachment; my growing years abolished the distance that might yet remain between a parent and a son, and my behaviour satisfied my father, who was proud of the success, however imperfect in his own lifetime, of my litterary talents. Our solitude was soon and often enlivened by the visit of the friend of my youth, of Mr. Deyverdun, whose absence from Lausanne I had sincerely lamented. About three years after my first departure he had migrated from his native lake to the banks of the Oder in Germany. The res angusta domi, the waste of a decent patrimony by an improvident father, obliged him, like many of his countrymen, to confide in his own industry; and he was entrusted with the education of a young prince, the grandson of the Margrave of Schwedt, of the Royal family of Prussia. Our friendship was never

cooled, our correspondence was sometimes interrupted:
but I rather wished than hoped to obtain Mr. Deyverdun
for the companion of my Italian tour. An unhappy
though honourable passion drove him from his German
court, and the attractions of hope and curiosity were
fortified by the expectation of my speedy return to
England. [I was allowed to offer him the hospitality of
the house:] during four successive summers he passed
several weeks or months at Buriton, and our free conversations on every topic that could interest the heart or
understanding would have reconciled me to a desert or a
prison. In the winter months of London my sphere of
knowledge and action was somewhat enlarged by the
many new acquaintance which I had contracted in the
Militia and abroad; and I must regret, as more than an
acquaintance, Mr. Godfrey Clarke of Derbyshire, an
amiable and worthy young man, who was snatched away
by an untimely death. A weekly convivial meeting was
instituted by myself and my fellow-travellers under the
name of the Roman Club; * [and I was soon ballotted into
Boodle's (the school of virtue, as the Earl of Shelburne
had first named it), where I found the daily ressource of
excellent dinners, mixed company, and moderate play.
I must own, however, with a blush, that my virtues of
temperance and sobriety had not compleately recovered
themselves from the wounds of the militia, that my

---

* The members were Lord Mountstuart (now Marquis of Bute), Colonel Edmonstone, William Weddal, Rev. Mr. Palgrave, Earl of Berkley, Godfrey Clarke (Member for Derbyshire), Holroyd (Lord Sheffield), Major Ridley, Thomas Charles Bigge, Sir William Guise, Sir John Aubrey, the late Earl of Abingdon, Hon. Peregrine Bertie, Rev. Mr. Cleaver, Hon. John Damer, Hon. George Damer (late Earl of Dorchester), Sir Thomas Gascoygne, Sir John Hort, E. Gibbon.—LORD SHEF-FIELD.

T

connections were much less among women than men,
and that these men, though far from contemptible in
rank and fortune, were not of the first eminence in the
litterary or political World.]

The renewal, or perhaps the improvement, of my
English life was embittered by the alteration of my own
feelings. At the age of twenty-one I was, in my proper
station of a youth, delivered from the yoke of education,
and delighted with the comparative state of liberty and
affluence. My filial obedience was natural and easy; and
in the gay prospect of futurity, my ambition did not
extend beyond the enjoyment of my books, my leisure,
and my patrimonial estate, undisturbed by the cares of a
family and the duties of a profession. But in the militia
I was armed with power, in my travels I was exempt
from controul; and as I approached, as I gradually transcended my thirtieth year, I began to feel the desire of
being master in my own house. The most gentle authority
will sometimes frown without reason, the most chearful
submission will sometimes murmur without cause; and
such is the law of our imperfect nature, that we must
either command or obey; that our personal liberty is
supported by the obsequiousness of our own dependents.
While so many of my acquaintance were married, or in
parliament, or advancing with a rapid step in the various
roads of honours and fortune, I stood alone, immoveable
and insignificant; for after the monthly meeting of 1770
I had even withdrawn myself from the militia, by the
resignation of an empty and barren commission. My
temper is not susceptible of envy, and the view of successful merit has always excited my warmest applause.
[A matrimonial alliance has ever been the object of my <

terror rather than of my wishes. I was not very strongly pressed by my family or my passions to propagate the name and race of the Gibbons, and if some reasonable temptations occurred in the neighbourhood, the vague idea never proceeded to the length of a serious negociation.] The miseries of a vacant life were never known to a man whose hours were insufficient for the inexhaustible pleasures of study. But I lamented that at the proper age I had not embraced the lucrative pursuits of the law or of trade, the chances of civil office or India adventure, or even the fat slumbers of the Church; and my repentance became more lively as the loss of time was more irretrievable. Experience shewed me the use of grafting my private consequence on the importance of a great professional body—the benefits of those firm connections which are cemented by hope and interest, by gratitude and emulation, by the mutual exchange of services and favours. From the emoluments of a profession I might have derived an ample fortune or a competent income, instead of being stinted to the same narrow allowance, to be encreased only by an event which I sincerely deprecated. The progress and the knowledge of our domestic disorders aggravated my anxiety, and I began to apprehend that I might be left in my old age without the fruits either of industry or inheritance.

In the first summer after my return, whilst I enjoyed at Buriton the society of my friend Deyverdun, our daily conversations exspatiated over the field of ancient and modern litterature, and we freely discussed my studies, my first Essay and my future prospects. The decline and fall of Rome I still contemplated at an awful distance : but the two historical designs which had

balanced my choice were submitted to his taste, and in
the paralel between the revolutions of Florence and
Switzerland, our common partiality for a country which
was *his* by birth and *mine* by adoption inclined the scale
in favour of the latter. According to the plan, which
was soon conceived and digested, I embraced a period of
two hundred years from the association of the three
peasants of the Alps to the plenitude and prosperity of
the Helvetic body in the sixteenth century. I should
have described the deliverance and victory of the Swiss,
who have never shed the blood of their tyrants but in a
field of battle; the laws and manners of the confederate
states; the splendid trophies of the Austrian, Burgundian,
and Italian wars; and the wisdom of a nation who, after
some sallies of martial adventure, has been content to
guard the blessings of peace with the sword of freedom.

"Manus hæc inimica Tyrannis
Ense petit placidam sub libertate quietem."

My judgement, as well as my enthusiasm, was satisfied
with the glorious theme; and the assistance of Deyverdun
seemed to remove an insuperable obstacle. The French
or Latin memorials, of which I was not ignorant, are
inconsiderable in number and weight; but in the perfect
acquaintance of my friend with the German language I
found the key of a more valuable collection. The most
necessary books were procured; he translated for my
use the folio volume of Schilling, a copious and contemporary relation of the war of Burgundy; we read and
marked the most interesting parts of the great chronicle
of Tschudi; and by his labour, or that of an inferior
assistant, large extracts were made from the History of
Lauffer and the Dictionary of Leu. Yet such was the

distance and delay, that two years elapsed in these preparatory steps; and it was late in the third summer (1767) before I entered, with these slender materials, on the more agreable task of composition. A specimen of my history, the first book, was read the following winter in a litterary society of foreigners in London; and as the author was unknown, I listened, without observation, to the free strictures and unfavourable sentence of my judges.* The momentary sensation was painful, but their condemnation was ratisfied (*sic*) by my cooler thoughts; I delivered my imperfect sheets to the flames,† and for ever renounced a design in which some expence, much labour,

---

* Mr. Hume seems to have had a different opinion of this work.

From Mr. Hume to Mr. Gibbon.

Sir,—It is but a few days ago since M. Deyverdun put your manuscript into my hands, and I have perused it with great pleasure and satisfaction. I have only one objection, derived from tho language in which it is written. Why do you compose in French, and carry faggots into the wood, as Horace says with regard to Romans who wrote in Greek? I grant that you have a like motive to those Romans, and adopt a language much more generally diffused than your native tongue: but have you not remarked tho fate of those two ancient languages in following ages? The Latin, though then less celebrated, and confined to more narrow limits, has in some measure outlived the Greek, and is now more generally understood by men of letters. Let the French, therefore, triumph in the present diffusion of their tongue. Our solid and increasing establishments in America, where we need less dread the inundation of Barbarians, promise a superior stability and duration to the English language.

Your use of the French tongue has also led you into a style more poetical and figurative, and more highly coloured, than our language seems to admit of in historical productions: for such is the practice of French writers, particularly the more recent ones, who illuminate their pictures more than custom will permit us. On the whole, your History, in my opinion, is written with spirit and judgment; and I exhort you very earnestly to continue it. The objections that occurred to me on reading it were so frivolous that I shall not trouble you with them, and should, I believe, have a difficulty to recollect them. I am, with great esteem,

Sir, your most obedient
and most humble servant,
(Signed) David Hume.
London,
24th of Oct. 1767.

† He neglected to burn them. He left at Sheffield Place the introduction, or first book, in forty-three pages folio, written in a very small hand, besides a considerable number of notes. Mr. Hume's opinion, expressed in the letter in the last note, perhaps may justify the publication of it.—Sheffield.

and more time had been so vainly consumed. I cannot regret the loss of a slight and superficial Essay; for such the work must have been in the hands of a stranger, uninformed by the scholars and statesmen, remote from the libraries and archives of the Swiss Republics. My ancient habits, and the presence of Deyverdun, encouraged me to write in French for the Continent of Europe; but I was conscious myself that my style, above prose and below poetry, degenerated into a verbose and turgid declamation. Perhaps I may impute the failure to the injudicious choice of a foreign language. Perhaps I may suspect that the language itself is ill adapted to sustain the vigour and dignity of an important narrative. But if France, so rich in litterary merit, had produced a great original historian, his Genius would have formed and fixed the idiom to the proper tone, the peculiar mode of historical eloquence.

It was in search of some liberal and lucrative employment that my friend Deyverdun had visited England: his remittances from home were scanty and precarious. My purse was always open, but it was often empty; and I bitterly felt the want of riches and power, which might have enabled me to correct the errors of his fortune. His wishes and qualifications solicited the station of the travelling governor of some wealthy pupill; but every vacancy provoked so many eager candidates, that for a long time I struggled without success; nor was it till after much application that I could even place him as a clerk in the office of the Secretary of state. In a residence of several years he never acquired the just pronunciation and familiar use of the English tongue, but he read our most difficult authors with ease and taste;

his critical knowledge of our language and poetry was such as few foreigners have possessed, and few of our countrymen could enjoy the Theatre of Shakespeare and Garrick with more exquisite feeling and discernment. The consciousness of his own strength and the assurance of my aid emboldened him to imitate the example of Dr. Maty, whose *Journal Britannique* was esteemed and regretted; and to improve his model, by uniting with the transactions of litterature a philosophic view of the arts and manners of the British nation. Our Journal for the year 1767, under the title of *Memoires Litteraires de la Grande Bretagne*, was soon finished and sent to the press. For the first article, Lord Lyttleton's history of Henry II., I must own myself responsible; but the public has ratified my judgement of that voluminous work, in which sense and learning are not illuminated by a ray of Genius. The next specimen was the choice of my friend, *the Bath Guide*, a light and whimsical performance, of local and even verbal pleasantry. I started at the attempt; he smiled at my fears: his courage was justified by success, and a master of both languages will applaud the curious felicity with which he has transfused into French prose the spirit, and even humour, of the English verse. It is not my wish to deny how deeply I was interested in these Memoirs, of which I need not surely be ashamed; but, at the distance of more than twenty years, it would be impossible for me to ascertain the respective shares of the two associates. A long and intimate communication of ideas had cast our sentiments and style in the same mould: in our social labours we composed and corrected by turns, and the praise which I might honestly bestow would fall perhaps on some article or passage most properly my own. A second volume (for the year 1768) was published of these Memoirs: I will presume to say that their merit was superior to their reputation, but it is not less true that they were productive of more reputation than emolument. They introduced my friend to the protection, and myself to the acquaintance, of the Earl of Chesterfield, whose age and infirmities secluded him from the World; and of Mr. David Hume, who was under-Secretary to the office in which Deyverdun was more humbly employed. The former accepted a dedication (April 12, 1769), and reserved the author for the future education of his successor; the latter enriched the Journal with a reply to Mr. Walpole's historical doubts, which he afterwards shaped into the form of a note. The materials of the third volume were almost compleated, when I recommended Deyverdun as Governor to Sir Richard Worsley, a youth, the son of my old Lieutenant-Colonel, who was lately deceased. They set forwards on their travels, nor did they return to England till some time after my father's death.

My next publication was an accidental sally of love and resentment; of my reverence for modest Genius, and my aversion to insolent pedantry. The sixth book of the Æneid is the most pleasing and perfect composition of Latin poetry. The descent of Æneas and the Sybill to the infernal regions, to the world of spirits, expands an awful and boundless prospect, from the nocturnal gloom of the Cumæan grot—

> " Ibant obscuris solâ sub nocte per umbram "—

to the meridian brightness of the Elysian fields—

> " Largior hic campos æther et lumine vestit
>   Purpureo——"

from the dreams of simple nature to the dreams, alas! of Ægyptian Theology and the Philosophy of the Greeks. But the final dismission of the Hero through the Ivory gate, from whence

"Falsa ad cœlum mittunt insomnia manes,"

seems to dissolve the whole enchantment, and leaves the reader in a state of cold and anxious scepticism. This most lame and impotent conclusion has been variously imputed to the haste or irreligion of Virgil; but, according to the more elaborate interpretation of Bishop Warburton, the descent to hell is not a false, but a mimic scene, which represents the initiation of Æneas, in the character of a Law-giver, to the Eleusinian mysteries. This hypothesis, a singular chapter in the Divine legation of Moses, had been admitted by many as true, it was praised by all as ingenious; nor had it been exposed, in a space of thirty years, to a fair and critical discussion. The learning and abilities of the author had raised him to a just eminence; but he reigned the Dictator and tyrant of the World of Litterature. The real merit of Warburton was degraded by the pride and presumption with which he pronounced his infallible decrees; in his polemic writings he lashed his antagonists without mercy or moderation, and his servile flatterers (see the base and malignant *delicacy of friendship*),* exalting the master critic far above Aristotle and Longinus, assaulted every modest dissenter who refused to consult the oracle and to adore the Idol. In a land of liberty such despotism must provoke a general

* By Hurd, afterwards Bishop of Worcester. See Dr. Parr's Tracts by Warburton, and a Warburtonian.—LORD SHEFFIELD.

opposition, and the zeal of opposition is seldom candid or
impartial. A late Professor of Oxford (Dr. Lowth), in a
pointed and polished Epistle * (August 31, 1765), defended
himself and attacked the bishop; and, whatsoever might
be the merits of an insignificant controversy, his victory
was clearly established by the silent confusion of Warburton and his slaves. *I* too, without any private offence,
was ambitious of breaking a lance against the Giant's
shield; and in the beginning of the year 1770, my
Critical observations on the sixth book of the Æneid
were sent, without my name, to the press. In this short
Essay, my first English publication, I aimed my strokes
against the person and the Hypothesis of Bishop Warburton. I proved, at least to my own satisfaction, *that*
the ancient Lawgivers did not invent the mysteries, and
that Æneas was never invested with the office of law-
giver. *That* there is not any argument, any circumstance, which can melt a fable into allegory, or remove
the scene from the lake Avernus to the temple of Ceres.
That such a wild supposition is equally injurious to the
poet and the man. *That* if Virgil was not initiated he
could not, if he were he would not, reveal the secrets of
the initiation. *That* the anathema of Horace (Vetabo qui
Cereris sacrum, vulgârit, etc.) at once attests his own
ignorance and the innocence of his friend. As the
Bishop of Gloucester and his party maintained a discreet
silence, my critical disquisition was soon lost among the
pamphlets of the day; but the public coldness was over-
balanced to my feelings by the weighty approbation of

---

* This letter of Lowth's is a
masterpiece of its kind, and, if our
calmer judgment is offended by
the unseemly spectacle of two
Christian prelates engaged in this
fierce intellectual gladiatorism,
the chief blame must fall on the
aggressor, Warburton.—Milman.

the last and best Editor of Virgil, Professor Heyne of Gottingen, who acquiesces in my confutation, and styles the unknown author doctus . . . et elegantissimus Britannus. But I cannot resist the temptation of transcribing the favourable judgement of Mr. Hayley, himself a poet and scholar: "An intricate hypothesis, twisted into a long and laboured chain of quotation and argument, the Dissertation on the sixth book of Virgil, remained some time unrefuted. . . . At length, a superior but anonymous critic arose, who, in one of the most judicious and spirited Essays that our nation has produced on a point of Classical literature, completely overturned this ill-founded edifice, and exposed the arrogance and futility of its assuming architect." He even condescends to justify an acrimony of style, which had been gently blamed by the more unbyassed German, " Paullo acrius quam velis ". . . "perstrinxit." * But I cannot forgive myself the contemptuous treatment of a man who, with all his faults, was entitled to my esteem; † and I can less forgive, in a personal attack, the cowardly concealment of my name and character.

In the fifteen years between my Essay on the study of literature and the first Volume of the decline and fall (1761-1776), this criticism on Warburton, and some

---

* The editor of the Warburtonian tracts, Dr. Parr (p. 192), considers the allegorical interpretation "as completely refuted in a most clear, elegant, and decisive work of criticism; which could not, indeed, derive authority from the greatest name, but to which the greatest name might with propriety have been affixed."—Lord Sheffield.

† The *Divine Legation of Moses* is a monument, already crumbling in the dust, of the vigour and weakness of the human mind. If Warburton's new argument proved anything, it would be a demonstration against the legislator who left his people without the knowledge of a future state. But some episodes of the work, on the Greek philosophy, the hieroglyphics of Egypt, etc., are entitled to the praise of learning, imagination, and discernment.—Lord Sheffield.

articles in the Journal, were my sole publications. It is
more specially incumbent on me to mark the employment, or to confess the waste of time, from my travels
to my father's death, an interval in which I was not
diverted by any professional duties from the labours and
pleasures of a studious life. i. As soon as I was released
from the fruitless task of the Swiss revolutions, I more
seriously undertook (1768) to methodize the form, and
to collect the substance of my Roman decay, of whose
limits and extent I had yet a very inadequate notion.
The Classics, as low as Tacitus, the younger Pliny, and
Juvenal were my old and familiar companions : I
insensibly plunged into the Ocean of the Augustan
history; and in the descending series I investigated,
with my pen almost always in my hand, the original
records, both Greek and Latin, from Dion Cassius to
Ammianus Marcellinus, from the reign of Trajan to
the last age of the western Cæsars. The subsidiary rays
of Medals and inscriptions of Geography and Chronology
were thrown on their proper objects; and I applied the
collections of Tillemont, whose inimitable accuracy almost
assumes the character of Genius, to fix and arrange within
my reach the loose and scattered atoms of historical
information. Through the darkness of the middle ages
I explored my way in the Annals and Antiquities of
Italy of the learned Muratori; and diligently compared
them with the parallel or transverse lines of Sigonius
and Maffei, Baronius and Pagi, till I almost grasped the
ruins of Rome in the fourteenth Century, without suspecting that this final chapter must be attained by
the labour of six quartos and twenty years. Among the
books which I purchased, the Theodosian Code, with the

commentary of James Godefroy, must be gratefully remembered. I used it (and much I used it) as a work of
history rather than of Jurisprudence; but in every light
it may be considered as a full and capacious repository
of the political state of the Empire in the fourth and
fifth Centuries. As I believed, and as I still believe,
that the propagation of the gospel and triumph of the
Church are inseperably connected with the decline of
the Roman Monarchy, I weighed the causes and effects
of the Revolution, and contrasted the narratives and
apologies of the Christians themselves, with the glances
of candour or enmity which the Pagans have cast on the
rising sect. The Jewish and Heathen testimonies, as they
are collected and illustrated by Dr. Lardner, directed,
without superseding my search of the originals; and in
an ample dissertation on the miraculous darkness of the
passion, I privately drew my conclusions from the silence
of an unbelieving age. I have assembled the preparatory studies directly or indirectly relative to my
history; but, in strict equity, they must be spread beyond
this period of my life, over the two summers (1771 and
1772) that elapsed between my father's death and my
settlement in London. ii. In a free conversation with
books and men, it would be endless to enumerate the
names and characters of all who are introduced to our
acquaintance, but in this general acquaintance we may
select the degrees of friendship and esteem. According
to the wise maxim, "*Multum* legere potius quam *multa*,"
I reviewed again and again the immortal works of the
French and English, the Latin and Italian Classics.
My Greek studies (though less assiduous than I designed) maintained and extended my knowledge of that

incomparable idiom. Homer and Xenophon were still my favourite authors; and I had almost prepared for the press an Essay on the Cyropædia, which in my own judgement is not unhappily laboured. After a certain age the new publications of merit are the sole food of the many; and the most austere student will be often tempted to break the line, for the sake of indulging his own curiosity and of providing the topics of fashionable currency. A more respectable motive may be assigned for the triple perusal of Blackstone's commentaries, and a copious and critical abstract of that English work was my first serious production in my native language. iii. My litterary leisure was much less compleat and independent than it might appear to the eye of a stranger: in the hurry of London I was destitute of books; in the solitude of Hampshire I was not master of my time. [By the habit of early rising I always secured a sacred portion of the day; and many precious moments were stolen and saved by my rational avarice. But the family hours of breakfast and dinner, of tea and supper, were regular and tedious: after breakfast Mrs. Gibbon expected my company in her dressing-room; after tea my father claimed my conversation and the perusal of the Newspapers. In the heat of some interesting pursuit, I was called down to receive the visits of our idle neighbours; their civilities required a suitable return; and I dreaded the period of the full moon, which was usually reserved for our more distant excursions.] My quiet was gradually disturbed by our domestic anxiety; and I should be ashamed of my unfeeling philosophy, had I found much time or taste for study in the last fatal summer (1770) of my father's decay and dissolution.

The disembodying of the Militia at the close of the
War (1762) had restored the Major—a new Cincinnatus
—to a life of Agriculture. His labours were useful, his
pleasures innocent, his wishes moderate; and my father
seemed to enjoy the state of happiness which is celebrated
by poets and philosophers as the most agreeable to
Nature, and the least accessible to Fortune—

> "Beatus ille, qui procul negotiis
> (Ut prisca gens mortalium)
> Paterna rura bubus exercet suis,
> Solutus omni fœnore." *

But the last indispensable condition, the freedom from
debt, was wanting to my father's felicity; and the vanities
of his youth were severely punished by the solicitude
and sorrow of his declining age. The first mortgage, on
my return from Lausanne (1758), had afforded him a
partial and transient relief: the annual demand of
interest and allowance was an heavy deduction from
his income: the militia was a source of expence: the
farm in his hands was not a profitable adventure; he
was loaded with the costs and damages of an obsolete
lawsuit; and each year multiplied the number and
exhausted the patience of his creditors. Under these
painful circumstances, [my own behaviour was not only
guiltless but meritorious. Without stipulating any
personal advantages,] I consented, [at a mature and
well-informed age,] to an additional mortgage, to the
sale of Putney, and to every sacrifice that could
alleviate his distress; but he was no longer capable
of a rational effort, and his reluctant delays postponed,
not the evils themselves, but the remedies of those evils,

---

* Hor. *Epod.* ii. 1.

(*remedia malorum potius quam mala differebat*). The pangs of shame, tenderness, and self-reproach incessantly preyed on his vitals; his constitution was broken; he lost his strength and his sight; the rapid progress of a dropsy admonished him of his end, and he sunk into the grave on the tenth of November, 1770, in the sixty-fourth year of his age. A family tradition insinuates that Mr. William Law has drawn his pupil in the light and inconstant character of *Flatus,* who is ever confident and ever disappointed in the chace of happiness. But these constitutional failings were amply compensated by the virtues of the head and heart, by the warmest sentiments of honour and humanity. His graceful person, polite address, gentle manners, and unaffected chearfulness, recommended him to the favour of every company; and in the change of times and opinions, his liberal spirit had long since delivered him from the zeal and prejudice of a Tory education. [The tears of a son are seldom lasting.] I submitted to the order of Nature, and my grief was soothed by the conscious satisfaction that I had discharged all the duties of filial piety. [Few, perhaps, are the children who, after the expiration of some months or years, would sincerely rejoyce in the resurrection of their parents; and it is a melancholy truth, that my father's death, not unhappy for himself, was the only event that could save me from an hopeless life of obscurity and indigence.]

Section III.

As soon as I had paid the last solemn duties to my father, and obtained from time and reason a tolerable composure of mind, I began to form the plan of an independent life most adapted to my circumstances and inclination. Yet so intricate was the net, my efforts were so awkward and feeble, that near two years (November, 1770—October, 1772) were suffered to elapse before I could disentangle myself from the management of the farm, and transfer my residence from Buriton to an house in London. During this interval I continued to divide my year between town and the country; but my new freedom was brightened by hope: [nor could I refuse the advantages of a change, which had never (I have scrutinized my conscience)—which had never been the object of my secret wishes. Without indulging the vanity and extravagance of a thoughtless heir, I assumed some additional latitude of lodging, attendance, and equipage; I no longer numbered with the same anxious parsimony my dinners at the club or tavern:] my stay in London was prolonged into the summer, and the uniformity of the summer was occasionally broken by visits and excursions at a distance from home. [That home, the house and estate at Buriton, were now my own; I could invite without controul the persons most agreable to my taste; the horses and servants were at my disposal; and in all their operations my rustic ministers solicited the commands and smiled at the ignorance of their master. I will not deny that my pride was flattered by the local importance of a country gentleman: the busy scene of the farm, productive of seeming plenty, was embellished in my eyes by the partial sentiment of property; and, still adhering to my original plan, I expected the adequate offers of a tenant, and postponed without much impatience the moment of my departure. My friendship for Mrs. Gibbon long resisted the idea of our final separation.

After my father's decease, she preserved the tenderness, without the authority, of a parent : the family, and even the farm, were entrusted to her care; and as the habits of fifteen years had attached her to the spot, she was herself persuaded, and she tryed to persuade me, of the pleasures and benefits of a country life. But, as I could not afford to maintain a double establishment, my favourite project of an house in London was incompatible with the farm at Buriton, and it was soon apparent that a woman and a philosopher could not direct with any prospect of advantage such a complex and costly machine. In the second summer my resolution was declared and effected; the advertisement of the farm attracted many competitors; the fairest terms were preferred : the proper leases were executed; I abandoned the mansion to the principal tenant, and Mrs. G., with some reluctance, departed for Bath, the most fashionable azylum for the *sober singleness* of widowhood. But the produce of the effects and stock was barely sufficient to clear my accounts in the country, and my first settlement in town : from the mischievous extravagance of the tenant I sustained many subsequent injuries; and a change of ministry could not be accomplished without much trouble and expense.

Besides the debts for which my honour and piety were engaged, my father had left a weighty mortgage of seventeen thousand pounds : it could only be discharged by a landed sacrifice, and my estate at Lenborough, near Buckingham, was the devoted victim. At first the appearances were favourable; but my hopes were too sanguine, my demands were too high. After slighting some offers by no means contemptible, I rashly signed an agreement with a worthless fellow (half knave and half madman), who, in three years of vexatious chicanery, refused either to consummate or to relinquish his bargain. After I had broken my fetters, the opportunity was lost; the public distress had reduced the value of land : I waited the return of peace and prosperity; and my last secession to Lausanne preceded the sale of my Buckinghamshire estate. The delay of fifteen years, which I may impute to myself, my friends, and the times, was accompanied with the loss of many thousand pounds. A delicious morsel, a share in the New river company, was cast, with many a sigh, into the gulph of principal, interest, and annual expence; and the far greater part of the inadequate price of poor Lenborough was finally devoured by the insatiate monster. Such remembrance is bitter; but the temper of a mind exempt from avarice suggests some reasonable topics of consolation. My patrimony has been diminished in the enjoyment of life.] The gratification of my desires (they were not immoderate) has been seldom disappointed by the want of money or credit; my pride was never insulted by the visit of an importunate tradesman; and any transient anxiety for the past or future was soon dispelled by the studious or social occupation of the present hour. My conscience does not accuse me of any act of extravagance or injustice : the remnant of my estate affords an ample and honourable provision for my declining age, [and my spontaneous bounty must be received with implicit gratitude by the heirs of my choice.] I shall not expatiate [more minutely] on my œconomical affairs, which cannot be instructive or amusing to the reader. It is a rule of prudence, as well as of politeness, to reserve such confidence for the ear of a private friend, without exposing our situation to the envy or pity of strangers; for envy is productive of hatred, and pity borders too nearly on contempt. Yet I may believe, and even assert, that in circumstances more indigent or more wealthy, I should never have accomplished the task, or acquired the fame, of an historian; that my spirit would have been broken by poverty and contempt; and that my industry might have been relaxed in the labour and luxury of a superfluous fortune. [Few works of merit and importance have been executed either in a garret or a palace. A gentleman, possessed of leisure and independence, of books and talents, may be encouraged to write by the distant prospect of honour and reward; but wretched is the author, and wretched will be the work, where daily diligence is stimulated by daily hunger.]

MY OWN LIFE.*

[My family is ancient and honourable in the county of Kent.[1] As early as the year 1326 the Gibbons, who still bear the same arms as myself,[2] were possessed of lands in the parish of Rolvenden,[3] and their successive alliances connect them with many worthy names of the English

---

[1] I have obtained much domestic information from an English treatise of Heraldry (with a Latin title), composed by John Gibbon, Blue-mantle Poursuivant, and the brother, as I believe, of my great-grandfather Matthew—*Introductio ad Latinam Blazoniam*, London, 1682, in 12mo. The author of this odd and even original work is deeply tinctured with the prejudices of his age and his art. After observing the colours and symbols on the painted bodies of the Indians of Virginia, he logically concludes that "Heraldry is ingrafted naturally into the sense of human race" (p. 156). I wish to insert his *diabolical* scutcheon for the Whigs (p. 165). The Gibbons were high Tories.

[2] *A Lyon, rampant, gardant, between three Schallops.* Blue-mantle tells a whimsical story of Edmond Gibbon, who changed the three schallops of his arms into three ogresses, or female monsters, the emblems of three cousins with whom he had a law-suit (p. 161).

[3] "Nedum mentionem sum facturus" (he modestly talks Latin) "Gibbonos terras tenuisse et possedisse in Rolvenden, anno 1326." Fourteen years afterwards, King Edward III. granted to his *Murmorarius*, John Gibbon, the profits of the passage between Sandwich and the isle of Thanet, the reward of no vulgar architect. He is supposed to have built Queensborough Castle (p. 160).

* Memoir E; from the early history of the family to July, 1789. The numbered notes to this Memoir are Gibbon's own.

gentry.[4] About the beginning of the last century, a younger branch appears to have migrated from the country to the city. My grandfather, Edward Gibbon, was Commissioner of the Customs (1710–1714), and a Director of the South Sea Company. In the calamitous year twenty, he was stripped of his apparent fortune (£106,543 5s. 6d.) by an arbitrary vote of the house of commons, which reduced him to an allowance of ten thousand pounds;[5] yet such were his dexterity and diligence, that he died, sixteen years afterwards, in very affluent circumstances. My father, Edward Gibbon (born in 1707), enjoyed the advantages of education and travel, and successively represented in Parliament the borough of Petersfield (1734) and the town of Southampton (1740). In the opposition to Sir Robert Walpole and the Pelhams he was connected with the Tories—shall I say the Jacobites? With them he gave many a vote, with them he drank many a bottle. But the prejudices of youth were gradually corrected by time, temper, and good sense.

---

[4] See the Introductio ad Blazoniam, pp. 157–160. Our most respectable ancestor in the female line is Lord Say and Seale, Lord High Treasurer of England in the reign of Henry VI. According to Shakespeare, he may be considered as a martyr of Litterature. My grandfather was allied by his wife and sister to the Actons of Shropshire, who now claim the Minister of the Sicilian Monarchy.

[5] See the whole course of these iniquitous proceedings in Rapin and Tindal's History of England (vol. iv. pt. ii. pp. 629–644, folio Edition). The offence of the South Sea Directors was not defined in law; their guilt was not proved, in fact: they were refused the common right of being heard by their council against a bill of pains and penalties, and their fate was decided by hasty and passionate votes on the character and fortune of each individual. It may be added, as a last aggravation, that the legal existence of the Parliament which condemned them is extremely questionable.

I was born at his house at Putney, in Surry, the eldest child of his marriage, a marriage of inclination, with Judith Porten. My five brothers and my sister all died in their infancy, and the premature decease of my mother (1746) left her fond husband a disconsolate widower.[6] Some years afterwards (1755) he was married to his second wife, Mrs. Dorothea Patten, whose tender friendship has often made me forget that I had scarcely known the blessing of a mother.

From my birth to the age of fifteen, my puny constitution was afflicted with almost every species of disease and weakness; and I owe my life to the maternal tenderness of my aunt, Mrs. Catherine Porten, at whose name I feel a tear of gratitude trickling down my cheek: My first domestic tutor was Mr. John Kirkby, the author of an English Grammar and the Philosophical Romance of Automathes.[7] But my progress at Kingston and West-

---

[6] In an agreable little poem, in which Mr. Mallet invites some friends to the anniversary of his wedding-day, my father is thus introduced—

"But first a pensive love forlorn,
    Who three long weeping years has borne
    His torch revers'd, and all around,
    Where once it flam'd with Cypress bound,
    Sent off to call *a neighbouring friend*,
    On whom the mournful train attend;
    And bid him, this one day at least,
    For such a pair, at such a feast,
    Strip off the sable vest, and wear
    His once gay look and happier air."

[7] A self-taught Youth who discovers Religion and Science in a desert island, is indeed a Romance. The characters of a Philosopher and a Bigot are blended in my old tutor; but the story of Automathes (London, 1745, in 12mo) is agreably told. The original idea is borrowed, however, from the life of Hai Ebn Yokdhan, composed in

minster Schools was too often interrupted by my returns of illness; and the want of public discipline was imperfectly supplied by private instruction. It is fashionable for the *man* to envy and regret the happiness of the *boy*, but I never could understand the happiness of servitude; [8] and my want of agility and strength disqualified me for the joyous play of my equals. The long hours of confinement to my chamber or my couch were soothed, however, by an early and eager love of reading. Some books of fiction, Pope's Homer and the Arabian Nights, were the first food of my mind; but I soon began to devour, with indiscriminate appetite, the history, chronology, and geography of the ancient and modern world.

A.D. 1752. April 3.   At an unripe age I was matriculated as a Gentleman-commoner at Magdalen College, in the University of Oxford, where I lost fourteen valuable months of my youth. The reader will ascribe this loss to my own incapacity, or to the vices of that ancient institution. [9]

A.D. 1753. March.   Without a master or a guide, I unfortunately stumbled on some books of Popish controversy; nor is it a matter of reproach that a boy should have believed that he

---

the twelfth century by Abû Jaafar Ebn Tophaïl, and translated from Arabic into Latin by Dr. Pocock (Oxon, 1700, in 4to, secundâ edit.). There is a very good abstract in the Bibliothèque Universelle (tom. iii. pp. 76–98) of Le Clerc.

[8] A similar opinion is ascribed by d'Alembert (Éloges des Academiciens, tom. iii. p. 24) to Boileau, who had suffered, indeed, many hardships in his childhood and youth. The life of a schoolboy is by no means exempt from care or passion, and he is yet unripe for the highest enjoyments of the mind and body.

[9] The revenues, monopoly, and idleness of these Ecclesiastical corporations are justly censured by Dr. Adam Smith (Riches of Nations, vol. ii. pp. 340–374), who affirms that most of the professors of Oxford have given up even the pretence of public teaching.

believed, etc. I was seduced like Chillingworth and Bayle,[10] and, like them, my growing reason soon broke through the toils of sophistry and superstition.

Most fortunately my father was persuaded to fix my exile and education at Lausanne, in Switzerland, under the care of Mr. Pavillard, a Calvinist Minister. I would praise his virtue above his learning, his learning above his genius: yet a pupil might imbibe from his lessons the love, the method, and the rudiments of science, and I shall always esteem that worthy man as the first father of my mind.

At the end of five years I was recalled home—of five years which my voluntary and rational diligence had profitably employed. It was at Lausanne that I acquired the perfect knowledge and use of the French language; that I read almost all the Latin Classics in prose and verse; that I made some progress in Greek litterature; and that I finished a regular course of Philosophy and Mathematics. It was there that my taste and reason were expanded; that I formed the habits of being pleased (I will not say of pleasing) in good company; and that I eradicated the prejudices which would have ripened in the Atmosphere of an English Cloyster. A tour of Switzerland enlarged my views of Nature and man: I enjoyed the singular amusement of seeing Voltaire an actor

---

[10] When these masters of argument were seduced by Popery, the Frenchman was near twenty-two, the Englishman above twenty-eight years of age. In their retrograde motion, the logic of Chillingworth paused on the last verge of Christianity; the genius of Bayle pervaded the boundless regions of Scepticism. See the article CHILLINGWORTH in the third Volume of the new Edition of the Biographia Britannica; and Vie de Pierre Bayle, by Mr. des Maizeaux, in the first volume of the Dictionary.

in his own tragedies;[11] and, before the age of twenty, I solicited and sustained a learned correspondence with several professors in foreign universities.[12]   I should blush if the season of youth had passed away without love or friendship.   My connection with Mr. George Deyverdun, a young gentleman of Lausanne, has been terminated only by the death of my friend.   A lover's wishes reluctantly yielded to filial duty;[13] time and absence produced their effect; but my choice has been justified by the virtues of Mademoiselle C—— (now Madame N——) in the most humble and the most splendid fortune.

---

[11] Voltaire had lately escaped from the dangers of Royal friendship, and now began, at the age of threescore, to enjoy his freedom and fortune.   His letters, dated from Lausanne, repeatedly praise, in 1757 and 1758, the country, the people, his audience, his actors, etc. (Correspondance générale, tom. iv. pp. 396, 408, 410, 414, 419, 421–424, 429, 430, 431, 439; tom. v. pp. 6, 9, 15, 16, 19, 21–23, 26, 34; Edition de Beaumarchais).

[12] Crevier of Paris, Gesner of Gottingen, and Breitinger of Zurich are known as Authors or Editors.   But the most valuable of my correspondents was Mr. Allamand of Bex, whose learning and philosophy were buried in a Swiss village.

[13] See Œuvres de Rousseau, tom. xxxiii. pp. 88, 89, octavo Edition.   As an author, I shall not appeal from the judgement, or taste, or caprice of *Jean Jacques*; but that extraordinary man, whom I admire and pity, should have been less precipitate in condemning the moral character and conduct of a stranger.*

   * "*Lettre à Mr. M[oult]u.*

"A Motiers, le 4 Juin 1763.

"Vous me donnez pour Mlle. C—— une commission dont je m'acquitterai mal, précisément à cause de mon estime pour elle. Le refroidissement de M. G—— me fait mal penser de lui; j'ai revu son livre; il y court après l'esprit, il s'y guinde: M. G—— n'est point mon homme; je ne puis croire qu'il soit celui de Mlle. C—— qui ne sent pas son prix, n'est pas digne d'elle; mais qui l'a pu sentir, & s'en détache, est un homme à mépriser. Elle ne sait ce qu'elle veut, cet homme la sert mieux que son propre cœur. J'aime cent fois mieux qu'il la laisse pauvre & libre au milieu de vous, que de l'emmener être malheureuse & riche en Angleterre. En vérité je souhaite que M. G—— ne vienne pas. Je voudrois me déguiser, mais je ne saurois, je voudrois bien faire, & je sens que je gâterai tout."

On my return home I was indulged with a decent allowance of money and liberty; and the two following years were unequally divided between a short visit to London, and a long calm residence in my father's house at Buriton, near Petersfield, in Hampshire. For rural sports and agriculture I had no taste; and all the hours that I could steal from family duties were deliciously passed in a library, which soon became my own. By practise and study I recovered the purity of my native tongue; and the English, Greek, and Latin Classics were the best companions of my solitude. My pen was seldom idle, and I began to write for the public eye as well as for my own.

From these studies I was called away by the sound of the militia drum, by the embodying of the South Battalion of the Hampshire, in which I had rashly accepted a Captain's commission, and in which I was afterwards promoted to the rank of Major and Lieutenant Colonel-Commandant. At the first outset I was dazzled and fired by the play of arms, the exercise, the march, and the camp, and my present acquaintance will smile when I assure them that I was once a very tolerable officer. I read Homer in my tent, I compared the theory of ancient with the practise of modern tactics; and the Captain of Grenadiers (they may again smile) has not been useless to the historian of the Roman Empire. By degrees our mimic Bellona unveiled her naked deformity, and before our final dissolution I had long sighed for my release.[14]

---

[14] In an old pocket-book of the time I find the satirical lines of Dryden, which thus conclude —

> "Of seeming arms they make a short essay;
> Then hasten to be drunk—the business of the day."

1761.
June.

In the midst of this military life, I published my *Essai sur l'étude de la Litterature,* which was extorted from me by my father's authority, and the advice of Dr. Maty[15] and Mr. Mallet,[16] after it had slept two or three years in my desk. The vanity of being the first English author in the French language[17] might perhaps be excused ; but, in sober truth, I wrote, as I thought, in the most familiar idiom. The journals of Paris[18] and Holland have praised the style and spirit, the learning and judgement, of this juvenile performance, with which, at the distance of thirty years, I am not absolutely displeased. But in England my Essay was slowly

---

In the qualifications of dexterity and discipline our embodied regiments were far superior to the old militia. But the exercise of the field was still succeeded by that of the bottle, and the habit of intemperance too long survived my discharge from the service.

[15] The eighteen volumes of the *Journal Britannique,* which he sustained six years (1750–1755), almost alone had displayed the moderation and taste of Dr. Maty. A flattering epistle which he prefixed to my Essay is so cautiously worded, that, in case of a defeat, he might have excused his indulgence to a *young English gentleman.*

[16] The author of a Life of Bacon (which has been rated above its value), of some forgotten poems and plays, and of the pathetic ballad of William and Margaret. An enemy, and a stern enemy (Johnson's Lives of the Poets), acknowledges that Mallet's conversation was elegant and easy.

[17] The French letters of Sir William Temple, Lord Bolingbroke, Lord Chesterfield, etc., were not composed for the public. The writings of the Chevalier Ramsay and Count Hamilton may form an exception ; but the latter, who is indeed a model of original style, had been educated from his infancy in France.

[18] The copious extracts which were given in the *Journal Etranger* by Mr. Suard, a judicious critic, must satisfy both the author and the public. I may here observe that I have never seen, in any literary review, a tolerable account of my History. The manufacture of Journals, at least on the Continent, is miserably debased.

circulated, little read, and soon forgotten; till the fame of the historian enhanced the price of the remaining copies, which I refused to multiply by a new edition. After this first experiment, I meditated some historical composition. Many subjects were examined and rejected: an *history of the freedom and victories of the Swiss* was the theme on which I dwelt with the longest pleasure, and which I abandoned with the most reluctance.[19]

The hour of peace and national triumph was propitious to my design of visiting the continent. The arts and public buildings, the libraries and theatres of Paris, might have occupied more than four months the curiosity of a stranger. But the favourable reception of my Essay, and some weighty recommendations, introduced me into the societies of Helvetius, of the Baron d'Holbach, of Mr. de Foncemagne, of Madame Geoffrin, and of Madame du Bocage. At these elegant Symposia, to which I was wellcome, without invitation, almost every day of the week, I saw and heard the most eminent of the wits, scholars, and philosophers of France; and it was amusing, as well as instructive, to compare the writings with the characters of the men.

1763.
January—
May.

In my second voluntary visit I was received at Lausanne as a native, who, after a long absence, returns to his friends, his family, and his country. The simple charms of Nature and society detained me at the foot of the Alps till the ensuing spring; and I justified my

1763.
May—
1764.
April.

---

[19] By the assistance of Mr. Deyverdun I obtained many extracts and translations from the German originals of Tschudi, Stetler, Schilling, Lauffer, Leu, etc.; but I soon found, on a tryal, that these materials were insufficient. An historian should command the language, the libraries, and the archives of the country of which he presumes to write.

delay by the useful study of the Italian and Roman antiquities.

1764.
April—
1765.
June.
The pilgrimage of Italy, which I now accomplished, had long been the object of my curious devotion. The passage of Mount Cenis, the regular streets of Turin, the Gothic cathedral of Milan, the scenery of the Boromean Islands, the marble palaces of Genoa, the beauties of Florence, the wonders of Rome, the curiosities of Naples, the galleries of Bologna, the singular aspect of Venice, the amphitheatre of Verona, and the Palladian architecture of Vicenza, are still present to my imagination. I read the Tuscan writers on the banks of the Arno; but my conversation was with the dead rather than the living, and the whole college of Cardinals was of less value in my eyes than the transfiguration of Raphael, the Apollo of the Vatican, or the massy greatness of the Coliseum. It was at Rome, on the fifteenth of October, 1764, as I sat musing amidst the ruins of the Capitol, while the barefooted fryars were singing Vespers in the temple of Jupiter, that the idea of writing the decline and fall of the City first started to my mind. After Rome has kindled and satisfied the enthusiasm of the Classic pilgrim, his curiosity for all meaner objects insensibly subsides. My father was impatient, and I returned home by the way of Lyons and Paris, enriched with a new stock of images and ideas, which I could never have acquired in the solitude of the Closet.

1765.
June—
1770.
November.
After this various and delightfull excursion, I again settled, in the dull division of my English year, between London and Buriton. But in the militia I had been used to command, in my travels I was free from controul. The most gentle authority will sometimes frown without

reason, the most chearful obedience will sometimes murmur without cause; and, at the age of thirty, I felt the natural wish of being master in my own house. The love of study secured me against the tediousness of an idle life, but I sometimes regretted that I had not consulted my interest and independence by the timely choice of a lucrative profession.

The greatest part of the seven years which elapsed after my return home was seriously employed in preparing the materials of my Roman history, of whose nature and extent at first I had a very inadequate idea. i. From the Augustan age to the fall of the western Empire, I studied, almost always with my pen in my hand, the original records, both Greek and Latin, both Ecclesiastical and profane. I have never denied or dissembled my obligations to modern glasses, more especially to the incomparable microscope of Tillemont; but as it was my privilege to think with my own reason, so it was my duty to see with my own eyes. ii. In the Italian history of the middle ages, Muratori and Pagi, Sigonius and Maffei, were my faithful and assiduous guides; and I grasped the ruins of Rome in the fourteenth century, without suspecting that the distant object would fly before me to the end of a sixth quarto.

Yet in the progress of my work I was often diverted by the amusements of the World, and the avocations of old and new books; of the ancient Classics of Greece and Rome, of the annual publications of France and England. During this period I twice gave my thoughts, without giving my name, to the public. I joyned with my friend Mr. Deyverdun, who resided several years in England: we published two volumes of a litterary

1765–
1772.

Journal or review, *Memoires Litteraires de la Grande
Bretagne*, for the years 1767 and 1768 ; but in this social
work I am not ambitious of ascertaining my peculiar
property. In the year 1770 I sent to the press some
Critical Observations on the Sixth Book of the Æneid. This
anonymous pamphlet was pointed against Bishop Warburton, who demonstrates that the descent of Æneas
to the shades is an Allegory of his initiation to the
Eleusinian mysteries. The love of Virgil, the hatred
of a Dictator,[20] and the example of Lowth,[21] awakened

---

[20] Our litterary Sylla was encompassed with a guard of flatterers
and slaves ready to execute every sentence of proscription which
his arrogance had pronounced. The assassination of Jortin by Dr.
Hurd, now Bishop of Worcester (see the Delicacy of Friendship), is
a base and malignant act, which cannot be crazed by time or expiated
by *secret* pennance.[*]

[21] See a letter from a late Professor in the University of Oxford
(1766, fourth Edition). The public adjudged the prize to the chaste
and temperate spirit of Dr. Lowth (since Bishop of London), who had
been furiously attacked by Warburton and his bloodhounds. As long
as the dispute is connected with the taste and knowledge of Hebrew
poetry, the Oxford professor fights on his own ground. But his
argument is often weak ; and how can it be strong, when he pleads
the cause of bigotry and persecution ?[†]

[*] Dr. John Jortin, in 1755, in a dissertation *On the State of the Dead
as described by Homer and Virgil*, had strongly opposed the theory of
Warburton mentioned in the text, and was thereupon attacked with
considerable severity by Hurd in his treatise *On the Delicacy of
Friendship, a Seventh Dissertation, addressed to the Author of the Sixth.*
Hurd again took up the cudgels on behalf of his patron, Warburton, in
1764, when his *Doctrine of Grace* was controverted by Dr. Thomas
Leland. and Dr. Warburton on the use made of the Book of Job in support of a chronological argument in the lectures. The dispute was
apparently at an end, till Warburton, in 1765, renewed the
attack in the sixth book of his *Divine Legation*, and was answered
by Lowth in his *Letter to the Author of the Divine Legation*, which is
described by Gibbon as " a pointed and polished epistle."

" This letter of Lowth's is a masterpiece of its kind, and if our
calmer judgment is offended by the unseemly spectacle of two Christian
prelates engaged in this fierce gladiatorism, the chief blame must
fall on the aggressor, Warburton."
—Milman.

[†] In 1741 Robert Lowth, when Professor of Poetry at Oxford, delivered a series of *Lectures on Hebrew Poetry*. In 1756 some controversy took place between him

me to arms.   The coldness of the public has been amply compensated by the esteem of Heyne,[22] of Hayley,[23] and of Parr;[24] but the acrimony of my style has been justly blamed by the Professor of Gottingen.   Warburton [25] was *not* an object of contempt.

---

[22] That incomparable scholar, who, after so many hundred editions has enriched the world with the *first* edition of Virgil, declines the examination of Warburton's hypothesis, " Otium fecit vir doctus, qui eam in singulari libello paullo acrius quam velis perstrinxit" (Virgilii Opera, tom. ii. p. 804, Lipsiæ, 1787).   He afterwards (p. 821) approves a conjecture, " elegantissimi Britanni," etc.

[23] "At length a superior but anonymous critic arose, who, in one of the most judicious and spirited essays which our nation has produced on a point of classical literature, compleatly overturned this ill-founded edifice, etc." (Hayley's Works, vol. iii. p. 152, etc.).   He then transcribes several passages, from an idea that the circulation of the pamphlet had not been equal to its merit.

[24] The editor of the Warburtonian Tracts (p. 192) considers the Allegorical interpretation " as completely refuted in a most clear, elegant, and decisive work of criticism, which could not indeed derive authority from the greatest name, but to which the greatest name might with propriety have been affixed."

[25] The Divine Legation of Moses * is a monument, already crumbling into dust, of the vigour and weakness of the human mind. If Warburton's new argument proved any thing, it would be a demonstration against the Legislator, who left his people without the knowledge of a future state.   But some episodes of the work on the Greek philosophy, the Hieroglyphics of Egypt, etc., are entitled to the praise of learning, imagination, and discernment.

* *The Divine Legation of Moses Demonstrated, on the Principles of a Religious Deist, from the Omission of the Doctrine of a Future State of Rewards and Punishments in the Jewish Dispensation*, bks. 1-3, 1738; bks. 4-6, 1741; bk. 9, 1788. "That the doctrine of a future state of reward and punishment was omitted in the Book of Moses had been insolently urged by infidels against the truth of his mission, while divines were feebly occupied in seeking what was certainly not to be found there, otherwise than by inference or implication.   But Warburton, with an intrepidity unheard of before, threw open the gates of his camp, admitted the host of his enemy within his works, and beat them on a ground which was now become both his and theirs.   In short, he admitted the proposition in its fullest extent, and proceeded to demonstrate from that very omission, which in all instances

1770.
Nov. 10.

At the time of my father's decease I was upwards of thirty-three years of age, the ordinary term of an human generation. My grief was sincere for the loss of an affectionate parent, an agreeable companion, and a worthy man. But the ample fortune which my grandfather had left was deeply impaired, and would have been gradually consumed by the easy and generous nature of his son.[26] I revere the memory of my father, his errors I forgive, nor can I repent of the important sacrifices which were chearfully offered by filial piety. Domestic command, the free distribution of time and place, and a more liberal measure of expence, were the immediate consequences of my new situation; but two

1772.
October.

years rolled away before I could disentangle myself from the web of rural œconomy, and adopt a mode of life agreeable to my wishes. From Buriton Mrs. Gibbon withdrew to Bath; while I removed myself and my books into my new house in Bentinck Street, Cavendish Square, in which I continued to reside near eleven years. The clear untainted remains of my patrimony have been always sufficient to support the rank of a Gentleman, and to satisfy the desires of a philosopher.]

1773.
January—
1783.
September.

I had now attained [the solid comforts of life—a convenient well-furnished house, a domestic table, half

---

[26] In his Hampshire retirement, my father might seem to enjoy the state of primitive happiness—"Beatus ille qui procul negotiis, etc." But, alas! he was not "solutus omni fœnore," and without such freedom there can be no content.

of legislation, merely human, had been industriously avoided, that a system which could dispense with such a doctrine, the very bond and cement of human society, must have come from God, and that the people to whom it was given must have been placed under His immediate superintendence."—Dr. Whittaker, in *Quarterly Review*, vii. 398.

a dozen chosen servants, my own carriage, and all those
decent luxuries whose value is the more sensibly felt
the longer they are enjoyed. These advantages were
crowned by] the first of earthly blessings, independence.
I was the absolute master of my hours and actions; nor
was I deceived in the hope that the establishment of
my library in town would allow me to divide the day
between study and society. Each year the circle of my
acquaintance, the number of my dead and living companions, was enlarged. To a lover of books the shops
and sales in London present irresistible temptations, and
the manufacture of my history required a various and
growing stock of materials. The Militia, my travels, the
House of Commons, the fame of an author, contributed
to multiply my connections. I was chosen a member
of the fashionable clubs; [27] and before I left England
there were few persons of any eminence in the litterary
or political World to whom I was a stranger. [28] By my
own choice I passed in town the greatest part of the

---

[27] From the mixed, though polite, company of Boodle's, White's
and Brooks's, I must honourably distinguish a weekly society which
was instituted in the year 1764, and which still continues to flourish
under the title of the Literary Club (Hawkins's life of Johnson,
p. 415; Boswell's Tour to the Hebrides, p. 97). The names of
Dr. Johnson, Mr. Burke, Mr. Garrick, Dr. Goldsmith, Sir Joshua
Reynolds, Mr. Colman, Sir William Jones, Dr. Percy, Mr. Fox,
Mr. Sheridan, Mr. Adam Smith, Mr. Steevens, Mr. Dunning, Sir
Joseph Banks, Dr. Warton, and his brother, Mr. Thomas Warton,
Dr. Burney, etc., form a large and luminous constellation of British
stars.

[28] It would most assuredly be in my power to amuse the reader
with a gallery of portraits and a collection of anecdotes; but I have
always condemned the practise of transforming a private memorial
into a vehicle of satire and praise.

year; but whenever I was desirous of breathing the air of the Country, I possessed an hospitable retreat at Sheffield Place, in Sussex, in the family of Mr. Holroyd, a valuable friend, whose character, under the name of Lord Sheffield, has since been more conspicuous to the public.

1773.
February,
etc.

No sooner was I settled in my house and library than I undertook the composition of the first Volume of my history. / At the outset all was dark and doubtful—even the title of the work, the true æra of the decline and fall of the Empire, the limits of the Introduction, the division of the chapters, and the order of the narrative; and I was often tempted to cast away the labour of seven years. The style of an author should be the image of his mind, but the choice and command of language is the fruit of exercise; many experiments were made before I could hit the middle tone between a dull Chronicle and a Rhetorical declamation; three times did I compose the first chapter, and twice the second and third, before I was tolerably satisfied with their effect. In the remainder of the way I advanced with a more equal and easy pace; but the fifteenth and sixteenth Chapters have been reduced, by three successive revisals, from a large Volume to their present size, and they might still be compressed without any loss of facts or sentiments. An opposite fault may be imputed to the concise and superficial narrative of the first reigns from Commodus to Alexander, a fault of which I have never heard except from Mr. Hume in his last journey to London. Such an oracle might have been consulted and obeyed with rational devotion; but I was soon disgusted with the modest practise of reading the manuscript to my friends. Of such friends some will praise from politeness, and some will criticise from vanity. The author himself is the best Judge of his own performances; none has so deeply meditated on the subject, none is so sincerely interested in the event.

By the friendship of Mr. (now Lord) Eliot, who had married my first cousin,[29] I was returned at the general election for the borough of Leskeard. I took my seat at the beginning of the memorable contest between

---

[29] Catherine Elliston, whose mother, Catherine Gibbon, was my grandfather's second daughter. The education of Lady Eliot, a rich heiress, had been entrusted to the Mallets; and she is thus invited to their Hymenæal feast.

> "Last comes a virgin—Pray admire her!
> Cupid himself attends to squire her:
> A welcome guest! we much had mist her;
> For 'tis our Kitty, or his sister.
> But, Cupid, let no knave or fool
> Snap up this lamb to shear her wool;
> No Teague of that unblushing band,
> Just landed, or about to land;
> Thieves from the womb, and train'd at nurse
> To steal an heiress, or a purse.
> No scraping, saving, saucy cit,
> Sworn foe of breeding, worth, and wit;
> No half-form'd insect of a peer,
> With neither land nor conscience clear,
> Who, if he can, 'tis all he can do,
> Just spell the motto on his Landau.
> From all, from each of these defend her,
> But thou and Hymen both befriend her,
> With truth, taste, honour in a mate,
> And much good sense, and some estate."

The poet's wishes were soon accomplished, by her marriage with Mr. Eliot, of Port Eliot, in Cornwall. In the year 1784 he was raised to the honour of an English peerage, and their three sons are all Members of the house of Commons.

Great Britain and America; and supported, with many
a sincere and *silent* vote, the rights, though not perhaps
the interests, of the mother-country. After a fleeting
illusive hope, prudence condemned me to acquiesce in
the humble station of a mute. I was not armed by
Nature or education with the intrepid energy of mind and
voice—

" Vincentem strepitus, et natum rebus agendis."

timidity was fortified by pride, and even the success
of my pen discouraged the tryal of my voice. But I
assisted at the debates of a free assembly, [which agitated
the most important questions, of peace and war, of Justice
and Policy :] I listened to the attack and :defence of
eloquence and reason; I had a near prospect of the
characters, views, and passions of the first men of the
age. The eight sessions that I sat in Parliament were
a school of civil prudence, the first and most essential
virtue of an historian.

1775.
June.
      The volume of my history, which had been somewhat
delayed by the novelty and tumult of a first session, was
now ready for the press. After the perilous adventure
had been declined by my timid friend Mr. Elmsley, I
agreed, on very easy terms, with Mr. Thomas Cadell, a
respectable bookseller, and Mr. William Strahan, an
eminent printer; and they undertook the care and risk
of the publication, which derived more credit from the
name of the shop than from that of the author. The
last revisal of the proofs was submitted to my vigilance;
and many blemishes of style, which had been invisible
in the manuscript, were discovered and corrected in the
printed sheet. So moderate were our hopes, that the
original impression had been stinted to five hundred, till

the number was doubled by the prophetic taste of **Mr.** Strahan.   During this awful interval I was neither elated by the ambition of fame, nor depressed by the apprehension of contempt.   My diligence and accuracy were attested by my own conscience.   History is the most popular species of writing, since it can adapt itself to the highest or the lowest capacity.   I had chosen an illustrious subject; Rome is familiar to the schoolboy and the statesman, and my narrative was deduced from the last period of Classical reading..   I had likewise flattered myself that an age of light and liberty would receive, without scandal, an enquiry into the *human* causes of the progress and establishment of Christianity.

I am at a loss how to describe the success of the work without betraying the vanity of the writer.   The first impression was exhausted in a few days; a second and third edition were scarcely adequate to the demand, and the bookseller's property was twice invaded by the pyrates of Dublin.   My book was on every table, and almost on every toilette; the historian was crowned by the taste or fashion of the day; nor was the general voice disturbed by the barking of any profane critic.   The favour of mankind is most freely bestowed on a new acquaintance of any original merit, and the mutual surprize of the public and their favourite is productive of those warm sensibilities which, at a second meeting, can no longer be rekindled.   If I listened to the music of praise, I was more seriously satisfied with the approbation of my Judges.   The candour of Dr. Robertson embraced his disciple; a letter from Mr. Hume[30] overpaid the

1776.
February
17.

---

[30] That curious and original letter will amuse the reader; and his

labour of ten years; but I have never presumed to accept a place in the triumvirate of British historians.

My second excursion to Paris was determined by the

---

gratitude should shield my free communication from the reproach of vanity.

" Edinburgh, 18th of March, 1776.

" Dear Sir,

        " As I ran through your Volume of History with great avidity and impatience, I cannot forbear discovering somewhat of the same impatience in returning you thanks for your agreeable present, and expressing the satisfaction which the performance has given me. Whether I consider the dignity of your style, the depth of your matter, or the extensiveness of your learning, I must regard the work as equally the object of esteem, and I own that, if I had not præviously had the happiness of your personal acquaintance, such a performance from an Englishman in our age would have given me some surprize. You may smile at this sentiment; but as it seems to me that your countrymen, for almost a whole generation, have given themselves up to barbarous and absurd faction, and have totally neglected all polite letters, I no longer expected any valuable production ever to come from them. I know it will give you pleasure (as it did me) to find that all the men of letters in this place concur in their admiration of your work, and in their anxious desire of your continuing it.

        " When I heard of your undertaking (which was some time ago) I own that I was a little curious to see how you would extricate yourself from the subject of your two last chapters. I think you have observed a very prudent temperament; but it was impossible to treat the subject so as not to give grounds of suspicion against you, and you may expect that a clamour will arise. This, if anything, will retard your success with the public; for in every other respect your work is calculated to be popular. But, among many other marks of decline, the prevalence of superstition in England prognosticates the fall of Philosophy, and decay of taste; and though nobody be more capable than you to revive them, you will probably find a struggle in your first advances.

        " I see you entertain a great doubt with regard to the authenticity of the poems of Ossian. You are certainly right in so doing. It is indeed strange that any men of sense could have imagined it possible that above twenty thousand verses, along with numberless historical

pressing invitation of Mr. and Madame Necker, who had
visited England in the preceding summer. On my
arrival I found Mr. Necker, Director-general of the
finances, in the first bloom of power and popularity; his
private fortune enabled him to support a liberal establishment; and his wife, whose talents and virtues I had
long admired, was admirably qualified to preside in the
conversation of her table and drawing-room. As their
friend, I was introduced to the best company of both
sexes; to the foreign ministers of all nations, and to the
first names and characters of France, who distinguished
me by such marks of civility and kindness as gratitude
will not suffer me to forget, and modesty will not allow

---

facts, could have been preserved by oral tradition, during fifty generations, by the rudest perhaps of all the European nations, the most
necessitous, the most turbulent, and the most unsettled. Where a
supposition is so contrary to common sense, any positive evidence for
it ought never to be regarded; men run with great avidity to give
their evidence in favour of what flatters their passions and their
national prejudices. You are, therefore, over and above indulgent to
us in speaking of the matter with hesitation.

"I must inform you that we are all very anxious to hear that you
have fully collected the materials for your second volume, and that
you are even considerably advanced in the composition of it. I speak
this more in the name of my friends than in my own, as I cannot
expect to live so long as to see the publication of it. Your ensuing
Volume will be still more delicate than the preceding, but I trust in
your prudence for extricating you from the difficulties; and in all
events you have courage to despise the clamour of Bigots.

"I am, with great regard,

"Dear Sir,

"Your most obedient and most humble servant,

"DAVID HUME."

Some weeks afterwards I had the melancholy pleasure of seeing
Mr. Hume in his passage through London; his body feeble, his mind
firm. On the 25th of August of the same year (1776) he died at
Edinburgh, the death of a Philosopher.

me to enumerate. The fashionable suppers often broke into the morning hours; yet I occasionally consulted the Royal Library, and that of the Abbey of St. Germain; and in the free use of their books at home I had always reason to praise the liberality of those institutions. The society of men of letters I neither courted nor declined; but I was happy in the acquaintance of Mr. de Buffon, who united with a sublime Genius the most amiable simplicity of mind and manners. At the table of my old friend, Mr. de Foncemagne, I was involved in a dispute [31] with the Abbé de Mably, [32] and his jealous

---

[31] As I might be partial in my own cause, I shall transcribe the words of an unknown critic (Supplément à la manière d'écrire l'histoire, p. 125, etc.), observing only that this dispute had been preceded by another on the English constitution at the house of the Countess de Froulay, an old Jansenist Lady. " Vous étiez chez M. de Foncemagne, mon cher Theodon, le jour que M. l'Abbé de Mably et M. Gibbon y dinerent en grande compagnie. La conversation roula presque entierement sur l'histoire. L'Abbé etant un profond politique, la tourna sur l'administration, quand on fut au dessert; et comme par caractère, par humeur, par l'habitude d'admirer Tite-Live, il ne prise que le système Républicain, il se mit à vanter l'excellence des Républiques; bien persuadé que le savant Anglois l'approuveroit en tout, et admireroit la profondeur de génie, qui avoit fait deviner tous ces avantages à un François. Mais M. Gibbon, instruit par experience des inconvéniens d'un gouvernement populaire, ne fut point du tout de son avis, et il prit généreusement la defense du gouvernement monarchique. L'Abbé voulut le convaincre par Tite-Live, et par quelques argumens tirés de Plutarque en faveur des Spartiates. M. Gibbon, doué de la memoire la plus heureuse, et ayant tous les faits présens à la pensée, domina bien-tôt la conversation; l'Abbé se fâcha, il s'emporta, il dit des choses dures. L'Anglois, conservant le flegme de son pays, prenoit ses avantages, et pressoit l'Abbé avec d'autant plus de succès que la colère le troubloit de plus en plus. La conversation s'echauffoit, et M. de Foncemagne la rompit en se levant de table, et en passant dans le sallon, où personne ne fut tenté de la renouer."

[2] Of the voluminous writings of the Abbé de Mably (see his *Eloge*

irascible spirit revenged itself on a work which he was incapable of reading in the original.[33]

Near two years had elapsed between the publication of my first and the commencement of my second Volume; and the causes must be assigned of this long delay. 1. After a short holyday I indulged my curiosity in some studies of a very different nature; a course of Anatomy which was demonstrated by Dr. Hunter, and some lessons of Chemistry which were delivered by Mr. Higgins: the principles of these sciences, and a taste for books of Natural history, contributed to multiply my ideas and images, and the Anatomist or Chemist may sometimes track me in their own snow. 2. I dived perhaps too deeply into the mud of the Arian controversy; and many days of reading, thinking, and writing were consumed in the pursuit of a phantom. 3. It is difficult to arrange with order and perspicuity the various transactions of the age of Constantine; and so much was I displeased

1777.
December,
etc.

---

by the Abbé Brizard), the *Principes du Droit public de L'Europe*, and the first part of the *Observations sur l'histoire de France*, may be deservedly praised; and even the *Manière d'ecrire l'histoire* contains several useful precepts and judicious remarks. Mably was a lover of virtue and freedom; but his virtue was austere, and his freedom was impatient of an equal. Kings, Magistrates, Nobles, and successful writers were the objects of his contempt, or hatred, or envy; but his illiberal abuse of Voltaire, Hume, Buffon, the Abbé Raynal, Dr. Robertson, and *tutti quanti*, can be injurious only to himself.

[33] "Est-il rien de plus fastidieux" (says the polite Censor), "qu'un M. *Guibbon*, qui, dans son eternelle histoire des Empereurs Romains, suspend à chaque instant son insipide et lente narration, pour vous expliquer la cause des faits que vous allez lire?" (Maniere d'ecrire l'histoire, p. 184; see another passage, p. 280). Yet I am indebted to the Abbé de Mably for two such advocates as the Anonymous French Critic (Supplément, pp. 125–134), and my friend Mr. Hayley (vol. ii. pp. 261–263).

with the first Essay, that I committed to the flames above
fifty sheets. 4. The six months of Paris and pleasure
must be deducted from the account. But when I resumed my task I felt my improvement. I was now
master of my style and subject; and while the measure
of my daily performance was enlarged, I discovered less
reason to cancel or correct. It has always been my
practise to cast a long paragraph in a single mould, to
try it by my ear, to deposit it in my memory, but to
suspend the action of the pen till I had given the last
polish to my work. Shall I add that I never found my
mind more vigorous or my composition more happy
than in the winter hurry of society and Parliament?

1779.
Feb. 3.

Had I believed that the majority of English readers
were so fondly attached even to the name and shadow
of Christianity, had I foreseen that the pious, the timid,
and the prudent would feel, or affect to feel, with such
exquisite sensibility, I might perhaps have softened the
two invidious Chapters, which would create many enemies
and conciliate few friends. But the shaft was shot, the
alarm was sounded, and I could only rejoyce that if
the voice of our priests was clamorous and bitter, their
hands were disarmed of the powers of persecution. I
adhered to the wise resolution of trusting myself and
my writings to the candour of the Public, till Mr. Davies
of Oxford presumed to attack, not the faith, but the good
faith, of the historian. My *Vindication*,[34] expressive of

---

[34] *A Vindication of some passages in the fifteenth and sixteenth
chapters of the History of the Decline and Fall of the Roman Empire,
by the Author : London*, 1779, *in octavo*—for I would not print it in
quarto, lest it should be bound and preserved with the History itself.
At the distance of twelve years, I calmly affirm my judgement of

less anger than contempt, amused for a moment the busy and idle metropolis; and the most rational part of the Laity, and even of the Clergy, appears to have been satisfied of my innocence and accuracy. My antagonists, however, were rewarded in this World: poor Chelsum * was indeed neglected, and I dare not boast the making Dr. Watson †
a Bishop;[85] but I enjoyed the pleasure of giving a Royal pension to Mr. Davies,‡ and of collating Dr. Apthorpe §
to an Archiepiscopal living. Their success encouraged the zeal of Taylor ‖ the Arian[36] and Milner the Me-

Davies, Chelsum, etc. A victory over such antagonists was a sufficient humiliation.

[35] Dr. Watson, now Bishop of Llandaff, is a prelate of a large mind and liberal spirit. I should be happy to think that his apology for Christianity had contributed, though at my expence, to clear his Theological character. He has amply repaid the obligation by the amusement and instruction which I have received from the five Volumes of his Chemical Essays. It is a great pity that an agreable and useful science should not yet be reduced to a state of *fixity*.

[36] The stupendous title, *Thoughts on the Causes of the Grand Apostacy*, at first agitated my nerves, till I discovered that it was the apostacy of the whole Church since the Council of Nice, from Mr. Taylor's private Religion. His book is a strange mixture of *high* enthusiasm, and *low* buffoonery, and the *Millennium* is a fundamental article of his creed.

* James Chelsum, D.D. (1740–1801), Fellow of Christ's College, Cambridge, author of *Remarks on Mr. Gibbon's History*, 1772 and 1778; *Reply to Gibbon's Vindication*, 1785. He also wrote a *History of the Art of Engraving*.

† Richard Watson (1737–1816), Fellow of Trinity College, Cambridge, Professor of Chemistry, Regius Professor of Divinity; Archdeacon of Ely, 1780; Bishop of Llandaff, 1782. *An Apology for Christianity, in a Series of Letters to Edward Gibbon*, appeared in 1776.

‡ Henry Edwards Davis (1756–1784) published an attack on the fifteenth and sixteenth chapters of Gibbon's *History*, within a few months of taking his B.A. degree at Balliol in 1778. His work displayed ability, but he was no match for the historian as a controversialist.

§ East Apthorp (1732–1816), a native of Boston, U.S.A, came to Jesus College, Cambridge, and was appointed Prebend of Finsbury, 1790.

‖ Henry Taylor (died 1785), Rector of Crawley and Vicar of Portsmouth. His *Thoughts on the Nature of the Grand Apostacy, with Reflections on the Fifteenth Chapter of Mr. Gibbon's History*, was published in 1781-2.

thodist,[37] with many others whom it would be difficult to remember and tedious to rehearse : the list of my adversaries was graced with the more respectable names of Dr. Priestley,[38] Sir David Dalrymple,[39] and Dr. White,[40] and

---

[37] From his Grammar school at Kingston-upon-Hull, Mr. Joseph Milner * pronounces an anathema against all rational Religion. *His* faith is a divine taste, a spiritual inspiration; *his* Church is a mystic and invisible body : the *natural* Christians, such as Mr. Locke, who believe and interpret the Scriptures, are in his judgement no better than profane infidels.

[38] In his History of the Corruptions of Christianity (vol. ii.), Dr. Priestly throws down his two gauntlets to Bishop Hurd and Mr. Gibbon. I declined the challenge in a polite letter, exhorting my opponent to enlighten the World by his philosophical discoveries, and to remember that the merit of his predecessor Servetus is now reduced to a single passage, which indicates the smaller circulation of the blood through the lungs, from and to the heart (Astruc de la structure du Cœur, tom. i. pp. 77–79). Instead of listening to this friendly advice, the dauntless philosopher of Birmingham continues to fire away his double battery against those who believe too little and those who believe too much. From *my* replies he has nothing to hope or fear; but his Socinian shield has repeatedly been pierced by the spear of the mighty Horsley, and his trumpet of sedition may at length awaken the magistrates of a free country.

[39] The profession and rank of Sir David Dalrymple (now a Lord of Session) † have given a more decent colour to his style. But he scrutinizes each separate passage of the two chapters with the dry minuteness of a special pleader; and as he is always solicitous to make, he may sometimes succeed in finding, a flaw. In his Annals of Scotland he has shewn himself a diligent Collector and an accurate Critic.

[40] I have praised, and I still praise the eloquent sermons which were preached in St. Mary's pulpit at Oxford by Dr. White.‡ If he

* Joseph Milner (1744–1797), Head-master of Hull Grammar School, and subsequently Vicar of Holy Trinity, Hull, was a voluminous writer; his best-known work is his *History of the Church of Christ*, which he did not live to complete. His *Gibbon's Account of Christianity Considered* appeared in 1781.

† Afterwards Lord Hailes (1726–1792).

‡ Joseph White, D.D. (1746–1814), son of a weaver at Gloucester, became Fellow of Wadham College, Laudian Professor of Arabic, and Regius Professor of Hebrew in Oxford. The allusion to Gibbon

every polemic of either University discharged his sermon or pamphlet against the impenetrable silence of the Roman historian.[41] Let me frankly own that I was startled at the first vollies of this Ecclesiastical ordnance; but as soon as I found that this empty noise was mischievous only in the intention, my fear was converted to indignation, and every feeling of indignation or curiosity has long since subsided in pure and placid indifference.

The prosecution of my history was soon afterwards checked by another controversy of a very different kind. At the request of the Chancellor and of Lord Weymouth, then Secretary of State, I vindicated against the French

1779.
May.

---

assaults me with some degree of illiberal acrimony, in such a place and before such an audience, he was obliged to speak the language of the country. I smiled at a passage in one of his private letters to Mr. Badcock: "The part where we encounter Gibbon must be brill[i]ant and striking."

[41] In a sermon lately preached before the University of Cambridge, Dr. Edwards compliments a work "which can only perish with the language itself," and esteems the author as a formidable enemy. He is indeed astonished that more learning and ingenuity has not been shewn in the defence of Israel; that the prelates and dignitaries of the Church (alas! good man) did not vie with each other whose stone should sink the deepest in the forehead of this Goliah. "But the force of truth will oblige us to confess that in the attacks which have been levelled against our Sceptical historian, we can discover but slender traces of profound and exquisite erudition, of solid criticism and accurate investigation; but are too frequently disgusted by vague and inconclusive reasoning, by unseasonable banter and senseless witticisms, by unlettered bigotry and enthusiastic jargon, by futile cavils and illiberal invectives. Proud and elated by the weakness of his antagonists, he condescends not to handle the sword of controversy, etc." (*Monthly Review* for October, 1790, vol. iii. p. 237).

was made in his *Bampton Lectures on Mahometanism and Christianity.* We need not here dwell on the use he made of the works of the Rev. Samuel Badcock, who is mentioned in Gibbon's note; the question is dealt with in the life of Dr. Samuel Parr.

manifesto the justice of the British arms. The whole correspondence of Lord Stormont, our late Ambassador at Paris, was submitted to my inspection, and the *Memoire Justificatif*, which I composed in French, was first approved by the Cabinet Ministers, and then delivered as a state paper to the Courts of Europe. The style and manner are praised by Beaumarchais himself, who, in his private quarrel, attempted a reply ; but he flatters me by ascribing the *Memoire* to Lord Stormont, and the grossness of his invective betrays the loss of temper and of wit.[42]

1779.
July 3.

Among the honourable connections which I had formed, I may justly be proud of the friendship of Mr. Wedderburne, at that time Attorney-General, who now illustrates the title of Lord Loughborough, and the office of Chief Justice of the Common pleas. By his strong recommendation, and the favourable disposition of Lord North, I was appointed one of the Lords Commissioners of trade and plantations, and my private income was enlarged by a clear addition of between seven and eight hundred pounds a year. The fancy of an hostile Orator may paint in the strong colours of ridicule "the perpetual virtual adjournment and the unbroken sitting vacation of the board of trade;"[43] but it must

---

[42] See Œuvres de Beaumarchais, tom. iii. pp. 299–355 : "Le style ne seroit pas sans graces ni la logique sans justesse," etc., if the facts were true, which he undertakes to disprove. For these facts my credit is not pledged—I spoke as a lawyer from my brief; but the veracity of Beaumarchais may be estimated from the assertion that France, by the treaty of Paris (1763), was limited to a certain number of ships of war. On the application of the Duke of Choiseul he was obliged to retract this daring falsehood.

[43] See Mr. Burke's Speech on the bill of reform, pp. 72–80. I can never forget the delight with which that diffusive and ingenious Orator was heard by all sides of the House, and even by those whose

be allowed that our duty was not intolerably severe, and that I enjoyed many days and weeks of repose without being called away from my library to the office. My acceptance of a place provoked some of the Leaders of opposition, with whom I lived in habits of intimacy, and I was most unjustly accused of deserting a party in which I had never been enlisted.

The aspect of the next Session of parliament was stormy and perilous: County meetings, petitions, and committees of correspondence announced the public discontent; and instead of voting with a triumphant majority, the friends of government were often exposed to a struggle and sometimes to a defeat. The house of Commons adopted Mr. Dunning's motion, "that the influence of the Crown had encreased, was encreasing, and ought to be diminished;" and Mr. Burke's bill of reform was framed with skill, introduced with eloquence, and supported by numbers. Our late president, the American Secretary of State, very narrowly escaped the sentence of proscription, but the unfortunate board of trade was abolished in the committee by a small majority (207 to 199) of eight votes. The storm, however, blew over for a time. A large defection of Country Gentlemen eluded the sanguine hopes of the patriots; the Lords of trade were revived; administration recovered their strength and spirit; and the flames of London, which were kindled by a mischievous madman, admonished all thinking men of the danger of an appeal to the people. In the præ-

A.D. 1780. March 13.

June 2, etc.

---

existence he proscribed. The Lords of Trade blushed at their own insignificancy, and Mr. Eden's appeal to the two thousand five hundred volumes of our reports served only to excite a general laugh. I take this opportunity of certifying the correctness of Mr. Burke's printed speeches, which I have heard and read.

Sept. 1. mature dissolution which followed this Session of parliament I lost my seat. Mr. Eliot was now deeply engaged in the measures of opposition, and the Electors of Leskeard are commonly of the same opinion as Mr. Eliot.

1781.
March 1. In this interval of my Senatorial life, I published the second and third Volumes of the decline and fall. My Ecclesiastical history still breathed the same spirit of freedom; but Protestant zeal is more indifferent to the characters and controversies of the fourth and fifth Centuries; my obstinate silence had damped the ardour of the polemics; Dr. Watson, the most candid of my adversaries, assured me that he had no thoughts of renewing the attack, and my impartial balance of the virtues and vices of Julian was generally praised. This truce was interrupted only by some animadversions of the Catholics of Italy,[44] and by some angry letters from Mr. Travis,[45] who made me personally responsible for

---

[44] The piety or prudence of my Italian translator * has provided an antidote against the poison of his original. The vth and vii[th] Volumes are armed with five letters from an anonymous Divine to his friends, Foothead and Kirk, two English students at Rome, and this meritorious service is commended by *Monsignore* Stonor, a prelate of the same nation, who discovers much venom in the *fluid* and nervous style of Gibbon. The critical Essay at the end of the iii[d] Volume was furnished by the Abbate Nicola Spedalieri, whose zeal has gradually swelled to a more solid confutation in two quarto Volumes. Shall I be excused for not having read them?

[45] The brutal insolence of his challenge can only be excused by the absence of learning, judgement, and humanity; and to that excuse he has the fairest or foulest title. Compared with Archdeacon Travis,† Chelsum and Davis assume the character of respectable enemies.

* Dean Milman states in his notes that he was never able to find the Italian translation. It was published in Pisa, 1779–86, under the title *Istoria della decadenza e rovina dell' Imperio Romano tradotta dall' Inglese* (by A. Fabbroni and — Poggi).

† George Travis (1740–1797), of St. John's College, Oxford, wrote *Letters to Edward Gibbon . . . in Defence of the Authenticity of 1 John v. 7 in 1784.*

condemning with the best Critics the spurious text of the three heavenly Witnesses. The bigotted advocate of Popes and monks may be turned over even to the bigots of Oxford, and the wretched Travis still howls under the lash of the mercyless Porson.[46] But I perceived, and without surprize, the coldness and even prejudice of the town; nor could a whisper escape my ear that, in the judgement of many readers, my continuation was much inferior to the original attempt. An author who cannot ascend will always appear to sink: envy was now prepared for my reception, and the zeal of my religious [47] was fortified by the malice of my political enemies. I was, however, encouraged by some domestic and foreign

---

[46] I consider Mr. Porson's answer to Archdeacon Travis as the most acute and accurate piece of criticism which has appeared since the days of Bentley. His strictures are founded in argument, enriched with learning, and enlivened with wit, and his adversary neither deserves nor finds any quarter at his hands. The evidence of the three heavenly witnesses would now be rejected in any court of Justice; but prejudice is blind, authority is deaf, and our vulgar Bibles will ever be polluted by this spurious text, "Sedet æternumque sedebit." The more learned Ecclesiastics will, indeed, have the secret satisfaction of reprobating in the Closet what they read in the Church.

[47] Bishop Newton (see his Life in Posthumous works, vol. i. pp. 173, 174, octavo edition) was at full liberty to declare how much he himself and two eminent brethren were disgusted by Mr. G.'s prolixity, tediousness, and affectation. But the old man should not have indulged his zeal in a false and feeble charge against the historian, who had faithfully and even cautiously rendered Dr. Burnet's meaning by the alternative "of sleep *or repose.*" That philosophic Divine supposes that in the period between death and the resurrection human souls exist without a body, endowed with internal consciousness, but destitute of all active or passive connection with the external World. "Secundum communem dictionem Sacræ Scripturæ, Mors dicitur *somnus*, et morientes dicuntur *obdormire:* quod innuere mihi videtur statum mortis esse statum quietis, silentii, et ἀεργασίας" (De statû Mortuorum, C. v. p. 98).

testimonies of applause, and the second and third volumes insensibly rose in sale and reputation to a level with the first. But the public is seldom wrong; and I am inclined to believe that, especially in the beginning, they are more prolix and less entertaining than the first: my efforts had not been relaxed by success, and I had rather deviated into the opposite fault of minute and superfluous diligence. On the continent my name and writings were slowly diffused: a French translation of the first volume had disappointed the booksellers of Paris, and a passage in the third was construed as a personal reflection on the reigning Monarch.[48]

A.D.
1781.
June.

Before I could apply for a seat at the general Election, the list was already full; but Lord North's promise was sincere, his recommendation was effectual, and I was soon chosen on a vacancy for the borough of Lymington, in Hampshire. In the first Session of the new parliament, administration stood their ground; their final overthrow was reserved for the second. The American War had once been the favourite of the Country; the pride of England was irritated by the resistance of her Colonies; and the executive power was driven by national clamour into the most vigorous and coercive measures. But the length of a fruitless contest, the loss of armies, the

---

[48] It may not be generally known that Louis XVI. is a great reader, and a reader of English books. On the perusal of a passage of my History (vol. iii. p. 636), which seems to compare him with Arcadius or Honorius, he expressed his resentment to the Prince of B——, from whom the intelligence was conveyed to me. I shall neither disclaim the allusion nor examine the likeness; but the situation of the *late* King of France excludes all suspicion of flattery, and I am ready to declare that the concluding observations of my third Volume were written before his accession to the throne.

accumulation of debt and taxes, and the hostile con-
federacy of France, Spain, and Holland, indisposed the
public to the American War and the persons by whom it
was conducted. The representatives of the people followed
at a slow distance the changes of their opinion, and the
ministers who refused to bend were broken by the tempest.
As soon as Lord North had lost, or was about to lose, a
majority in the house of Commons, he surrendered his
office, and retired to a private station, with the tranquil
assurance of a clear conscience and a chearful temper ;
the old fabric was dissolved, and the posts of Government
were occupied by the victorious and veteran troops of
opposition. The Lords of Trade were not immediately
dismissed ; but the board itself was abolished by Mr.
Burke's bill, which decency compelled the patriots to
revive, and I was stripped of a convenient salary after I
had enjoyed it about three years.

1782.
May 1.

So flexible is the title of my history, that the final æra
might be fixed at my own choice, and I long hesitated
whether I should be content with the three Volumes, the
fall of the Western Empire, which fullfilled my first
engagement with the public. In this interval of sus-
pense, near a twelvemonth, I returned by a natural impulse to the Greek authors of antiquity. In my library
in Bentinck street, at my summer lodgings at Bright-
helmstone, at a country house which I hired at Hampton
Court, I read with new pleasure the Iliad and Odyssey,
the histories of Herodotus, Thucydides, and Xenophon,
a large portion of the tragic and comic theatre of Athens,
and many interesting dialogues of the Socratic school.
Yet in the luxury of freedom I began to wish for the
daily task, the active pursuit which gave a value to every

1782.
March 1.

book, and an object to every enquiry : the preface of a new edition announced my design, and I dropt without reluctance from the age of Plato to that of Justinian. The original texts of Procopius and Agathias supplied the events, and even the characters, of his reign ; but a laborious winter was devoted to the Codes, the Pandects, and the modern interpreters before I presumed to form an abstract of the Civil law. My skill was improved by practise, my diligence perhaps was quickened by the loss of office, and, except the last chapter, I had finished my fourth Volume before I sought a retreat on the banks of the Leman lake.

1783.

It is not the purpose of this narrative to expatiate on the public or secret history of the times—the schism which followed the death of the Marquis of Rockingham, the appointment of the Earl of Shelburne, the resignation of Mr. Fox, and his famous coalition with Lord North. But I may affirm with some degree of assurance that in their political conflict those great antagonists had never felt any personal animosity to each other; that their reconciliation was easy and sincere ; and that their friendship has never been clouded by the shadow of suspicion or jealousy. The most violent or venal of their respective followers embraced this fair occasion of revolt; but their alliance still commanded a majority in the House of Commons: the peace was censured; Lord Shelburne resigned, and the two friends knelt on the same cushion to take the oath of Secretary of State. From a principle of gratitude I adhered to the coalition; my vote was counted in the day of battle, but I was overlooked in the division of the spoil. There were many claimants more deserving and importunate than myself:

the board of trade could not be restored; and while the list of places was curtailed, the number of candidates was doubled. An easy dismission to a secure seat at the board of customs or excise was promised on the first vacancy; but the chance was distant and doubtful, nor could I solicit with much ardour an ignoble servitude which would have robbed me of the most valuable of my studious hours.* At the same time, the tumult of London and the attendance on Parlia[ment] were grown more irksome, and without some additional income I could not long or prudently maintain the style of expence to which I was accustomed.

From my early acquaintance with Lausanne I had always cherished a secret wish that the school of my youth might become the retreat of my declining age. A moderate fortune would secure the blessings of ease, leisure, and independence : the country, the people, the manners, the language, were congenial to my taste ; and I might indulge the hope of passing some years in the domestic society of a friend. After travelling with several English,† Mr. Deyverdun was now settled at home in a pleasant habitation, the gift of his deceased aunt : we had

1783.
May 20.

---

* About the same time, it being in contemplation to send a secretary of embassy to Paris, Mr. Gibbon was a competitor for that office. The credit of being distinguished and stopped by government when he was leaving England, the salary of 1200*l.* a year, the society of Paris, and the hope of a future provision for life, disposed him to renounce, though with much reluctance, an agreeable scheme on the point of execution; to engage, without experience, in a scene of business which he never liked; to give himself a master, or at least a principal, of an unknown, perhaps an unamiable character : to which might be added the danger of the recall of the ambassador, or the change of ministry. Mr. Anthony Storer was preferred. Mr. Gibbon was somewhat indignant at the preference ; but he never knew that it was the act of his friend Mr. Fox, contrary to the solicitations of Mr. Craufurd, and other of his friends.—SHEFFIELD.

† Sir Richard Worsley, Lord Chesterfield, Broderick Lord Midleton, and Mr. Hume, brother to Sir Abraham.

long been separated, we had long been silent; yet in my
first letter I exposed with the most perfect confidence my
situation, my sentiments and my designs. His immediate
answer was a warm and joyful acceptance: the picture of
our future life provoked my impatience; and the terms of
arrangement were short and simple, as he possessed the
property and I undertook the expence of our common house.
Before I could break my English chain, it was incumbent
on me to struggle with the feelings of my heart, the indolence of my temper, and the opinion of the World, which
unanimously condemned this voluntary banishment. In
the disposal of my effects, the library, a sacred deposit,
was alone excepted: as my post-chaise moved over
Westminster bridge, I bid a long farewell to the "fumum,
et opes, strepitumque Romæ." My journey by the direct
road through France was not attended with any accident,
and I arrived at Lausanne near twenty years after my
second departure. Within less than three months the
Coalition struck on some hidden rocks; had I remained
aboard I should have perished in the general shipwreck.

A.D.
1783.
September
27—
1787.
July 29.

Since my establishment at Lausanne more than seven
years have elapsed, and if every day has not been equally
soft and serene, not a day, not a moment has occurred in
which I have repented of my choice. During my absence,
a long portion of human life, many changes had happened:
my elder acquaintance had left the stage; virgins were
ripened into matrons, and children were grown to the
age of manhood. But the same manners were transmitted from one generation to another: my friend alone
was an inestimable treasure; my name was not totally
forgotten, and all were ambitious to welcome the arrival
of a stranger, and the return of a fellow-citizen. The

first winter was given to a general embrace, without any nice discrimination of persons and characters : after a more regular settlement, a more accurate survey, I discovered three solid and permanent benefits of my new situation. 1. My personal freedom had been somewhat impaired by the house of commons and the board of trade; but I was now delivered from the chain of duty and dependence, from the hopes and fears of political adventure : my sober mind was no longer intoxicated by the fumes of party, and I rejoyced in my escape as often as I read of the midnight debates which preceded the dissolution of Parliament. 2. My English œconomy had been that of a solitary batchelor who might afford some occasional dinners. In Switzerland I enjoyed at every meal, at every hour, the free and pleasant conversation of the friend of my youth; and my daily table was always provided for the reception of one or two extra-ordinary guests. Our importance in society is less a positive than a relative weight : in London I was lost in the crowd; I ranked with the first families of Lausanne, and my style of prudent expence enabled me to maintain a fair balance of reciprocal civilities. 3. Instead of a small house between a street and a stable-yard, I began to occupy a spacious and convenient mansion, connected on the north side with the City, and open on the south to a beautiful and boundless horizon. A garden of four acres had been laid out by the taste of Mr. Deyverdun; from the garden a rich scenery of meadows and vineyards descends to the Leman lake, and the prospect far beyond the lake is crowned by the stupendous mountains of Savoy. My books and my acquaintance had been first united in London; but this

happy position of my library in town *and* country was
finally reserved for Lausanne. Possessed of every comfort
in this triple alliance, I could not be tempted to change
my habitation with the changes of the seasons.

My friends had been kindly apprehensive that I
should not be able to exist in a Swiss town at the foot
of the Alps, after so long conversing with the first men
of the first cities of the World. Such lofty connections
may attract the curious and gratify the vain, but I am
too modest or too proud to rate my own value by that
of my associates; and whatsoever may be the fame of
learning or genius, experience has shewn me that the
cheaper qualifications of politeness and good sense are
of more useful currency in the commerce of life. By
many conversation is esteemed as a theatre or a school;
but after the morning has been occupied by the labours
of the library, I wish to unbend rather than to exercise
my mind, and in the interval between tea and supper
I am far from disdaining the innocent amusement of a
game at cards. Lausanne is peopled by a numerous
gentry, whose companionable idleness is seldom disturbed
by the pursuits of avarice or ambition; the women, though
confined to a domestic education, are endowed for the
most part with more taste and knowledge than their
husbands or brothers; but the decent freedom of both
sexes is equally remote from the extremes of simplicity
and refinement. I shall add, as a misfortune rather than
a merit, that the situation and beauty of the Pays de
Vaud, the long habits of the English, the medical reputation of Dr. Tissot, and the fashion of viewing the
mountains and *glaciers*, have opened us on all sides to
the incursions of foreigners. The visits of Mr. and

Madame Necker,[49] of Prince Henry of Prussia,[50] and of Mr. Fox [51] may form some pleasing exceptions; but, in general, Lausanne has appeared most agreable in my eyes when we have been abandoned to our own society.

My transmigration from London to Lausanne could not be effected without interrupting the course of my historical labours. The hurry of my departure, the joy of my arrival, the delay of my tools, suspended their progress, and a full twelvemonth was lost before I could resume the thread of regular and daily industry. A number of books, most requisite and least common, had been præviously selected; the Academical library of Lausanne, which I could use as my own, contains at least the fathers and councils, and I have derived some occasional succour from the public collections of Bern and Geneva. The fourth volume was soon terminated

A.D.
1784.
July, etc.

---

[49] I saw them frequently in the summer of 1784, at a country house near Lausanne, where Mr. Necker composed his treatise of the administration of the Finances. I have since (in October, 1790) visited them in their present residence, the castle and barony of Copet, near Geneva. Of the merits and measures of that Statesman various opinions may be entertained, but all impartial men must agree in their esteem of his integrity and patriotism.

[50] In the month of August, 1784, Prince Henry of Prussia, in his way to Paris, passed three days at Lausanne. His military conduct is praised by professional men; his character has been vilified by the wit and malice of a Dæmon (Memoires secrets de la cour de Berlin); but I was flattered by his affability, and entertained by his conversation.

[51] In his tour of Switzerland (September, 1788), Mr. Fox gave me two days of free and private society. He seemed to feel and even to envy the happiness of my situation; while I admired the powers of a superior man, as they are blended in his attractive character, with the softness and simplicity of a child. Perhaps no human being was ever more perfectly exempt from the taint of malevolence, vanity, or falsehood.

by an abstract of the controversies of the Incarnation,[52]
which the learned Dr. Prideaux* was apprehensive of
exposing to profane eyes.[53]   In the fifth and sixth
Volumes the revolutions of the Empire and the World
are most rapid, various, and instructive; and the Greek
or Roman historians are checked by the hostile narratives
of the Barbarians of the East and West.   It was not till
after many designs and many tryals that I preferred, as
I still prefer, the method of groupping my picture by
nations,[54] and the seeming neglect of Chronological order
is surely compensated by the superior merits of interest
and perspicuity.   The style of the first Volume is, in my
opinion, somewhat crude and elaborate; in the second

---

[52] In one of the Dialogues of the dead (xvi.) Lucian turns into
ridicule the Pagan theology concerning the double Nature of Hercules,
God and Man (Opp., tom.ii. pp. 402–405, edit. Reitz).   As truth and
falsehood have sometimes an apparent similitude, I am afraid that
even the Synods of Ephesus and Chalcedon would not have been safe
from the arrows of his profane wit.

[53] It had been the original design of the learned Dean Prideaux
to write the history of the ruin of the Eastern Church.   In this work
it would have been necessary not only to unravel all those controversies
which the Christians made about the Hypostatical Union, but also to
unfold all the niceties and subtile notions which each sect did hold
concerning it.   The pious historian was apprehensive of exposing that
incomprehensible Mystery to the cavils and objections of unbelievers,
and he durst not, considering the nature of this book, venture it abroad
in so wanton and lewd an age (see Preface to the Life of Mahomet,
p. xxi.).

[54] I have followed the judicious precept of the Abbé de Mably
(Manière d'écrire l'histoire, p. 110), who advises the historian not to
dwell too minutely on the decay of the Eastern Empire, but to consider the Barbarian conquerors as a more worthy subject of his
narrative.   "Fas est et ab hoste doceri."

* Humphrey Prideaux (1648–   Dean of Norwich, 1702.   His *Life*
1724), Christ Church, Oxford;   *of Mahomet* was published in 1697

and third it is ripened into ease, correctness, and numbers; but in the three last I may have been seduced by the facility of my pen, and the constant habit of speaking one language and writing another may have infused some mixture of Gallic idioms. Happily for my eyes, I have always closed my studies with the day, and commonly with the morning, and a long but temperate labour has been accomplished without fatiguing either the mind or body. But when I computed the remainder of my time and my task, it was apparent that, according to the season of publication, the delay of a month would be productive of that of a year. I was now straining for the goal, and in the last winter many evenings were borrowed from the social pleasures of Lausanne. I could now wish that a pause, an interval, had been allowed for a serious revisal.

I have presumed to mark the moment of conception; I shall now commemorate the hour of my final deliverance. It was on the day, or rather the night, of the 27th of June, 1787, between the hours of eleven and twelve, that I wrote the last lines of the last page in a summer-house in my garden. After laying down my pen I took several turns in a *berceau*, or covered walk of Acacias, which commands a prospect of the country, the lake, and the mountains. The air was temperate, the sky was serene, the silver orb of the moon was reflected from the waters, and all Nature was silent. I will not dissemble the first emotions of joy on the recovery of my freedom, and perhaps the establishment of my fame. But my pride was soon humbled, and a sober melancholy was spread over my mind by the idea that I had taken my ever-lasting leave of an old and agreable companion, and that, whatsoever might be the future date of my history, the life of the historian must be short and precarious. I will add two facts which have seldom occurred in the composition of six, or at least of five, quartos. 1. My first rough manuscript, without any intermediate copy, has been sent to the press.[55] 2. Not a sheet has been seen by any human eyes except those of the Author and the printer; the faults and the merits are exclusively my own.

A.D.
1787.
July 29.After a quiet residence of four years, during which I had never moved ten miles from Lausanne, it was not without some reluctance and terror that I undertook, in a journey of two hundred leagues, to cross the mountains and the sea. Yet this formidable adventure was atchieved without danger or fatigue, and at the end of a fortnight I found myself in Lord Sheffield's house and library, safe, happy, and at home. The character of my friend (Mr. Holroyd) had recommended him to a seat in Parliament for Coventry, the command of a regiment of light Dragoons, and an Irish peerage. The sense and spirit of his political writings have decided the public opinion on the great questions of our commercial intercourse with America[56]

---

[55] I cannot help recollecting a much more extraordinary fact, which is affirmed of himself by Rétif de la Bretonne, a voluminous and original writer of French novels. He laboured, and may still labour, in the humble office of Corrector to a printing-house. But this office enabled him to transport an entire volume from his mind to the press; and his work was given to the public without ever having been written with a pen.

[56] *Observations on the commerce of the American states, by John Lord Sheffield: the sixth edition, London,* 1784, *in octavo.* Their sale was diffusive, their effect beneficial. The Navigation act, the Palladium of Britain, was defended, and perhaps saved, by his pen; and he proves, by the weight of fact and argument, that the mother-

and Ireland.[57] He fell * (in 1784) with the unpopular coalition, but his merit has been acknowledged at the last general election (1790) by the honourable invitation and free choice of the city of Bristol. During the whole time of my residence in England, I was entertained at Sheffield place and in Downing Street by his hospitable kindness, and the most pleasant period was that which I passed in the domestic society of the family. In the larger circle of the Metropolis, I observed the country and the inhabitants with the knowledge and without the prejudices of an Englishman; but I rejoyced in the apparent encrease of wealth and prosperity which might be fairly divided between the spirit of the nation and the wisdom of the minister. All party resentment was now lost in oblivion; since I was no man's rival, no man was my enemy: I felt the dignity of independence, and as I asked no more, I was satisfied with the general civilities of the World. The house in London which I frequented with the most pleasure and assiduity was that

---

country may survive and flourish after the loss of America. My friend has never cultivated the arts of composition, but his materials are copious and correct, and he leaves on his paper the clear impression of an active and vigorous mind.

[57] *Observations on the trade, manufactures, and present state of Ireland, by John Lord Sheffield: the third edition, London,* 1784, *in cctavo.* Their useful aim was to guide the industry, to correct the prejudices, and to asswage the passions of a country which seemed to forget that she could only be free and prosperous by a friendly connection with Great Britain. The concluding observations are expressed with so much ease and spirit, that they may be read by those who are the least interested in the subject.

* It is not obvious from whence ho fell: he never held nor desired any office of emolument whatever, unless his military commissions, and the command of a regiment of light dragoons, which he raised himself, and which was disbanded on the peace, 1783, should be deemed such.—*Note in Lord Sheffield's edition.*

of Lord North : after the loss of power and of sight, he was still happy in himself and his friends, and my public tribute of gratitude and esteem could no longer be suspected of any interested motive. Before my departure from England I assisted at the august spectacle of Mr. Hastings's tryal in Westminster hall : I shall not absolve or condemn the Governor of India, but Mr. Sheridan's eloquence demanded my applause; nor could I hear without emotion the personal compliment * which he paid me in the presence of the British nation.[58]

As the publication of my three last volumes was the principal object, so it was the first care of my English journey. The prævious arrangements with the bookseller and the printer were settled in my passage through London, and the proofs which I returned more correct were transmitted every post from the press to Sheffield Place. The length of the operation and the leisure of the country allowed some time to review my manuscript : several rare and useful books, the Assises de Jerusalem, Ramusius de bello C. P^aro, the Greek Acts of the Synod of Florence, the Statuta Urbis Romæ, etc., were procured, and I introduced in their proper places the supplements

---

[58] From this display of Genius, which blazed four successive days, I shall stoop to a very mechanical circumstance. As I was waiting in the Manager's box, I had the curiosity to enquire of the short-hand writer how many words a ready and rapid Orator might pronounce in an hour. From 7000 to 7500 was his answer. The medium of 7200 will afford one hundred and twenty words in a minute, and two words in each second. But this computation will only apply to the English language.

* Sheridan alluded to certain facts as being unparalleled in atrociousness and criminality "either in ancient or modern history, in the correct periods of Tacitus or the luminous page of Gibbon." He is credited with having explained in private that he meant *vo-luminous*.

which they afforded. The impression of the fourth volume had consumed three months; our common interest required that we should move with a quicker pace, and Mr. Strahan fullfilled his engagement, which few printers could sustain, of delivering every week three thousand copies of nine sheets. The day of publication was, however, delayed, that it might coincide with the fifty-first anniversary of my own birthday: the double festival was celebrated by a chearful litterary dinner at Cadell's house, and I seemed to blush while they read an elegant compliment from Mr. Hayley,[59] whose poetical talent had more than once been employed in the praise of his friend. As most of the former purchasers were naturally desirous of compleating their sets, the sale of the quarto edition was quick and easy; and an octavo size was printed, to satisfy, at a cheaper rate, the public demand. The conclusion of my work appears to have diffused a strong sensation; it was generally read and variously judged. The style has been exposed to much Academical criticism; a religious clamour was revived; and the reproach of indecency has been loudly echoed by the rigid censors of morals.[60] Yet, upon the whole,

1788.
May 8.

---

[59] Before Mr. Hayley inscribed with my name his Epistles on History, I was not personally acquainted with that amiable man and elegant poet. He afterwards thanked me in verse for my second and third Volumes; and in the summer of 1781 the Roman Eagle (a proud title) accepted the invitation of the English sparrow, who chirped in the groves of Eartham, near Chichester.

[60] I never could understand the clamour which has been raised against the indecency of my three last Volumes. (1) An equal degree of freedom in the former part, especially in the first Volume, had passed without reproach. (2) I am justified in painting the manners of the times; the vices of Theodora form an essential feature in the reign and character of Justinian, and the most naked tale in my history

the history of the decline and fall seems to have struck a root both at home [61] and abroad,[62] and may, perhaps, an hundred years hence, still continue to be abused.   The French,* Italian, and German transla-

---

is told by the Reverend Mr. Joseph Warton, an instructor of Youth (Essay on the Genius and Writings of Pope, pp. 322–324).   (3) My English text is chaste, and all licentious passages are left in the obscurity of a learned language.

"Le Latin dans ses mots brave l'honnêteté,"
says the correct Boileau in a country and idiom more scrupulous than our own.

[61] I am less flattered by Mr. Porson's high encomium on the style and spirit of my History than I am satisfied with his honourable testimony to my attention, diligence, and accuracy—those humble virtues which Religious zeal has most audaciously denied.   The sweetness of his praise is tempered by a reasonable mixture of acid (see his preface, pp. xxviii.–xxxii.).

[62] As the book may not be common in England, I shall transcribe my own character from the Bibliotheca Historica of Meuselius, a learned and laborious German (Vol. iv. P. i. pp. 342–344): "Summis ævi nostri historicis Gibbonus sine dubio adnumerandus est.   Inter Capitolii ruinas stans primùm hujus operis scribendi consilium cepit.   Florentissimos vitæ annos colligendo et laborando eidem impendit.   Enatum inde monimentum ære perennius, licet passim appareant sinistre dicta, minus perfecta, veritati non satis consentanea.   Videmus quidem ubìque fere studium scrutandi veritatemque scribendi maximum: tamen sine Tillemontio duce, ubi scilicet hujus historia finitur, sœpius noster titubat atque hallucinatur.   Quod vel maxime fit, ubi de rebus Ecclesiasticis vel de Juris prudentiâ Romanâ (tom. iv.) tradit, et in aliis locis.   Attamen nævi hujus generis haud impediunt quo minus operis summam et οἰκονομίαν præclare dispositam, delectum rerum sapientissimum, argutum quoque interdum, dictionemque seu stilum historico æque ac philosopho dignissimum, et vix a quoque alio Anglo, Humio ac Robertsono haud exceptis, prærepto (*præreptum?*), vehementer laudemus, atque sæculo nostro de hujusmodi historiâ gratulemur . . . Gibbonus adversarios cum in tum extra patriam nactus est, quia propagationem Religionis Christianæ, non, ut vulgo fieri solet, aut more Theologorum, sed ut historicum et philosophum decet exposuerat."

* The French edition was subsequently revised by M. Guizot.

tions [63] have been executed with various success; but instead of patronizing, I should willingly suppress such imperfect copies which injure the character while they propagate the name of the author. The Irish pyrates are at once my friends and my enemies, but I cannot be displeased with the two numerous and correct impressions of the English original, which have been published for the use of the Continent at Basil in Switzerland.[64] The conquests of our language and litterature are not confined to Europe alone; and the writer who succeeds in London is speedily read on the banks of the Delaware and the Ganges.

In the preface of the fourth Volume, while I gloried in the name of an Englishman, I announced my approaching return to the neighbourhood of the lake of Lausanne. This last tryal confirmed my assurance that I had wisely chosen for my own happiness; nor did I once, in a year's visit, entertain a wish of settling in my native country. Britain is the free and fortunate island, but where is the spot in which I could unite the comforts and beauties of my establishment at Lausanne? The tumult of London astonished my eyes and ears; the

---

[63] The first Volume had been feebly though faithfully translated into French by M. Le Clerc de Septchênes, a young Gentleman of a studious character and liberal fortune. After his decease the work was continued by two manufacturers of Paris, MM. Desmeuniers and Cantwell; but the former is now an active member in the national assembly, and the undertaking languishes in the hands of his associate. The superior merit of the Interpreter, or his language, inclines me to prefer the Italian version; but I wish it were in my power to read the German, which is praised by the best Judges.

[64] Of their fourteen octavo Volumes, the two last include the whole body of the notes. The public importunity had forced *me* to remove them from the end of the Volume to the bottom of the page, but I have often repented of my complyance.

amusements of public places were no longer adequate to the trouble; the clubs and assemblies were filled with new faces and young men; and our best society, our long and late dinners, would soon have been prejudicial to my health. Without any share in the political wheel, I must be idle and insignificant; yet the most splendid temptations would not have enlisted me a second time in the servitude of parliament or office. At Tunbridge, some weeks after the publication of my history, I tore myself from the embraces of Lord and Lady Sheffield, and, with a young Swiss friend * whom I had introduced to the English world, I pursued the road of Dover and Lausanne. My habitation was embellished in my absence, and the last division of books which followed my steps encreased my chosen library to the number of six or seven thousand volumes. My Seraglio was ample, my choice was free, my appetite was keen. After a full repast on Homer and Aristophanes, I involved myself in the philosophic maze of the writings of Plato, of which the dramatic is perhaps more interesting than the argumentative part; but I stept aside into every path of enquiry which reading or reflection accidentally opened.

Alas! the joy of my return and my studious ardour were soon damped by the melancholy state of my friend, Mr. Deyverdun. His health and spirits had long suffered a gradual decline; a succession of Apoplectic fits announced his dissolution, and before he expired, those who loved him could not wish for the continuance of his life. The voice of reason might congratulate his deliverance, but the feelings of Nature and friendship could be subdued only by time: his amiable character was still alive in

---

* M. Wilhelm de Severy.

my remembrance; each room, each walk, was imprinted with our common footsteps, and I should blush at my own philosophy if a long interval of study had not preceded and followed the death of my friend. By his last will he left me the option of purchasing his house and garden, or of possessing them during my life on the payment either of a stipulated price, or of an easy retribution to his kinsman and heir. I should probably have been tempted by the Dæmon of property,[65] if some legal difficulties had not been started against my title. A contest would have been vexatious, doubtful, and invidious; and the heir most gratefully subscribed an agreement which rendered my life-possession more perfect, and his future condition more advantageous. The certainty of my tenure has allowed me to lay out a considerable sum in improvements and alterations; they have been executed with skill and taste, and few men of letters, perhaps, in Europe, are so desirably lodged as myself. But I feel, and with the decline of years I shall more painfully feel, that I am alone in paradise. Among the circle of my acquaintance at Lausanne, I have gradually acquired the solid and tender friendship of a respectable family: the four persons of whom it is composed are all endowed with the virtues best adapted to their age and situation; and I am encouraged to love the parents as a brother, and the children as a father. Every day we seek

---

[65] Yet I had often revolved the judicious lines in which Pope answers the objection of his long-sighted friend—

> " Pity to build without or child or wife!
> Why, you'll enjoy it *only* all your life.
> Well, if the use be mine, does it concern one
> Whether the name belong to Pope or Vernon? "

and find the opportunities of meeting, yet even this valuable connection cannot supply the loss of domestic society.

Within the last two or three years our tranquillity has been clouded by the disorders of France: many families of Lausanne were alarmed and affected by the terrors of an impending bankruptcy; but the revolution or rather the dissolution of the Kingdom,[66] has been heard and felt in the adjacent lands. A swarm of emigrants of both sexes, who escaped from the public ruin, has been attracted by the vicinity, the manners, and the language of Lausanne, and our narrow habitations in town and country are now occupied by the first names and titles of the departed Monarchy. These noble fugitives are entitled to our pity; they may claim our esteem, but they cannot, in the present state of their mind and fortune, much contribute to our amusement. Instead of looking down, as calm and idle spectators, on the theatre of Europe, our domestic harmony is somewhat embittered by the infusion of party spirit; our ladies and gentlemen assume the character of self-taught politicians, and the sober dictates of wisdom and experience are silenced by the clamours of the triumphant *Democrates*. The fanatic missionaries of sedition have scattered the seeds of discontent in our cities and villages, which had flourished above two hundred and fifty years without fearing the approach of war, or feeling the weight of government.

---

[66] I beg leave to subscribe my assent to Mr. Burke's creed on the Revolution of France. I admire his eloquence, I approve his politics, I adore his Chivalry, and I can almost excuse his reverence for Church establishments. I have sometimes thought of writing a dialogue of the dead, in which Lucian, Erasmus, and Voltaire should mutually acknowledge the danger of exposing an *old* superstition to the contempt of the blind and fanatic multitude.

Many individuals, and some communities, appear to be infected with the [French disease *], the wild theories of equal and boundless freedom : but I trust that the body of the people will be faithful to their sovereign and themselves ; and I am satisfied that the failure or success of a revolt would equally terminate in the ruin of the country. While the Aristocracy of Bern protects the happiness, it is superfluous to enquire whether it is founded in the rights of man : the œconomy of the state is liberally supplied without the aid of taxes ;[67] and the magistrates *must* reign with prudence and equity, since they are unarmed in the midst of an armed nation. For myself (may the omen be averted) I can only declare that the first stroke of a rebel drum would be the signal of my immediate departure.

When I contemplate the common lot of mortality, I must acknowledge that I have drawn a high prize in the lottery of life. The far greater part of the globe is overspread with barbarism or slavery ; in the civilized world the most numerous class is condemned to ignorance and poverty, and the double fortune of my birth in a free and enlightened country, in an honourable and wealthy family, is the lucky chance of an unit against millions. The general probability is about three to one that a new-born infant will not live to compleat his fiftieth year.[68] I have

---

[67] The revenue of Bern (I except some small duties) is derived from Church lands, tythes, feudal rights, and interest of money. The Republic has near 500,000 pounds sterling in the English funds, and the amount of their treasure is unknown to the Citizens themselves.

[68] See Buffon, Supplément à l'histoire naturelle, tom. vii. pp. 158–164. Of a given number of new-born infants, one-half, by the fault of Nature or Man, is extinguished before the age of puberty and reason. A melancholy calculation !

* " Gallic frenzy " in Lord Sheffield's edition.

now passed that age, and may fairly estimate the present value of my existence in the threefold division of mind, body, and estate.

i. The first indispensable requisite of happiness is a clear conscience, unsullied by the reproach or remembrance of an unworthy action.

> " Hic murus aheneus esto
> Nil conscire sibi, nullâ pallescere culpâ."

I am endowed with a chearful temper, a moderate sensibility, and a natural disposition to repose rather than to action : some mischievous appetites and habits have perhaps been corrected by philosophy or time. The love of study, a passion which derives fresh vigour from enjoyment, supplies each day, each hour, with a perpetual source of independent and rational pleasure, and I am not sensible of any decay of the mental faculties. The original soil has been highly improved by labour and manure ; but it may be questioned whether some flowers of fancy, some grateful errors, have not been eradicated with the weeds of prejudice. ii. Since I have escaped from the long perils of my childhood, the serious advice of a physician has seldom been requisite. "The madness of superfluous health" I have never known ; but my tender constitution has been fortified by time ; [the play of the animal machine still continues to be easy and regular,] and the inestimable gift of the sound and peaceful slumbers of infancy may be imputed both to the mind and body. [About the age of forty I was first afflicted with the gout, which in the space of fourteen years has made seven or eight different attacks ; their duration, though not their intensity, appears to encrease, and after each fit I rise and walk with less strength and agility than before. But the gout has hitherto been confined to my feet and knees; the pain is never intolerable; I am surrounded by all the comforts that art and attendance can bestow; my sedentary life is amused with books and company, and in each step of my convalescence I pass through a progress of agreable sensations.] iii. I have already described the merits of my society and situation; but these enjoyments would be tasteless and bitter, if their possession were not assured by an annual and adequate supply. [By the painful method of amputation, my father's debts have been compleatly discharged; the labour of my pen, the sale of lands, the inheritance of a maiden aunt (Mrs. Hester Gibbon [69]), have improved my property, and it will be exonerated on some melancholy day from the payment of Mrs. Gibbon's jointure.] According to the scale of Switzerland I am a rich man; and I am indeed rich, since my income is superior to my expence, and my expence is equal to my wishes. My friend Lord Sheffield has kindly relieved me from the cares to which my taste and temper are most adverse:* [the œconomy of my house is settled without avarice or profusion; at stated periods all my bills are regularly paid, and in the course of my life I have never been reduced to appear, either as plaintiff or

---

[69] My pious aunt and her profane sister are described under the names of Miranda and Flavia in Law's Serious Call, a popular and powerful book of Devotion. Mr. William Law, a Nonjuror, a Saint, and a wit, had been my father's domestic Tutor. He afterwards retired, with his spiritual daughter Miranda, to live and dye in a Hermitage at Cliffe, in Northamptonshire.

* This read originally, "My friends, more especially Lord Sheffield, kindly relieve me." It has been altered in ink, but not by Gibbon, to "My friend Lord Sheffield has kindly relieved me."

defendant, in a court of Justice.] Shall I add that, since the failure of my first wishes, I have never entertained any serious thoughts of a matrimonial connection?

I am disgusted with the affectation of men of letters, who complain that they have renounced a substance for a shadow, and that their fame (which sometimes is no insupportable weight) affords a poor compensation for envy, censure, and persecution.[70] My own experience, at least, has taught me a very different lesson: twenty happy years have been animated by the labour of my history; and its success has given me a name, a rank, a character, in the World, to which I should not otherwise have been entitled. The freedom of my writings has, indeed, provoked an implacable tribe; but as I was safe from the stings, I was soon accustomed to the buzzing of the hornets: my nerves are not tremblingly alive: and my litterary temper is so happily framed, that I am less sensible of pain than pleasure. The rational pride of an author may be offended rather than flattered by vague indiscriminate praise; but he cannot, he should not, be indifferent to the fair testimonies of private and public esteem. Even his social sympathy may be gratified by the idea that, now in the present hour, he is imparting some degree of amusement or knowledge to *his friends* in a distant land; that one day his mind will be familiar to the grandchildren of those who are yet

---

[70] Mr. d'Alembert relates that, as he was walking in the gardens of Sans-souci with the King of Prussia, Frederic said to him, "Do you see that old woman, a poor weeder, asleep on that Sunny bank? She is probably a more happy Being than either of us." The King and the Philosopher may speak for themselves; for my part, I do not envy the old woman.

unborn.[71] I cannot boast of the friendship, or favour of princes; the patronage of English litterature has long since been devolved on our booksellers, and the measure of their liberality is the least ambiguous test of our common success. Perhaps the golden mediocrity of my fortune has contributed to fortify my application : [few books of merit and importance have been composed either in a garret or a palace. A Gentleman, possessed of leisure and competency, may be encouraged by the assurance of an honourable reward; but wretched is the writer, and wretched will be the work, where daily diligence is stimulated by daily hunger.]

The present is a fleeting moment: the past is no more; and our prospect of futurity is dark and doubtful. This day may *possibly* be my last; but the laws of probability, so true in general, so fallacious in particular, still allow me about fifteen years,[72] and I shall soon enter into the

---

[71] In the first of ancient or modern Romances (Tom Jones, l. xiii. c. 1) this proud sentiment, this feast of fancy, is enjoyed by the Genius of Fielding. "Foretell me that some future maid whose grandmother is yet unborn, etc." But the whole of this beautiful passage deserves to be read.*

[72] See Buffon, p. 224. From our disregard of the possibility of death within the four and twenty hours, he concludes (pp. 56–58) that a chance which falls below or rises above ten thousand to one, will never affect the hopes or fears of a reasonable man. The fact is true,

* "Come, bright love of fame, &c., fill my ravished fancy with the hopes of charming ages yet to come. Foretel me that some tender maid, whose grandmother is yet unborn, hereafter, when, under the fictitious name of Sophia, she reads the real worth which once existed in my Charlotte, shall from her sympathetic breast send forth the heaving sigh. Do thou teach me not only to foresee but to enjoy, nay even to feed on, future praise. Comfort me by the solemn assurance that, when the little parlour in which I sit at this moment shall be reduced to a worse furnished box, I shall be read with honour by those who never knew nor saw me, and whom I shall neither know nor see."—Book xiii. chap. 1.

period which, as the most agreable of his long life, was selected by the judgement and experience of the sage Fontenelle. His choice is approved by the eloquent historian of Nature, who fixes our moral happiness to the mature season, in which our passions are supposed to be calmed, our duties fullfilled, our ambition satisfied, our fame and fortune established on a solid basis.[73] I am far more inclined to embrace than to dispute this comfortable doctrine: I will not suppose any præmature decay of the mind or body; but I must reluctantly observe that two causes, the abbreviation of time and the failure of hope, will always tinge with a browner shade the evening of life. 1. The proportion of a part to the whole is the only standard by which we can measure the length of our existence. At the age of twenty, one year is a tenth, perhaps, of the time which has elapsed within our consciousness and memory; at the age of fifty it is no more than a fortieth, and this relative value continues to decrease till the last sands are shaken by the hand of death. This reasoning may seem metaphysical, but on a tryal it will be found satisfactory and just. 2. The warm desires, the long expectations of youth, are founded on the ignorance of themselves and of the World: they are gradually damped by time and experience, by disappointment or possession;

---

but our courage is the effect of thoughtlessness rather than of reflection. If a public lottery was drawn for the choice of an immediate victim, and if our name were inscribed on one of the ten thousand tickets, should we be perfectly easy?

[73] See Buffon, p. 413. In private conversation, that great and amiable man added the weight of his own experience; and this autumnal felicity might be exemplified in the lives of Voltaire, Hume, and many other men of letters.

and after the middle season the crowd must be content to remain at the foot of the mountain, while the few who have climbed the summit aspire to descend or expect to fall. In old age, the consolation of hope is reserved for the tenderness of parents, who commence a new life in their children; the faith of enthusiasts who sing Hallelujahs above the clouds,[74] and the vanity of authors who presume the immortality of their name and writings.

LAUSANNE, *March* 2, 1791.

---

[74] This cœlestial hope is confined to a small number of the Elect, and we must deduct: (1) All the *mere* philosophers, who can only speculate about the immortality of the soul. (2) All the *earthly* Christians, who repeat without thought or feeling the words of their Catechism. (3) All the *gloomy* fanatics, who are more strongly affected by the fear of Hell, than by the hopes of Heaven. " Strait is the way and narrow is the gate, and *few* there be who find it."

THE MEMOIRS

OF

THE LIFE

OF

EDWARD GIBBON

WITH

VARIOUS OBSERVATIONS AND EXCURSIONS

BY HIMSELF.

[MEMOIRS OF MY OWN LIFE.*

CHAPTER I.

Introduction—Account of my family—My grandfather—My father—My birth in the year 1737—My infancy—My first education and studies.]

In the fifty-second year of my age, after the completion of a toilsome and successful work, I now propose to employ some moments of my leisure in reviewing the simple transactions of a private and litterary life. Truth, naked unblushing truth, the first virtue of more serious history, must be the sole recommendation of this personal narrative: the style shall be simple and familiar; but style is the image of character, and the habits of correct writing may produce, without labour or design, the appearances of art and study. My own amusement is my motive, and will be my reward; and if these sheets are communicated to some discreet and indulgent friends, they will be secreted from the public eye till the author shall be removed from the reach of criticism or ridicule.†

---

* Memoir A. The earliest, 1788-9. Lord Sheffield printed from this only pars. 1, 2, and 3, partially.

† This passage is found in this alone of the sketches. "Mr. Gibbon, in his communications with me on the subject of his Memoirs, a subject which he had not mentioned to any other person, expressed a determination of publishing them in his lifetime; and never

[The reasons and examples which may furnish some Apology will be reserved for the last chapter of these Memoirs, when the order of time will lead me to account for this vain undertaking.

A Philosopher may reasonably despise the pride of ancestry; and, if the philosopher himself be a plebeian, his own pride will be gratified by the indulgence of such contempt. It is an obvious truth that parts and virtue cannot be transmitted with the inheritance of estates and titles; and that even the claim of our legal descent must rest on a basis not perhaps sufficiently firm, the unspotted chastity of *all* our female progenitors. Yet in every age and country the common sense or common prejudice of mankind has agreed to respect the son of a respectable father, and each successive generation is supposed to add a new link to the chain of hereditary splendour.] Wherever the distinction of birth is allowed to form a superior order in the state, education and example should always, and will often, produce among them a dignity of sentiment and propriety of conduct which is guarded from dishonour by their own and the public esteem. If we read of some illustrious line, so ancient that it has no beginning, so worthy that it ought to have no end, we sympathize in its various fortunes; nor can we blame the generous enthusiasm or even the harmless vanity of those who are associated to the honours of its name. In the study of past events our curiosity

---

appears to have departed from that resolution, excepting in one of his letters, in which he intimates a doubt, though rather carelessly, whether in his time, or at any time, they would meet the eye of the public.—In a conversation, however, not long before his death, I suggested to him that, if he should make them a full image of his mind, he would not have nerves to publish them, and therefore that they should be posthumous. He answered, rather eagerly, that he was determined to publish them *in his lifetime.*"—Sheffield.

is stimulated by the immediate or indirect reference to ourselves; [within its own precincts a local history is always popular, and the connection of a family is more clear and intimate than that of a kingdom, a province, or a city. For my own part, could I draw my pedigree from a General, a statesman, or a celebrated author, I should study their lives or their writings with the diligence of filial love, and I suspect that from this casual relation some emotions of pleasure—shall I say of vanity?—might arise in my breast. Yet I will add that I should take more delight in their personal merit than in the memory of their titles or possessions, that I should be more affected by litterary than by martial fame; and that I would rather descend from Cicero than from Marius, from Chaucer than from one of the first Companions of the Garter. The family of Confucius is, in my opinion, the noblest upon Earth. Seventy *authentic* Generations have elapsed from that Philosopher to the present Chief. of his posterity, who reckons one hundred and thirty-five degrees from the Emperor Hoang-ti, the father, as it is believed, of an illustrious line which has now flourished in China four thousand four hundred and twenty-five years. I have exposed my private feelings, as I shall always do, without scruple or reserve—— Let every reader, whether noble or plebeian, examine his own conscience on the same subject.]

That these sentiments are just, or at least natural, I am the more inclined to believe, since I do not feel myself interested in the cause, since I can derive from my ancestors neither glory nor shame.* [I had long and

---

* From this point onward this Memoir has not hitherto been published.

modestly acquiesced in the knowledge of my two immediate predecessors, a country gentleman and a wealthy merchant. Beyond these I found neither tradition nor memorial; and as our Genealogy was never a topic of family conversation, it might seem probable that my grandfather, the Director of the South Sea Company, was himself a son of the Earth, who by his industry— his honest industry perhaps—had raised himself from the Work-house or the Cottage. It is not two years since I acquired in a foreign land some domestic intelligence of my own family, and this intelligence was conveyed to Switzerland from the heart of Germany. I had formed an acquaintance with Mr. *Langer*, a lively and ingenious Scholar, while he resided at Lausanne as preceptor to the Hereditary prince of *Brunswick*. On his return to his proper station of librarian to the Ducal library of *Wolfenbuttel*, he accidentally found among some litterary rubbish a small, old English Volume of Heraldry, inscribed with the name of *John Gibbon*. From the title only, Mr. *Langer* judged that it might be an acceptable present to his friend: and he judged rightly, for I soon convinced myself that the author was not only my namesake, but my kinsman. To his book I am indebted for the best and most curious information; but in my last visit to England I was tempted to indulge a curiosity which had been excited by this odd discovery. Some Wills, parish-registers, and monumental inscriptions were consulted at my request, and my enquiries were assisted by Mr. *Brooke*, the Somerset Herald, whose knowledge deserves my applause, and whose friendly industry is entitled to my thanks.

The first authentic record of my family shall be given

in the disqualifying words of *John Gibbon*, Blue-mantle
Poursuivant, who will soon become an acquaintance of
the reader.   After renouncing the vanities of this world,
and closing by an et cætera the mention of some titles
and alliances, *Ne videar vanitati* Genealogicæ nimis-
nimium indulgere.

> " Et genus et proavos et quæ non fecimus ipsi
>   Vix ea nostra voco "—

he adds with a modest cunning, " Nedum mentionem
sum facturus *Gibbonos* terras tenuisse et possedisse in
Rolvenden, Anno 1326, vicesimo Edwardi secundi, *Gib-
bonorum* familiæ meminit, Villare Anglicanum, pp. 72,
73, 120, 206, 296, ter 391, et inter errata prioris tabulæ
ad p. 299 respicientia." He afterwards mentions their
possessions in the neighbouring parish of Benenden; and
I have endeavoured to form some idea of the ancient
state of the Country in which they appear to have been
seated since the beginning of the fourteenth Century.
The adjacent hundreds of Rolvenden and Tenterden form
one of the most southern districts of Kent, with Sussex
to the West, the isle of Oxney to the south, and Romney
Marsh to the East.   A part of the maritime coast has
been gradually acquired by the retiring of the sea; since
the village of Newenden, now at the distance of some
miles, is supposed by *Cambden* to be the Roman *Anderida*, a town and harbour which had been chosen for a
naval station against the incursions of the Saxon pyrates.
The more inland tract, still denominated the *Weald*, was
a portion of the great forest of Anderida, which overspread the adjacent counties of Kent, Sussex, Surrey,
and Hampshire, and long afforded a retreat to the fugitive
Britons.   By the wise policy of Edward III., a Cloth

manufactory, long since decayed, was established in the towns of Cranbroke, Tenterden, and Benenden, and the rude natives were instructed by a colony of Flemings about the time of the first appearance of my ancestors.

From that period to the present day the Gibbons have flourished, or at least subsisted, near five hundred years in the same district of Kent. Their rank in society is defined by the appellation of Esquire, in an age when that title was less promiscuously bestowed. The property of the elder branch, the Gibbons of Rolvenden, now amounts to about five hundred pounds a year, without much encrease, as it should seem, or much diminution of their ancient patrimony. They do not appear to have been distinguished by the virtues or vices of an active spirit. From father to son they succeded each other in rural obscurity; and if I am asked about their lives and characters, I can only answer—

> "Go! search it there, where to be born and dye
> Of rich and poor makes all the history."

One only of the name left behind him a monument more conspicuous than the gravestone of a parish church-yard. In a grant of the thirteenth year of the reign of Edward III. (A.D. 1340) John Gibbon is styled Marmarius, (Marmorarius) Regis, the King's chief Marbler, master-mason, or Surveyor of his stone-works: no contemptible office, says Blue-mantle, who is jealous of the honour of his namesake. "For Weaver (p. 582) of his funeral monuments tells you, that such a one, a Marmorarius was Armiger Illustrissimi principis Richardi secundi Regis Angliæ." It is more than supposed (says he) that John Gibbon was the principal architect in the building Queensborough Castle. At a time when the English coast was infested by the French and Flemings, this strong and stately fortress was erected on the west side of the isle of Sheppey, to guard the entrance of the river Medway. It was denominated from the heroic *Queen*, Philippa of Hainault, and it is praised by the royal founder as a castle in a pleasant situation, a terror to his enemies and a comfort to his subjects. The reward which he bestowed on the Architect bespeaks him no vulgar mechanic. By a grant, which is still exstant, Edward III. invested John Gibbon with the profits of the passage between Sandwich and Stonar, in the isle of Thanet. I know not how long this favour was enjoyed by the Architect or his family, but it has long since been abolished by the lapse of time.

In the primitive institution a coat of arms was the symbol of real armour, a representation of the shield and helmet of the Warrior. His motto was the cry of battle, at whose well-known sound the followers were accustomed to charge and rally under the banner of their Chief. In these days of freedom the unmeaning badge of vanity is assumed by all and disputed by none; and every man who has money to buy a carriage may blazon, if he please, his fancied arms on the pannels. But there was an intermediate period in which the Gentry of England was discriminated by the use of armorial coats, when the science of quarters and colours was defined by the College of Heralds, and when a plebeian usurper would have been rejected and punished by the Court of the Earl-Marshal. I do not challenge the honours of ancient chivalry; but as early as the reign of Elizabeth the Gibbons of Kent were entitled to the same arms which I now claim by descent, though I may not perhaps describe them with the accuracy of technical language. " A Lyon, rampant, gardant, between three scallop-shells, silver on a field azure."   They are thus translated by the Bluemantle-poursuivant in his Latin verses which he subjoins to a picture of the arms—

" Symbola vera super data sunt auctoris honesti ;
  Erectus Leo stans inter conchylia terua
  (Ora sua obvertens) onus album, cærula parma est."

He records a whimsical instance of the revenge of his Godfather, Edmond Gibbon, who, with the license of Sir William Segar, King-at-arms, exchanged the three scallop-shells for three Ogresses. " He assumed this new coat out of distaste against three ladies, his kinswomen, daughters of Gervase Gibbon, of the Pump. Frances married Sir Robert Points, Knight of the Bath ; Elianor married to Sir John Crook: and Grizeld married to Sir John Lawrence, Knight and Baronet, who lies buried at Chelsy in Middlesex, in a chappel belonging to (and re-edified by) herself, with a fair mural monumental remembrance. The falling out was about the will of Edmund Gibbon, founder of the free school in Benenden, the next parish to Rolvenden aforesaid." The three Ladies were uncourteously described under the form of Gigantic cannibals, and their adversary reserved the Lyon as the emblem of his own warfare and defence against the female monsters. But this unchristian vindictive spirit was renounced by Edmond Gibbon himself or by his heir : he lyes buried in the Temple Church, London (in the walks or western part) ; with a fair monument, against a pillar ; and the harmless scallop-shells are restored to their place in the first quarter of his armorial coat.

My lineal ancestor in the fifth degree, Robert Gibbon

of Rolvenden, Esquire, was Captain of the Kentish militia;
and as he died in the year 1618, it may be presumed that
he had appeared in arms at the time of the Spanish
invasion. His wife was Margaret Phillips, daughter of
Edward Phillips de la Weld in Tenterden, and of Rose
his wife, daughter of George Whetnal of East-Peckham,
Esqre. By this last marriage John Gibbon the Herald—
did his modesty allow him—might connect his family
with many respectable names of the Gentry of England:
"Omitto Berclêos de Beauston, Hextallos, Ellenbriggòs,
Claverlêos, et Whetnallos Cestrenses, Equestri dignitate
olim nobiles." Peckham, the seat of the Whetnalls of
Kent, is mentioned—not, indeed, much to its honour—in
the Memoires du Comte de Grammont; a classic work, the
delight of every man and woman of taste to whom the
French language is familiar. It was at Peckham, la
triste Peckham, that the fair and inanimate *Whitnell*
(poupée jusqu'à la mort resta la blanche Whitnell)
passed so many gloomy hours with an husband qui aimoit
mieux feuilleter de vieux livres que de jeunes appas. It
was there that she received the visit of Mademoiselle
Hamilton, her cousin; that she sighed in the absence of
George Hamilton; that she felt the propriety of rewarding a faithful lover. If her marriage had preceded our
alliance, I would not so confidently boast of my descent
from the Whetnals of Peckham.

Yet it is from this union that I claim the most
illustrious of my ancestors, James, Lord Say and Sele,
who, in the reign of Henry VI., was Governor of Dover,
Warden of the Cinq-ports, Constable of the Tower,
Lord Chamberlain and Lord High Treasurer of England.
After the marriage of Queen Margaret he was accused by

the commons of delivering Maine and Anjou to the
French ; and to appease the popular discontent, this
favourite and perhaps innocent Minister was sequestered
from his office and then committed to the Tower. But
neither his dignity nor his disgrace could save him from
the blind rage of the Kentish Insurgents and their leader,
Jack Cade. Lord Say was dragged from the asylum of
his prison, and after a mock-tryal at Guild-hall, more
illegal, than any act of which he was accused, his head
was struck off, and borne in triumph about the street.
The charge against him, as it is stated by Jack Cade in
the words of Shakespeare, cannot, I believe, be strictly
maintained ; but it is of such a nature as would make a
man of letters proud of his descent from a martyr of
learning. "Thou hast most traiterously" (says the rude
clown) " corrupted the youth of the realm, in erecting a
grammar school : and whereas, before, our forefathers had
no other books but the score and the tally, thou hast
caused printing to be used ; and, contrary to the King, his
crown, and dignity, thou hast built a paper-mill. It will
be proved to thy face that thou hast men about thee that
usually talk of a noun and a verb, and such abominable
words as no christian ear can endure to hear." The
name of the Lord Treasurer, beheaded in the year 1450,
was Fiennes, and his family, which is still enrolled in the
British, had been settled in England from the time of
King Stephen. From the Co-heiress of a family still
more ancient and honourable than his own, he inherited
the Barony of Say, to which he was restored in full
parliament. Elizabeth, his daughter, married William
Cromer, twice Sheriff of Kent, and the son of a Lord
Mayor of London. Their son, Sir James Cromer, was the

father of Anne, the wife of William Whetnal of Peckham; George, their son, was the father of the above-mentioned Rose, the mother of Margaret Phillips, the wife of Robert Gibbon of Rolvenden. And thus, through the medium of four female alliances, I derive my lineage in the eleventh degree from the Lord Treasurer.

But, alas! these honours are obliterated, and my scutcheon is irretrievably stained if we adopt the lofty prejudices of French and German nobility. I cannot deny that the younger branch of the Gibbons of Kent migrated, in the reign of James I. from the Country to the City, and that they persevered during three generations in the profession of trade. Robert, the younger son of the above-mentioned Robert Gibbon of Rolvenden, Esqre, became a citizen of London and a member of the Cloth-workers' company. His son Matthew was a Linnen-draper in Leadenhall street in the parish of St. Andrew, Undershaft; and the son of Matthew, Edward Gibbon, my grandfather, was engaged in various branches of foreign and domestic commerce before he was elected a Director of the South sea Company. These facts I can relate without a blush: the good-sense of the English has embraced a system more conducive to national prosperity; the character of a merchant is not esteemed incompatible with that of a Gentleman; and the first names of the peerage are enrolled in the books of our trading Corporations. The descent of landed property to the eldest son is secured by the common law, and though Kent, under the name of *Gavelkind,* retains a more equal partition, this provincial custom is defeated by the practise of settlements and entails. The pride and indolence of younger brothers might frequently acquiesce in the life

of a William Wimble, so incomparably described by the
Spectator: but a more rational pride must often prevail
over their indolence, and urge them to seek in the World
the comforts of independence.   Since the auspicious reign
of Elizabeth the commerce of England had opened a
thousand channels of industry and wealth, and the more
splendid ressources which now divert a Gentleman's
younger sons from the mercantile profession were much
less frequent and beneficial.   After the reformation the
Church assumed a graver and less attractive form, and
though many might be content to sleep in the possession
of a patrimonial living, the bench of bishops was long
filled by indigent scholars, before the gentry, or at least
the nobility, became fully sensible of the value of a calling
which bestows riches and honours without requiring either
genius or application.   In every age the youth of England
has been distinguished by a martial spirit, and the
subjects of Elizabeth and her successors sought every
occasion of danger and glory by sea and land.   But these
occasions were rare and voluntary; nor could they afford
such an ample and permanent provision as is now supplied
by an hundred regiments, and an hundred ships of the line.
Our civil establishment has gradually swelled to its
present magnitude; nor did India unfold her capacious
bosom to the merit or fortune of every needy adventurer.
The common alternative was the bar and the counter;
but the success of a lawyer, unless he be endowed with
superior talents, is difficult and doubtful; the various
occupations of commerce are adapted to the meanest
capacity, and a modest competency is the sure reward of
frugality and labour, since those humble virtues have so
often sufficed for the acquisition of riches.

Robert Gibbon the younger died in London in the year 1643, and his alliance may prove that he had not degraded himself by the profession of a Citizen and a clothier. He married the sister of Thomas Edgar, Esqre, Justice of Peace and Recorder of Ipswich, and their son, the Blue-mantle poursuivant, is well pleased to blazon his maternal with his paternal coat

" Maternus clypeus comitatur jure paternum
Cujus subsequitur Latiâ descriptio prosâ."

But this poetical vein was exhausted, and he is content to describe in Latin and English prose the modern arms of the Edgars, which they assumed by patent in the reign of Henry VIII., and afterwards to depict the armorial bearings of their ancient and primitive coat. But enough of these solemn trifles—I had rather observe that the Edgars, who spread into three branches, had flourished more than four hundred years in the County of Suffolk. The most eminent person of the race appears to have been Sir Gregory Edgar, a wealthy Serjeant-at-law, who died in the year 1506. "He took to wife Anne one of the daughters of Simon Wiseman, a man valiant and noble. This Woman was graced with modesty, manners, innocency, affability, and good parentage : and acceptable to all, and so liberal to the poor as was incredible." Such women at all times are rare, and it is a pleasure to descend from one of them.

Of the life and character of Matthew Gibbon, the son of Robert, I am totally ignorant, and must be content to repeat that he was a Linnen-draper in Leadenhall Street. After his decease, Hester, his relic, remarried with Richard Acton, third son of Sir Walter Acton, Baronet, who exercised the same trade, in the same street ; and in due time their union was confirmed by the marriage of the son of Hester and the daughter of Richard by their former marriages. This lady, who survived both her husbands, and lived to a great age, was of an active and notable spirit. While her son, my Grandfather Edward Gibbon, was in Flanders, where he had a contract for supplying King William's arms, his mother managed all his mercantile affairs at home; and I have seen some of her letters, in a character no longer legible, and on business no longer interesting. Besides my grandfather, she had another son, Thomas Gibbon, who became Dean of Carlisle. In my childhood I have known *his* son, Williams Gibbon, a drunken Jacobite parson, who obtained by party-interest the Rectory of Bridewell.

Another son, I know not whether elder or younger, of Matthew * Gibbon was John the Herald, without whose friendly aid I should be a stranger to my own family. In his book he has contrived to scatter many hints of his own life, and he thus records, in Latin verse, the important event of his birth, on the 3rd of November, of the year 1629—

> " Tertia lux *Noni*, mihi vitam contulit imbris,
> Anno millesimo Christi sexcentesimoque,
> Vigesimo nono (præ nonâ vesperis horâ),
> *Martyris et Caroli* quarto sub *Sole Beati.*"

After passing through the studies of the Grammar school, a necessary step, John Gibbon became a member of Jesus College at Cambridge, and the blazon of its coat and crest, which he received from the President Dr. Sherman, is piously inserted in his work. With the same

---

* Gibbon evidently wrote " Matthew " here in error for " Robert."

gratitude he celebrates the retired content with which he was blessed at Allesborough, in Worcestershire, at the seat of his good Lord Thomas, Lord Coventry; and from the comparison of his own felicity with that of Mr. Hobbes in the Devonshire family, I should guess that my kinsman exercised the office of a domestic tutor. From this peaceful retreat he launched into the World, and though he would not, or more probably could not, relate his battles and sieges, he finds or makes an opportunity of deciding a point of military discipline. " I remember " (says he) " when I was a soldier, I have heard some of the *Veterani* discourse concerning the fashion of belts, who averred that the shoulder-belt is very dangerous for a horseman; for a strong man, taking advantage of it, easily dismounts his adversary, whereas the waist- or middle-belt prevents this inconvenience." He must have been soon released from the service, since he could indulge his curiosity in visiting foreign countries; he mentions France and the Netherlands with the pleasure and knowledge of a traveller, and expresses his gratitude to the Isle of Jersey, " ubi me quondam jucunde vixisse jam nunc juvat meminisse." But his excursions were not confined to Europe. " A great part of 1659, till February of the year following, I lived (says John Gibbon) in Virginia, being most hospitably entertained by the Honourable Colonel Richard Lee, sometime Secretary of State there, and who, after the King's martyrdom, hired a Dutch vessel, freighted her himself, went to Brussels, surrendered up Sir William Barcklaie's old commission for the government of the province, received a new one from his present Majesty—a loyal action and well deserving my commendation." In that rising

colony he once saw a war-dance acted by the natives.
The Dancers performed their martial evolutions, sometimes retreating and sometimes advancing towards the
Spectators, with ferocious countenances and brandishing
their Tamahawks. But what most forcibly affected his
eye and fancy was the painting of their shields and
bodies, in which he recognized the regular blazon of
colours and symbols. " Some of the dancers were painted
from forehead to foot—*Party per pale, Gules and sable ;*
others, *party per fesse of the same colours :* At which I
exceedingly wondered, and concluded that Heraldry was
ingrafted naturally into the sense of human race.
If so, it deserves a greater esteem than is nowadays put
upon it." Such an idea, when applied to the vainest institution of modern art, displays a degree of enthusiasm
for a favourite study, which is at once ridiculous and
respectable.

I know of no purer felicity than that of a man who
can gratify his taste in the exercise of his profession, and
such was the good fortune of my kinsman after his return
to England, his marriage, and his settlement (in February,
1665) in a house in the cloyster of St. Catherine's
hospital, near the tower, which devolved to his nephew,
my grandfather. In the year 1671 he was admitted into
the College of Heralds by the style and title of Blue-
Mantle Poursuivant; and it is with a mixture of gratitude
and pride that he owns his obligations to a Judge as well
as a patron, the learned Sir William Dugdale, Garter
King-at-Arms, and the first English Antiquarian of the
age. He glories in the friendship of the curious Mr.
Ashmole, and of respectable Physicians, Dr. John Betts
and Dr. Nehemiah Grew; and acknowledges the courteous

encouragement which himself and his book received from Sir Stephen Fox, one of the Lords of the Treasury. This trusty servant of Charles II., in his exile and after his restoration, is compared to the faithful Achates; and John Gibbon applies a prophecy of Solomon (" As-tu vû un homme habile en son travail? il sera au service des Rois," of the French version of the Proverbs), which has been more conspicuously verified in the son and grandson of Sir Stephen Fox. The happiness of Blue-mantle would have been compleat, if already in his time the art and fashion of Heraldry had not been somewhat decayed. The ceremony of funerals, as accompanied with officers of arms began to be in the wane: in eleven years it was his hard hap to have no more than five turns; but he gratefully commemorates the worthy and noble families who so generously conducted their relation. His leisure was employed in smoothing a difficulty which had been felt by Cambden himself—the definition in Latin of the terms and symbols of heraldry; and his technical language, were the object of more use and importance, might deserve as much praise as the Botanical idiom of Linnæus. In the Introductio ad Latinam blazoniam published at London, 1682, the Author displays some wit and much zeal, a perfect knowledge of English Genealogy, and a familiar acquaintance with the French and Spanish languages. An English text is adorned with many Latin sentences and verses of his own composition; his quotations from the poets are apt and frequent; but in his own practise he claims an exemption from the laws of prosody. Of the intrinsic merit of his work I am not qualified to decide, and I much doubt whether the more rigid heralds would approve his heresy of inscribing metal on metal, and colour on colour. I am apprehensive that on this question they will not be satisfied with the authorities of Ovid and of Scripture; with the shield of Nileus in the Metamorphoses (lv.)—

> " Clypeo quoque flumina septem
> Argento partim, partim cœlaverat auro "—

nor with the silver apples on a golden ground in the Proverbs (xxvii.); yet, as Solomon was the wisest of Kings, he could not, says the Author, be an ignorant herald. From this small volume, a duodecimo of one hundred and sixty-five pages, John Gibbon appears to have expected high and lasting reputation. In the title-page he loudly proclaims, " No work of this nature extant in our English tongue, nor, absit gloriari, of its method and circumstances in any foreign language what-soever." And at the conclusion of his labours he sings in a strain of self-congratulation—

> " Usque huc corrigitur *Romana Blasonia* per me,
> Verborumque dehinc Barbara forma cadat.
> Hic liber in meritum si forsitan incidet usum
> Testis rite meæ sedulitatis erit
> Quicquid agat Zoilus ventura fatebitur ætas.
> *Artis* quod fueram non *Clypearis* inops."

But the succeeding age was ignorant of his name; and had I not by a strange accident discovered his book, the memory of John Gibbon would have been obliterated in his own family.

In the last years of Charles II. it was difficult, between the Whigs and Tories, for an Englishman to remain neuter; the science of hereditary honours is favourable to Monarchy, and the Herald was strenuously attached to the Royal brothers of the house of Stuart. " Tutus sit " (he devoutly exclaims) "Augustissimus Rex Carolus Sancti Felicis festo prospere natus! Celsissimus Illustrissimus Dux Jacobus, quem stellam borealem ante multos annos [prædicere vates], et universa stirps Regia a turbâ fanaticâ Anti-monarchicâ!" He commemorates several pamphlets, such as the *Swan's Wellcome*, the *Flagellum Mercurii Antiducalis*, the warm effusions of his loyalty, and mentions with some bitterness, his Antagonist, "the little Mr. Harry Care, that great writer who scommatically affronts the dread reverence and awe due to Kings and Princes." His enemies, if we may trust his complaints, employed against [him] a base and treacherous stratagem : they interpolated his text, spoilt his Latin ; and when he hailed the *aus*picious return of the Duke of York, the unlucky epithet of *sus*picious was substituted by a Whig printer, on whom he most heartily bestows the curse of Judas. After such provocations, no wonder if he sought for revenge ; and, as every animal is conscious of its weapons, his revenge is that of an Herald : he blazons, whimsically enough, the coat of the Republican faction "Quibus symbolum et insigne est, *Bellua multorum capitum,* coloris Diabolici (viz. nigri) in campo sanguineo. Clamor bellicus, *Iste est hæres, trucidemus eum et obtineamus hæreditatem.* Genius tutelaris non Sanctus Georgius, S. Andreas, S. Patricius. Sed iste *Draco magnus, rufus* in Apocalypsi memoratus. Dissipentur autem ut palea coram vento. AMEN." The Revolution was adverse to his principles, his feelings, and his fortune ; the Blue-mantle Poursuivant could never ascend to an higher station in the College ; and after the accession of George I. he was suspended from his office till he could bend his conscience to the oath

of allegiance. The age which he attained, of almost
ninety years, is a fair presumption that he was endowed
with the health of mind as well as body; and his
Philosophic temper is expressed in the following lines—

> " Mortis at incertum cum tempus, det Deus aptâ
> Conditione siem, semper stans mente paratus
>   Interea
> Magna mihi in votis haud sunt; dent numina tantum
> Exiguum Censum servem, simul integra membra;
> Mens virtute fruens addatur et insuper illis."

Of his wife and children I am ignorant; of his posterity
there is no trace. From some letters and traditions in
the College, I understand that John Gibbon was a lover
of Astrology, and a member, with Ashmole, Dugdale, etc.,
of an Astrological Club. Their two favourite sciences
were long supported by the vanity and curiosity of Mankind, and the second of these passions is still more
universal and powerful than the first.

From the singular character of the Herald, my uncle
in the third ascending degree, I now return to the direct
line. By Hester, the wife and widow of his brother
Matthew, three links were formed between the Gibbons
and the Actons: by her second nuptials with Richard
Acton, by the marriage of their children of the first
adventure, and by the union of her daughter with Sir
Whitmore Acton. This triple alliance, and especially
the second, gives me a deep and domestic interest in
the name and honours of a worthy family, which has
flourished in Shropshire since the thirteenth and fourteenth Centuries, which has been propagated by a series
of adequate connections, and of which the younger
branches have been supported without being disgraced

by the profession of trade. In the eyes of the Tories, the Actons may claim the merit of firm and untainted loyalty, not only in their distant province far from the vortex of new opinions, but even in the occupations and offices of the Capital. Sir Richard Acton, of a branch now extinct, was created a baronet in 1629; in the year 1643 he was chosen Lord Mayor of London, and was removed by the House of Commons for his attachment to the King, and his opposition to their proceedings. His cousin, Edward Acton of Aldenham the Chief of the elder, was created a Baronet by Charles I. in 1643, a few months after he had erected his standard at Nottingham. Sir Edward was succeeded by Sir Walter, his eldest son, and the father of seven sons, who all exceeded the ordinary proportion of the human stature. One of these, Francis, who died a bachelor in my grandfather's (his nephew's) house at Putney, confessed or boasted that he was a pygmey of six feet two inches, the least of the seven, and he added, in the true spirit of party, that such men had not been born since the Revolution. Of the other brothers, I shall mention three who left a numerous posterity: Sir Edward, the father of Sir Whitmore, who married my grandfather's sister, by whom he had Sir Richard, the present baronet, now almost fourscore years of age; Richard, the father of my grandmother; and Walter, whose descendants, by strange accidents, have migrated to foreign Countries. Walter himself and his son Edward passed their lives, a Mercer, and a Goldsmith, in the city of London; but of the two sons of Edward, the one, who accompanied my father on his travels, was tempted to marry and settle at Besançon in France, while the other, a Captain in the East India Company's service, was invited to command at Leghorn the fleet of the Emperor, Great Duke of Tuscany. The Commodore died a bachelor: the two younger sons of the Physician are still, if they are alive, in the French service; but the fortune of the elder has been much more singular and splendid. After a visit to England in the year 1762, with the design, perhaps, of obtaining the daughter and heiress of his kinsman, Sir Richard Acton, he devoted himself with spirit and success to the naval service of Tuscany and Naples. In the expedition against Algiers, the Chevalier Acton, who commanded a Frigate, was distinguished by his courage and conduct, and his abilities have since raised him to the first honours of the State. The Courts of Versailles and Madrid have laboured in vain to drive him from his station; and he still enjoys, with the title, or at least the power, of prime Minister, the entire confidence of the King—I should rather say of the Queen—of the two Sicilies.

Were I possessed of the books and papers of my grandfather, Edward Gibbon, I should not feel much pleasure in stating the balance of his accounts, or the progress of his fortune. Yet he moved in an higher sphere than his two predecessors of commercial and even of political life. Under Lord Oxford's administration he held near four years the office of one of the Commissioners of the Customs; he was afterwards elected one of the Directors of the South-sea Company, and partook of its transient glory; but in the year 1720 he was buried in its ruins, and the labours of thirty years were blasted in a single day. The act of Parliament which stripped the Directors of the greatest part of their property has been condemned by the more impartial judgement of posterity, and, without suspicion of personal resentment, I may be allowed to prove that the proceedings against those unfortunate men were *unjust, illegal,* and arbitrary. i. In the year 1711 the South-sea Company had been incorporated by Lord Oxford; their original stock was composed of near ten millions of the unfunded debt, and the creditors, now transformed into merchants, were invested with an exclusive charter of trade and establishment in the South Seas. But their ambition was soon checked by the conclusion of the peace; the treaty of Utrecht did not afford an adequate compensation; their commercial privileges were eluded or infringed by the jealousy of Spain; nor could these new adventurers pretend to rival the firm credit of the Bank, or the rising greatness of the East India Company. Yet they were encouraged by the favour of the crown and the people, and a project was adopted in the year 1720 for consolidating in their hands the greatest part of the national debt. They were authorized by parliament to encrease their stock, and to acquire, by subscription or purchase, the redeemable and irredeemable debts on such terms as they should be able to stipulate with the public creditors. Their first operations were seconded by the enthusiasm of the times; the rapid rise in the price of their stock enabled them to conclude an advantageous bargain; all parties were united by the lust of gold, and all men rushed forwards to grasp those ideal treasures which were realized only for those who had prudence to withdraw before the impending ruin. In these wonderful transactions, I am at a loss to discern the precise and specific crime of the Directors; nor could it be very obvious to the majority of Country Gentlemen who sat as their

Judges in the house of commons. The least justifiable of their measures, the vague letter of Attorney which was inserted in their books, and unknowingly signed by the thoughtless subscribers, was afterwards ratified at *their* expence by the authority of parliament. If the directors promised an enormous dividend, if they opened a subscription at one thousand per cent., they were countenanced and almost compelled by the popular frenzy; nor are they accused, at least they are not convicted, of inflaming that frenzy for their private emolument. They acted under the legal controul of the Lords of the Treasury; and whatever might be the guilt, the largest share must be assigned to the Earl of Sunderland, the first Lord, and, above all, to Mr. Aislabie, Chancellor of the Exchequer. Yet these Ministers were peaceably dismissed or imperfectly punished. Their resignation attoned for their offences, and the friendless directors were the victims to appease the blind vehemence of popular resentment. ii. Lord Molesworth, the author of the state of Denmark, confessed in the house of Commons that there was no law to punish the Directors; but he appealed to the practise of the Romans, who having neglected to provide against the incredible guilt of parricide, applied a new remedy to a new disease, and cast the first criminal into the River, inclosed in a sack. And with this penalty, he mildly added, he himself should be content, were it inflicted on the authors of the present mischief. This inhuman speech was received with applause; and that every form of justice might be violated, the Directors were refused the common privilege of being heard by their council against a bill which blasted their characters and confiscated their fortunes.

I will not deny that an ex post facto law, a bill of attainder, may be excused by public necessity. But the state could not be saved by the disgrace or ruin of these men; nor can the use of example be urged; since their guilt, were it proved, could scarcely be repeated. iii. It had been first proposed that each director should be allowed, for his future support, one-eighth of his estate. But it was replied with some shew of reason, that, considering the difference of their characters and fortunes, such an equal penalty would be too light for many, and perhaps too heavy for some of these offenders. The case of each man was separately weighed; but instead of the calm solemnity of judicial proceedings, their honour and fortune were made the topic of hasty conversation, the sport of a lawless majority; and each member, by a malicious word or a silent vote, might indulge his general spleen or personal malevolence. Injury was aggravated by insult, and insult was embittered by pleasantry. Allowances of twenty pounds or of one shilling were facetiously moved; and a vague story that such a Director had been formerly concerned in another project, by which some unknown persons had lost their money, was admitted as an evidence of his present guilt. One man was ruined because he had dropt a foolish speech, that his horses should feed upon gold; and another, because he was grown to such an height of pride and insolence, that he once behaved with impertinence at the treasury, and refused to give a civil answer to persons much above him. All were condemned, absent and unheard, in various and arbitrary fines, which swept away the far greater part of their fortunes.

Such were once the proceedings of a British parliament: but it was the same house of Commons which had forfeited the trust of their constituents, and voted their own continuance four years beyond their legal term of existence ; it was the same parliament which passed the Riot-Act, and introduced Martial law in time of peace ; which stripped the Irish peerage of their right of judicature, and had almost stripped the Scotch peerage of their right of election.   It must be lamented that the Whigs have too often sullied the principles of freedom by the practise of violence and tyranny.

From these general reflections I must now return to the particular case of my grandfather. When the South-sea Directors were obliged to deliver upon the value of their whole property, he stated his own at the ample sum of one hundred and six thousand five hundred and forty-three pounds five shillings and six pence. The question put in the house of Commons whether Mr. Gibbon's allowance should be ten or fifteen thousand pounds, and it was carried without a division for the smaller sum.

[Pages 25-30 (inclusive) of the original MSS. are missing.]

he saw me after the fatal event—the awful silence, the room hung with black, the midday tapers, his sighs and tears, his praises of my mother, whom he called a Saint in Heaven; his solemn exhortation that I would cherish her memory and copy his (*sic*) virtues, and the fervour with which he kissed and blessed me as the sole remaining pledge of their loves. That interesting romance of the Abbé Prevot d'Exiles, the Memoires d'un homme de qualité, had lately been translated into English; and as soon as I read them, the grief of the Marquis on the death of his beloved Selima most forcibly brought to my mind the situation and behaviour of my poor father. After he could persuade himself to try, not the pleasures, but the consolations of friendship and society, the two houses at Putney which he most familiarly frequented were those of the Gilberts and the Mallets. The former were three maidens of middle age and small fortunes, the sisters of the *leaden* Gilbert stigmatized by Pope, and who, without either talents or virtue, could ascend the Ecclesiastical ladder as high as the station of Archbishop of York. The younger sister, Emily Gilbert, was a Lady of some spirit and accomplishments, who had been the intimate friend of my mother; and she secretly aspired to supply as well as to alleviate the widower's loss. But he was exasperated at the first suspicion of her design; and as his indignation was artfully fomented, he threw himself without reserve into the arms of the Mallets. The Poet's conversation (we may trust Dr. Johnson, an unforgiving enemy) was easy and elegant; and his wife, though far different from my mother in character and person, was not deficient either in wit or cunning. Their society soothed and occupied his grief; and as they both thought with freedom on the subjects of Religion and Government, they successfully laboured to correct the prejudices of his education. My father is introduced in one of Mallet's most agreable poems, entitled, THE WEDDING DAY. The place of the scene is thus described—

> "Just then, where our good-natured THAMES is
> Some four short miles above ST. JAMES'S
> And deigns with silver-streaming wave
> Th' abodes of Earth-born pride to lave;
> Aloft in air two Gods were soaring,
> While PUTNEY cits beneath lay snoring."

After some smart dialogue between Cupid and Hymen, the latter points with his torch to the happy couple, and the two Deities agree to invite some select friends—Mr. Waller, Mr. Mitchell (afterwards Minister to the King of Prussia), Colonel Caroline, and his brother, Mr. George Scott, etc.—to celebrate, on the third of October, 1750, the eighth anniversary of their nuptials. While Cupid flies to London—

> "His brother too, with sober cheer
> For the same end did westward steer.
> But first a pensive love forlorn
> Who three long weeping years has borne
> His torch revers'd, and all around
> Where once it flam'd with cypress bound,
> Sent off, to call a neighbouring friend,
> On whom the mournful train attend:
> And bid him, this one day, at least,
> For such a pair, at such a feast,
> Strip off the sable veil, and wear
> His once gay look and happier air."

On such a day, at a convivial meeting of his friends, the sorrowful widower might assume or affect his former chearfulness. But his plan of happiness was destroyed: his faithful companion was no more, and my father found himself alone in a World of which the business and amusement were now grown insipid or irksome. At the end of the parliament, he dropt his interest at Southampton, renounced all thoughts of a seat in the house of Commons. London he seldom visited; he soon forgot the associates of his politicks and pleasures, and by them he was soon forgotten. The residence of Putney was too near and public, and, after some tryals, he resolved to bury himself in a solitude at his estate of Buriton, near Petersfield, in Hampshire. Society he wished to avoid, books could not amuse his leisure; but he depended on the perpetual occupation, the labor actus in orbem of agriculture. To this art he was no stranger, and even at Putney he had delighted in the character of a curious and fashionable farmer.

Such was truly the most interesting and respectable cause of my father's retirement; but I may not dissemble that it was precipitated by a motive of a baser alloy, the encreasing disorder of his circumstances. By a wise dispensation, which preserves the balance of riches, idleness is the heir of industry; and the thirst of gain is succeeded by the desire of enjoyment. Œconomy is seldom the virtue of a gay and sanguine temper; my father's youth had been penuriously stinted; he was dazzled by a sudden influx of gold; but his possessions proved inadequate to his *hopes*, and his expences soon exceeded the measure of his income. To this illusion my grandfather had in some degree been accessory, by leaving to his daughters the clearest and most solid parts of his personal fortune, while he bequeathed to his son such unsettled accounts, such complicated plans, as might have been productive in his own hands, but which tended rather to deceive than to enrich a less careful manager. Among these was a lucrative contract for supplying the Court of Spain with naval stores, of which large quantities were already deposited in his ware-houses at Cadiz. In spite of the most solemn engagements, these effects were sequestered on the rupture between the two nations; and in the vote which my father gave against the Spanish convention, I must admire either his patriotism or his credulity. He anticipated the payment of his debt, with a large arrear of interest and

damages, which he confidently expected from the justice
of the Catholic King; but, alas! on the return of peace,
our agents and memorials were referred by the Ministers
to the Judges, and by the judges to the ministers, till the
obsolete demand has finally evaporated in delay, disappointment, and fruitless cost. Of dress and diversions, of house
and equipage, the expences may be foreseen, and must be
limited; but the gaming-table is a dark and slippery
precipice. My father did not enjoy with impunity the
honour of being a member of the old club at White's:
his contemporaries seemed to think less highly than
himself of his skill at Whist; some large and nameless
charges in his books must be placed to the Debtor side
of play; and the tryals to which I have alluded were the
anxious hours and sleepless nights of his wife, while she
felt that too much of her children's fortune was depend-
ing on a card or a die. By these means his ready money
was speedily exhausted, his landed estate was entailed,
and as soon as the first debts were contracted, the rapid
accumulation of principal and interest increased the want,
and diminished the facility of new supplies. His temper
was soured by pecuniary embarassments; and had my
mother lived, he must have withdrawn, with more comfort,
but with less grace, from a public life in which he could
not support or retrench his customary figure. But if
we search still deeper, we shall discover a third motive
of retirement in the natural inconstancy of his disposition,
which, perhaps, has been painted by his tutor, Mr.
William Law, under the name of *Flatus*. "Flatus" (says
the devout satirist) "is rich and in health: yet always
uneasy, and always searching after happiness. Every
time you visit him you find some new project in his

head; he is eager upon it, as something that is more worth his while, and will do more for him than anything that is already past. Every new thing so seizes him, that if you were to take him from it, he would think himself quite undone. His sanguine temper and strong passions promise him so much happiness in everything, that he is always cheated, and satisfied with nothing." Mr. Law's wit then pursues him through the various pursuits of dress, gaming, diversions, drinking, hunting, building, riding, and travelling, with each of which Flatus is by turns delighted and disgusted. All these features cannot, indeed, be applied to the same person; and as the second Edition of The serious call to a devout and holy life was published in the year 1732, the prophetic eye of the tutor must have discerned the butterfly in the caterpillar. But our family tradition attests his laudable or malicious design, and from my own observation, I can acknowledge the skill of the painter and the likeness of the portrait.

I have mentioned my two aunts on the father's side— the two Ogresses, as my old kinsman would have styled them—who were so plentifully endowed at our expence. Their names were Catherine and Hester, though I do not pretend to ascertain the order of their respective births. Their characters were widely different, and the profane Flavia (in the Serious call) is the sister of the holy Miranda. The character of the former is not marked by any scandalous vice, and, to aggravate her guilt, the artful satirist allows her a decent sense and practise of the externals of Religion. But she was devoid of true piety. Vanity was the idol of her heart, and her time, her thoughts, and her expences were all devoted to herself and to the World.   After an humorous picture of her Sunday, Mr. Law makes the following calculation: "If Flavia lives ten years longer, she will have spent about fifteen hundred and sixty Sundays after this manner.   She will have wore above two hundred different suits of Cloaths.   Out of this thirty year of her life fifteen of them will have been dispo[sed] off in bed: and of the remaining fifteen, fourteen of them will have been consumed in eating, drinking, dressing, visiting, conversation, reading and hearing plays and romances; at Opera's assemblies, balls, and diversions.   For you may reckon all the time that she is up thus spent, except about an hour and half that is disposed of at Church most Sundays in the year.   With great management, and under mighty rules of œconomy, she will have spent sixty hundred pounds" (he much underrates her fortune) "upon herself; bating only some shillings, crowns, or half-crowns that have gone from her in *accidental* charities."—Her eternal damnation he will not absolutely pronounce, but he is bold to say that she can have no hopes of being saved. Wherever she be at present, both Flavia and her husband were deceased before my remembrance.   Miss Catherine Gibbon had married Captain Edward Elliston, whom my grandfather in his Will calls his nephew—a Gentleman who had acquired a competent fortune for those times in the service of the East India Company.   They left one only daughter, Catherine Elliston, about two years older than myself; and from both her parents, as well as from the savings of a long minority, she was possessed, on the day of her own marriage, of more than sixty thousand pounds.   My father was left one of her guardians; but as he was ill qualified, in his widowed state, for the care of a young heiress, he entrusted her education to his friends, the Mallets, with whom Miss Elliston resided several years. At the age of fifteen she is prettily introduced in the poem of the *Wedding-day*—

> " Last comes a virgin—pray admire her!
> Cupid himself attends to squire her.
> A welcome guest! we much had mist her;
> For 'tis our Kitty, or his sister.
> But, Cupid, let no knave or fool
> Snap up this lamb, to shear her wool;
> No teague of that unblushing band,
> Just landed, or about to land;
> Thieves from the womb, and train'd at nurse
> To steal an heiress or a purse.
> No scraping, saving, sawcy Cit,
> Sworn foe of breeding, worth, and wit.
> No half-form'd insect of a peer
> With neither land nor conscience clear :
> Who, if he can, 'tis all he can do
> Just spell the motto on his landau.
> From all, from each of these defend her !
> But thou, and Hymen, both befriend her
> With truth, taste, honour in a mate,
> And much good sense, and some estate."

By all these monsters was the heiress successively assailed: she escaped, however, from their pursuit, and was saved from herself by the coldness of Sir William Peere Williams, afterwards killed at Belleisle: an high-spirited Youth, whose talents might have been the glory, but whose passions would have proved the curse, of her life. The poet's wish was *apparently* fulfilled by her marriage, in 1756, with Edward Eliot Esqre (now Lord Eliot), of Port Eliot, in the County of Cornwall. They are both alive, and their three sons, now grown to man's estate, are my nearest relations on the father's side.

While my poor aunt Flavia resigned herself to the World and the Devil, her sister, Mrs. Hester Gibbon, walked in the way of salvation, under the guidance of Mr. Law; and her devout life is either the original or the copy of his character of Miranda. By severe penance she laboured to attone for the faults of her youth, for the scenes of vanity into which she had been led or driven by authority or example. But no sooner was she mistress of her own actions and a plentiful fortune, than the pious Virgin abandoned her brother's house, and retired, with her Director, and a widow lady of the name of Hutchinson, to Cliffe, near Stamford, in Northamptonshire, where she still survives, many years after the loss of her two friends. I shall not pretend to enumerate the Christian virtues of Miranda. Her charity, even its excess, commands our respect: "Her fortune is divided between herself and several OTHER poor people; and she has only her part of relief from it." The sick and lame, young children and aged persons, are the first objects of her benevolence; but she seldom refuses an alms to a common beggar, "and instead of driving him away as a cheat, because she does not know him, she relieves him, because he *is* a stranger and unknown to her. Excepting her victuals, she never spent ten pounds a year upon herself. If you was to see her, you would wonder what poor body it was, that was so surprizingly neat and clean. She eats and drinks only for the sake of living; and with so regular an abstinence, that every meal is an exercise of self-denial, and she humbles her body every time, that she is forced to feed it." Her only study is the bible, with some legends and books of piety, which she reads with implicit faith. Her prayers are repeated five times each day; and as singing, according to Mr. Law, is an essential part of devotion, she rehearses the Psalms and hymns of thanksgiving which she will hereafter chant in a full chorus of Saints and Angels. Such was the portrait, and such the life, of that holy maiden, who by Gods is Miranda called, and by men Mrs. Hester Gibbon. Of the pains and joys of a spiritual life *I* am ill qualified to speak; yet I am inclined to hope that her lot has not been unhappy in this World. Her pennance is voluntary, and in her eyes meritorious; her time is constantly employed, and instead of the insignificance of an old maid, she is surrounded by dependants (poor and abject as they are) who solicit her bounty and adopt her sentiments. Christianity has not shed it's mildest influence on her temper, naturally proud and morose; she hates all the enemies of God, and how can *her* enemies be *his* friends? After their separation, she seldom saw and never forgave my father; his connection with the Mallets marked him as a reprobate, and when I notified his death, the sister did not drop a tear of sorrow or sympathy. That event, however, renewed our correspondence, which had been interrupted from my childhood, and I have been admitted to her presence in her two short and necessary visits to London. I found her external appearance such as has been described; her health confirmed by temperance, her natural understanding clear and manly, and her attention to the interest of this World as keen and intelligent as if she had never thought of another. My aunt Hester has now lived above eighty-five years on this earth, an improper habitation; and if she survives to the conclusion of these

Memoirs, I shall mention my hopes and fears which may depend on her final dispositions.

At an advanced age, about the year 1761, Mr. William Law departed this life, at the house of his favourite Miranda. In his last days his Religion degenerated into the visions of Jacob Behmen; but he always esteemed himself a true son of the Church of England, though he was separated from her visible communion by the unfortunate quality of a Nonjuror. As such, he could disclaim all obedience to the new Usurpers of the Crown and Mitre, and might avow his loyalty to the indefeasible right, the banished heir of the house of Stuart. After the Revolution, oaths of allegiance had been multiplied and imposed by the foolish jealousy of the reigning party. Did they hope, by such cobwebs, to bind the conscience of Sunderland or Marlborough, of Bolingbroke or Atterbury? The majority of Jacobites was resolved to *ab*jure and *per*jure, as occasion might serve; and the persecution fell on some harmless, honest Enthusiasts, who can never be formidable to any Government. The sacrifice of interest to principle or prejudice is an act of virtue; and Mr. Law has left in our family the reputation of a pious and austere Clergyman, who believed all that he professed, and who practised all that he enjoyned. I can pronounce with more confidence on his writings than on his person, as I have found and perused several of his books in my father's library. His argument is specious, his wit is lively, his style forcible; and had not enthusiasm clouded his vigorous understanding, he might have ranked with the most agreable and ingenious writers of the Age. While the Bangorian controversy was a popular theme, he entered the lists on the subject of Christ's Kingdom and the authority of the priesthood; and long afterwards, he engaged the great Hoadley in single combat against his plain account of the Sacrament of the Lord's supper. The friend of reason and liberty who struggles, ut cum ratione insaniat is foiled by the high church Champion; and at every weapon of attack and defence the Nonjuror is superior to a Prelate who has been magnified by Whig-Idolatry far above his real size. On the publication of the Fable of the Bees, Mr. Law drew his pen—a sharp pen—against that licentious treatise, and Morality as well as Religion must joyn in his applause. After these praises, which are sincerely bestowed, I have a right to despise his extravagant declamation on the absolute unlawfulness of Stage-entertainments. "The Actors, and Spectators must be all damned: the playhouse is the porch of Hell, the place of the Devil's abode where he holds his filthy court of evil Spirits: a play is the Devil's triumph, a sacrifice performed to his glory, as in the Heathen temples of old," etc. etc. etc. Far different. in composition and effect is the master-work of Mr. Law, *his serious Call to a devout and holy life.* His maxims are rigid, but his eloquence is powerful; and if he finds in the reader's breast a spark of devotion, he will soon kindle it to a flame. He points his reasoning and his ridicule against the nominal Christians who forfeit their salvation for the business or pleasures of a transitory world. Some of his portraits of men and manners are not unworthy of the pencil of La Bruyere. His principles are true, either in themselves, or in the opinion of those for whom he writes. Philosophy will teach that all our actions should be conformable to the dignity and happiness of our present Nature; religion may describe the present life as no more than a passage, a preparation to an eternal state of reward or punishment. But the Sage who rejects the truth, and the Saint who obeys the law of the Gospell must equally disdain the absurd contradiction between the faith and practise of the Christian World.]

*[I was born at Putney, in the County of Surry, of the marriage of Edward Gibbon, Esqre, and his first wife, Judith Porten; and was the eldest of their seven children, all of whom, except myself, died in their infancy. My lot in this World might have been that of a peasant, a slave, or a savage!

My family is ancient and honourable, in the County of Kent, where they were possessed of lands as early as the year 1326, in the parish of Rolvenden. In the beginning of the seventeenth century a younger branch migrated from the Country to the City; nor can I be ashamed of the counter, or even the shop, of my ancestors; since English Gentility has never been degraded by the profession of trade. My grandfather, a man of sense and spirit, was a Commissioner of the Customs in the last Tory Ministry of Queen Anne, and was afterwards chosen one of the Directors of the South sea company. In the calamitous year one thousand seven hundred and twenty, he was stripped of his property, one hundred and six thousand five hundred and forty-three pounds five shillings and sixpence, and reduced, by a most arbitrary vote of the house of Commons, to an allowance of ten thousand pounds. Yet something had been secreted by his foresight, much was restored by his industry; and he died about Christmas, 1736, in the enjoyment, or at

---

* Memoir D, from his birth to his father's death. Written 1790–91; not hitherto published.

least in the possession, of a fortune not inferior to that which he had lost. By his wife, of the ancient family of the Actons of Shropshire, he left one son and two daughters—Hester, who preferred a life of celibacy and devotion, and Catherine, the wife of Edward Elliston, and the mother of the present Lady Eliot, of Port Eliot in the County of Cornwall. My father, who was born in the year 1707, enjoyed the advantages of Academical education and foreign travel; he successively represented in Parliament the borough of Petersfield (1734) and the town of Southampton (1740); and gave a strenuous though silent support to the Tory opposition against Sir Robert Walpole and the Pelhams. Had he trod in the mercantile path of his predecessors, he would have been an happier, and I might be a richer man. But his temper was gay, his life was dissipated; his sisters had been too liberally endowed at his expence; his income was inadequate to his hopes; his expences were superior to his income; and his prudent retreat (1748) to his estate in Hampshire was dignified by pious grief for the loss of a beloved consort.

A.D.
1737–
1752.
The weakness and infirmities of my childhood afforded little hope that I should reach the age which I have already attained; and I am indebted for my preservation to the maternal care of my aunt, Mrs. Catherine Porten, at whose name I feel a tear of gratitude trickling down my cheek. During the first years of my life my tender frame was afflicted by almost every disorder to which human nature is exposed; and every practitioner, from Sloane and Mead to Ward and the Chevalier Taylor, was successively summoned to torture or relieve me. From these ills and their remedies I have wonderfully

escaped, and though I have never known the insolence of active and vigorous health, I have seldom required, since the age of fifteen, the serious advice of a Physician. But the care of my body had already been pernicious to that of my mind, and the progress of my education was often relaxed by indulgence and often interrupted by disease.

In my seventh year I imbibed the rudiments of science from the domestic tuition of Mr. John Kirkby, a Nonjuring Clergyman, the author of an English Grammar, which he dedicated to my father, and of a moral romance, entitled the life of Automathes (1745). In my eighth year I was dismissed from the tenderness and luxury of my own family to the discipline and tumult of a school, from whence, however, I was often recalled to a bed of sickness. At Kingston, and afterwards in the more public seminary of Westminster, I acquired, with much sweat and some blood, a competent knowledge of the Latin tongue; but my frequent absence and early departure would not allow me to reap the full harvest of a Classical institution and the society of my equals. During the last two years which preceded my settlement at Oxford (1750–1752), I was moved from place to place for the benefit of the waters or of medical assistance, and, except some rare occasional lessons, the child was abandoned to his own pursuits. From the dawn of reason I had discovered a taste, or rather a passion, for books; my infirmities disqualified me for the rough play of the school, and while I was confined to the chamber or the couch, reading—free desultory reading—was the solace of my leisure hours. My young fancy was first captivated by works of fiction, the Arabian nights, and

Pope's Homer; but I soon fixed on my proper food : all the volumes of history, Chronology, and Geography which I could procure in English were eagerly devoured; and though I read without choice or judgement, the ancient and modern World were gradually opened to my view. Several projects of composition already floated in my mind, and I arrived at Oxford with a stock of erudition that might have puzzled a Doctor, and a degree of ignorance of which a schoolboy would have been ashamed.

A.D.
1752.
April 3. Before I had accomplished my fifteenth year I was matriculated as a Gentleman-Commoner of Magdalen College, in the ancient and famous university of Oxford, in which I consumed fourteen months, the most barren and unprofitable of my whole life. After every fair abatement for my tender age, unripe studies, and hasty removal, the reader will impute this loss of time either to my own incapacity or to the misconduct of my Academical guides. Yet I will take leave to repeat, after a philosopher and a friend, that "in the university of Oxford the greater part of the public professors, for these many years past, have given up, altogether, even the pretence of teaching" (Riches of Nations, vol. ii. p. 343). The monks or fellows of our wealthy foundation were immersed in Port wine and Tory politics; no model, or motive, or example of study was proposed to the under-graduates, and the silk gown, the velvet cap, was a badge of protection against the formal exercises of the common hall. The diligence of my College Tutors was confined to a morning lecture of an hour, which I was at full liberty to attend or forget: with the first, one of the best of the tribe, I read in two or three months two or three plays of Terence; but I was never called, in a much longer space, to visit the chambers of the second. The idleness of a boy was easily betrayed into some irregularities of company and expence ; but after my foolish, frequent excursions to London, Bath, etc., I never felt the hand of authority, or ever heard the voice of admonition—I shall rejoyce to learn that, since my time, any reformation has taken place either in the university or in the college.

As the university of Oxford had contrived to unite the opposite extremes of bigotry in her doctrines and of indifference in her practise, the religion of her pupils was not less neglected than their litterature ; and I was left, by the dim light of my Catechism, to grope my way to the Chappel and the Communion-table. But the dull weight of the Atmosphere had not totally broken the elasticity of my mind. Accident threw into my hands, and curiosity tempted me to peruse, some Popish treatises of Controversy. I read till I was deluded by the specious sophistry, till I believed that I believed all the tremendous mysteries of the Catholic creed ; and my folly may be excused by the examples of Chillingworth and Bayle, whose acute understandings were seduced at a riper age by the same arguments. With the ardour of a youth and the zeal of a proselyte, I was impatient to enter into the pale of the Church ; some acquaintance in London introduced me to a priest, and at his feet I solemnly abjured the heresy of my ancestors. My father was neither a bigot nor a philosopher, but this rash step compelled him to remove me without delay from Oxford, and even from England. The Protestant Religion and French language recommended Lausanne as a proper place of exile and education. I was delivered into the hands of a Swiss Gentleman; after a journey of eleven days through France, we reached the banks of the Leman Lake, and I found myself established in the house and under the tuition of Mr. Pavillard, one of the ministers of the town.

At the distance of thirty-seven years I can still remember the melancholy impression of my first arrival at Lausanne—at Lausanne, the beloved school of my youth, and the chosen retirement of my declining age. My spacious apartments in the new buildings of Magdalen College were exchanged for a dark ill-furnished room in the most dreary street of an unhandsome city; our domestic œconomy was dirty and penurious; from the liberty and affluence of a Gentleman-Commoner, I was reduced, by my father's displeasure, to the humiliating dependence of a schoolboy, and my ignorance of the language deprived me at once of the use of hearing and of speech. Yet of these hardships, some were removed by time, others were alleviated by habit, and many were conducive to my wellfare and improvement. A severe course of abstinence and discipline invigorated the temper of my mind and body; poverty and pride estranged me from my rich and idle countrymen, and forced me to seek my amusement in myself and my books: in the easy and familiar society of the natives of both sexes, I gradually lost the awkward shame and narrow prejudices which in an English Cloyster would have adhered to my whole life. The Academy of Lausanne was not then distinguished by the fame of the professors or the emulation of the students; nor will my gratitude for the virtuous Pavillard allow me to extend his praise beyond the merits of kindness, assiduity, and a pleasing method of inculcating the general principles of human learning. But my first steps were animated and directed by his judicious advice; and as soon as I advanced beyond his speed and measure, he had the modesty and good sense to leave me to my own impulse. My vague love of reading, which had been damped at Oxford, was now transformed into regular and rational application, and the hours of lecture were soon melted into the voluntary labour of the morning or of the day. The first use of my growing reason was to reject the dreams of superstition, and my father rejoyced in the intelligence that I had again professed myself a member of the Protestant Church.

My litterary obligations to Lausanne during a residence of near five years, at the interesting age from sixteen to twenty-one, may be enumerated under the following heads. 1. I went through a compleat course of Logic, Metaphysics, and Ethics. After digesting with my worthy Tutor the preparatory Logic of his master, M. de Crousaz, I ascended, without a guide, to writers of an higher class; and in my solitary meditations I was successively the disciple, but not the slave, of Locke and Malebranche, of Grotius and Puffendorf, of Bayle and Montesquieu. 2. In the private lectures of a Professor of the Academy I imbibed, as far as the Conic sections inclusively, the Elements of Algebra and Geometry. 3. By conversation and study I acquired the free use and critical knowledge of the French language, which became not less familiar to my ear, my pen, and my tongue. 4. The constant exercise of translating and re-translating from French into Latin, from Latin into French, accustomed me to write with ease and purity in both idioms. My serious occupation and favourite amusement was the study of

the Classics, more especially of the writings of Tully;
and before my departure I had *almost* executed the plan
of reading in a Chronological series all the Poets and
historians, the Orators [and] Philosophers, of ancient
Rome.   5. I entered on the study of Greek, subdued the
difficulties of the Grammar, tasted some easy authors, and
prepared my arms for a more serious attack.   From the
notes still in my possession, I could recapitulate many
books of instruction and amusement, the various food
from which I was now qualified to extract the nutritive
particules.   I am tempted to describe the Theatre of
Voltaire, on which that extraordinary man represented
his own plays (Correspondence Générale, tom. iv. pp. 396,
408, 410, 414, 419, 421, 422, 423, 424, 429, 430, 431,
439 ; tom. v. pp. 5, 6, 9, 15, 16, 19, 21, 22, 23, 26, 34 ;
Edition de Beaumarchais) ; a tour of Switzerland, which
diversified my views of mankind ; and a litterary correspondence with Messieurs Breitinger, Gesner, and Crevier,
three learned professors of Zurich, Gottingen, and Paris,
which I provoked and sustained.   When I was recalled
home by my father, England was almost obliterated from
my memory ; I was naturalized in the Pays de Vaud,
nor was it without a sigh that I tore myself from the
dearest objects of my affection.   My friendship for Mr.
George Deyverdun, a young Gentleman of Lausanne, has
ended only with his life.   I felt (and I am proud that
I felt) the beauty and merit of a Lady who has supported
with equal propriety the scenes of fortune, from the
daughter of a country clergyman to the wife of the first
minister of the Finances of France.

A.D.
1758.
April 11—
May 4.   After an easy journey through France and Holland,
I landed in England at the age of twenty-one.   That

period had been expected with some impatience for the accomplishment of a legal sacrifice not unknown to the heirs of entailed estates, and my filial obedience was rewarded with an annuity of three hundred pounds. My father, with evident marks of satisfaction, embraced me as a friend and a man, and we lived till the hour of his death on the most cordial terms of confidence and affection. The amiable character of his second wife, whom he had married in my absence, soon dispelled the jealousy of prejudice; and as Mrs. Gibbon had neither children, nor hopes of children, we adopted the tender names and genuine sentiments of mother and son. The two first years of my residence in England were unequally divided between London and our family mansion at Buriton, near Petersfield, in Hampshire. But the first aspect of the Metropolis did not correspond with my sanguine expectations. My solitary lodging in Bond Street was destitute of books, and I disliked the idle round of the Tavern and the Coffee-house. The Theatre was my favourite amusement, my best resource; but my foreign education had left me a stranger in my own country, and amidst the crowds of London I often regretted the society of Lausanne. From this costly and tumultuous scene I retired, at the approach of spring, to the hospitable entertainment of Buriton, and as my stay was unconstrained, I was always wellcomed and dismissed with a smile. Some portion of the day was devoted to filial duties, and the forms of a family, but many hours were my own; and a tolerable library, of which I obtained the key, was gradually enriched by my care and expence. The love of learning was now matured into a constant passion, and a rational habit: by the exercise of reading and writing I recovered the freedom and purity of my own language, while I prosecuted with ardour the study of the Greek and Latin Classics. Several researches were pursued, several plans of composition were formed and prepared: my *Essai sur l'etude de la Litterature* was finished in the first six weeks of my first summer campaign; and the rude sketch was altered and revised in several Manuscript Editions. For the sports of the country I had no relish: I seldom mounted an horse, I never handled a gun; and when my father galopped away on a fleet hunter to join the Duke of Richmond's fox-hounds, *my* walk was soon terminated by some shady bench, where I forgot the hours in the conversation of Horace or Xenophon. In this tranquil retreat, in this torpid state, the circulation of expence was suspended during several months, and the œconomy of the purse most happily contributed to the improvement of the understanding.

A.D. 1760. May 10— 1762. December 23. But, alas! we were soon summoned, my father from his farm, and myself from my books, by the sound of the militia drum. We had rashly given our names to that popular service, and when the order came down for embodying the South-Battalion of the Hampshire, it was too soon to repent, and too late to retreat. In this corps, which consisted of four hundred and seventy-six officers and men, my proper station was that of first Captain; but as the Major was my father, and the Lieutenant-Colonel-Commandant (Sir Thomas Worsley) was my friend, as they were often absent and always inattentive, I exercised the effective government of the Battalion, to the titular command of which I was promoted after the resignation of the one and the death of the other. The history of our bloodless campaigns may be dispatched in a few words: we moved our quarters from Dover to the Devizes; we guarded some thousands of French prisoners in Porchester and Sissinghurst castles; we formed a part of a summer camp near Winchester; and had the war continued another year, we might have vied in appearance and discipline with the best of our brethren. A youth of any spirit is fired even by the play of arms, and my enthusiasm aspired to the character of a *real* soldier; but the martial feaver was cooled by the enjoyment of our mimic Bellona, who soon revealed to my eyes her naked deformity, and I seriously panted for a life of liberty and letters. A larger introduction into the English World was a poor compensation for such company and such employment—for the loss of time and health in the daily and nocturnal exercises of the field and of the bottle.

> " Of seeming arms they make a short essay;
> Then hasten to get drunk—the business of the day."

From a service without danger I might have fled without disgrace; but my father's authority and the entreaties of the Colonel kept me chained to the oar, till, at the end of two years and seven months, I was released by the final dissolution of the Militia. Yet even in the tumult of an Inn, a barrack, or a Camp I had stolen some moments of litterary amusement: I read Homer in my tent; and in our more settled quarters, I forced my rude companions to respect those studies of which they were ignorant. My accidental profession invited me to examine the best authors on military tactics: I compared the theory of the ancients with the practise of the moderns; and the Captain of the Hampshire Grenadiers (the reader may smile) has not been useless to the historian of the Roman empire. A rare and short leave of absence, I sometimes snatched; and in my excursions to Buriton each precious hour was diligently occupied.

A.D.
1761.
June, It was in this period of a military life that I first gave myself to the public in the character of an author. My Essai sur l'etude de la Littérature still reposed in my desk, and I might long have balanced between the fears and wishes of virgin modesty, had not my father's pressing exhortation been enforced by the advice of Dr. Maty, the author of the *Journal Britannique*, and of Mr. Mallet, whose name still lives among the English poets. The præposterous mixture of an English dedication was enjoyned by Mr. Mallet; in my absence from town Dr. Maty corrected the press, and it was without my knowledge that he prefixed an elegant and flattering Epistle—so prudent, however, that, in case of a defeat, he might have excused his indulgence to my age, my rank, and my country. My first work was printed as I was marching into Winchester camp, and in the distribution of presents I offered a grateful tribute to my old Tutor and my friends of Lausanne. I had soon the satisfaction of reading the copious extracts, warm praises, and fair predictions of the Journals of Paris and Holland, and a new edition (I believe at Geneva) diffused the circulation of my Essay. At home this foreign production was little read, and speedily forgotten: the bookseller murmured that a small impression was slowly dispersed, and the author (had his feelings been more exquisite) might have wept over the baldness and blunders of his English translation. Fifteen years afterwards (such is the power of a name) the first volume of my history revived the

memory of my Essay : the shops were eagerly searched, and when a copy occurs in some auction, the fanciful price is raised from half a crown to a guinea or thirty shillings : a new Edition was hastily published by the Dublin pyrates; but as I was still proprietor of the copy, I denied Becket the permission of reprinting it in London. Yet, on a cool impartial review, thirty years after the first effusion, I am not ashamed of this juvenile performance. The want of order and perspicuity, the ardent style, and the affectation of wit (Œuvres de Rousseau, tom. xxxiii. p. 88) are the errors of an ambitious youth. But the substance is the fruit of sound, though superficial, reading and thinking, the spirit is liberal, and my Essay contains the seeds of some ideas, especially on the Polytheism of the ancients, which might deserve the cultivation of a riper judgement. The merit of language remains ; and the merit is singular—the examples of Count Hamilton and the Chevalier Ramsay are inadequate ; and I may esteem myself the first Briton who has aspired to the purity and elegance of a French style. Yet this motive of vanity did not influence my choice ; I wrote as I thought in the most familiar idiom. After this first attempt I resolved to embrace some design of history or biography, to which, even from my childhood, I had been prompted by a secret instinct. Many books were consulted, several subjects were investigated, some sketches were delineated ; but as long as I dragged the militia chain, the execution was impracticable ; and the first use of my freedom was a second visit to the Continent.

In this visit two years and an half were employed ; and though I supported the dress, appearance and equipage

of an English Gentleman, my expence did not exceed the
sum which had been præviously stipulated. So lively
was my impatience, that in forty days I shifted the scene
from a guard-house at Gosport to the Faubourg St.
Germain at Paris, where I passed between three and
four months, which I reckon among the most agreable
of my life. In the morning round of Churches, palaces,
and manufactures I visited with peculiar devotion the
Royal and public libraries. Four times a week I was
invited to seat myself, an unbidden guest, at the tables
of Mesdames Geoffrin and du Bocage, of the celebrated
Helvetius and Baron d'Holbach, which were frequented
by the first litterary characters of France, and enlivened
by the free conflict of Wit, learning, and philosophy.
From these *Symposia* I usually repaired to the Theatre,
and my evenings were spent in the houses of my
acquaintance, where I was received with favour and
perhaps with friendship. From the metropolis it had
been my design to view the southern provinces of
France, but I was diverted from this costly and circuitous
journey by the recent expences of Paris and the ancient
love of Lausanne. After five years absence virtuous
Pavillard embraced with tears of joy a pupil whose
success he ascribed to his own lessons, and my voluntary
return was hailed by the warm and sincere acclamations
of the friends of my youth. I chose my lodging and
table in the house of Mr. de Mesery, who entertained his
boarders (his *pensionaires*) with the spirit and liberality
of a Gentleman. Such were the simple attractions of the
place, so delightful was the alliance of study and society,
that the summer and autumn were lost in the succeeding
winter; nor could I accomplish till the return of Spring

my passage of the Alps. A tour of Italy had long been the object of my hopes and wishes; but I shall not expatiate on a country which has been seen by thousands and described by hundreds of our modern travellers. From the regular streets of Turin, the Gothic Cathedral of Milan, and the marble palaces of Genoa, I proceeded by the ordinary road to the beauties of Florence, the wonders of Rome, and the curiosities of Naples. After a winter of enchantment in the eternal City, I again ascended along the Adriatic coast to the galleries of Bologna and the canals of Venice, bestowed a rapid glance on the Palladian architecture of Vicenza and the amphitheatre of Verona, and again repassing Mount Cenis I returned home by the way of Lyons and Paris. During my stay at Florence I read the classics of the country with a Tuscan master; but as I never could acquire a liberty of speech, my intercourse with the natives was rare and formal, and my leisure was idly wasted with the English Colony, the pilgrims of the year. For the harmony of Music I had no ear, and I beheld the capital works of painting and sculpture with the eyes of Nature rather than of art. But I was not ignorant of the science of medals and manuscripts, I had accurately surveyed the Geography of Italy, and the Topography of ancient Rome; her heroes and her writers were present to my mind, and the flame of enthusiasm was blended with the light of critical enquiry. I must not forget the day, the hour, the most interesting in my litterary life. It was on the fifteenth of October, in the gloom of evening, as I sat musing on the Capitol, while the barefooted fryars were chanting their litanies in the temple of Jupiter, that I conceived the first thought of my history. My original plan was confined to the decay of the City; my reading and reflection pointed to that aim; but several years elapsed, and several avocations intervened, before I grappled with the decline and fall of the Roman Empire.

After my first (1758) and my second (1765) return home the forms of the English picture were nearly the same, but the colours had been darkened by time, and the five years and an half from my travels to my father's death is the period of my life which I passed with the least enjoyment, and which I recollect with the least satisfaction. The militia and my travels had, indeed, multiplied the number of my acquaintance both in town and country: the *Romans* of the same year had agreed to form a weekly society; and in a new Club (Boodle's) into which I was balotted I found the daily ressource of excellent dinners, mixed company, and moderate play. The aspect of Buriton and of my family was still the same, and a month of every year, till I broke the inglorious chain (1770), was consumed at Southampton in the exercise and command of the Hampshire militia. But in the spring of life I felt my liberty rather than my dependence, and the enjoyment of the present hour was animated by the hopes without being disturbed by the cares of futurity. In the militia I was armed with power, in my travels abroad I was exempt from controul: the most gentle authority will sometimes frown without reason ; the most chearful obedience will sometimes murmur without cause; and as I approached, as I transcended, my thirtieth year, I began to wish to be master in my own house. While so many of my contemporaries were pushing forwards in the various paths of honours and riches, I was

left alone and immovable, the idle and insignificant spectator of the agitations of the state and the business of the
World. Experience had shewn me the use of grafting my
personal consequence on the importance of a professional
body, the benefits of those connections which are cemented
by the mutual exchange of services and obligations. I
repented, when it was too late, that I had not embraced
at a proper age some lucrative calling, of trade, of the
law, or even of the Church, which might have defined
my character, assured my independence, and improved
my fortune. My scanty annuity of three hundred pounds
was a charge on our private estate, and I was afflicted by
the discovery that my pecuniary circumstances might be
impaired by the life, and could only be enlarged by the
loss, of a parent. From these painful reflexions I found
the best refuge and consolation in my library; but I
should abhor my own unfeeling philosophy had I been
capable of much study in the last fatal summer which
preceded my father's death.

Among the several plans of historical compositions
which I had weighed and compared, *two* were selected
of a convenient size and interesting nature—the Revolutions of the Republic of Florence till it's final submission to the house of Medicis; and the Wars and
alliances of the Swiss, from the first conspiracy of the
three peasants to the defeat and death of Charles, Duke
of Burgundy. My choice, which already inclined in
favour of my *second* countrymen, was decided by the
arrival and advice of Mr. George Deyverdun, whose long
and frequent visits enlivened the solitude of Buriton. I
soon discovered the insufficiency of my French and Latin
memorials; but my friend, who had resided in one of the

courts of Germany, was a master of the idiom in which the annals of the Swiss cantons are for the most part recorded. Some necessary books, the Chronicles of Tschudi and Schilling, the history of Lauffer, the Dictionary of Leu, etc., were gradually collected; and a decent stock of extracts and materials, a heap of bricks and stones, was prepared for the [use] of the architect. My associate, my own habits, and the scene itself recommended the French language; and in the summer of 1767 the first book was undertaken, and finished with the ardour of a new adventure. But in the following winter my Essay was read, judged, and condemned in a society of ingenious foreigners in London; and the author, of whom they were ignorant, acquiesced in the justice of their sentence. I cannot repent of desisting from an enterprize in [which] some expence, more labour, and much time had been fruitlessly employed. At a distance from the archives and libraries, without any correspondents among the scholars and statesmen of Switzerland, I could have produced only a superficial sketch, an abridgement rather than an history, a declamation rather than an abridgement. Nor would the elegance of the fashion have attoned for the slightness of the substance: the French language, so rich in litterary merit, has not produced any great models of historical composition; and I was conscious that I had not attained the genuine style, the middle tone, of that species of writing. After this failure I engaged with my friend in a periodical work of more merit than reputation, but of more reputation than emolument. The *Journal Britannique* of Dr. Maty was esteemed and regretted, and our *Memoires litteraires de la Grande Bretagne* embraced a larger field—the arts and manners as well as the litterature of the British Nation. It is needless, and it would be difficult, to ascertain the shares of our respective property: but the taste and knowledge of my fellow-labourer may be esteemed by the singular felicity with which he has transfused into a foreign idiom the local and even verbal wit of the *Bath Guide*. After publishing two Volumes for the years 1767 and 1768, the work was interrupted by Mr. Deyverdun's leaving England. I had recommended him as Governor to Sir Richard Worsley, the son of my deceased Colonel; he afterwards travelled in the same character with the present Earl of Chesterfield, Lord Middleton, and Mr. Alexander Hume: in the intervals of these continental tours he resided chiefly in my house, till an annuity from the last of his pupils, and the inheritance of an aunt, enabled him to fix his final abode in his native country.

A youth of liberal education may be allowed to make a tryal of his strength in a foreign language, and some applause will attend the successful adventure; but his riper judgement will teach him that it is in his own country, and in his mother-tongue, that he must build the solid fabric of his fame. After my second return I gradually adopted the style and sentiments of an Englishman: it was in my power to act as a magistrate; it might be my fortune to sit in Parliament: I investigated with some care the principles and history of the British constitution; and a copious, rational abstract of Blackstone's Commentaries was the first and, indeed, the sole fruit of my legal studies. The generality of readers feed only on the popular publications of the winter, and the most austere student will often break the line to indulge his curiosity, and provide the fashionable topics of conversation. But I was ever mindful of the adage, "old wine, old friends, *old books*," the classics of Greece and Rome were my perpetual feast, and the *Critical observations on the sixth book of the Æneid* arose perhaps from the thirtieth perusal of Virgil. I presumed to examine and refute the learned and fanciful hypothesis of the Bishop of Gloucester, "That the descent of Æneas to the shades is a figurative description, an allegorical picture of the Hero's initiation to the Eleusinian mysteries." During a space of thirty years this conjecture, a strange episode in the Divine legation of Moses, was adopted by many and contradicted by none ; and even those scholars who doubted the truth, admired the ingenuity of Warburton's interpretation. But the insolence of the tyrant and the idolatry of his slaves (see the base and malignant *delicacy of friendship*) had provoked a general opposition among the freemen of the Republic of letters, and I was encouraged by the triumph of Lowth (*Letter from a late professor in the University of Oxford*) to break a lance against the Giant's shield. My critical observations, a small pamphlet which I printed in the beginning of the year 1770, was received by the public with coldness and neglect ; but the public neglect has been amply compensated by the honourable testimonies of Heyne (Virgilii Opera, tom. ii. p. 804, edit. secunda, Lipsiæ, 1787), of Hayley (see his Works, vol. iii. pp. 152–162, octavo edition of Parr ; preface to the Warburtonian tracts, p. 192). The warm feelings of Mr. Hayley even prompt him to vindicate the acrimony of style which had been so justly censured ("Paullo acrius quam velis . . . perstrinxit ") by the incomparable editor of Virgil. But the Genius of Warburton was not an object of contempt ;

nor can I forgive myself the cowardice of suppressing my name in a personal attack.

Between my Essay and the first volume of the decline and fall, fifteen years (1761–1776) of strength and freedom elapsed, without any other publications than my criticism on Warburton and some articles in the *Mémoires Littéraires*. The four first years may be deducted for the militia and foreign travel, the three last for the actual composition of my first volume; but in the intermediate period (1765–1772) I gradually advanced from the wish to the hope, from the hope to the design, from the design to the execution, of my historical work, of whose nature and limits I had yet a very inadequate notion. The Classics, as low as Tacitus, the younger Pliny, and Juvenal, were my old and familiar companions; and from this æra I insensibly plunged into the Ocean of the Augustan history. The subsidiary rays of laws, of medals, and of inscriptions were cast on their proper objects; and in the descending series I investigated, with my pen almost always in my hand, the original records, both Greek and Latin, from Dion Cassius to Ammianus Marcellinus, from the reign of Trajan to the last age of the Western Cæsars. Through the darkness of the middle ages I explored my way, in the Annals and Antiquities of Italy of Muratori, and compared them with the paralel or transverse lines of Sigonius and Maffei, of Baronius and Pagi, till I almost grasped the ruins of Rome in the fourteenth Century, without suspecting that this final chapter must be attained by the labour of six quartos and twenty years. The connection of the Church and state compelled me to assume the character of a Theologian : I read my Greek Bible, with the notes of the best Interpreters; and the Ecclesiastical history of Eusebius was accompanied by the Apologies of the primitive Christians. I am not ashamed to acknowledge a debt of gratitude to the inimitable accuracy of Tillemont, the learned paradoxes of Dodwell, the sagacity of Mosheim, the candour of Beausobre, the free spirit of Middleton, the good sense of Le Clerc, the just morality of Barbeyrac, and the honest diligence of Lardner; but the labours of the moderns have served to guide, not to supersede, my enquiries; and as I have presumed to think with my own reason, so I have endeavoured to see with my own eyes. These various studies were productive of many remarks and memorials, and in this supplement I may perhaps introduce a Critical dissertation on the miraculous darkness of the Passion.

My father's death, A.D. 1770. November 10.

The dissolution of the militia at the close of the War (1762) had restored my father, a new Cincinnatus, to his Hampshire farm. His labours were useful, his pleasures innocent, his wishes moderate: the neighbourhood enjoyed the presence of an active magistrate and charitable landlord; his polite address and chearful conversation recommended him to his equals; he was not dissatisfied with his son, and he had been fortunate, or rather judicious, in the choice of his two wives. In this retirement he *seemed* to enjoy the state of life which is praised by philosophers and poets as the most agreable to Nature, and the least accessible to Fortune—

> " Beatus ille qui procul negotiis
> (Ut prisca gens mortalium)
> Paterna rura bubus exercet suis
> *Solutus omni fænore.*"

But the last indispensable condition, the freedom from

debt, was wanting to my father's happiness; and the vanities of his youth were severely expiated by the accumulation of solicitude and sorrow on his declining. There can be no merit in the discharge of a duty; but alone, in my library, at such a distance of time and place, without a witness or a judge, I should be pursued by the bitterness of remembrance had I not obeyed the dictates of filial piety, had I not consented to every sacrifice that might promise some relief to the distress of a parent. His mind, alas! was no longer capable of a rational effort, and his reluctant delays postponed, not the evils themselves, but the remedies of those evils (*remedia malorum potius quam mala differebat*). The pangs of tenderness and self-reproach incessantly preyed on his vitals; he lost his strength and his sight; a rapid dropsy admonished him of his end, and he sunk into the grave, in the sixty-fourth year of his age. His death was the only event that could have saved me from a life of obscurity and indigence; yet I can declare to my own heart that, on such terms, I never wished for a deliverance.

A prosperous or thoughtless heir may indulge in the use and abuse of his new wealth; but, at the sober age of three and thirty it is was (*sic*) incumbent on me to measure the limits of my income and the extent of my obligations. My temper is not susceptible of avarice: but even my youth had been exempt from vice and folly; and I may alledge as a singular evidence of discretion, that during the lifetime of my father my narrow annuity was never burthened with any debts of my own contracting. The heavy mortgages which he left could only be discharged by the sale of a considerable part of my landed property.

The victims were brought to the altar; but so un-
skillful or unsuccesful were my efforts, so untoward were
the circumstances of the times and the characters of
men, that a long train of difficulties and delays, of
disappointments and losses, preceded the consumma-
tion of the sacrifice and the final settlement of my
affairs. While I struggled with these embarrassments,
the balance of receipt and expenditure could not be
very correctly observed. But I always continued to
enjoy the comforts of decent luxury, and to maintain
an honourable rank in the society of my equals and
superiors. I have seldom been mortified by the denial
of any reasonable gratification; my credit was never
sullied by any act of meanness or injustice; and the
annual deficiencies of my revenue were readily provided
by some accidental ressource or some extraordinary
supply.—I shall not expatiate more minutely on a
subject, unpleasant to myself, uninteresting to the reader.
It is a rule of prudence as well as of politeness to
reserve such confidence for the ear of a friend, without
exposing our private situation to the envy or pity of
strangers: for envy is productive of hatred, and pity
borders too nearly on contempt. Yet I am disposed
to believe that the mediocrity of my life and fortune,
above poverty and below riches, has powerfully contributed to the application and success of the historian.
Few books of merit and importance have been composed
either in a garret or a palace. A lofty station and
superfluous estate are too closely connected with the
cares, the pleasures, and the vanities of the world; while
the Genius of indigence will be depressed and occupied
by the humble labours of some necessary calling. The

distant hope of honour and reward may excite the industry of a liberal mind, but wretched is the author and wretched will be the work where daily diligence is stimulated by daily hunger.

After my father's decease the plan of an independent life was soon decided in my own choice. But I was still involved in the management of a large estate; a rural net which could not be torn without loss nor disentangled without skill. I was apprehensive of wounding the feelings of Mrs. Gibbon, as she fondly adhered to a spot which was consecrated by her husband's memory; and whilst I hesitated, two winters and two summers rolled away in the same distribution of my time between London and Hampshire. But the new prospect was brightened by liberty and hope; my town residence was improved and prolonged; the uniformity of the country was broken by invitations and excursions; I could now indulge myself in some latitude of expence; and my favourite expence was always applied to the prosecution of my studies. At length, with the assistance of a friend, I disposed of my stock, let a long lease of Buriton, and bid an everlasting farewell to the country. Mrs. Gibbon had chosen Bath, the best retreat for the *sober singleness* of widowhood; and my books, the most valuable of my effects, accompanied my own removal to the metropolis.]

1753, June—1754, December.

1. Journey to L.—Eliot—Chesterfield.

2. First aspect horrid—house, slavery, ignorance, exile.

3. Benefits—separation, language—health, study, exercises.

4. Pavillard—character—use—lectures—conversation—French and Latin—double translations—Logic.

5. Return to the Protestant Church.

1755, Jan.—December.

6. Mental puberty—voluntary study—habits—Cicero, my gratitude to him and Xenophon.

7. Greek grammar and Testament.

8. Rational reading—commonplace.

9. Tour of Switzerland.

1756, Jan.—1758, April.

10. My series of Latin Classics—criticisms—Greek fragment.

11. Mathematics—Metaphysics—Ethics public and private.

12. Correspondence, with Breitinger, Allamand, etc.

13. Taste and compositions—seeds of the Essay.

14. Love.

15. Friendship and society.
16. Voltaire Theatre.
17. The World.
18. Recall and Estimate.

A lively desire of knowing and recording our ancestors so generally prevails, that it must depend on the influence of some common principle in the minds of men. Our imagination is always active to enlarge the narrow circle in which Nature has confined us. Fifty or an hundred years may be alotted to an individual; but we stretch forwards beyond death with such hopes as Religion and Philosophy will suggest, and we fill up the silent vacancy that precedes our birth by associating ourselves to the authors of our existence. [We seem to have lived in the persons of our forefathers: it is the labour and reward of Vanity to extend the term of this ideal longevity, and few there are who can sincerely despise in others an advantage of which they are secretly ambitious to partake. The knowledge of our own family from a remote period will be always esteemed as an abstract pre-eminence, since it can never be promiscuously enjoyed; but the longest series of peasants and mechanics would not afford much gratification to the pride of their descendant. We wish to discover our ancestors; but we wish to discover them possessed of ample fortunes, adorned with honourable titles, and holding an eminent rank in the class of hereditary nobles, which has been maintained for the wisest and most beneficial purposes, in almost every climate of the Globe and in almost every form of political society. If any of these have been conspicuous above their equals by personal merit and glorious atchievments, the generous feelings of the heart will sympathize in an alliance with such characters; nor does the man exist who would not peruse with warmer curiosity the life of an hero from whom his name and blood were lineally derived.] The Satirist may laugh, the Philosopher may preach; but reason herself will respect the prejudices and habits which have been consecrated by the experience of mankind.

Our calmer judgement will rather tend to moderate than to suppress the pride of an ancient and worthy race : but in the estimate of honour we should learn to value the gifts of Nature above those of fortune; to esteem in our ancestors the qualities that best promote the interest of Society, and to pronounce the descendant of a King less truly noble than the offspring of a man of Genius, whose writings will instruct or delight the latest posterity. The family of Confucius is, in my opinion, the most illustrious in the World. After a painful ascent of eight or ten Centuries, our Barons and Princes of Europe are lost in the darkness of the middle age; but in the vast equality of the Empire of China, the posterity of Confucius has maintained above two thousand two hundred years its peaceful honours and perpetual succession; and the Chief of the family is still revered by the Sovereign and the people, as the living image of the wisest of mankind. The nobility of the Spencers has been illustrated and enriched by the trophies of Marlborough; but I exhort them to consider the *Faery Queen* as the most precious jewel of their coronet.

"Nor less praise-worthy are the ladies there,
The honour, of that noble familie
Of which I meanest boast myself to be."

Our immortal Fielding was of a younger branch of the Earls of Denbigh, who draw their origin from the Counts of Habsburgh, the lineal descendants of Ethico in the seventh Century, Duke of Alsace. Far different have been the fortunes of the English and German divisions of the family of Habsburgh. The former, the Knights and Sheriffs of Leicestershire, have slowly risen to the dignity of a peerage; the latter the Emperors of Germany and Kings of Spain, have threatened the liberty of the old and invaded the treasures of the new World. The successors of Charles the fifth may disdain their humble brethren of England, but the Romance of Tom Jones, that exquisite picture of human manners, will outlive the palace of the Escurial and the Imperial Eagle of the house of Austria.

WILL OF EDWARD GIBBON MADE IN 1788.*

CONSCIOUS of the uncertainty of human life, I, Edward Gibbon, do make my last Will and testament in the following manner :—

I constitute and appoint the Right Honourable John Lord Sheffield and John Batt, Esqre, of the Adelphi, London, the joint Executors of this my last Will and testament, requesting only, that in all matters to be performed in Switzerland they will consult with Monsieur Victor de Saussure, Judge of the city of Lausanne, in whose honour, friendship, and ability they may safely confide.

It is at present my intention to dispose of my landed property at Buriton, in the County of Southampton, but in case I should die without effecting that purpose, I give and devise all the said lands to my two Executors, or the survivor of them, in trust to be by them sold, and the monies arising from such sale to be carried to the general account of my personal estate. And I give to the said Executors, their heirs, Executors, administrators, and assigns, the whole of my personal estate, of whatsoever nature it may be, in trust to be applied by

---

* Endorsed, *not* in Gibbon's writing : " The last Will and Testament of Edward Gibbon, Esq., *dated* the 14th July, 1788; cancelled by last Will, 1791."

them to the following uses, according to the order in which they are hereafter specified.

I will that my funeral be regulated with the strictest simplicity; and that if I should dye abroad, my remains, instead of being transported to England, be decently interred at the place of my decease—Shall I be accused of vanity if I add that a monument is superfluous?

I will that all my funeral expences, just debts, and legacies be paid by my Executors, as soon as may be after my decease. And in case my personal property, exclusive of the sale of Buriton, shall not be found sufficient for the discharge of the same, I will that the remaining deficiency be charged on the produce and purchase-money of my real estate.

As a mark of filial gratitude and regard, I give to Mrs. Dorothea Gibbon, of the Belvidere at Bath, an annuity for her life of two hundred pounds over and above any jointure, or equivalent for a jointure, to which she may be entitled as the widow of my deceased father.

I give to my friend Mr. George Deyverdun, of Lausanne, the interest of a sum of four thousand pounds; and after his death, the aforesaid sum to Mr. William de Severy of the same place, to him and his heirs for ever. But in case the said William de Severy should die before me, I give the same sum, after the death of Mr. George Deyverdun, to be equally divided between my two cousins, the children of my uncle, Sir Stanier Porten.

I give to the two children of my aforesaid uncle, or to the survivor of them, the sum of four thousand pounds: to wit, to Stanier Porten two thousand pounds, and to

Charlotte Porten two thousand pounds, to be paid on the day of their marriage, or of their respectively attaining the age of twenty-one years. And in case they should both die before that time, I give their shares, together with the four thousand pounds which may accrue to them by the death of William de Severy, to the Honourable John and William Eliot, younger sons of the Right Honourable Edward Lord Eliot, share and share alike.

I give to the above-mentioned John and William Eliot the sum of eight thousand pounds, to be equally divided between them, and the whole to the survivor and his heirs for ever.

I give to each of my two executors the sum of two hundred pounds. They will not refuse this slight acknowledgment of their good offices; but I can never discharge my debt of gratitude to the warm and active friendship of Lord Sheffield.

I give to Monsieur Victor de Saussure one hundred pounds, as an inadequate recompense for his trouble.

I give to the Right Honourable Abigail Lady Sheffield, to Madame de Montalieu (born Polier de Bottens) of Lausanne, to Dr. William Robertson and Dr. Adam Smith of Edinburgh, to the Right Honourable Alexander Lord Loughborough, and Sir Reynolds Knight, the sum of one hundred guineas each, to be laid out by them in such way as will best recall to their minds the memory of a departed friend.

I give to Mr. Peter Elmsley, bookseller, the sum of fifty pounds, from the same motive and to the same purpose.

I give to Richard Caplen, who lived with me many

years in the capacity of a butler, the sum of three hundred pounds, and recommend him to all my friends as a man of sense and integrity, not unworthy of a higher station.

I give to Phœbe Ford, who formerly lived with me in the capacity of a housekeeper, an annuity of twenty-five pounds for her life.

of my servants a year's wages; and to each of those   lived with me seven years at the time of my decease, I give an annuity for their lives of the value of one year of their respective wages.

I give to my friend Mr. George Deyverden, of Lausanne, all my plate, china, pictures, linen, and household furniture whatsoever, requesting only that he would bestow all my wearing apparel on the valet de chambre who shall live with me at the time of my decease.

I give all my library of printed books to Mr. George Deyverden, and after his decease to the Academy of Lausanne for the public use: reserving only a copy in red morocco of my History, which I give to Madame de Severy, together with one hundred volumes such as she shall please to select.

I will that all my Manuscript papers found at the time of my decease be delivered to my executors, and that if any shall appear sufficiently finished for the public eye, they do treat for the purchase of the same with a Bookseller, giving the preference to Mr. Andrew Strahan and Mr. Thomas Cadell, whose liberal spirit I have experienced in similar transactions. And whatsoever monies may accrue from such sale and publication I give to my much-valued friend William Hayley, Esq., of Eastham, in the County of Sussex. But in case he shall

dye before me, I give the aforesaid monies to the Royal
Society of London and the Royal Academy of Inscriptions of Paris, share and share alike, in trust to be by
them employed in such a manner as they shall deem most
beneficial to the cause of Learning.

And I give all the rest and residue of my property, of
whatsoever nature it may be, to the Honourable John
Eliot and his heirs for ever : whom I appoint my
residuary legatee, by this my last will and testament,
written and subscribed with my own hand at Sheffield
Place, in the county of Sussex, on the fourteenth day of
July, of the year one thousand seven hundred and eighty-
eight.

Signed, sealed, and published in the
    presence of

JOHN CRAUFURD,
JOS. BANKS,   } Witnesses.
NORTON NICHOLLS,

Seal

INDEX.

THE END.

LONDON: PRINTED BY WILLIAM CLOWES AND SONS, LIMITED, STAMFORD STREET AND CHARING CROSS.